CROWNS OF
BLOSSOM
& FIRE

K.T. HARRIS

To my real-life MMC— You are the steady
flame in every storm. The heartbeat beneath my
every word. The quiet hero whose strength I
carry in these pages. You believed in this dream
when it was only a whisper and stood beside me
as it found its voice. I have found the kind of
love I write about. Fierce and achingly beautiful.
You are my forever plot-line.

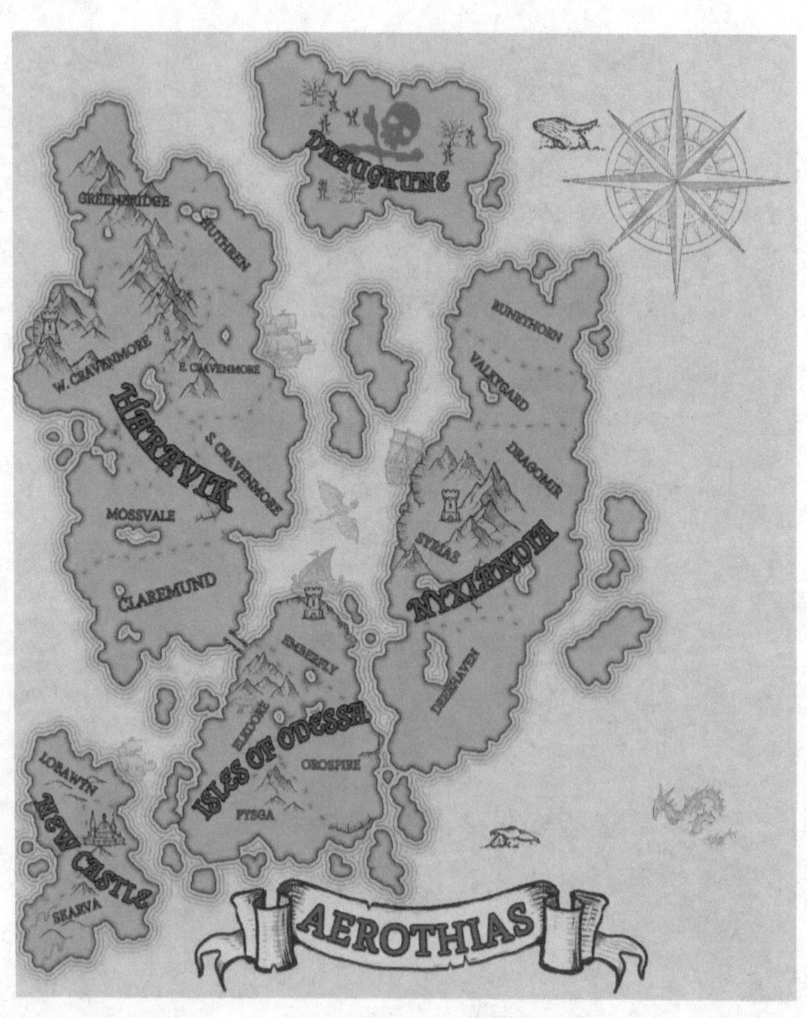
DRAUGTUNE
GREENRIDGE
AUTHREN
RUNETHORN
W. CRAVENMORE
E. CRAVENMORE
VALKYGARD
DRAGOMIR
HARVIK
S. CRAVENMORE
STRAS
MOSSVALE
NYXLANDIA
CLAREMUND
ELMORE
BRIARFLY
GRIMHAVEN
LORAWYN
ISLES OF ODESSA
OROSPIRE
NEW CASTLE
FYSGA
SKARVA
AEROTHIAS

CHAPTER ONE

I close my eyes, inhaling the briny air, letting the feel of sand beneath my toes etch itself into my memory. I bend down, picking up a smooth, gray shell to feel its cool surface against my palm.

This shore, these cliffs, this wild untamed sea, it's the only home I've ever known. I don't know how to say goodbye. They've heard every little dream I've had about wanting a life that's actually mine, not just what's expected of me. Soon, I'll be nothing more than a symbol of unity between nations: the princess who unites nations with her charm.

But not yet.

In this moment, I am just a girl standing on the edge of the world, feeling the pulse of the ocean on my skin. Today and every day for the next six moons, I am just Winnie.

The sun dips lower, painting the sky in shades of orange and violet, a vivid reminder that if I don't hurry back, I'll never escape Mom's scolding.

Reluctantly, I turn from the sea. The crashing of waves now sounds like a warning. My mother won't forgive tardiness tonight. I'm meeting the adviser and guard who will travel with me to Haravik—the place that I'll soon call home.

I gather my skirts, the damp fabric clinging to my legs, and start the trek back to the castle. Each step is further away from the freedom I crave.

Just as I quicken my pace, the familiar giggle of my favorite little cakile breaks the silence.

"Hello!" I chirp, unable to resist greeting my botanical friends.

It waves its succulent leaves and periwinkle-colored petals in excitement.

"I'll be back tomorrow!" I tell it and turn away, careful not to step on my little herbaceous friend. In long strides, I hurry toward the tall, white stone castle.

Breathless, I sprint across the grass. The soft thud of my steps is lost beneath the rustling leaves. I race up the worn stone stairs two at a time, with my skirts gathered in one hand. My heart pounds with urgency.

The garden blurs around me. Roses, lavender, and wild thyme snag on my skirts until I burst past the iron gate and into the cool shadows of the archway.

As I step through the heavy oak doors, the cool echoing halls settle around me. The scent of baked bread and roasted meats hits me, a cue that I'm later than I thought. I hurry through the castle halls, doing my best to go unnoticed.

Suddenly, I run into a familiar soft frame.

"Princess!" My lady's maid's voice rings out, sharp and unmistakable, cutting through the air like a bell.

She grabs my forearms and yanks me through the doorway to my rooms. Maya stands ready, her usual sweetness overshadowed by the anxious crease between her brows. Her pale blue eyes scan me over.

"You're cutting it close, Princess," she frets. "They're already here, waiting in the dining hall," she says with quiet urgency, gently steering me toward my wardrobe.

Maya begins to unlace my damp gown.

The wet fabric is replaced with a soft, silk gown of deep emerald green that accentuates every dip and curve my body has to offer. The bodice hugs my waist with such tightness I can hardly breathe.

The silhouette of the dress is flowing over my broad hips, and the hemline pools at my feet. The gown is embroidered with delicate silver thread in patterns reminiscent of vines and leaves.

The sleeves are long and flowing, made of a lighter silk in the same emerald hue with silver embroidery at the cuffs.

Without hesitation, I settle into the chair at the vanity, heart still racing. Maya manages to untangle and assemble my exceptionally long hair into a braid in record time, leaving waves of my dark auburn hair to frame my round face.

She paints my full lips with a mauve colored gloss and applies silver glitter to my eyelids to complement my naturally rosy cheeks and smoke-gray eyes.

As soon as I rise from the vanity, she gives me a quick once over before gently ushering me out of the room.

I hurry down the cool, dim halls of the castle, passing portraits of the princes and princesses who came before me, whispering a quick "hello" to the potted florals nestled beneath each frame.

I shouldn't stop, but the painting catches me again, just as it always does.

I pause beneath the gaze of a girl frozen in time.

She has wild auburn curls that frame her face, a smile too bright to forget, and those unmistakable silver-flecked eyes. It's almost like staring into a mirror. Emerald-green and silver accents frame her, echoing the colors of our kingdom, a quiet reminder of why I'm doing this.

A wave of sadness washes over me, a familiar ache from the void she left behind.

I take a breath, straighten my shoulders, and continue down the dining hall.

The dining hall doors open. A hush falls over the room as I feel all eyes gravitate to me.

A strange buzzing sensation courses through my body, a magnetic pull or static energy forcing me to the table and pulling every breath from my lungs.

Anxiety grips me as I scan the room, suddenly too aware of how tight this bodice is. The weight of responsibility presses down on me, making it harder to breathe.

Time seems to slow to a crawl when our eyes meet—the man I can only assume is my new guard. He stands tall behind his chair, waiting with disciplined stillness for me to sit so he might follow suit.

Suddenly, the buzzing increases, hitting my senses like a wall of every emotion I've ever known. He is, without question, the most captivating man I've ever seen. Taller than anyone I've come across in this kingdom. Is everyone from Haravik this tall? Is everyone from Haravik this impossibly handsome?

His dark brown hair is braided into a single tight plait that runs down the center of his head. The sides are shaved clean to reveal the sharp angles of his skull. His jawline is strong. His brow is masculine and pronounced... He has this intensity that's impossible to ignore.

Everything about him radiates strength and masculinity, from his broad shoulders and massive hands to the bright amber eyes that seem to see straight through me.

His face is dusted with dark stubble, only enhancing the rugged beauty that looks as if it were hand-carved by Freya herself.

"Your Highness?"

Maya's soft voice breaks me from my stupor, as she's waiting to push my chair in.

After I sit, everyone else follows suit. My father begins introductions. Each name is a blur as I politely nod to each person, trying to appear composed.

The buzzing feeling intensifies when my father's introductions reach the man sitting across from me, and our gazes meet once again.

"Larkin Steelborn, Your Highness."

His voice booms over my father's words. His eyes never leave mine.

The man seated to Larkin's right is introduced by my father as one of his oldest and most trusted friends, Igor Wynfir.

He's an older man, with deep-set wrinkles that gather at the corners of his eyes, hair streaked with black with gray, like salt and pepper, and a sharp, hawkish nose.

"Hello, Winifred," he says, his voice warm but firm. "I met you many years ago when you were once just a babe."

I wince at the sound of my full name. *Winifred* is usually reserved for moments when I'm being scolded.

"Hi, nice to meet you... or, erm, see you again," I reply with a polite smile. "Just *Winnie* will do."

He returns the favor, though a thin line of tension pinches the skin around his eyes.

"What is the real reason you're here six moons before Winnie is to be wed, Igor?" Father asks from across the table.

"Alasdair, I have a report of rumors buzzing around Haravik that Odesa is conspiring to conquer all of Aerothias."

"That is news to me. I have no intentions of taking Haravik. Surely, you know this, Igor," my father retorts.

"Yes, of course, Your Highness. My loyalty lies with the Salem family and the kingdom of Odesa. That is why I wanted to warn you of Prince Rome Riftrage's craft. My spies have informed me the prince has the ability to read intentions and emotions. I'm simply wanting to heed the warning, Alasdair. King Veric is an immensely powerful and ruthless man. He is weary of your intentions, and Prince Rome will know once Winif— Winnie arrives if she has ulterior motives."

"Ulterior motives?" my mother bites out. "Winnie is helping Verik's crops with her craft. She is being wed to seal the treaty. She has no ulterior motives!"

Igor shifts in his seat.

"Yes, Queen Esme, I understand. Word in the streets of West Cravenmore is, you're conspiring with Syrias, Your Highness."

Larkin stiffens at his proclamation.

Igor takes a sip from his ale. "My spies have reported that Prince Rome possesses a very dangerous lumina. The ability is unknown. It's clear that it's meant to be a secret," he adds as he wipes the ale out of his mustache. "There is also talk about the Isles of Odesa lacking a male heir, Your Highness. It is in the kingdom's best interest to produce an heir if Winnie is to wed."

"Esme is with child, Igor. We had plans to announce this to the kingdom at her birthday ball," my father announces with a grin.

My heart leaps with joy for a beat, then a wave of guilt washes over me.

My sister, Brynn, would be ecstatic. Here we are celebrating this joyous news without her. Would she have felt replaced?

The thought brings a pang of sadness.

After the announcement, I rise from my seat and excuse myself. I can feel Larkin's gaze on me, unfaltering and warm. My emotions twist and gather, a slow storm building behind my ribs as I finally reach the quiet of my chambers.

Maya draws me a hot bath as I ready myself to bathe.

I step over the lip of the rose quartz bathtub. The warmth of the water closes around me as I sink into the water. The fragrant oils do little to soothe my troubled thoughts.

I close my eyes, replaying the events that occurred in the dining hall tonight. My thoughts drift to those amber eyes.

Larkin Steelborn.

The memory of his gaze lingers as I go over tonight's conversation. King Veric thinks my father wants his kingdom. What am I getting myself into? How can I live under a man who is convinced that my kingdom seeks to usurp his throne?

He will be eyeing me with suspicion at every turn. Has the king gone mad with paranoia? Is it fear, born from years of border skirmishes and political maneuvering? Or is there more, some hidden plot that fuels his distrust?

My gaze moves to the romance novel sitting on the stool beside the foot of the tub.

Brynn could read a whole book just by holding it in her hands. I was always so jealous of her craft. She would sneak around the library at night and bring every piece smutty literature she could find and leave it at my door. She would even place small pieces of colored paper in the book marking all the steamy parts.

She loved her plants, and I loved my books. I tended to her flowers so well, her room was a small reflection of the castle's great gardens outside. I cared for every one of them, keeping them happy and at full bloom. And even now, I still keep them flourishing.

We always joked about how we should have been born with each other's crafts instead.

My craft of plant work is a gift and it's a responsibility to be a voice for those who cannot speak for themselves.

That's why the Riftrages want me so badly. Their crops are failing; their people are starving.

Neither Brynn nor I were blessed with a lumina. Nor was my mother, though her craft is a useful one. Mother can sense when a person is nearby. It made sneaking around the castle past bedtime almost impossible.

Luminas are both revered and feared, their abilities setting them apart, marking them as different.

And my future husband has one.

That would mean that King Veric or the late Queen Ari might have had one as well. Lumina abilities are sometimes passed down through families, a legacy of power inherited from one generation to the next.

But it's not always the case, like me. My father has the extraordinary ability to manipulate the weather. He commands the winds, summons the rain, and stills the storms.

It's a formidable power, one that has protected our kingdom from famine and drought. It's a dangerous ability that has the potential to cause unimaginable disaster.

He can create tornadoes that could level a city. He could cause an earthquake and separate kingdoms. But I'm just ordinary. Between my father and me, the Isles of Odesa have never known hunger.

CHAPTER TWO

I stir from a heavy sleep, groaning, desperate for just a few more moments of peace. But it is no use. The sound of boots echoes outside my door, followed by a sharp knock.

"Princess, it's time to wake up. Training begins in an hour." Larkin's voice booms through the door.

Training?

"What training, Larkin?" I yell from beneath my heavy covers, but receive no response.

I reluctantly drag myself out of bed.

I splash cold water on my face to shock myself awake. I open my door to find a pile of clothes neatly folded on the floor at my feet. I take it I'm supposed to wear this.

I hurry back into my rooms and strip myself of my nightwear. I quickly slide on the brown leather pants that strain over my wide hips and throw the cream-colored tunic over my head.

The tunic is embroidered with vines and flowers along the sleeves and down the sides. I fasten the boots tightly and head out the door.

I grab a quick breakfast from the kitchens and head to the courtyard, where Larkin waits with a stern expression. Our gazes meet. I half expect to have my senses assaulted with that intense buzzing again, but there was nothing.

"Larkin, what's this about?"

"If we're to be traveling, you need to know how to defend yourself," he says.

I frown. "But isn't that why you're here?"

He smiles. "Yes... but every lady should know how to defend herself."

The hours that follow are a blur of sweat and exertion. Larkin pushes me relentlessly, demanding perfection with every strike and parry.

"I take it you've done this before?" he asks with a surprised tone.

"I will take that as a compliment. My sister and I would spar when she was alive."

Larkin nods in understanding.

My arms are weighty lead. My breaths come in ragged gasps, and my body screams in protest.

The weight of the sword strains my arm. He circles me slowly. His expression is unreadable, but his eyes are sharp. Sweat drips down my spine, and my muscles burn. But I grit my teeth and hold my ground.

When he lunges, I block, barely, and the clash of wood jolts through my bones. I meet his gaze, breathless but unwavering.

"Fix your stance, too wide," he says, voice low and calm.

I adjust, shifting my heel slightly inward.

"Better. I'd hate to see you fall on your royal backside."

Larkin's tunic is soaking wet with sweat, clinging to his colossal form. Each muscle tightens with every movement. His back muscles are straining every thread of his tunic. It's a miracle it has lasted this long. My thoughts are cut short as my body collides with the hard ground.

"Distracted, Princess?" Larkin smirks from above me.

He's close enough I can feel his breath on my face.

"Get some rest," he suggests as he climbs off me. "Same time tomorrow," he says, extending a hand out to help me up from the ground.

I glare up at him, but take it anyway. His grip is calloused and warm as he pulls me to my feet like I weigh nothing.

I nod once and turn away, placing my training sword back on the rack.

The training yard fades behind me as I walk the path toward the castle. A few guards nod as I pass, and I offer them a tired smile.

My boots echo along the worn stone as I push open the heavy doors and step inside. The cooler air wraps around my sweat-damp skin like a sigh.

The castle kitchens are still bustling when I slip in through the side door. The cooks barely glance at me, used to my quiet raids by now, and I help myself to a simple meal and head out of the tall glass doors.

The midday sun warms my face as I sit by the shore, the familiar scent of saltwater filling my senses. My friends, the cakile plants, rustle contentedly beside me as we enjoy a quiet lunch together. I snagged some sourdough discharge from the kitchens for my herbaceous friends to feast on while I enjoy my turkey leg, soft cheese, and bread.

Training today has made me ravenous.

"Tide's high today," I murmur.

The cackile's leaves sway gently.

My botanical friends continue to talk among themselves, their voices quieting as my thoughts drift. As I look out into the horizon, Larkin's amber eyes linger in my mind. The salty breeze carries my wayward thoughts to the place where his hard body was pressed against mine. His lips were less than an inch from my own.

The sun beats down, and the plants rustle beside me, pulling me from my thoughts.

Suddenly, a shadow passes over the water. I squint, my heart skipping a beat. "Did you see that?" I whisper.

There, in the distance, a dark shape soars against the bright sky. It couldn't be... could it? "Is that a dragon?"

I blink, thinking it must be a trick of the light, a figment of my imagination fueled by too much sun and too little sleep. Fear mixed with a strange sense of wonder washes over me. I stand to better my view, but it's gone.

Dragons were creatures of legend, ancient beings thought to be long gone.

Heart pounding, I gather my things, leaving my half-eaten lunch and my startled cakile friends behind.

I start sprinting toward the castle. The image of the dragon sears itself into my mind, a surreal and unsettling vision.

Bursting through castle doors, I hurry toward my chambers, eager to share what I saw, to find some explanation for the impossible.

I find Maya, humming softly, her long brown waves hugging her cheeks as she lays out my evening gown.

"Maya, you won't believe what I just saw!" I exclaim, breathless.

Maya turns, her brow furrowing with concern. "What's the matter, Your Highness? You're flushed. Are you okay?"

"A dragon, Maya! I saw a dragon flying over the sea!"

Maya's pale blue eyes widen, then drop to an amused expression. She chuckles as she leads me toward the bathing chamber.

"You've been reading too many of your fantasy books. Now, come, let us get you ready for a bath. A good soak will calm those nerves," she orders.

"But Maya, I'm serious! It was huge, with wings like sails!"

Sinking into the warm, lavender-scented water, I try to relax, but the sight of the dragon keeps replaying in my head.

"Maya," I say as she begins to wash my hair, "could you check the library for any books about dragons? Legends, histories, anything at all?"

Maya sighs, but her eyes soften with understanding. "Of course, Princess. I'll see what I can find, but keep this between us, will you?"

"Yeah, of course, it was probably just a large bird or a cloud formation."

I know in my heart that was no bird or cloud.

Stepping out of the fragrant bath, I feel a little calmer, though the image of the dragon still dances in my mind. Maya bustles around me, with her brow furrowing with concern.

"Dragons, Your Highness? Are you sure?" she asks, her voice trembling with worry.

"Please, Maya," I insist, "check the library. There must be something about them."

As Maya begins braiding my hip-length hair into a thick rope, its hues of auburn glint in the sunlight streaming through the tall windows. I dab on a bit of rose water and a touch of color to my eyelids to make my pale gray eyes pop. No need to add anything to my cheeks, as they are always a natural bright pink peppered with many freckles.

I pick a silver gown that flows like moonlight, catching the light with every subtle movement. It was stitched from the finest silk, so light, it's a whisper against my skin.

The bodice is fitted, accentuating my curves, particularly my wide hips and full bust, before gently flaring out into a floor-length skirt. Delicate vines, embroidered with shimmering silver thread, climb across the fabric, their tendrils winding around the bodice and cascading down the skirt. Tiny flowers bloom amid the vines, each petal like light dewdrops.

The sleeves are long and flowing, tapering slightly at the wrists, where they were finished with a delicate lace trim. The gown is a masterpiece.

Khristea, my royal seamstress, her craft is extraordinary. She can imbue fabrics with her magic, using the elements and nature. The silver silk of the gown feels unusually light and fluid because Khristea wove strands of moonlight into the very fibers.

The vines and flowers weren't just embroidered. They were enchanted to subtly shift and shimmer, creating an ethereal effect that seemed to breathe with life. I can only dream she'll accept my invitation to join me across kingdoms in my new home.

"Now, hurry before you're late for your mother's birthday ball," Maya orders as she secures my crown crafted of rose gold vines and flowers. Each petal is adorned with shimmering silver diamonds.

The doors behind me creak open, and the muffled music from the ballroom spills into a warm cascade of sound.

With one last glance over my shoulder, I lift my chin, gather the flowing train of my gown, and step forward through the tall oak doorway.

The castle staff has transformed the ballroom into a shimmering wonderland, with crystal chandeliers casting a warm glow on the meticulously arranged tables.

All eyes turn toward me as I enter the ballroom with a familiar rush of adrenaline. Courtiers bow, ladies curtsy, and whispers of admiration follow my every step.

I scan the crowd, looking for any familiar face. Among the swirling gowns and twinkling lights, my gaze sweeps across the ballroom.

My heart skips a beat when I spot the most exquisite man in the room, the one with the amber eyes that sear into my gaze like hot iron.

He stands out, towering over the crowd.

Larkin begins to move, with the crowd parting at his every step. He's like a shark gliding through a sea of lesser fish, his presence demanding a clear path for his colossal form.

He reaches me, the murmur of conversation fading as he bows. His eyes hold mine captive.

"Princess," he murmurs, his voice a low caress that sends shivers down my spine. "May I have this dance?"

The shock of it steals my breath. I extend my hand. The soft skin of my palm meets the calloused strength of his.

He pulls me to his solid form. His hand finds the small of my back, with a grounding touch that sends a jolt of electricity through me.

The waltz begins, and we start to move as one. His lead is firm yet gentle. My steps instinctively follow his.

Where did a guard learn to dance like this?

I wonder as we glide across the dance floor. Around us, the court watches. Their whispers are like a rustle of leaves in a storm. The intrigued expressions, glued to our flowing movements as they watch us in awe, prove I'm not wrong to be shocked that a guard has dancing abilities to this caliber.

The magic of our dance comes to a halt when the sound of trumpets echoes in the ballroom, announcing the arrival of a noble. No, a prince.

Not just any prince.

My heart drops.

"Rome Riftrage the Prince of Haravik." The name escapes the majordomo's lips and lingers in the air like a winter storm.

Larkin's hand tenses on the small of my back in response to the introduction.

I quickly push away from Larkin. The sudden absence of his warmth makes me too aware of the cold air.

As the prince makes his grand entrance, my throat tenses. This is the man my parents have chosen, the one I'm to marry for the sake of alliances and power. He is handsome, with sharp eyes and a smooth smile. Everything about him screams wealth and power.

He's impeccably groomed, with short, onyx colored hair and a clean-shaven face. Even his eyebrows are scrupulously shaped into perfect ridges above his piercing ice-blue eyes. Not a hair is astray on his fair-skinned face.

Does he recognize me, I wonder.

Then his gaze settles on mine, and the corner of his lips curls up in a way that makes me certain he does.

He approaches me. His smile widens into a softer, less lethal curve.

"Princess," he greets, bowing.

The scent of pine and snow clings to him— an echo of the kingdom I'll soon call home.

"I trust you are enjoying the festivities?" His eyes flicker to Larkin, with a brief expression of annoyance crossing his face before he forces a polite smile.

"Larkin, Isle of Odesa's newest captain of the guard," Larkin says, before I get the chance to introduce them to one another. "I didn't see your name on the attendee sheet, Your Highness," Larkin says with a sourness to his tone.

"I'm simply passing through," he replies smoothly. "Official business calls me to New Castle, and this is the most direct route."

His eyes meet Larkin's.

"When I heard of Queen Esme's celebration, I figured I would stop by to give my best wishes. She is *my* future mother-in-law after all, Captain." He dismisses Larkin with a subtle nod.

The prince extends his hand, and with a strange sadness, I place mine in his.

"Nervous, Princess?" he asks, pulling me against his chest. "That guard of yours reeks of desire, poor lad."

Oh, shit.

I had nearly forgotten about my betrothed's craft. I don't even know what I'm feeling. No chance he does, I assure myself.

Wait, desire can't be right. Larkin is my guard, nothing more.

He moves with skill as we glide across the dance floor. Something feels amiss. His touch is polite, his movements nimble, but the exhilarating thrill I felt with Larkin is absent. It's a fine dance, and Rome is handsome. But it lacks the raw, untamed energy that sets my heart racing.

My skirts flare around us as he twirls me across the dance floor. We laugh, breathless as the music speeds up, and he spins me again, our hands never parting.

"You're a wonderful dancer," he says, leaning in just enough for only me to hear.

I smile, cheeks flushed. "You're not so bad yourself, Your Highness."

He chuckles, his gaze lingering on me like a caress. "The portraits didn't do you justice, you know."

"Oh?" I arch a brow.

"Just... they're not nearly as beautiful."

The music slows, and he dips me just slightly, grinning like he has won the world. I laugh, breathlessly, as he pulls me upright again.

"Well," he says, brushing an imaginary speck from his shoulder. "I think we have thoroughly dazzled the room. Shall we reward ourselves with a sweet treat? A drink? A stolen tart from the table?"

I nod.

He offers his arm with a roguish gleam in his eye.

Rome returns with two flutes of sparkling wine and a tiny plate stacked with pastries.

"I see you've gone with the 'bribery by sugar' approach," I say, accepting the glass.

"I find it incredibly effective," he replies, offering me the plate with a slight bow. "Especially with charming princesses who clearly have a weakness for lemon tarts."

I take one. "You don't know that."

"I suspect it. And now I'm testing my theory." He takes a sip of his drink, watching me over the rim with narrowed eyes.

I raise my glass to him. "To your tireless dedication to pastry-based research."

He clinks his flute against mine.

The balcony doors swing open, and we step into the cool night air. Moonlight spills over the balustrade, painting the marble silver. The sounds of music and laughter drift out in waves, soft and distant.

"Finally." I sigh, leaning against the railing. "Fresh air and no shoes stepping on mine."

"I'd never step on your feet," he says, feigning offense.

"You came dangerously close during the waltz."

"I was distracted. I had a very compelling view."

I laugh, shaking my head.

Rome turns to face me fully, with one elbow still resting on the balcony railing. For a moment, the teasing fades from his expression, replaced by a softer warmth.

"You know," he says, his voice low. "Your smile's the kind that makes people forget what they were about to say."

I glance at him, caught off guard. "That so?" I try to hide my smile behind another sip of wine. "Well," I murmur, trying not to blush, "you can certainly remember what to say just fine."

"Only because I've been rehearsing clever things all evening," he says with a wink. "But if you keep smiling like that, I'm bound to forget them all."

The hours slip by like silk through fingers, with glasses refilled and laughter spilling freely between us as the music carries on.

We return to the ballroom more than once, spinning beneath the chandeliers with flushed cheeks and light steps. The world narrows to stolen glances and shared smiles.

By the time the final notes fade, and the guests begin to drift away, the candles have burned low, and my heart feels strangely full.

CHAPTER THREE

She's going to die if I don't get there in time.

My boots slam against the stone floor. The sound is swallowed by the suffocating dark of the castle halls. The air is cold and stale, but my lungs burn. My heart hammers so violently I feel it in my ears, drowning out everything but the thought pounding through my skull: *I just have to get to her.*

The hall stretches ahead, impossibly long. Each flicker of dying torchlight throws my path into stuttering darkness. My legs ache. My chest feels like it's caving in. I have been running for an eternity.

The shadows lean toward me, clawing at my sides, slowing me. My pulse is the only thing that moves fast anymore.

The door is here. Finally.

My arms are heavy as stone when I reach for the latch. My fingers shake, slick with sweat. Time crawls, mocking me.

My fingers close, trembling, around the cold iron knob. The door groans open.

The room is empty.

The window gapes open. The night wind hisses through it. Curtains whip and snap. My stomach plunges. My heart jolts upward, threatening to leap out and follow the figure that has just gone through.

I lunge forward toward the sill.

And there she is.

A figure plummeting into darkness. Her hair streams auburn ribbons. Her face is turned upward. A face so similar to the one I see in every reflection. She's staring back at me as she falls. Down into blackness.

My hand shoots out, but the cold swallows her. My fingers close on air.

I jolt awake.

Gasping. Skin clammy, my long hair plastered to my forehead. My ceiling stares down at me, unmoved. My bed is beneath me. But my pulse doesn't slow. The moonlight spills pale and cold across the floor.

I roll over, pull the blanket to my chin, and squeeze my eyes shut. I tell myself it's just a dream. The same one that has been plaguing me for years.

Sunlight streams through the gap in my curtains, stabbing at my eyelids. Groaning, I roll over, burying my face in my pillow. My head pounds like someone's banging pots and pans inside my skull. My feet ache with a dull throb, souvenirs from last night's revelry. Wine and dancing with the prince, who would have thought I would have enjoyed myself *that* much.

The thought flickers through my mind, a tiny ember of hope. Maybe marrying him won't be the torturous ordeal I've been dreading.

I force myself out of bed. The silk sheets whisper against my skin, begging me to stay in my nest of comfort.

No time for lingering, the day is upon me.

After a quick change into my training wear, I head down to the kitchens. The aroma of baking bread and roasting meat pulls me forward. A hearty breakfast is exactly what I need to face training today, and coffee, definitely coffee.

I grab a toasted breakfast bread and two links of poultry sausage, down my coffee, and head to the training grounds.

Larkin is already here, his broad shoulders tense as he adjusts some targets. He throws the training swords into the sparring pit with more force than necessary.

"Good morning," I say, trying to keep my tone light.

Larkin says nothing as he turns toward me, expressionless.

"Talking to myself today, am I?" I bite out.

We start our usual light warm-up exercises with no words and tension in the air so tight you could feel it in your bones.

He launches us into a grueling set of exercises, each one more demanding than the last. The weight of the training sword feels heavier than the last, and my muscles scream in protest.

Every parry, every thrust, every block is met with unwavering intensity. He pushes me harder than before.

That guard of yours reeks of desire.

"Larkin, is everything okay?" I say between my ragged breaths.

"Everything is great, Princess," he mumbles.

I know with a sinking feeling this is his way of showing his displeasure. He then opens his mouth and closes it.

"How was last night? Seemed like you had a great time," he scowls.

Is that jealousy?

Okay, I'll take the bait.

"Last night *was* a great time, thanks for asking," I say through my teeth as I slam my training sword into his ribs.

A crack of wood against wood thunders through the courtyard as we exchange emotion-filled blows. I grit my teeth, parrying his strike with more force than finesse. The impact jolts up my arm.

Larkin's eyes are molten, narrowed beneath damp stands of hair stuck to his brow.

He removes his tunic in a single, irritated motion and tosses it aside.

His solid chest, carved arms, and the tension in his strong torso flex with each breath.

My pulse skips.

And I hate that it does. He lunges, and I meet him with a sharp crack of our swords, shaking myself from the distraction.

"You're angry," I breathe, forcing the words through clenched teeth as I deflect another blow.

I twist, duck, counter. "Why is that, Larkin?" I say with a sarcastic smirk.

He drops his sword and backs away as he says

"Laps. We're done here."

"What?" I ask, catching my breath.

"Laps, three laps around the grounds," he commands.

"Okay, no problem… I was planning to do that anyhow," I say with a polite smile.

I will *not* let him think he won. I will *not* let him see me falter.

After three grueling laps around the castle grounds, I trudge myself back to my room. I nearly collapse into the bath Maya prepared for me. My legs shake so bad the water is vibrating around me.

"Tough day today, Princess?" Maya asks as she washes my hair with lavender-scented soap.

"That's an understatement," I mumble.

My muscles are throbbing with every beat of my heart. If I stay here enveloped in this warmth any longer, I will fall asleep.

"Maya, could you have my dinner brought to my room, please?" I ask her as I pull myself up out of the bath.

"Yes, Your Highness, and I've brought the books you've requested."

I dress in my cozy, oversized, kit sweater, and get comfortable in my bed with a tray of lamb, greens, pepper sourdough bread, spicy cheese, and a big cup of berry juice. I'm ready to tackle the big pile of books sitting on my side table. I pick up the first book in the stack, *Dragons of the Realm.*

Each page is filled with whispers of dragons, tales of fire and scales—fiction.

Sighing, I toss it to the side. The next book is a graphic novel filled with illustrations of a wide variety of dragons. History books, fantasy novels, and graphic novels, I've scoured them all. A rumor here, a legend there, but no solid proof. With heavy eyelids, I replace the empty space on my stool with the heavy stack of books, roll onto my side, and drift off to sleep.

It's been a few words and awkward silence between Larkin and me. Despite his silence, my heart still does a little flutter every time we share a breath on the training mat, or every time our bodies collide.

The sun warms my face; a gentle breeze carries the scent of saltwater and blooming jasmine.

"Princess," a voice calls from over the flower-covered hill.

I see Maya waving her hand in the air, running toward me.

"The queen's midwife is requesting your presence in her chambers, immediately."

My stomach clenches.

"Did she say what it's about?" I ask, trying to keep my voice even.

Maya shakes her head.

"Only that it's urgent, Your Highness."

I hike my skirts up and run toward the castle, my heart quickens with a mix of apprehension and curiosity. Mother rarely calls for me so urgently.

My feet pound against the cobblestone path, each step echoing my growing unease. The castle looms closer, its stone walls seeming to watch me, waiting as a violent storm crests the horizon.

I burst through the heavy oak doors, nodding to the guards as I rush through the familiar corridors.

My eyes meet Larkin's as I pass him in the halls.

"Princess, what's the matter?" he bellows from behind me.

"Why do you care?" I yell over my shoulder as I reach the bottom of the winding staircase.

I run up the stairs past the portraits of stern-faced ancestors until I reach the door to my mother's chamber.

I pause, take a deep breath to compose myself, and then knock.

"Enter," her midwife calls from the other side of the door.

I push open the door, ready to face whatever awaits me.

The scene that greets me in my mother's room is one of hushed chaos. A circle of faces surrounds her bed. Concern and desperation are etched on each one. Every healer in the castle is here, along with my father. His brow is furrowed with worry, and Kestral, my mother's midwife, has her hands clasped tightly in her lap.

Confusion washes over me. What's *going on?*

Before I can speak, the head healer, Master Eshmun, turns toward me. His eyes are filled with urgency.

"Princess Winifred," he says, his voice grave, "your mother is at risk of losing the baby, maybe even her life."

My breath stills in my throat.

No.

He holds out a piece of aged parchment, an illustration inked delicately upon it.

"This," he says, pointing to the drawing of a sky-blue flower with large open pointed petals freckled with bright yellow specks, long red filaments, and anthers shooting from the middle. The sepals are long, thin, and curl into coils beneath the striking petals. "Is the only thing that can save them now."

"Do you know what this is, Princess?" he asks in desperation.

"Lapis Moon Camellia," I whisper under my breath, still processing everything that has been said in this room.

"And, more importantly, do you know where to find it?"

"How long?" I blurt.

"Three suns at most, Your Highness."

I run down the winding staircase, trying to calm my dizzying worry. The healers' words have me reeling.

The baby.

My mother.

The heir to the throne. The fate of the Isles of Odesa is on my shoulders once again. The weight of it all presses down on me. I burst out of the castle, desperate for air, for clarity.

"Princess! Are you all right?" Larkin's voice, sharpened with concern, cuts through my panic.

He's running after me, with his hand outstretched. But I can't face him now, not with this burden. His silence, his distance these past weeks, it all feels like a wall between us.

"I'm fine, Larkin," I manage to say, my voice strained. "There's just something I need to do, and everything will be fine. She will be okay," I say, trying to convince myself more so than him.

I don't wait for his response; I turn and head for the gardens.

My boots are trampling across the cobblestone faster than my heart beats. I need to consult the wisest being I know—the ancient willow tree. It has stood in the heart of the gardens for centuries. Its branches weep with untold stories. Its roots run deep with secrets. If anyone knows where to find a lapis moon camellia, it's the old willow.

And I'm the only person who can speak to it.

I reach the tree. Its leaves rustle in the breeze like whispered words. I drop to my knees before the tree. My hands tremble as I press them into the soil, digging deep, as if the answers are buried deep beneath its roots.

Tears spill freely now. My sobs are muffled by my shaky breaths.

"Please," I whisper through the ache in my throat. "I need your help,"

The willow's leaves rustle, a sighing sound that seems to echo my own turmoil.

"Do you know where I can find a lapis moon camellia? The queen's life depends on it, and the heir of the Isles of Odesa."

The willow's branches groan, its long, silvered leaves begin to stir. They hum, a low, melodic sound that vibrates through the ground and into my bones.

Images blurred and slow, like a dream folding around me. Jagged peaks of the Elkdore Mountains, a field of crimson poppies, and a narrow stream winding through pale stone. The flower is tucked into the shadows, surrounded by shimmering blue butterflies. I clutch at the vision, breath caught in my chest.

The willow hums again, more deeply this time, and its voice scrapes the inside of my mind.

You will find what you seek...but it is not the only item you will need.

I lean forward, desperate, dirt clinging to my hands.

"What else?" I demand.

But the tree offers no more. Its branches still, its voice fades, and I'm left with silence.

"Tell me," I beg, my hands still clutched in its soil.

The willow's leaves usher me away in silence.

I slowly rise to my feet, brushing soil from my palms. My voice is quiet, almost lost to the grove.

"The foot of the Elkdore Mountains," I murmur, gaze drifting to Larkin's.

I make it back to my rooms to change into something more practical: my training clothes. Maya braids my hair into a tight knot that sits on the top of my head.

"Thank you, Maya"

With a sharp knock at the door, my father opens the door and steps through the doorway. His gray eyes are red from stress, and his long white hair is disheveled.

"Your Highness." Maya bows.

"Leave us, please," my father politely commands.

"Dad, what are—"

"Winnie, someone poisoned your mother." His voice is barely audible over the sounds of thunder cracking outside my window. "A hellebore tonic, they wanted her to lose the baby," my dad says with furrowed brows, his face etched with worry.

"Who would do such a thing?" I ask, my voice trembling. "Why would someone want to hurt a baby? To hurt her?"

"I don't know, Winnie." His voice is grave.

He grabs my shoulders and pulls me into a hug. "Keep an eye out, stay on guard, okay," he asks while squeezing me tight.

"Of course, Dad."

I run down the castle halls, almost reaching the heavy doors, when Larkin's voice booms from behind me.

"I'm coming with you," he says with determination.

"Larkin!" I turn and throw my arms around him.

I'm surprised by the warmth of the embrace, how it seems to ease the knot of stress and worry in my chest. It feels...nice. Pulling away, I look at him, hardening my gaze.

"No, Larkin," I say, my voice stronger now. "I need you to stay here. Watch over my mother. Protect her." I take his hands in mine, with my eyes pleading. "And Larkin... find out who did this. Who poisoned her?"

CHAPTER FOUR

The forest welcomes me with open arms. Its tall trees stand as silent guardians. Their leaves rustle in the gentle breeze. Sunlight filters through the canopy, dappling the forest floor in shifting patterns of light and shadow.

As I ride deeper, the air grows cooler. The scent of damp earth and blooming honeysuckle fills my senses. The sounds of the forest surround me with the chirping of unseen birds, the rustling of leaves, and the distant trickle of a hidden stream.

With each step of my mare, I feel myself becoming more attuned to the forest, more connected to its inhabitants. It's as if the trees are guiding me. Their roots hum with a silent energy that resonates within my own soul.

I follow the winding path. The air grows thick with anticipation.

The faint rush of water slapping against stone leads the way toward the whispering willows. The trees appear before me. Their branches are a wall of curtains. Their leaves rustle in the breeze, creating a soft, melodic whisper.

As I pass through the willows, I see it—the river. Its waters shimmer in the sunlight, bending toward the east as if it's guiding me.

And beyond the river is a sight that makes my heart soar, a vast field of poppies, their vibrant petals dancing in the wind like flames. My mare halts, throwing her head back in protest, refusing another step.

"Tally, what's wrong?" I ask, but she only snorts and refuses to budge. Annoyed, I dismount, determined to continue on foot.

"Fine, I'll go myself," I mutter, jaw tight as I push forward.

The plants around me whisper in a frantic tone, with their leaves trembling. A thick unease curls around my chest, tightening with every breath.

Tally shrieks from the tree line and slams her hooves into the ground, warning me of an unseen threat.

Then, from the shadows comes a low, guttural growl.

It slithers through the air like a paralyzing smoke.

My lungs seize. Slowly, I turn.

And see it.

A panther.

Sleek. Silent. Death in motion. Its eyes are fixed on mine like glowing embers in the dim light. Its shoulders coil to strike.

Panic explodes through me.

I run.

Branches tear at my arms, and roots claw at my boots. My lungs burn. My breath tears in ragged gasps. The ground blurs beneath me. Every rustle, every snapped twig sounds like the panther's breath on my neck.

As I pump my arms, my eyes dart across the terrain for any sign of escape.

I spot it. A hollowed-out log, half buried in moss and rot. A chance. Maybe. If I can reach it. Maybe I can slide inside, draw my blade, and fight like hell.

The panther is gaining. Its low snarl and the thud of its paws are pounding closer with the sharp snap of twigs beneath its weight.

It's relentless as powerful strides eat up the distance between us.

My legs scream, and my vision blurs with sweat. The log is closer now, close enough to taste.

My foot catches on a root, and I stumble, falling to the ground with a thud. The breath is knocked from me in one brutal rush. I hit the earth, dirt in my mouth. My heart thunders like it's trying to escape my chest.

I brace for teeth. For claws. For the end.

Instead, darkness. A shadow. Massive. Wings blotting the sun.

I look up.

And a dragon drops from the sky.

Its scales shimmer a deep green so dark it's nearly black. Its eyes are a molten gold.

With a roar that rattles the very ground, it snatches the panther midair in its claws, bone, blood, and fur and lifts off, vanishing into the trees with a single, thunderous wingbeat.

Silence crashes in behind it.

I lay there, trembling, staring into the sky.

What just happened?

I pick myself up from the ground, trying to ease my still pounding heart.

I stumble toward the river's edge, with my hands shaking.

Crouching down, I splash my face with the chilly water. The shock helps to clear my dizzying thoughts.

As I lift my head, a shimmer sweeps across the air. Blue light reflects off the wings of countless moon drop swallowtail butterflies, their buzzing creating a soothing melody.

It has to be close by.

I begin my search, venturing into the shadows. My eyes scan the undergrowth.

Finally.

I spot them—a cluster of lapis moon camellia. Their delicate blue petals glow faintly in the dim light.

But as I get closer, I realize something's wrong.

The flowers are sickly. Their petals are drooping, their glow fades.

A sense of disappointment washes over me. They will never make the trek back to the castle, not like this. Kneeling beside the moon flowers, I reach out and gently touch one of the drooping petals.

"What's wrong?" I whisper. "What do you need?"

I whistle for Tally.

My mare comes trudging through the forest, greeting me with an apologetic whinny. I reach for the satchel fastened at her side. From within it, I pull out a small vial.

There you are.

A yeast tonic I prepared for my botanical friends when they are ill.

I pour the contents of the vial into the flower's soil. Digging deep from my core, I reach for my magic. Drawing it out like a long breath, I center my palms over the moon flowers and let my magic flow. It whirls around, caressing each petal and diving down deep into the soil.

I watch, holding my breath in desperation. A few moments pass by, feeling like an eternity. The moon flowers start to hum. Their petals slowly start to perk and glow brighter with my every breath as if my lungs are pushing life into them.

The moon flowers reach a healthy glow, high on my magic and giggling in unison. The entire forest feels lighter. Its inhabitants whisper praises. I uproot two of the flowers and gently place them in my leather bag half full of cool, damp soil.

"Let's get you two to the castle."

I mount Tally, and we gallop down the path back to the castle.

I burst into my mother's chambers, breathless and clutching my backpack. Eshmun rushes forward, with relief etched on his face as I hand over one of the moon flowers.

The moon flower is not the only thing you will need to save them.

The willow's words echo in my mind.

A wave of panic washes over me.

"There's something else we need!" I blurt out.

"What do you mean, child? What else could there be?" the midwife asks.

I shake my head. "I don't know."

I tell them everything the willow said.

The room falls silent.

I look at the healer who is holding the aged parchment.

"Can I see that?" I ask, reaching for the old parchment.

As I scan the recipe, my eyes catch a disturbing word.

Blood.

But just before it, a large smudge obscures the preceding word.

"What does that say?" I ask, pointing to the smudge.

The healer squints, trying to decipher the faded writing.

"It's hard to tell, but we always assumed it said, 'father's blood.' In most recipes for maternal care, the father's blood is required for the tonics," Master Eshmun explains.

I nod, returning the timeworn parchment.

I throw my backpack over my shoulder where the remaining flower is safely stored.

"I need to speak to the willow again," I say, my voice firm.

I don't wait for a response.

I close my mother's door behind me as a wave of exhaustion washes over me.

Larkin stands right beside the door. His expression is a mix of concern and determination. Relief floods through me. He stayed and watched over her.

"Thank you, Larkin," I say, my voice softer than before.

Without waiting for a response, I turn and start heading to the gardens. My mind races with the cryptic words on the parchment and the healer's assumption.

Larkin falls in step beside me.

"Did you find anything? Any leads?" I whisper.

His face clouds over with frustration. "Nothing, Princess. I'm sorry."

We rush through the castle halls, the tapestries blurring into streaks of color as we pass.

We burst through the tall glass doors that lead to the gardens, cloaked in twilight.

I make a beeline for the arcane willow, its branches swaying gently in the breeze.

I drop to my knees and bury my hands into its soil once more.

"I need answers," I say, my voice pleading. "The cure... It mentions blood, but it's illegible."

The willow's leaves rustle, as if in thought. They pulse in a low rhythmic tremor that echoes in my chest. The hum returns, familiar and thrumming with unseen power.

My vision blurs, and then images come.

Blood.

Thick and red, dripping slowly from an unseen wound. A pool of it, rippling as if someone just stepped through. Glass vials, sealed and filled with that same dark red life.

Scales. Gleaming. Iridescent. A flash of massive wings cutting through stormy skies. Large, clawed feet covered in scales.

"Dragon's blood?"

The words sound absurd even to my own ears.

The willow's hum deepens. Its leaves rustle with finality, and the connection snaps. I sit there, breathless and shaken. The taste of earth is on my tongue. The echo of the images is still seared into my mind.

"How am I supposed to get dragon's blood?" I say out loud to myself.

Images of my hero in the poppy fields flood my memories.

Larkin follows me back to the door of my rooms. His presence is a comforting weight beside me.

"Get some rest, Princess. We'll figure this out tomorrow," he says with his hands cupping my cheeks and his amber eyes never leaving my own.

He pulls me into a hug, and I sink into his embrace. The warmth and security are a welcome balm to my frayed nerves. It feels so nice, so right, that I almost forget the impossible task that lies ahead.

I reluctantly pull away, offering him a small, grateful smile.

I leave him standing in the hallway as I step into my room. The weight of the day settles heavily on my shoulders. Sinking down at my writing desk, I pen a message, explaining the impossible words the willow spoke.

I hand the letter to Maya and tell her to deliver it to Master Eshmun.

I take a hot bath, recalling the memories in the poppy field.

The blood of a dragon.

The images replay in my mind over and over. As I mull over how to approach the dragon, a ridiculous image flashes through my mind. Do I just waltz up to this magnificent beast, curtsy politely, and say, *Excuse me, dragon, may I have some of your blood?*

The thought is so absurd that a nervous giggle escapes my lips.

I need a plan, a strategy. Perhaps I can retrace my steps, revisit the places I have encountered this creature. Maybe it will sense my presence and reveal itself once more. But, even if it does, what do I do then? How do I get its precious blood?

I dive into the discarded books once again in hopes of finding any guidance or clue to help with the impossible that I've been tasked with.

I jolt awake, with my heart pounding in my chest. Disoriented, I glance around the room, realizing I must have fallen asleep while poring over the literature. The scattered pages and heavy tomes serve as a testament to my desperate search for answers.

As I sit up, a glint of something catches my eye. On my nightstand, where just hours ago there was nothing, sits a small ornate box. Confusion washes over me as I reach for it, my fingers tracing its surface. With a deep breath, I lift the lid, and my eyes widen in disbelief.

Nestled inside, cushioned by parchment, is a vial filled with a thick, viscous liquid as dark as midnight.

The glass shimmers with an otherworldly sheen, and sloppily etched, looks as if an old dagger carved on the side, an unmistakable image of a dragon.

I stare at the vial, my mind reeling.

Where did this come from?

Dragon's blood.

Maya? No. Not. Possible.

Driven by a surge of adrenaline, I waste no time in getting dressed.

I run through the castle halls, my footsteps echoing against the old stone walls as I make my way to my mother's rooms. The vial of black liquid is clutched tightly in my hand, as if it holds the key to her salvation.

I burst into the room, where the royal healers are gathered around my mother's bedside. Their faces are etched with worry and exhaustion.

I thrust the vial toward them.

The healers examine the liquid with curiosity. Their expressions are filled with skepticism.

"Princess, dragons have not roamed this realm in centuries," Master Eshmun declares.

"I have seen one! Just yesterday." I admit.

Everyone in the room exchanges worried glances.

"We cannot be certain, Master," the midwife states. "Using this to create a cure could have unforeseen consequences."

I pull the last moon flower from my bag.

"But what choice do we have?" My voice trembles with desperation. The flower shakes in my grasp.

"We tried to use King Alasdair's blood, and she failed to make improvements," the short, rotund healer says to Master Eshmun. "Maybe we try it. As the princess said, what choice do we have?"

With a sigh, Eshmun nods, with a flicker of determination in his eyes. "Very well, we will proceed with the tonic."

As Master Eshmun begins the delicate process of creating the healing tonic, he laces his bright white, wispy magic with the healing ingredients twirling around inside the mortar.

I watch his every move, my heart pounding in my chest as he carefully measures and mixes the ingredients with the pestle. I move myself out of the way to the corner of the room, stopping when I catch Larkin suddenly at my elbow.

I never even knew he was in the room. He brushes the back of my hand in reassurance, and I appreciate the nice gesture. Together, we watch as the tonic is administered to the queen.

My gaze drifts around the room to the plush emerald-green carpets, the ornate tapestries, and the delicate porcelain figurines displayed on the shelves.

Memories flood my mind, images of Brynn and me playing together on the floor of this very room as little girls. Laughter, games, endless hours of innocent fun. A tear escapes my eye, then another, and another.

Larkin gently wipes each one away.

His touch is comforting, and I lean into his presence, drawing strength from his unwavering support.

As the tonic and Eshmun's magic take effect, I watch in amazement as my mother's condition begins to improve. Her color returns, her breathing becomes more regular, and her blue eyes reveal a spark of life that had been absent just moments before.

I step closer to the bedside, my heart pounding with trepidation. Kestral, the midwife, stands beside the queen, with her eyes closed and her brow furrowed in concentration. Her hands hover over her mother's belly, her magic flowing and swirling beneath her palms.

Kestral lifts her head. Her eyes snap open, and a look of relief washes over her face. The babe's heart is beating with much strength."

The queen stirs, her eyes focusing on Kestral, and a smile touches her lips. I nearly collapse in relief, my knees weak with emotion.

The mood in the room shifts. A sense of calm replaces the earlier tension. Master Eshmun instructs everyone to leave the queen to rest, allowing her body to continue its healing process.

After I place a small kiss on my mother's forehead, I reluctantly leave the room. My heart is filled with gratitude.

CHAPTER FIVE

Larkin turns to me with his eyes filled with concern.

"Princess, you've been through a lot these past few days. You need to get a good meal in you."

I nod, realizing I haven't eaten. My stomach rumbles in agreement.

"How about we get out of the castle for a bit?" Larkin suggests. "Get some fresh air, clear our heads. You could show me around town, and we could get some lunch."

The idea of escaping the castle walls, even for a little while, is appealing. But I need to find out who poisoned my mother.

"Larkin, we have so much to do. Maybe just something from the kitchens?" I suggest.

"Princess, please, let's just go relax, get a change of scenery, and fill our bellies. I could really go for a whiskey. We will come back and face this all with fresh minds," he pleads. "Together."

"Okay," I say, managing a weak smile. "That sounds nice, Larkin."

He escorts me to my room, his presence a comforting reassurance.

"I'll call for a carriage," he says as I reach my door. "Take your time and get ready."

I enter my room to find Maya already at work, hanging my dresses neatly in the large closet.

"Oh, I'll wear that one!" I exclaim, spotting a light pink gown that catches my eye.

Maya smiles as her pale blue eyes meet mine. She hands me the gown.

It's an ideal choice for a casual outing, the sleeves are short and trimmed with delicate lace, the waist is fitted to accentuate my figure, and the skirt flows daintily around my legs. The fabric is lightweight and simple, perfect for a warm day in town.

I slip into the gown and have a seat at the vanity table. Maya busies herself with my hair. She skillfully braids it into two neat twin braids plastered to my scalp that run down my back.

I gaze at my reflection in the mirror and take in the toll the past few days have marked on me. My eyes are shadowed, and my skin looks pale and drawn.

A wave of self-consciousness crashes into me.

I reach for my cosmetics. A touch of concealer to brighten my dark circles, a hint of blush to restore some color to my cheeks, and a swipe of gloss to add a touch of life to my lips. It's a small effort, but it makes a world of difference. As I look at myself again, I see a hint of myself returning, the one who isn't weighed down by worry and responsibility.

I step outside my door, and I find Larkin in the hall waiting for me.

"Princess, you look beautiful," Larkin says with a breath.

I nod in appreciation at his kind words.

We head down the castle halls, and Larkin easily pushes open the heavy oak doors.

We make our way down the grand stairs. The front of the castle is a sight to behold. Towering white stone walls are softened by ivy climbing toward the sky. Manicured bushes are shaped into spheres and pyramids line the walkway, and roses of every color bloom in neat rows, their fragrance sweet in the air.

I often forget how beautiful my home is.

We reach the carriage, Larkin helps me get in, and we set off down the winding road that hugs the edge of the cliffs. From up here, the view is breathtaking.

The shoreline stretches out as far as I can see, with the waves crashing against the rocks far below. The air is fresh and salty. The cries of seagulls echo in the distance.

The carriage rocks gently as it winds down the cobbled road, the castle fading behind us like a ghost in the mist. I sit across from Larkin. He watches the passing trees with a bored expression, one leg casually crossed over the other.

But I can feel his eyes flick to me every few moments, just brief enough to pretend it didn't happen. A low rumble escapes from my stomach, completely betraying me in the quiet of the carriage.

Larkin's head turns sharply, and his brows lift with surprise.

"Was that... thunder? Or is the princess starving to death in front of me?"

I groan.

He grins, far too pleased with himself.

"I told you, you need to get some food in you, Princess."

The trees thin, and the rooftops of the town begin to peek through the haze ahead. The town is immaculate, clearly very well cared for.

I find myself feeling a surge of pride. I know how much my father values maintaining such a kingdom. He always says a happy kingdom is a beautiful kingdom, and he works tirelessly to ensure both.

Colorful flowers spill from window boxes and line the cobblestone streets. Brightly painted shops stand side by side, bakeries with the aroma of fresh-baked bread wafting out, and little boutiques displaying handcrafted goods.

Tall stone buildings housing libraries, coffee shops, restaurants, haberdasheries, and houseware shops line the streets facing the shoreline where fisherman have docked their boats.

The carriage comes to a stop in front of an eatery named Sands XXI.

"This place has the best fish and chips!" I exclaim.

Larkin exits the carriage, extending his hand to help me down the steps.

The doorway shines with brass accents and frosted glass.

We make our way down into the eatery. The cool air kisses my face in contrast to the beating sun we just evaded. A soft piano melody drifts through the air, mingling with the hushed conversation of diners.

The lighting is dim and flattering, with crystal chandeliers throwing a warm glow over the room. Tables are draped in crisp white linens, topped with delicate china, gleaming silverware, and a single rose in a slender vase. Muted gold walls are decorated with tasteful artwork. Large windows offer a view of the town square, lively with activity.

We slip into our seats at the table, and almost at once, a barmaid drifts over. Her smile is as warm as the hearth fire.

"Good afternoon, Princess," she says with a bow. "Would you care for a Brumble Berry Ale?"

My eyes widen slightly.

"Yes, please," I reply, glancing at Larkin, who raises an eyebrow in surprise.

The barmaid turns to him. "And for you, sir, might I suggest a Dragon's Breath Whiskey?"

Larkin chuckles.

"I think I would."

We exchange another curious look.

The barmaid continues, "And for your meal, Princess, our famous fish and chips perhaps?"

"Yes! That sounds wonderful," I exclaim, a bit too eagerly.

"And for you, sir, a pulled beef sandwich?"

"Perfect," Larkin replies, still clearly puzzled.

I can't contain my curiosity any longer.

"Excuse me," I say to the barmaid. "How did you know what we wanted? It's as if you read our minds!"

She smiles knowingly. "Well, Princess," she says, leaning in slightly. "My craft allows me to see each person's likes and dislikes. It makes serving my guests a little easier, and hopefully, a lot more enjoyable for them." She smiles, turns, and takes her leave.

"Speaking of crafts, Larkin, what is yours?" I ask with curiosity.

Some people consider asking this rude because it suggests that a person's worth is defined by their magic.

He leans in as close as the table will allow. His hand glides over mine in a gentle grasp, his voice low and silky.

"Princess, my powers could neutralize every living body in this room before they even knew they were in danger."

The sheer power and protectiveness in his voice is a physical force curling around me like a shield.

Air stutters in me, and a shiver runs down my spine.

It isn't just the words themselves, but the way he says them, the confidence that spills from him.

Warmth spreads through my core, in a mix of admiration and a feeling I can't quite grasp. I'm utterly speechless, my heart pounding in my ears.

I stare at him, completely captivated. My mind reels with wonder.

Our barmaid returns with our drinks, placing a tall, slender mug in front of me. Its contents are a pink, amber hue, the liquid bubbling. The scent of brumble berry hits my nostrils, and I'm suddenly drooling.

Larkin takes a long sip of his whiskey, with his eyes closing for a moment as if savoring the taste.

"Mmm," he murmurs, setting the glass down. "Have you been here before, Princess?"

I nod. The memory brings a bittersweet smile to my lips. "Yes, I used to come here quite often, actually. My sister and I loved this place."

His expression softens, and a hint of sadness flickers across his face. "I bet you miss her very much." His gaze is sincere and empathetic.

"This is my first time I've been here since... since before she took her own life."

"Princess, I'm sorry. I... I just asked the coachman to take us somewhere. I didn't know," he says, with his voice coated with empathy. "We can go somewhere else."

"No, no, it's fine. I promise. It makes me feel more connected to her, if anything," I assure him.

The barmaid returns with our food in a welcome interruption.

She carefully places our plates in front of us. The aroma of the food momentarily distracts us from the heavy emotions that fill the air.

"Enjoy your meal," she says with a polite smile and a deep bow before retreating to the kitchen.

"I lost my sister, too, Princess," he says quietly.

My heart goes out to him, and I instinctively reach out to touch his hand.

"Oh, Larkin, I'm so sorry," I murmur, my voice full of genuine sympathy. "What happened?"

His jaw tightens, and a dark cloud seems to pass over his face. "She was murdered."

The words hang heavy in the air.

I gasp, my hand instinctively squeezing his.

"Oh, gods, Larkin, that's awful! Do you... Do you know who did it?"

He shakes his head slowly, his eyes filled with a mixture of grief and frustration.

"No, I don't. She was thirteen. Her name was Aurora."

"I'm so sorry, Larkin. That's a beautiful name, and I'm sure she was beautiful," I say. My voice is bound with sympathy.

"Speaking of beautiful women, Princess," he says with a teasing smile, "what are you doing for your birthday?"

My eyes flutter in surprise, momentarily forgetting the somber conversation we just had.

"How do you know my birthday is just coming up?" I ask, curiosity and amusement in my voice.

He shrugs. "Everyone knows when the princess's birthday is... So, spill. What plans do you have?"

I chuckle, shaking my head. "Knowing my parents, they're probably throwing some elaborate ball or something."

Larkin leans forward. His eyes sparkle with genuine interest. "What do *you* want to do for your birthday, Princess?"

I pause for a moment, considering the question. "Honestly," I say with a wistful tone creeping into my voice, "I just want to spend the day as a normal person. No royal obligations, no fancy gowns, no forced smiles."

Larkin raises an eyebrow, intrigued. "And what does a 'normal' day look like to you?"

I grin, my imagination taking flight. "I want to go to the hot springs and soak until my skin is pruned. I want to eat my weight in chocolate, drink berry ale, and read smut on a cliff's edge." I pause, then add, with a playful shrug, "Heck, I don't know, maybe even ride a dragon!"

I burst out laughing at the ridiculousness of the image, the sound echoing through the quiet restaurant.

"Okay, maybe not the dragon," I concede, still giggling. "But you get the idea. Just a day of simple pleasures, away from all the royal stuff."

"Ride a dragon, she says," Larkin teases, his fingers toying with his thick dark beard.

Our server approaches and places the tab on the table.

I dig into my coin purse and drop a handful of coins on the table, more than enough to cover the bill and feed the barmaid's family for months.

Larkin immediately protests, with his hand hovering over mine.

"Hey, let me get this," he insists. A playful frown creases his brow.

I shake my head, a gentle smile settling on my lips. "It's fine, Larkin. Really, it's my treat."

Digging deep into his pocket, he says, "I'm the one who dragged you out here, let me get this."

I sigh, placing a hand on his. "Exactly, I owe it to you for pulling me away from those castle walls. Plus, how does it make me look, my guard paying for my meal."

"All right, all right," he concedes, holding up his hands in surrender. "But at least let me buy you some chocolate and a new book when we leave."

My eyes light up at the mention of chocolate and books. "Well, if you insist," I say, feigning reluctance. "I suppose I could be persuaded to indulge in a little therapy."

With a shared grin, we gather our things and step out of the restaurant, ready to explore the charming shops that line the cobblestone streets.

We make our way down the lively street, passing a flower shop, an art studio, several boutiques, and we make a stop at a bookstore.

It is several stories high. Its brick facade is adorned with climbing ivy and overflowing window boxes bursting with colorful flowers.

The entrance is framed by two towering oak trees. Their branches intertwine to form a natural archway. Through the large glass windows, I glimpse towering shelves filled with books of all shapes and sizes. Their spines create a vibrant tapestry of colors and titles.

As we step inside, the aroma of books and freshly brewed coffee dances around us, creating a cozy environment. Sunlight streams from the skylights, illuminating the lush greenery that adorns every corner of the store.

Potted ferns hang from the ceilings, golden pothos sit perched upon pedestals, succulents on shelves nestled alongside literary treasures, and vines cascade down bookshelves, all whispering among themselves. It was as if the bookstore itself were a living, breathing garden.

"This place is beautiful," I whisper to myself.

"So, what kind of books do you like?" Larkin asks, his eyes scanning the towering shelves.

"I like epic tales, sweeping fantasies, and romance. What about you? Actually... let me guess, war novels, military fiction, political fiction, and historical," I say with a smile, teasing my lips.

"Wow, well, I do like the occasional political fiction," he admits. "But I really enjoy fantasy and romance, too."

I guess you really can't judge a book by its cover.

"Reads romance, he says," I say between giggles.

I began to browse books, my fingers trailing along the spines, and I now have a small stack of promising reads. Larkin offers to carry them for me, and I gratefully hand them over, freeing up my hands to continue my search.

As I turn a corner, a book with a striking cover catches my eye. It's titled *A History of Magnificent Beasts*, and emblazoned on the front is a dragon, with its scales shimmering in the light.

I pick it up without hesitation and add it to the pile.

Larkin, browsing a nearby shelf, chuckles and holds a book with a mischievous glint in his eyes.

"How about this one?" he asks, holding up the book titled *A Faerie's Orgy Experience.* Chuckling, he asks, "Sound like it's up your alley, eh?"

We both burst out laughing at the absurdity of the title.

"Why not?" I say, grabbing the book from his hand and starting for the checkout counter.

"Oh, hello," I greet the spider plant perched on the counter while Larkin pays for our loot.

"Ready?"

We turn and head for the exit.

"The spider plant would like some more sunlight," I say over my shoulder to the clerk.

The bell above the bookstore door chimes as we step out. Sunlight spills onto the street, warming my face as we stroll along. The quiet of the shop gives way to the gentle hum of the city.

"Sweets?" Larkin asks.

"Huh?"

"Sweets? Chocolate?" he repeats, jerking his chin toward the Chocolate House down the street.

Oh, sweets, the *food*. He's certainly not calling *me* sweets because that would be ridiculous.

I nod. My sweet tooth is always eager for a treat.

We make our way to the quaint shop a few doors down. Its windows display a tempting array of chocolates and pastries.

Larkin insists on buying me an assortment of chocolates. Each one is stuffed with something different. He also gets me a coffee, just the way I like it—strong, sweet, and creamy. We settle at a small table on the patio.

"My father tells me you're from Haravik. What's it like?"

"Oh, yeah, I've only been to West Cravenmore one time. I worked as a guard for a prison in Mossvale and moved to Deerhaven to work for a duke." He takes a sip from his steaming mug.

"Deerhaven, like *Nyxlandia* Deerhaven?" I ask in confusion.

"Yes, Princess."

"But where are you *from?*"

"I'm from Mossvale, Princess. Son of a fisherman."

"So why not follow in the family business?"

"Oh, the sea and I don't exactly get along. I get terribly seasick," he admits, with a hint of sheepishness in his eyes. "But I do enjoy fishing when I'm on solid ground."

A thoughtful expression crosses his face.

"I'm a very skilled fighter, and I wanted a job that would put my physical abilities to skillful use. So, I decided to go in a different direction."

His words hint at a strength and determination that I find incredibly intriguing.

I recall what he had said about his craft.

"Like your craft?" I ask, my voice bound with curiosity.

"Yes, Princess, like my craft." A subtle smile settles on his lips.

I wonder what kind of power he has that is so perilous, and why he keeps it hidden.

As we stand up from the table, we gather our things and head back to the carriage to return to the castle. My mind races with possibilities about Larkin's craft. Is he unnaturally fast? Does he have superhuman strength? Does he have laser beams for eyes that can incinerate anyone and everything?

These theories are getting out of hand, I think, as I fight back a laugh. The more I think about it, the more intrigued I become. I can't shake the desire to see his abilities firsthand.

As we settle into the carriage, I can't stop myself from stealing glances at Larkin, wondering what secrets he holds within him. The journey back to the castle feels longer than usual.

The carriage rocks gently as I stare out into the sea below. Larkin sits across from me, it's impossible to look at his hands without wondering what they can do. I try to busy my mind with the view, but the thought roots itself in me and refuses to loosen.

"My craft is plants," I blurt.

"Yes, Princess, the whole realm knows. You're truly one of a kind, in more ways than one." He pauses. "Your craft, Princess," his voice gentle, "it's a wellspring of life and light. It's beautiful and gentle."

He brushes the back of my hand with his fingers. He hesitates, his expression clouding over.

"Mine...mine is its antithesis. Death and destruction."

He looks at me, gently grabbing my chin. "You are purity and innocence. I hope you never have to witness the devastation I'm capable of."

Larkin's words resonate, stirring emotions I hadn't expected. The stark contrast he paints between us. Heat rushes low in my belly, catching me off guard. I am suddenly too aware of the tight space in this carriage. A blush creeps up my neck, warming my cheeks.

My eyes dart away as I suddenly find the seagulls remarkably interesting. After a subtle turn of my head, Larkin's hand releases his gentle grasp of my chin.

"That's very interesting," I manage to say, my voice barely a whisper.

My gods, why am I so awkward?

Back at the castle, Larkin escorts me to my room. We quietly walk the halls side by side, finally reaching my rooms.

I lean back against my door, tilting my head just enough to meet his amber eyes. My gaze drifts to his dark brown mustache and full lips. His scent of teakwood and smoke clouds my thoughts.

It isn't until a servant walks past that I realize I've been frozen here, staring at him in utter silence.

Before I can embarrass myself any further, I blurt out a hasty goodbye before darting inside. Grabbing my newly acquired stack of books, I make my way to the balcony, eager to lose myself in their pages.

The sun is beginning its descent, painting the sky in hues of fiery orange, soft pink, and deep violet. These colors dance across the water, creating a shimmering, liquid tapestry that stretches out to the horizon. The gentle waves lap against the shore, their low hush a soothing song.

My plant friends, nestled in their pots around the balcony, seem to bask in the fading sunlight. Their leaves are a vibrant green against the colorful backdrop.

"Isn't it beautiful tonight?" I murmur to the rose bush. Its pink petals open in response.

Yet, even amid this serene beauty, my thoughts keep drifting back to Larkin. His words, his eyes, and the way he carries himself all swirl in my mind.

I try to focus on the words of my book, but the letters seem to blur, rearranging themselves to spell out his name. My mind slips to the day we met. I recall the buzzing, electric feeling I felt coursing through my body when our eyes met. I wonder if that could have had something to do with his craft or my body warning me of the nearby threat.

A gentle knock at the balcony door interrupts my thoughts. Maya comes in, carrying a tray of chicken and wild rice soup, cheese, bread, and fruit.

"I thought you might enjoy eating out here, Princess," she says with a warm smile. "I will start a bath for you soon."

With a final curtsy, she leaves me to my meal and thoughts.

I open the book titled *A History of Magnificent Beasts* and jump into the pages, eager to escape my swirling thoughts. I become engrossed in a chapter detailing the legendary practice of dragon companionship in northern Nyxlandia. These people had formed deep bonds with dragons, living alongside them and even riding them into battle.

As I flip through the book, I stop—a log of the most recent dragon sightings all across the continent. Each entry is meticulously recorded with details about the dragon's appearance and location. Most logs end around fifty years ago, except for a few recent logs.

One small white dragon spotted on the coast of Syria and a large green dragon several years later in Mossvale, and West Cravenmore.

Green dragon.

I pen in at the bottom *Green dragon: Isles of Odessa, Emberfly,* and *Green dragon: Isles of Odessa, Elkdore Mountains.*

It's believed that the dragons are either extinct or in hiding due to fear of becoming extinct. There were no sightings in Nyxlandia logged outside of the one white dragon that was sighted ten years ago. The two most recent logs were sightings from five years ago.

It must be the same dragon.

I finish my food. The last bite leaves a pleasant warmth in my belly. I gather my books and head back inside, carefully placing them on my bookshelf. The bath is ready. The water is steaming and fragrant with lavender.

I sink into its warm embrace, letting the tension melt away from my muscles.

After a long soak, I hop over the lip of the quartz tub, and I towel myself off.

I slip into my nightgown and climb into bed. I stare up at the white stone ceiling, willing my heartbeat to slow. "I knew it. I fucking knew it." As if finding out who poisoned my mother wasn't enough, now I have to hunt down a dragon too.

CHAPTER SIX

I sit across from my mother in the sun-drenched gardens, a spread of pastries and fruits laid out between us. The air is filled with the sweet scent of blooming chrysanthemums.

"Your twenty-third birthday ball is fast approaching, darling. We'll have it on the corn moon," my mother begins, her voice gentle. "We must finalize the guest list and the arrangements. It will be quite the celebration, especially with news of the baby."

My mother places a hand on her swollen belly. "The midwife assures us it's a boy, and he's due in three months."

I offer her a smile. "That's great, Mother. I'm so happy."

The conversation shifts to the guest list, and my mother's tone becomes more pointed.

"Of course, Prince Rome Riftrage will be in attendance. It's an excellent opportunity for you two to become better acquainted before the wedding."

In the corner, Larkin shifts uncomfortably at her words. I'm not thrilled about the prospect of marrying Prince Rome, a man I barely know. It's simply my duty to my kingdom, a political alliance to benefit both kingdoms.

Yet still my mind keeps returning to the shared moments with Larkin. Maybe in a different realm, I could be with whomever I chose. Maybe then, I could marry for love. It was not that I could never come to love Rome. I'm sure he is a pleasant man. It's the lack of choice, the lack of freedom, that I hate.

As I sit here listening to my mother discuss the upcoming ball and the impending arrival of my baby brother, my mind drifts to the castle that has always been my home.

Its old white stone walls hold countless memories, echoing with laughter, whispered secrets, and Brynn. I'll be leaving it all for a place that's never heard Brynn's sweet laughs, cries, and feet pattering on the stone floors.

I'll be living in a castle that has never known her scent.

I picture the tapestries depicting our family's history and the cozy nooks where we spent countless hours together. Brynn would use her craft to pick all the books she knew I would love.

"Winnie, dear, don't you agree?"

My mother's voice pulls me from my stupor.

"What was that, Mother?" I look up, startled. I refocus my attention on her.

"I was saying that it would be a good idea for you to wear royal blue to the ball. It's Haravik's kingdom color, and it would be a lovely gesture," she repeats.

I nod slowly. "Royal blue, sure. I'll have Maya deliver a message to Khristea immediately."

I rise from the table. "There are a few things that I need to do. I'll see you at dinner."

I place a kiss on my mom's cheek and give her belly a soft rub.

As I hurry away, I sense Larkin falling into step beside me.

Turning to him, I ask, "Have you questioned any of the guards? They might have noticed something out of place the night of my mother's poisoning."

"I questioned the guards," Larkin says, with his brow furrowed with concern.

"But nobody saw anything?" I ask.

He pauses. "The castle's most trusted guards were on duty that night. They are adamant that no one entered or left the castle that entire day or night, not even the post."

I frown, my mind racing. Despite the setbacks, I refuse to lose hope.

"We can't let this discourage us," I say, my eyes meeting Larkin's. "We'll just have to dig deeper, look closer, and find the truth."

Larkin's eyes widen.

"Princess, the queen's birthday ball was the night before the night of the poisoning."

I turn to Larkin, my voice urgent. "Find the guest list and meet me on the cliff's edge in one hour. We'll go over it together and see if anything stands out."

With that, I turn and hurry away. My mind races with possibilities.

As Larkin goes to retrieve the guest list, I pay a visit to the stable boy.

"Hey," I say, approaching him with a friendly smile.

"Your Highness," he says with a bow. "Shall I get Tally ready for ya?"

"Oh, no, I was just wondering if, the night of the queen's ball, or the night after, did anything seem out of place?"

I lean in, lowering my voice. "Anything, at all, no matter how small. A strange horse, a whispered conversation. Anything that struck you as... odd?"

I watch his face intently, hoping he will remember something that could help.

"No, Princess. I'm sorry."

With a nod, I turn and head toward the cliff's edge, where I was supposed to meet Larkin.

The stable boy's lack of information was a setback, but I refuse to let it deter me. We still have the guest list to go through, and I was determined to find a trace that would lead us to the poisoner.

As I hurry toward the cliff's edge, I can't resist stopping in the kitchens to grab two cinnamon rolls. Larkin will appreciate the treat, and it will give us something to munch on while we go over the guest list.

When I finally arrive, I see Larkin standing there with his back toward me. He stands so tall against the backdrop of the ocean. His broad shoulders and towering height take my breath away. I can't stop the flutter of excitement as I step closer.

He turns as I approach. His face lights up with a big smile. He greets me with a bow. His eyes sparkle with warmth.

"I apologize for not bringing a blanket. But I can't let you sit on the bare ground." With a swift motion, he removes his shirt and carefully places it on the ground.

"Please make yourself comfortable," he says, gesturing toward the makeshift seat.

I can't help but blush at his thoughtfulness and chivalry... and carved torso.

"Thank you, Larkin," I say, my voice barely above a whisper. "You're too kind." I sit down on his shirt, feeling warmth spread through me that has nothing to do with the sun.

With each bite of cinnamon and sugar, my eyes wander to him, again and again, drawn to the strength in his features and the gentleness that softens them.

We search through the guest list, but nothing seems out of place. Every name is familiar, every title expected.

Just as we are about to give up.

"I remember Prince Rome Riftrage and his rangers showing up unannounced. They weren't on the original list," Larkin says.

"That is true, but no way he had a part in hurting my mother. He wouldn't risk this treaty, no way."

"No, but what about one of his men?"

"You will have to do some digging on them during my birthday celebration."

He nods in agreement.

"This is quite possibly the best cinnamon roll I've ever had," I say, wiping my face of its remnants.

"Agreed," Larkin says with a full mouth.

"Larkin, why do you never wear armor?" I ask in curiosity.

"Huh?"

"You're the only guard that I've seen that never wears armor."

"Well, Princess, the answer is..." He pauses. "I don't need to."

The dining hall buzzes with the usual castle sounds, clinking silverware, hushed conversations, and the distant echo of kitchen activity.

My father sits at the head of the table. His presence is as solid and dependable as the stone walls around us. My mother is beside him, with her elegant smile. Igor is perched on the edge of his seat, with his eyes darting between us all.

Larkin stands guard in the corner, nearly taller than the doorway beside him.

"Are you excited to see Prince Rome at the ball, Princess?"

Igor's voice cuts through my thoughts, pulling me back to the topic of my birthday celebration. "How did your last encounter with the prince go?"

"Winnie had so much fun she probably doesn't even remember," my mother says from a few seats down.

The table erupts in laughter.

"He's a very nice young man," my father chimes in. His voice is the same diplomatic tone he uses when discussing treaties and trade agreements.

The conversation shifts to the details of the upcoming trade negotiations with Rome's kingdom.

I try to focus, but the words seem to blur together, a monotonous drone that fades into the background as my gaze drifts toward Larkin.

He stands tall and imposing, cutting through the stuffy formality of the dining hall. Every bit of him shouts strength, with a ruggedness that draws me in. I find myself captivated by the way the candlelight flickers across his chiseled features, highlighting the sharp angles of his jawline.

My eyes trace the lines of his body, the broadness of his shoulders, the way his tunic stretches across his muscular chest.

He grips his canteen, and suddenly I'm paying far too much attention to the size of his hands. They are enormous, dwarfing the leather vessel in his grasp. He towers over everyone in this room, even my father, who I have always considered an excessively big man.

A strange warmth spreads through me, a sensation I can't quite explain. It's admiration, curiosity, and yearning… for something forbidden.

I quickly avert my gaze as our eyes met. A blush creeps up my neck as I realize I was staring.

The weight of my parents' expectations settles heavily on my shoulders. Prince Rome, trade agreements, treaties, and the future of the kingdom, it's all a distant dream compared to the magnetic pull of the guard standing silently in the doorway.

The clatter of silverware and polite conversation fades as dinner draws to a close. I breathe a sigh of relief, eager to escape the suffocating atmosphere of the dining hall and the dress that has grown too tight with far too many bites of peppered sourdough.

As I rise from my chair, Larkin steps forward. His presence is a comforting reassurance in the midst of my unease.

"I'll escort you back to your chambers, Your Highness."

I nod, grateful for his company.

We walk in silence through the winding corridors of the castle. The only sound is our footsteps against the white and gold marble floors.

I can't refrain from staring at him, admiring the way he carries himself. The sword swung easily at his side, appearing weightless.

We reach my rooms, and I turn to face my loyal guard.

"Goodnight, Larkin," I say softly, my voice barely above a whisper.

"Goodnight, Princess." His eyes meet mine for a brief, electrifying moment.

My hand is on the doorknob that I should be turning, but I am frozen, captivated by those amber eyes staring into my own.

Invite him in.

"Training at sunrise, Princess," Larkin says, breaking the silence.

"Right, see you then."

I step inside, the heavy oak door closing behind me with a soft thud. Leaning against the cool wood, I take a deep breath, trying to calm the frantic beating of my heart.

My room is a sanctuary, a haven of soft colors and plush fabrics. Bookshelves, ivy plants, and colorful tapestries line my walls.

I quickly change into my nightgown. The silk is cool against the heat of my skin.

I free my long hair from its tightly braided knot that sat at my nape, and I wash the cosmetics off my face.

I settle into my favorite armchair, where a stack of books waits for me on a nearby shelf. I reach for my newest romance novel, eager to lose myself in a world of passionate encounters and daring adventures. As I turn the pages, I imagine myself as the heroine, swept away by a handsome rogue, their love defying all odds.

The words blur before my eyes as my thoughts drift back to Larkin.

His strong hands, his piercing gaze, the way he makes my heart thud, it's all so intoxicating. I can't deny the attraction that simmers beneath the surface, a forbidden desire that threatens to consume me.

With a sigh, I close the book. The weight of my responsibilities settles heavily on my shoulders. I can't help but dream of a different life, where I am free to choose my own destiny, where I can be with a man who truly captures my heart.

But I am a princess, betrothed to a prince, destined to rule a kingdom.

There is no room for such foolish fantasies, no space for a love that can't be. I blow out the candle, plunging the room into darkness.
I crawl into bed and drift off to sleep.

CHAPTER SEVEN

I squint my eyes as the sun's rays fall on my face. I run along the cliff's edge, giggling as I chase butterflies. The wind whips through my copper hair.

I'm a child again, carefree and full of laughter, playing near the cliffs that border our castle. My caretaker is nearby, but her attention is elsewhere, leaving me to play on my own.

The plants and wildflowers are my playmates, their colors vibrant and cheerful.

Brynn must be in her studies.

There's a big, beautiful blue morpho butterfly. I've got to catch it, I think, as I playfully chase it down.

Suddenly, my foot slips on a loose rock.

I stumble, with my arms flailing as I lose my balance.

For a moment, I sway precariously. The ground slants beneath me.

With a sickening lurch, I plunge over the edge of the cliff

The air rushes past me as I fall. My heart pounds in my chest.

Just as I brace for the inevitable impact of the rocky shore, I feel a sharp jerk.

I'm suddenly suspended in midair, weightless and disoriented. All I can see is the aggressive slaps of the ocean waves against the big, sharp rocks below.

I am lifted in a tender ascent, carried up and up back toward the cliff's edge as if cradled by the wind.

I'm carefully dropped back onto solid ground.

Dazed and confused, I turn to see what had saved me.

A small, dark, emerald-green dragon is flying away, its wings shimmering in the faint light. I watch until it disappears on the horizon.

I awake with a gasp. My chest heaves, and my breath comes in ragged spurts.

The sun hasn't yet risen, but the dream feels so real that I can't stay in bed.

I slip out of bed. My bare feet pad softly against the cool stone floor. I dress quickly in my training clothes, pulling on a simple tunic and leggings. I lace my boots tightly and step through the large doorway of my bedroom.

My stomach rumbles with hunger, so I head toward the kitchens, hoping to find something to tide me over until breakfast.

The castle lies in silence, broken only by the whisper of wind and the faint, far-off chorus of birds. Candlelight dances along the walls, casting golden glimmers over green and silver tapestries that sway slightly with the breeze creeping in through the windows. Ivy hanging plants spill from carved sconces. Their leaves brush against the white stone.

The kitchens are dimly lit, but a warm, inviting aroma fills the air. A few-early rising cooks are already hard at work, preparing the day's meals. I'm greeted with wide smiles and deep bows.

I brew myself a cup of strong, hot coffee in my favorite ceramic mug. Its creamy off-white glaze gives it a rustic, comforting feel. The body of the mug is fairly simple, slightly rounded, and tapering gently toward the base. The handle is shaped like a delicate rose stem, and the stem curves away from the mug, providing a comfortable grip. On the bottom of the mug, it reads, *Love always, Brynn.*

I grab a cinnamon roll from a nearby tray, its sweet, spicy scent making my mouth water.

With my coffee and cinnamon roll in hand, I make my way to the greenhouse, my sanctuary, and a place where I feel most at peace.

The greenhouse is a sprawling structure of glass and steel, nestled against the castle walls.

Inside a lush, vibrant world thrives, shielded from the harsh elements.

The air is thick with the scent of damp earth, blooming flowers, and verdant foliage. Rows upon rows of plants line the shelves. Their leaves glisten with moisture.

Exotic orchids dangle from hanging baskets. Their delicate petals are painted in a riot of colors. Towering ferns unfurl their fronds, creating a verdant canopy overhead.

I move through the greenhouse with ease. My fingers gently brush against the leaves of my favorite plants. I check the moisture levels of the soil, prune away dead leaves, and water those in need.

I speak softly to the plants, encouraging them to grow and thrive. As golden rays of sunlight begin to dance over the blue irises and varied hues of roses, I lose myself in the rhythm of tending to them.

A sense of calm washes over me, with the worries and anxieties of my royal life fading into the background.

By the time the sun finally peeks over the horizon, casting a golden glow over the greenhouse, I've finished my tasks.

I savor the last bite of my cinnamon roll, the sweet sticky glaze melting in my mouth.

With a contended sigh, I head toward the training grounds. My heart fills with anticipation. It is time to meet with Larkin and begin my training for the day.

I make my way down the stone steps. The air brushes against my skin as the training yard comes into view below.

The clang of steel and barked commands fills the air, but my attention snags on Larkin instead of the group of rangers sparring.

He stands just beyond the sparring pit, tall and impossibly solid, speaking with a soldier, unaware that I'm watching. He towers over every man in the courtyard.

Gods, he is massive.

Even in the loose tunic, his muscles ripple beneath the fabric. His broad shoulders stretch the seams with every slight movement.

I should look away, I know I should, but my gaze clings to him like a secret.

The soldier nods and strides away. Larkin shifts, turning slightly to meet my gaze as I approach.

"Good morning, Larkin," I manage. My voice sounds a little too breathless from the hike here.

"Good morning, Princess."

His warm smile is enough to make my heart skip a beat.

"Ready to start?"

I nod.

We begin with stretching, and Larkin guides me through each movement, gently correcting my form. As he adjusts my stance, his hands brush against my back, sending a shiver down my spine.

Heat rises in my cheeks, and I focus on my breathing, trying to regain my composure. Dark strands of hair have escaped the knot at his nape. Faint lines crease the corners of his eyes when he smiles, and the strong line of his jaw is impossibly sharp.

And his scent, charred cedar, fills my senses, making it hard to concentrate on anything else.

"You're flexible, Princess," Larkin whispers close to my ear. "That will help make you a good fighter." He backs away.

We move on to some core strengthening exercises, planks, and push-ups.

"Ugh," I groan, trying to catch my breath after a particularly brutal set of jumping jacks.

"All the bread and cheese I eat definitely makes this a little more difficult." I wince.

Larkin chuckles, shaking his head. "Nonsense," he says, with a playful glint in his eyes. "If eating bread and cheese results in a body like that." He gestures to me, his eyes grazing my form. "Every woman in Aerothias should take notes."

Heat creeps up from between my thighs, and my cheeks redden at his words.

We move to the center of the training area, a large mat laid out on the ground.

As we immerse ourselves in more advanced techniques, my confidence grows.

Larkin shows me how to chain punches and kicks together, creating fluid combinations that flow seamlessly from one move to the next.

We practice parrying, blocking, and countering. Each movement becomes more instinctive with repetition.

The sweat pours down my face, my muscles burn, but I push through the pain, fueled by a sense of determination to impress Larkin.

He challenges me with increasingly complex drills, testing my speed, agility, and endurance.

He pushes me to my limits, but never beyond what I can handle.

With each successful maneuver, Larkin praises me. His words wash over me like a wave of warmth spreading through my chest.

It fills a space in my heart that has been empty for so long, a void my parents never quite manage to fill. Not that my parents aren't loving. They just don't express praise.

After several hours of grueling training, Larkin and I take a stroll around the castle grounds to cool down.

"How old are you, Larkin?"

"I am twenty-nine, Princess."

"When's your birthday?"

"Three days before the Hunter's moon."

"One moon cycle after mine."

"Yes, Princess."

"And what do *you* want to do for your birthday?" I ask as we make our way to the stables.

"Princess, I need nothing more than the privilege to serve you." His words softly escape his lips.

We approach Tally's stall, and she nickers in excitement.

Larkin explores the stables, greeting each horse while I braid Tally's thick blond mane.

"Did you bring a horse to court, Larkin?" I say, keeping my voice low enough not to spook Tally.

"My horse, he... he passed away a fortnight before I came to Odesa." His voice is threaded with sadness.

"Oh, Larkin, I'm so sorry," I say, letting the words come out gently.

He gives me a tight smile and a nod.

"Let's get you back to the castle, so you can eat something, Princess."

Larkin places his hand on the small of my back to guide me out of the stables.

We make it to the kitchens, where I serve myself a big bowl of chili and a wedge of sourdough thickly coated in butter.

Larkin grabs himself a serving.

We sit at a small table in the gardens, and I devour my food.

"Have you ever seen a dragon?" I blurt.

Larkin stares at me wide-eyed, and I'm suddenly feeling embarrassed by my question.

"Yes, Princess, I have."

My father comes through the doors leading to the gardens.

Larkin stands and bows as my father's shadow falls across our table.

"Your Highness," he says, returning to his seat.

"Winnie, I will be taking leave from the castle for a few days," he says, his voice carrying a weight I know too well.

"I need you to visit the farmers in Orospire tomorrow. Their crops are struggling, and they need your help. I'll see you at your birthday ball," he adds, his tone softening.

Before turning away, he leans down and kisses my cheek.

"Relax for the rest of the day, Larkin. We have a big day tomorrow, and there's a few things I need to do in preparation," I say, trying to sound casual.

I hurry down to the stables, where the scent of hay and horse fills my nostrils.

"Hey, Harry!" I call out. "I was wondering if your father has any horses for sale?"

Harry looks up in surprise.

"As a matter of fact, he does," he replies, a grin spreading across his face. "He's got a young gelding Shire, black as midnight. Just finished his training too."

My heart skips a beat. A Shire sounds perfect.

Without hesitation, I hand Harry a large sack of coins.

"Bring him to the stables by sunrise tomorrow," I instruct, my voice filled with excitement.

I turn on my heel and begin my trek back to the castle.

"Your Highness, you've given me way too much coin!" Harry exclaims.

I turn toward him.

"Harry, I want you to have it," I say, waving my hand dismissively. "Buy your mom something nice. Now, make sure that horse is ready for me tomorrow morning."

Finally making it back to my rooms, I'm overwhelmed with exhaustion. The day's events have taken their toll, and all I want to do is unwind.

I run a hot bath. The fragrant oils fill the air with a soothing aroma.

As I sink into the hot water, my muscles begin to relax. The tension slowly melts away.

I wash my hair and scrub my body. I feel my eyelids getting heavier by the moment.

The water is so relaxing. *I better head to bed before I fall asleep right here in this very bath.*

I decide to call it a night and pull myself up out of the bath.

As I wrap my towel around my body, there's a soft knock at my door.

I assume it's Maya.

"Come in," I yell from the closet.

The door opens, and in my peripheral vision, I see a colossal form filling the doorway.

My heart leaps in my chest as I turn and meet those familiar amber eyes.

"Oh, Princess, I'm sorry. I... I can come back," Larkin says with his head down.

I grab a nightgown and retreat to my bathroom.

"Just a moment!" I yell from the other side of the wall.

I slip the thin fabric over my head and return to my bedroom with Larkin still standing in the doorway.

"I'm sorry. Please come in, Larkin. What can I do for you?" I ask him, trying to keep my tone even.

"I actually... You left this at the training grounds." He stands in the doorway holding up my coffee mug.

"I took it to the kitchens, but the help said you prefer this one to stay in here, with you," he says with his arm outstretched, offering me my mug. "I washed it. They had chocolate cake, so I brought you some."

He smiles with a hefty slice of cake in the other hand.

"You... brought me my mug? And you washed it?" My heart swells in my chest. "That was very thoughtful, Larkin. Thank you so much."

"Yes... I did."

"Do you want to share this cake with me on the balcony?" I gesture toward the balcony doors.

"I'd love to, Princess," he says with a smile dancing on his lips as he moves to join me on the balcony.

As we settle onto the balcony, the air fills with the sweet aroma of chocolate cake and the gentle sounds of the waves crashing against the rocks below. The sun begins its descent, bleeding the sky with inks of orange, pink, and gold. The clouds drift lazily, catching the light and transforming into fiery shapes.

"This view is stunning," Larkin says with his eyes on me.

His gaze dips below my collarbone.

I nod in agreement.

The air is crisp and cool, carrying the scent of the sea below. We sit in a comfortable silence, enjoying the cake and the spectacular view, lost in our thoughts as the day slowly fades into night.

Just then, a thought struck me.

"Larkin, you said you've seen a dragon?"

"Mmhmm," he murmurs with a mouth full of cake. "I did, didn't I?"

"Can you tell me about it?"

He stares at me for a moment.

"It was a white dragon, off the shores of Deerhaven. It was one of the most beautiful things I've ever seen, second to you, Princess."

My cheeks turn a few shades redder than they already are.

Larkin's words hang in the air in a sweet melody that resonates with me.

I avert my gaze, suddenly finding the horizon far more interesting than usual. My heart flutters like a trapped bird, and I can't contain my smile. I can't help glancing at Larkin once more. He's smiling too, and it's a beautiful sight.

The setting sun casts a golden glow on Larkin's tanned skin. His long, dark-brown hair shines where the sun touches it.

"You should keep your hair down more often," I say, almost whispering.

"You as well, Princess." He leans back in his chair.

I catch myself admiring the way he fills the space around us.

And what a lot of space it was.

This balcony suddenly feels a whole lot smaller. His legs are stretched out and lean, and they are so close to mine that they are practically intertwined. Warmth radiates from his skin, a subtle reminder of his presence. It's a comfortable closeness, familiar and electrifying.

I cross my legs in an attempt to ease the warmth pooling in my core.

The sun has almost disappeared. Darkness replaces where it was just moments ago. The evening chill finally nudges us indoors.

I settle onto my bed, sinking into the soft mattress as Larkin wanders over to my bookshelf. He runs his fingers along the spines. I can't stop my mind from craving his fingers doing the same to my legs.

He pulls out a romance novel titled *The Knight and the Queen.*

"May I borrow this one?" he asks, holding up the well-worn novel.

"Of course," I reply, smiling. "Borrow any you'd like."

He grins, tucking the book under his arm as he continues to browse.

He pauses on *A History of Magnificent Beasts.* Turning to me, he walks over to the bed and sits on its edge. His gaze trails the length of my legs.

He eyes me all the way up my curvy form until our eyes meet. A shiver trails down my spine at the intensity, with a warmth that has nothing to do with the comfort of my blankets.

Larkin stands and makes his way toward me. He reaches for my face, stroking his thumb against my cheek and gently holding my chin.

"Goodnight, Princess," he says. My heart flutters as his eyes never break from mine. He leaves me lying there, his gaze a ghost that still warms my skin as he turns and walks out. The door closes softly behind him, and I press a hand to my chest, fighting to slow my heartbeat, my breaths coming thin.

CHAPTER EIGHT

As we enter the stables, Harry greets us with a knowing smile. My mare, Tally, is already saddled and ready for our travels.

But it's the sight across from her that makes my heart flutter with anticipation.

There stands the massive midnight-black Shire I purchased from Harry's father, a well-known breeder in Emberfly. The horse is magnificent, a true beast of beauty and strength. He towers over my Tally. His onyx black coat is a beautiful contrast to her gleaming white coat.

"Larkin, come acquaint yourself with the horse you'll be riding today," I say, as I run my hand along the horse's stark black mane. "What do you think of him?" I turn to Larkin

His smile is wide. "He's magnificent," he says in awe.

"Well, what are you gonna call him?" I ask, barely able to contain my excitement.

"What do you mean?" He chuckles.

"Larkin, he's yours. I got him for you. He's your new companion!" I say, unable to conceal my excitement.

His eyes widen in disbelief as he takes in the sight of the majestic creature.

I turn to Harry. "Thank you, he's lovely."

Harry nods and strides away.

Larkin is speechless, with gratitude evident in his eyes. "Princess, I can't accept this," he whispers.

"Yes, you can." I pause. "Call it an early birthday present."

Overcome with emotion, Larkin pulls me close and places a kiss on my mouth. His lips are so soft and warm.

He immediately pulls away, stunned, and apologizes. It's the first time I have ever been kissed by a man, and the sensation was magnificent, sweet, and utterly unexpected. I touch my lips, trying to savor the feeling of his on them.

"Don't apologize," I softly command, stepping in to kiss him back.

I gently grab the back of his neck, with my fingers intertwined with his long, soft strands of hair, pulling him down to meet my height.

He greedily accepts the invitation of my lips, opening his mouth to allow a deeper embrace. His hands roam the curves of my hips. His form is so solid and warm beneath my soft dips and curves.

The stables are quiet, save for the soft snorts and shifting of hooves.

Larkin and I stand between our horses, Tally and his new Shire. Their bodies act as a natural shield, cocooning us in our own little world. The kiss is electric, like a spark igniting a flame I didn't know was waiting to be lit.

We break apart, breathless, and we just look at each other.

His eyes are now so full with a tenderness that makes my heart ache. Time seems to stand still as we stand here, lost in the moment. The weight of the world outside the stables fades away.

Finally, he clears his throat, with a hint of his usual self returning. "We should probably get going." His voice is a little rough.

I nod, the spell broken. "Yup, time to go."

We mount our horses. The familiar motion grounds me slightly. But as we ride out of the stables and onto the path, my mind is racing. The kiss replays in my head, each touch, each sensation vivid and electric. I'm floating somewhere between reality and a dream.

I glance at Larkin. His profile is strong and handsome against the morning sun, and I know that nothing will ever be the same again.

As we ride, the wind whips through my hair, carrying away the scent of hay and horses. The memory of Larkin's lips on mine lingers. Is he thinking about what had just happened, too? I sneak a glance at him. His face is unreadable, and his gaze is fixed on the horizon. I couldn't begin to tell what he was thinking.

Panic starts to set in. I'm a princess, and he's my guard. That was not something princesses do with their guards.

It was just a kiss, I assure myself, a fleeting moment of weakness. I can't let it become anything more. The consequences would be disastrous, not just for me, but for him too. I have a duty to my kingdom, to my family. Love, especially with someone like Larkin, can't be a part of that equation.

I have to bury these feelings, lock them away. It is the only way.

But as I glance at Larkin again, the warmth of his gaze meets mine, and I know it won't be easy. The kiss has awakened a restless ache within me, and I'm not sure how to ignore it.

But I have to try.

For the sake of my crown, for the sake of Larkin's safety, I have to pretend it never happened.

The silence between us is thick, heavy with unspoken feelings and unresolved emotions. I need to break the tension, to find some semblance of normalcy before I completely unravel.

"Larkin, what's your favorite color?"

He turns to me, with a flicker of surprise in his eyes, as if he hadn't expected me to speak at all.

"Gray."

"Gray? That's not technically a color, ya know."

"Auburn."

"Huh?"

"If gray isn't an option, then my answer is auburn."

We sink into an easy silence, broken only by hooves striking the earth. I busy my hands with the ends of Tally's mane, weaving small braids to keep my thoughts from drifting back to the kiss.

I still can't refrain from stealing glances at him. There's a natural flow in the way Larkin rides, like he and his new horse have always belonged together.

"Well, what are you going to call him?" I ask, forcing a casual tone. "Have you decided on a name yet?"

He seems to consider the question for a moment, with a small smile playing on his lips.

"Actually, I think I have," he says, his voice lighter than it had been. "I'm going to call him Doc."

"Doc?" I repeat, a genuine smile on my lips. "I like it," I say, relieved that the awkwardness seems to have dissipated, at least for the moment.

The conversation shifts to lighter topics: the horses, the weather, the upcoming harvest, and my birthday ball. But under the surface, the memory of the kiss lingers, a soft reminder of the forbidden feelings I'm trying so hard to smother.

But, for some reason, I want more.

More kisses, more Larkin.

It is like an invisible tether connects us, drawing me to him with an irresistible force. He is my guard, sworn to protect me, never to love me. Too much stands in the way for us to ever meet in the middle.

And yet, I can't deny the longing, the unexplainable need to be near him, to feel his presence, and to bask in the warmth of his smile.

I'm caught in a web of my own making, and I don't know how to break free. I need to sort myself out before I'm to wed Prince Rome in two moons.

After hours of riding, we finally make it into town, and the aromas and sounds of busy streets greet us. My stomach rumbles, reminding me of my ever-present need for a snack.

"I need to stop for a snack," I announce, unable to resist the craving any longer. "And coffee, of course."

Larkin chuckles, with a familiar warmth spreading through me at the sound. "Of course, Princess," he says, his eyes twinkling with amusement.

We stop at the first little cafe we see, a charming place with outdoor seating and the smell of freshly baked goods wafting through the air.

Larkin, ever attentive, insists on ordering for me. I sit at a table on the patio, hoping not to be recognized.

Larkin returns with a sandwich, a delicate jellied pastry, and a hot, sweet, creamy coffee, just the way I like it. For himself, he simply ordered a black coffee with crackers and cheese.

After filling our bellies, Larkin refills our water containers and ensures our horses have a refreshing snack. It's a small act of care, but it speaks volumes about his character, his attentiveness to detail, and his nurturing nature.

As we mount our horses, I pause for a moment, staring at him.

His strong, capable hands adjust the reins, with his eyes focused on the path ahead. His presence is a constant reassurance, a silent promise of protection.

With a gentle nudge, we set off. The horses fall into a uniform stride as we make our way toward the first farmer.

The countryside stretches out before us in a tapestry of green and gold, dotted with quaint villages and rolling hills. It's a beautiful land, with subtle signs of the changing seasons. There's a crispness in the air, like a whisper of autumn carried on the breeze.

The leaves on the trees are just beginning to hint at their transformation. The edges of gold and crimson peek through the vibrant green.

As we arrive at the first farmer's land, the family rushes out to greet me, their princess. Their faces beam with relief and gratitude. Their eyes fill with hope.

Larkin stays close, ever vigilant. His presence is a silent reassurance.

The farmer has his withered hands clasped in front of him as he eagerly explains which crops need help. His voice trembles as he expresses his appreciation for my magic.

Without hesitation, I begin my work.

I walk along each row, with my hands outstretched and my eyes closed. A glow seeps from my fingertips as I breathe life into the struggling crops, encouraging each plant to produce big, healthy, meaty fruits.

The withered leaves unfurl, the stalks straighten, and the fields turn vibrant green, laden with the promise of abundance.

As the fields transform, the farmer and his family cheer. Their faces are alight with joy. The children, wide-eyed with wonder, run toward me. Their tiny hands clutch homemade gifts. One presents a crudely carved wooden bird, its wings outstretched in flight.

Their heartfelt appreciation fills me with warmth. It's such a simple craft, but it makes me feel good to help people. It's a reminder of the true purpose of my craft, a gift to be shared with those in need.

Which is exactly why I must wed Prince Rome

As we prepare to leave, their family gathers around us, their faces stamped with gratitude, their voices united in a chorus of thanks.

Larkin readies the horses. As I turn to thank him, I catch his gaze, a look I couldn't quite decipher. His eyes shine with wonder. A gentle smile plays on his lips, a silent acknowledgment of the work I had done.

We journey from one farmer's land to the next, spreading my magic across the countryside. The sun beats down on us, and the hours blur into a tapestry of golden fields and grateful smiles.

By sunset, exhaustion weighs heavily upon me. My limbs ache with fatigue.

"We should stop at an inn for the night," I suggest. "I can't ride another mile."

Larkin chuckles, a playful spark in his eyes. "Have you ever stayed beyond your comfy castle walls, Princess?"

I teasingly roll my eyes. "I'll take whatever meal and bed I can get."

Larkin nods with a smirk. "Don't say I didn't warn you."

With a shared laugh, we turn our horses toward the closest town. The promise of rest and a warm meal spur us onward. The thought of a cozy inn, far from the dusty roads and endless fields, fills me with a sense of anticipation.

The flickering light of the inn beckons us as we arrive at the edge of town.

"I'll go in and secure a room," I offer, eager to rest. "You can see to the horses."

Larkin's brow furrows, his gaze unwavering. "Absolutely not, you will not be left out of my sight, Princess. I won't leave you unprotected."

He dismounts and extends a hand. "You'll come with me, and we'll go in together."

A warmth spread through my chest at his words. It's a simple gesture, yet it truly shows his concern for my well-being.

"All right, Larkin," I reply. "Together it is then."

As we walk toward the inn, side by side. I feel the weight of his dedication. His desire to protect me lights a flame within my core.

The warm glow of the inn consumes us as we step inside. The scent of roasted meat and ale fills the air. A cheerful fire crackles in the hearth, casting dancing shadows on the roughhewn walls.

Behind the counter, a stout woman stands with rosy cheeks and a welcoming smile. "Good evening," she greets us, her voice hearty and kind.

"A room with two beds, please," Larkin says.

"All I've got is a master suite, one bed, one settee. It's got a lovely tub," she adds with a smile.

Larkin gives the nice lady some coin in exchange for the brass key.

"Want to get some food in the pub before heading to the room?" He nods his head toward the room littered with patrons drinking ale.

We settle in at a table in the corner of the tavern. The same lady from the front counter approaches our table and takes our order. Larkin orders us two ales, two roast specials, a loaf of bread, and a slice of chess pie.

A wave of shyness washes over me as every gaze in the room settles on me. I left my crown at home in hopes of not being recognized.

The hostess returns to the table with our ale and food, and I'm thankful for the diversion from the curious eyes around us.

The tavern buzzes back to life as patrons return to their conversations, but I can't shake the feeling of being watched.

A group of men sit at the table behind Larkin and keep casting glances my way, making me increasingly uneasy. They are probably just trying to decipher if I am *the* princess, or just someone who looks similar to her, I assure myself. Trying to ignore their unwelcome attention, I shift my focus to Larkin, who is layering a piece of bread with butter.

"Everything okay, Princess?" Larkin asks, offering me the generously buttered chunk of bread.

"Yeah, just exhausted."

As we finish our meal, Larkin glances over his shoulder toward the group behind us, and they quickly look away, trying to appear nonchalant.

We make our way upstairs to our room.

One of the men from the group downstairs walks down the hallway behind us, but he keeps a considerable distance.

We finally reach our room, with the man reaching his several rooms down from us.

The room is spacious and clean. The fireplace is the first thing that catches my eye, a grand stone structure that promises warmth and comfort.

The large bed is draped with heavy, velvet curtains that could be drawn for privacy and darkness. The settee is positioned near the window, offering a view of the street below. It's upholstered in a rich, floral fabric that adds a touch of elegance to the room. It's a nice room, no doubt, but it's not a room in my beloved castle.

As I glance over at the settee, a wave of concern washes over me. It was a lovely piece of furniture, no doubt, but it's hardly fit for a grown man to sleep on, let alone quite possibly the largest man known to the realm.

My eyes dart to Larkin, who is crouched in front of the fireplace, and I find myself imagining his tall frame trying to curl up on that small settee.

It simply won't do.

"Larkin, the settee is too small for you. You should take the bed. I can manage on the settee for the night."

His eyes meet mine. "Absolutely not, Princess," he replies firmly. "I would sooner sleep on the floor than allow you to sleep on the settee. It's out of the question."

"Okay, Larkin," I counter. "The bed is large enough for both of us. There's no need for either of us to be uncomfortable. We can just share the bed." I say, the sound of my beating heart nearly swallowing my words. "You can have the first bath. I'm going to enjoy this fire you so kindly started."

I settle back, watching as the flames dance and crackle, casting a warm glow around the room.

As the sound of water fills the room, signaling Larkin's retreat into the tub, a thought crosses my mind. Sharing a bed was one thing, but sharing a blanket? That might be a bit too intimate for a princess and her guard.

My eyes scan the room, searching for any sign of an extra blanket, and my search proves fruitless.

"Larkin, I'll be right back. I'm just going downstairs for a moment."

Whether he hears me over the sound of the running water, I can't be sure, but I'm sure I'll be back before he even notices I'm gone.

With that, I turn and make my way down the stairs. My mind is set on securing that elusive second blanket.

As I descend the stairs, the lively atmosphere of the pub surges around me. I glance around, taking in the familiar sights and sounds while I wait for the hostess to return with the extra blanket.

My gaze drifts toward the table where the men who had been staring at me earlier were still gathered, minus the one I spotted in the hall. A shiver runs down my spine when I realize they haven't moved.

Quickly, I avert my eyes, hoping to avoid any unwanted attention.

With the blanket finally in hand, I turn to head back upstairs, eager to return to our room.

As I reach the hallway, my heart skips a beat.

Standing there blocking my path is one of the men who was missing from the table.

"Nice necklace," he drawls, his eyes glinting in the dim light. "I wonder how much it's worth."

My blood runs cold as he takes a step closer, invading my personal space.

Instinctively, I recoil, taking a step back.

But to my horror, voices snake in from behind, trailed by a chorus of heavy footsteps. I look over my shoulder, mortified to see the rest of the men from the table, closing in on me, their intentions unclear. Panic surges through me as I realize I'm trapped, with nowhere to run.

My mind races as I replay the self-defense techniques Larkin taught me, desperately searching for a way out of this nightmare.

The man in front of me closes in, his presence suffocating me as he brushes a strand of my hair back with his hand. The stench of ale and unwashed skin fills my nostrils, intensifying my disgust and fear.

Reacting on instinct, I slam my fist into his ribs with all my might, hoping to create an opening for escape. He grunts in pain as I break free and make a desperate run for it.

My freedom is short-lived.

The other men quickly catch up to me, with their hands grabbing at my clothes, yanking me back with such force that dizziness washes over me.

"Where do you think you're going?" He grunts.

A yelp escapes my lips as one of them clamps a hand down over my mouth, silencing my cries for help.

Their voices, shadowed with malice and greed, echo in my ears as they speak among themselves, objectifying me, discussing my worth as if I'm nothing more than a commodity.

Panic surges through me, threatening to consume me as I struggle to comprehend the gravity of my situation.

The first man fists my necklace, Brynn's necklace, and rips it off my neck.

I fight with every ounce of strength I possess, kicking and thrashing against their grip as they drag me along the carpeted hallway. The coarse fibers scrape against my skin, adding to the torment of my struggle.

Panic claws at my throat, choking off any hope of escape.

"Hurry, get her in the room before someone comes looking for her," one of the men hisses, his voice quivering with urgency and fear.

"I'm trying, but the bitch is as weighty as a boar!"

His rough handling intensifies as they quicken their pace, dragging me closer to an unknown destination.

Suddenly, my head collides with the unforgiving surface of the wall.

A sharp, searing pain shoots through my skull, sending waves of dizziness crashing over me. My vision blurs. The edges of my surroundings fade into a hazy darkness. I struggle to maintain consciousness, to stay present in the midst of this terrifying ordeal.

But the pain is relentless, threatening to pull me under, to surrender me to the darkness that looms ever closer.

Through the haze of pain and fear, a familiar voice pierces the darkness, a sound so sweet it brings tears to my eyes.

Larkin.

My salvation has arrived.

Relief washes over me, but it's quickly replaced by a surge of worry.

Can Larkin handle four men on his own? The odds seem insurmountable.

I have to help him.

Get up.

Get up now.

His voice is weighted with a menacing tone I had never heard before. "Get your filth-stained hands off *my* princess before I send you back to Hel," he threatens. His words are a sharpened blade that cuts through the air.

The men chuckle at Larkin's words.

"None of you are leaving this hall alive. Now, you'll die choking on your own sins."

Forcing my eyes open, I catch a glimpse of Larkin standing before me. He's shirtless. His body glistens with moisture from his recent bath. His hair is wet and disheveled, and he is clad only in his underclothes. He has no visible weapon, yet his presence radiates an aura of power and determination.

A long, glistening dark sword materializes in his hand, pulled from the thin air. Larkin moves with impossible speed, a blur of motion that defies comprehension.

There are moments when he appears fully armored, a knight from Helheim, but my vision is too clouded to grasp the transformation.

What he does is magnificent. Larkin moves with unparalleled mastery. His sword is simply an extension of his will. He dances through the air, cutting through the men with a lethal skill.

One of the men begs and grovels.

Larkin's voice turns to ice. "There's no power in this realm that could save you from me."

In a matter of seconds, all four men lay on the ground, defeated and broken, with a pool of blood quickly turning the lush carpet a dark crimson.

The dizziness finally overwhelms me, and I succumb to the darkness. Larkin bends over me.

"I've got you, Princess," he whispers. His voice is a soothing balm against the storm raging within me.

And with those words, I surrender to the abyss, knowing I'm safe in his strong arms.

I wake to the gentle sound of running water filling my ears. A throbbing pain pulses in my head, a stark reminder of the brutal encounter. Larkin is next to me within seconds. His presence is a comforting reassurance. He carefully helps me sit up. His touch is so gentle, a contrast to the brutality I watched his hands commit moments ago.

"I have the bath ready for you, if you're up to it," he says softly. His eyes are filled with concern.

I nod.

He guides me toward the bathroom. His hand never leaves mine.

"I'm okay to get in myself," I say, offering a weak smile.

"Just yell if you need anything, I'll be right out here," Larkin replies. His voice is woven with tenderness.

As I settle into the warm water, a wave of relief washes over my aching body. The heat seeps into my muscles, easing the tension and calming my frayed nerves. Looking down, the damage sprawls across me. Bruises of all shapes and sizes mar my skin, reminding me of the violence I'd just endured. Unable to control myself, sudden sobs escape my lips.

Larkin bursts in, his face contorted with worry. "Princess, are you okay?" he asks frantically.

His eyes scan my body, and I see his jaw clench as he takes in the sight of the bruises. I cover myself, with my sobs intensifying.

Larkin, shaking with anger, sits down on the floor, his back turned to the tub, offering me a silent presence of support.

"My necklace!" I say in a panic, noticing its absence as I touch my neck.

"I've got your necklace, Princess," Larkin says, reaching into his pocket, presenting my necklace clutched in his large, calloused hand. "It's broken at the clasp, but I'll get it fixed for you as soon as we return to the castle," he says quietly.

Larkin helps me out of the tub, averting his gaze from my naked body. I towel myself off and accept the shirt Larkin offers me through the cracked door. I throw Larkin's shirt on over my head, wincing at the motion, straining my sore, battered arms. His shirt completely swallows me, smelling of oak and faint spices.

I wobble back to the plush mattress, allowing my broken body to sink into its warm embrace.

Larkin joins me on the bed, careful not to bump me. I scoot myself closer to him. The soft dips of my body press against his solid form. I rest my head on his chest. He gently wraps his strong arm around me, and the warmth of him encompasses me.

With each breath he draws, my worries unravel, and the thrum of his heart tethers me to peace. It feels like the safest place in the realm, like nothing could ever touch me as long as I'm here.

"Larkin, what is your craft?" I whisper.

He is quiet for a long moment. Just as I think he isn't going to answer, he does.

"I don't have a craft, Princess."

His words leave my mind reeling.

"So...you're powerless?" I ask, stunned.

What I witnessed tonight was not the actions of a powerless being. What Larkin did was unlike anything I have ever seen.

"No, Princess, I'm not powerless," he says, his voice soft.

"Then what are you, Larkin? What you did back there was... You were extraordinary."

Larkin leans in and places a gentle kiss on my forehead.

"Get some rest, Princess."

How could I possibly just *get some rest* after what I just watched him do?

His scent clings to me, his shirt soft against my skin. His warmth seeps into my back. Still, my mind refuses to rest. I'm lying this close to someone who still won't tell me what he is. My mind spins for what feels like an eternity, torn between fear and trust. But after that quiet war inside me finally burns itself out, his heartbeat guides me gently into sleep.

CHAPTER NINE

I stretch against the sheets, waking to a comforting weight pressed against my backside. Larkin lies behind me. His body is a warm haven. His arms are secure around my waist. A sense of peace settles over me, a feeling so profound that for a moment, I don't want to move, don't want to disrupt the tranquility of the morning.

With a reluctant sigh, I ease myself from Larkin's sweet embrace.

I change into my clothes, lace my boots, and throw my hair into a quick braid. I exit the bathroom, finding Larkin's shirtless form standing before me. My gaze lingers on the sculpted lines of his body longer than it should, and it takes more willpower than I care to admit to look away. I unenthusiastically hand over his shirt.

We make our way down the hallway. Someone removed the bodies, but the crimson stain remains in the plush carpet. Larkin gently brushes the back of my hand as we pass the bloody scene. Images of the brutal violence replay in my mind. We return the key to the front counter and head to the stables.

A wave of relief crashes over me the moment we step out of the inn. Every part of me aches to put as much distance as possible between me and that place. An overwhelming feeling of solace hits me as I settle into Tally's saddle.

The familiar rhythm of her gait pulls me closer to the feeling of home with every step. My body aches with every jolt of the road, and the journey ahead stretches out like an eternity.

"I want to talk to Father about posting more guards in Orospire. I would never want another woman to experience that horrific situation. They talked about... how much coin I'd be worth."

I shudder at the memory.

"If women in my kingdom are being sold like cattle, it needs to end," I say with a little more conviction in my voice.

"And those responsible need to suffer a fate worse than death," Larkin chimes in, his voice coated in steel. "I have already sent post, Princess, ordering a lance of rangers to transfer to Orospire, immediately... These atrocities won't be tolerated and will be investigated promptly."

My heart swells with Larkin's dedication to keep the women of this kingdom safe.

"Thank you, that was very thoughtful," I say, ready to rid my mind of the brutal violence I endured in my own kingdom. I push the memories away, to the farthest depths of my brain.

The journey back to the castle feels longer than the trip out. I tell Larkin I need to stretch my sore body, so we stop on the side of the road. Larkin busies himself watering the horses while I wander around a bit.

A handful of flowers fight to stay upright, their petals drooping sadly. Cupping my hands, I gather some water from the stream, lacing my magic within the water. I gently pour it into the flower's soil.

Each petal instantly perks up, and their colors become vibrant and alive.

I turn to see Larkin watching me, with a small smile playing on his lips. Feeling a bit refreshed, we continue on our way. With each step, the castle seems to grow closer. Its familiar towers are visible in the distance. I can't wait to be back within its walls, surrounded by the comforts of home. My tummy is rumbling with hunger, and I cannot wait to relax with some dinner and a nice novel.

I turn to Larkin. My voice is soft with gratitude. "Thank you for saving my life."

His eyes meet mine, with those warm amber eyes. He shakes his head gently. "You never have to thank me, Princess."

Then, his voice shifts, low and earnest. "Princess, your magic. It's incredible. Truly. I've watched you bring life where there was none. I've seen the way flowers bloom beneath your fingertips and how people smile when you walk past. You don't just use your craft, you *share* it. You leave a little piece of yourself in your every wake, the world flourishes in your mere presence," he continues, "It's...magnificent, everything in this realm notices how extraordinary you are, from the grains of sand beneath our feet to the stars far above and everything in between."

My lungs hiccup.

"I hope you never forget how extraordinary you are." His gaze is unwavering. "You embody life itself. And life, *your* life, should always be protected. This realm is a dark, cruel place. But you... Your existence makes even the darkest corners of this world shine brighter than the stars."

My heart flutters at his words, blooming with a warmth I can barely contain. I feel seen in a way I never have before, not as a princess, not as a daughter, not even from my own eyes.

Then, more solemnly, he adds, "I will protect you, always. With my last breath, if it ever comes to that. You never need to thank me for it."

Tears prick the corners of my eyes, but I blink them back, smiling instead. Because in this moment, wrapped in his voice and his vow, I have never felt safer or more cherished.

And somewhere deep in my chest, a part of me whispers that I'm already his. Yet, no matter how deeply I feel it, we both know this was something I will never be allowed to want.

By the time we reach the castle gates, exhaustion clings to my bones. Every step is a stinging ache. But Larkin stays close. His reliable presence is a lighthouse in the fog, guiding me through the corridors.

He walks me back to my chambers. His hand hovers just behind my back, not touching but near enough to anchor me if I falter.

When we reach my door, he turns to me, his brow knit with concern. "I'll send for a healer to look at your bruises," he says softly.

I nod, too tired to speak, but grateful for the way he always thinks of my well-being, always makes sure I am safe.

"I'll report everything to Igor." His jaw tightens.

Then, unexpectedly, he reaches up and brushes a strand of hair from my face. His fingertips linger just long enough to graze my cheek. The fleeting, gentle touch sends a tremor through me.

"I'll also follow up with the rangers I sent to Orospire," he adds. His hand falls reluctantly back to his side. "Get some rest, Princess. Drink some water, relax." His voice softens. "I'll see you later."

Then he was gone. His footsteps fade down the corridor.

CHAPTER TEN

My chambers are a flurry of soft voices and gentle rustling as Maya and the other maids work around me with intensity.

The windows are cracked just enough to let in the golden afternoon light and crisp autumn breeze, and it dances along the silk and crystal of the gown that hangs from the screen nearby.

My heart is fluttering, part nerves, part excitement. Tonight, the entire court will be watching Prince Rome and me. Every interaction, every dance, must be perfect.

Maya helps me step into my gown. The moment the fabric touches my skin, I feel transformed. The dress is a masterpiece—deep sapphire blue, a sky under candlelight glittering with its own stars.

It hugs my body in all the right places. The plunging neckline is daring but elegant, revealing just enough to draw attention without losing decorum. The bodice cinches at my waist, and the skirt falls in soft, shimmering folds that skim the floor with every step I take.

The fabric clings gently to my hips and frames my figure, highlighting the generous curve of my backside. Maya hums as she moves behind me. Her nimble fingers twist and pin my long hair into an elaborate updo around my glinting crown. It's beautiful. She leaves a few strands loose, carefully coaxed to fall down my back in cascading waves.

Another maid leans close, with her brush sweeping across my cheeks. I close my eyes, letting her work. My lips are painted a deep mauve shade. My cheeks are flushed just enough to look kissed by emotion. My eyes are lined with dark coal.

Maya steps back to admire her work. "You look breathtaking, Your Highness."

I rise slowly, smoothing the gown with both hands. My pulse quickens. The gown sparkles as I move. Each inch of fabric catches the light like stars sewn into silk.

A soft knock on my chamber door breaks the silence as the last pearl earring is fastened in place. My heart skips. It's time. Maya smooths the skirt of my gown one last time before opening the door.

And there he is, Larkin.

He stands tall, composed as ever, in his ceremonial uniform in dark emerald velvet and polished silver, with a sword at his hip. But the moment his eyes meet mine, that careful composure fractures. His gaze travels over me, slowly, like he's seeing me for the very first time. His mouth opens slightly, as if to speak, but nothing comes out.

His silence says more than words could ever. He shifts, as if trying to catch his breath. Then he clears his throat.

"You... look—" He falters again, eyes narrowing ever so slightly in disbelief. "You look... breathtaking, Princess."

The way he says it makes my cheeks warm.

But then, his expression shifts, just to show a flicker of uncertainty. His jaw tightens. "Your future husband will love that dress."

His voice is still soft, but there's a bite to it. A note of jealousy is buried under his usual formality. My heart does a strange twist in my chest. I give him a small knowing smile, brushing past him enough to let my perfume linger in the air between us.

We walk through the marble corridors. My heels click softly against the polished floor. As we approach the ballroom, strings swell in an elegant waltz. The low hum of conversation and laughter echoes beyond the high arched doors.

When the doors open, massive chandeliers glitter from the ceiling, casting warm light across the room in glimmering gold patterns. Every wall is draped in deep silks of silver and deep emerald. Tiny glass orbs float magically near the ceiling like starlight suspended in the air, shimmering and twinkling in time with the music. Ivy wraps around the marble columns, dotted with white blossoms that fill the air with a sweet, subtle perfume.

The floor is gleaming, polished so perfectly, I can see reflections in it. Tables wrapped in velvet are arranged around the edges, set with fine crystal and golden plates. Musicians in the gallery play from above, their sound a cascade of silk drifting down through the hall.

Guests already fill the space, nobles, foreign dignitaries, lords and ladies in their finest, but all eyes turn toward me the moment I step through the doors. And yet, the only gaze I feel is Larkin's, hot on my back, lingering longer than it should. I inhale slowly. Shoulders back. Chin high.

I move gracefully through the ballroom with the clink of crystal and soft rustle of silks all around me. Smiles greet me from every direction. Curtsies, bows, compliments, I've grown used to it all, and the way people speak to me as though I were made of porcelain and starlight. Tonight, I let myself enjoy it a little more than usual. Larkin's kind words linger, helping to lift my confidence. The Brumble Berry Ale doesn't hurt either.

I sip the sweet, spiced drink from a delicate silver goblet, letting the tartness linger on my tongue. Nearby, silver platters of pastries, sugared fruit, roasted meats, and buttered breads tempt every guest. I nibble on a bit of everything, savoring it all while exchanging pleasantries with the Duchess of Emberfly. The music shifts, lively and spirited. I glance toward the doors, and then I see him.

Prince Rome of Haravik.

He strides into the ballroom with his usual confidence. His smile is a polished blade, gleaming beneath the high arches. Every hair on his head is perfectly in place. He wears blue and gold. The threads of his tunic are embroidered with such detail they seem to shimmer. His crown catches the chandelier light and scatters it in every direction.

He is, objectively, handsome. *Regal*.

The kind of man who looks like he was carved to rule. Rome crosses the ballroom in smooth strides. People part for him like waves around a ship. When he reaches me, he bows with a flourish and takes my hand.

"Princess," he says, his voice pleasant. "You look exquisite. The gods themselves would be jealous."

I offer him a smile, the one I've practiced a hundred times. "You're too kind."

He straightens, eyes sweeping over me appreciatively. "May I have this dance?"

I nod, and he leads me onto the floor.

The music swells, and we begin to move. His hand is warm on my back. His steps are swift and fluid. We weightlessly sweep across the marble, spinning in sync with the music. It's all perfectly lovely, just as it should be. I catch glimpses of admiring eyes and whispered praise from onlookers as we twirl, a vision of unity and poise.

But even as I smile, even as I nod at his polite conversation, my thoughts begin to drift to the man standing at the edge of the ballroom, watching with unreadable eyes. Larkin. I wonder if he's thinking of me, too.

I bring myself back to the moment. Rome is speaking again. I try to focus. I want this to work. I *need* this to work. But Larkin's name echoes softly in my mind, a whispered secret I'm too afraid to say out loud.

As we glide across the floor, Rome leans in closer. The polished gold trim of his collar brushes against the bare skin of my collarbone. I catch the scent of pine and snow. Clean and sharp. It's a smell that reminds me of cool mountain winds and fire-lit halls, of a place I've never been, yet suddenly crave to see.

I tilt my head toward him.

"How's the weather in Haravik?" I ask, my voice low beneath the music.

He smiles, the corners of his ice-blue eyes crinkling.

"Getting chilly," he says. "The peaks are already dusted white. The first snowfall will come any day now."

"I've only seen snow once," I admit softly.

He looks at me, genuinely surprised.

"Truly?" Then, more warmly, he says, "You'll be seeing a lot of it soon, Princess."

There's a flicker of tenderness in his expression. For a moment, I think maybe this could work. Maybe he's more than just the gleam and polish of a crown.

"You smell lovely," he says, breathing me in. "And your hair, it's beautiful." His fingers trail a loose curl down my back.

I swallow, unsure of what to say.

His breath brushes the shell of my ear, his voice darkening. "You fill out that dress *very* nicely," he says as he moves his hand lower to the base of my spine.

A ripple of heat rolls up my neck, and I keep my expression poised.

"Thank you," I say, my voice level.

The song ends.

Rome releases me from his embrace. I step back, expecting the usual bow. But Rome holds my hand tightly. He lowers himself, dropping down onto one knee. Gasps ripple across the ballroom. The crowd shifts, opening up a circle around us.

From his coat, he pulls out a small black box. He opens it, revealing a gold glinting ring. A diamond is so large it catches every light in the room and throws it back a hundredfold. It's extravagant beyond belief, bigger than even my mother's.

I stare at it, momentarily stunned.

Rome looks up at me, his voice strong and certain.

"Princess Winnifred Salem of the Isles of Odesa, will you do me the honor of being my wife?"

A hundred eyes are on me. I feel Larkin's most of all.

I nod once. "Yes, I will."

The ballroom erupts in applause, cheers, and laughter. Rome slides the ring on my finger and rises, pulling me into an embrace. My hand and crown feel significantly heavier.

The ball continues in a blur of candlelight, music, and laughter. The air is warm with perfume and praise. Everyone wishes me joy. Their eyes flicker to the glittering ring onto my finger. My smile remains fixed in place, feminine and seasoned.

I sit among silken cushions beneath the stained glass windows, surrounded by gifts wrapped in velvets and gold-threaded ribbons. Boxes are opened one after the other. Maids are assisting me, presenting gowns of every imaginable color, delicate slippers, earrings carved from coral, and pendants. Piles of silk, lace, and glittering jewels grow at my feet.

And yet, I barely see any of it. My mind travels to a different place. Larkin Steelborn. And he's nowhere in my sights. My mind replays his kind words, gestures, the way his gaze lingers, and his jealousy.

My heart quickens as I realize, clear as candlelight, he feels something for me, more than just stolen kisses. Larkin is in love with me. Guilt creeps into my chest. Smoke curls and fills every corner. I try to push it down, to remind myself that Larkin could never be a choice. But the ache doesn't fade.

"Winifred." A voice breaks through my thoughts.

I turn, startled slightly, to see Prince Rome standing beside me.

He offers me a long, slender box wrapped in gleaming silver parchment.

"This one is from me," he says, flashing his bright white teeth in a smile.

I smile and take it gently, undoing the pale blue ribbon and lifting the lid.

Inside, nestled in white velvet, is a diamond bracelet. It's stunning, radiant, and bold. The stones catch the light just as my engagement ring does, clearly chosen to match.

It's breathtaking.

"Only the best for the future Queen of Haravik," he says, leaning in and kissing my cheek.

I laugh softly and let him fasten it around my wrist. The diamonds are cold against my skin. But even as I admire it, even as the music swells around us again and people raise glasses in my honor, I can't help but think of a pair of amber eyes and how they follow me quietly, faithfully, even when I'm not looking. And how they are nowhere to be found now.

The room is too warm. The music is too loud. The diamonds on my wrist and finger feel heavier with each passing moment.

I turn to Rome.

"If you'll excuse me," I say, touching his arm lightly, "I could use some fresh air."

He smiles, distracted but obliging.

"Of course, Little Flower."

Little Flower.

The words sit unexpectedly in my chest.

I slip away, careful not to draw attention, gliding past courtiers and dancers until I reach the tall doors leading to the gardens. The air beyond them is crisp and cool, a welcome contrast to the perfume of the ballroom.

The garden is quiet, lit by soft lanterns and the pale glow of the moon. The scent of jasmine and night roses floats on the breeze.

I breathe it in, slowly. Then I see him. Larkin. He's sitting on a stone bench near the fountain. His head is bowed. His elbows are on his knees, and a glass of amber liquid is cradled in his hand. His long hair falls forward, hiding most of his perfect face. But I can tell he's not just resting. He's unraveling.

I hesitate only a second before walking toward him. The train of my gown whispers across the stone floor.

He doesn't hear me at first. The garden is hushed; the world shrinks down to just the sound of my steps and the trickle of the fountain. When I reach him, I stop and slowly lower myself onto the bench beside him. He smells of whiskey, rich, bitter, burning. He shifts slightly, raising the glass, then letting it hang from his fingers.

His knuckles are white.

He mutters something, soft and slurred.

I can't make it out.

"Larkin?" I say gently.

He doesn't answer, just huffs a breath through his nose. A laugh that never made it past his throat. I look at him, really look at him. The careful guard's mask is gone. His eyes are half-lidded, distant. He looks tired.

Raw.

"Larkin, you should retire and get some rest," I suggest.

He doesn't look at me. "And miss the happy couples' celebration. Ha," he says with slurred words.

I rest my hands on my lap, unsure what to say. It's only a piece of metal, and yet the weight of the ring presses into my skin, reminding me of more than I want to carry.

I sit beside him in silence for a long moment. The night air curls cool around my bare shoulders. The scent of whiskey and damp stone fills my lungs. I glance down at the ring. Its surface is cold and gleaming, too perfect.

Then I look at him. His head still hangs low. His broad shoulders are tense beneath his suit jacket. He doesn't speak. Doesn't move. A hollow ache rips through my chest.

I rise to my feet slowly, smoothing the silk of my gown as I turn to him. He doesn't look up, but I lean in anyway, bending at the waist until my lips are near his ear.

"If I had a choice," I say softly, "I'd choose you, Larkin."

A shiver ripples through him as I whisper.

I turn, with my heart pounding. Each step away from him feels like it takes a piece from me.

The lantern light dances in my vision. I don't dare look back. But then, his voice follows me, a little louder, thick with whiskey but unmistakably clear.

"We always have a choice, Princess."

I stop.

My lungs falter.

But I don't turn around.

I let the words settle in the garden air, in a shower of leaves, soft, aching, final.

I keep walking.

CHAPTER ELEVEN

I awake to a knock at my door, the large oak door swings open, and Maya steps through holding a large box wrapped in parchment and tied with a silk pink ribbon.

"Good morning, Your Highness. This is a gift from Khristea," Maya says, placing the large box on my dresser.

She leaves my room, taking my soiled laundry with her.

I lift the lid, and my breath stills in my chest.

Inside is the most beautiful gown I've ever laid eyes on. It's solid white, delicate as snowfall, with embroidered vines and flowers stitched in white lace that shimmers faintly when the light catches them. It's long-sleeved and floor-length, with a train that seems to stretch for miles, elegant and regal. My fingers graze the fabric, marveling at the craftsmanship.

Tucked beneath the gown is a folded piece of parchment, sealed in wax. I open it carefully and recognize the seamstress's handwriting.

Princess, I am sorry I missed your celebration. I regrettably must inform you, I will not be accompanying you to the Kingdom of Haravik. I have just discovered I am with child. My husband and I are overjoyed. I wish you the best, and hope you love this wedding gown I made for you - Khristea

I sigh, with my heart warming.

Her absence will be deeply felt. As I fold the letter, something flutters to the floor, another, much smaller slip of paper. I pick it up and unfold it. The handwriting is the same, but this note is far shorter.

Trust no one. Not even your most faithful.

My brows pull together. What does that mean? I stare at the note, with my heart thudding heavier in my chest. I read it again.

Even your most faithful.

Is someone close to me not who they seem?

I carefully place the gown and both letters back in the box and slide it beneath my bed. My head is spinning, but I shake it off. I need to focus. I walk over to my dresser and pull out my training clothes.

But just as I reach for them, something catches my eye. Sitting on the chair beside the dresser is a small wooden box I don't recognize. I pause. It wasn't here last night. I lift the lid. Inside is a delicate bracelet, black metal and dainty, with two charms. One shaped like a horse and the other a tiny rose.

My lips part in surprise and then curve softly as realization dawns. It's from Larkin. I hold it up in the light, and the black color shifts to a beautiful shade of dark green.

I hold the bracelet in my palm for a long moment, feeling a gentle twist in my chest. Warmth, undeniable and true. And yet, that note echoes in the back of my mind.

Trust no one...

I glance at the heavy bracelet currently occupying my wrist. I pick up the new bracelet and fasten it around my other wrist. It feels light, almost like a secret. Like someone sees *me*, not just the title I carry.

I dress in my training clothes: the usual tunic, trousers, and tightly laced boots.

I braid my hair quickly, knotting it at the nape of my neck, and I head toward the training yard. The cool air bites pleasantly at my skin.

But when I arrive, Larkin isn't here. Instead, it's his general, General Jamie. A tall, broad-shouldered man with cold steel eyes and a scar that runs down the side of his face. He bows his head once, brisk and formal.

"Your Highness," he says. "Larkin isn't well. I'll be leading your session today."

My mouth opens slightly, instinctively wanting to ask what's wrong with Larkin, but

Jamie's expression is hard. Closed. Not welcoming questions.

I nod.

He doesn't go easy on me.

Every strike is fast. Each movement is meant to test me. There's no laughter, no teasing remarks like Larkin offers when he pushes me past my limits. No praise. Just silence, grunts, and the sounds of weapons clashing. My arms burn. My legs ache. Sweat drips down my back.

I finish the last sequence, panting, and bruised and sore in places I didn't know I could be sore. I squat, gasping to recover.

"Dismissed," Jamie says curtly, before turning on his heel. "Oh, Princess, the captain suggested you do your laps," he says over his shoulder.

I don't speak.

I just nod again and walk away. Every muscle screams, but images of the night in Orospire flash through my mind.

I run.

I take the path that winds around the back gardens, past the stables, through the thinning trees. My boots pound the earth in a thundering cadence. The wind catches strands of my hair.

I run until exhaustion claims me.

After my run, I'm drenched in sweat, lungs burning, skin flushed. The castle pool calls to me. I strip off my training clothes and slide into the water, cool and clear, letting it wash away the ache in my muscles and the knot tightening in my chest.

I float for a while, staring up at the sky through the glass ceiling and letting the silence settle me.

Once I'm clean and dry, I dress in a soft gown that a servant placed nearby. I head into the castle to my mother's chambers.

Her room is inviting, warm, and smells of lavender and honeysuckle. She's sitting in a plush chair by the window, crocheting something soft and blue. Her hands move quickly and efficiently.

She greets me with a warm smile. "Hello, dear."

I tend to her plants while we chat about the ball, Prince Rome, the engagement, and my upcoming farewell.

"Maybe the babe will arrive before you depart on the upcoming Sun's Day."

I nod, still tending to her many plants by filling each space in her bathing chamber and kissing each one with my magic. I leave on the sixth sunrise from today. I try to push my anxieties away and focus on what I'm doing.

My hand brushes the leaves of a tall fern, one of her oldest and tallest plants. The second my skin makes contact with the fern, the room blurs.

An intangible shift moves through the air.

A blinding white floods my vision.

My body locks. I can't move. I can't breathe.

A scene unfurls before me, a memory that is not mine, yet settles into me like a shadow.

Maya.

She's standing in this very spot, next to the sink in my mother's bathing chamber. In her grasp is a black vial. She pours the contents of the vial into a cup of tea that she then places back on the tray alongside an assortment of pastries, fruits, and meats. Her movements nimble and discreet, she slips the empty vial back into her skirts.

She carries the tray into my mother's room and places it on the table my mother sits at.

I want to scream, to lunge forward, but I can't move. My voice fails to escape my throat. I can't even blink.

I watch my mother accept the tray with a smile.

My heart violently beats within my chest as realization hits me.

I crash back into my body as if falling from great heights, gasping violently.

My knees feel like they're soon to buckle.

My hands collide with the cool stone of the counter, anchoring me as my lungs claw for air.

Wide-eyed and stunned, I look to my mother,

"I know who poisoned you," I say, breathless.

Fingers trembling, my vision swims. With my chest heaving, I manage to tell my mother of my vision between ragged breaths.

"Winnie, you do not tell anyone of this vision, and I mean *anyone*. Go to the captain, order him to question the servant," my mother quietly commands.

I nod, trying to calm my still racing heart.

CHAPTER TWELVE

After instructing Larkin to interrogate Maya, I head to the gardens to clear my spinning mind. The crisp autumn air meets me, an embrace that cannot smooth the fire crackling in my chest.

I wander past the fountain, past the fragrant roses, deeper into the hedges where the palace lights don't quite reach. My hands tremble. My chest still rises and falls too fast.

I stop near the stone bench where Larkin and I sat the night of my birthday celebration. I remember that night with painful clarity. He was brooding in the moonlight, like a man carrying too many shadows. He had barely looked at me.

We always have a choice, Princess.

That line echoed now like a prophecy.

Without thinking, I reach out and brush my fingers across a nearby bush. Its tiny green leaves are cool and damp with dew. Its presence calls to me like it wants to share a secret. White fills my vision, like a dense fog swallowing the world around me. I can't move. My body locks again. My breath freezes. But I *see*.

I'm suddenly back in that moment here with Larkin. But not through my eyes. Through the bush next to me. Through its small, rooted presence tucked beside the bench. I watch myself standing beside Larkin. I watch the whole scene unfold from the perspective of the bush inches away.

I walk away, disappearing back into the comfort of the castle. With a ragged cry, Larkin throws the glass of whiskey. I flinch from the sound of it shattering against the stone floor. He drops his face into his hands, and he sobs.

The air is thick with raw, unfiltered emotion. I feel my own tears pricking beneath my lashes. The urge to comfort him consumes me. He sobs, his heart unraveling with each shuddering breath. My heart twists in my chest.

I feel all of it.

His pain.

His longing.

His love.

In an instant, the vision fades like smoke swirling in the wind. I'm back, standing in the quiet garden.

My breath is shaky, with my lips parted, tears burning my vision. The urge to collapse into

Larkin's strong arms crashes into me, a wave in an unforgiving storm.

I have to go to him.

I pick up my skirts and scurry toward the tall glass doors of the castle. The large, colorful tapestries that line the walls are a blur as I hurry down the halls. The sound of my boots slapping the marble floors is a cadence between my ragged breaths.

I abruptly crash into a surface as solid as stone. I tilt toward the ground, then, that very same surface wraps itself around me, bracing my form.

Looking up, I meet a pair of frantic amber eyes.

"Princess, are you okay?" Larkin asks, his voice bound with concern. "I felt you—" He stops.

I unrestrainedly sob into his chest.

He silently holds me—his strong form an anchor—and I'm a ship rocking in the storm. I came to comfort him, and the tides have turned.

Larkin ushers me through the doorway to his room. We sit on his bed. I am finally able to catch my breath and ease my pounding heart.

"Princess, are you all right?" he asks again. "Did someone hurt you?" His voice turns to steel.

"No," I breathe. "No, I just, I needed to see you."

We sit in silence for a moment, the kind of silence that fills the space like warm water. My hands rest in my lap. The bracelet he gave me catches the light in a soft shimmer of green and charm. I consider telling him everything. About the visions. About the way my magic is changing in ways I don't understand. About the warning tucked into a seamstress's goodbye.

But my mother's voice rings in my mind. *Not a word to anyone.* I swallow the truth and keep it buried in the back of my throat.

Larkin watches me quietly, with his brows drawn with worry.

"What is it, Princess?" he asks, voice low.

I turn to him, meeting his eyes. Those resolute amber irises I've come to know better than my own reflection. My heart is aching and full all at once.

"I know you love me," I whisper.

He stills. His lips part like he wants to deny it or confirm it or say a hundred things at once.

But he says nothing. He just listens.

"I don't know what I'm supposed to do, because Larkin...I think I love you back."

For a second, everything stands still. The whole world holds its breath.

Then he exhales and pulls me into his arms, wrapping me tightly against his solid chest. His heartbeat thunders against my cheek.

"We'll figure it out," he says, voice muffled in my hair. "Whatever this is. Whatever comes next. We'll figure it out... together."

And in his arms, my heart starts to slow. My breath comes easier. For now... I am safe.

"Maya is gone," he whispers.

I pull away and find his gaze.

"What do you mean... gone?"

"She has left the castle," he replies. "I have guards searching for her, scouring every inch of Emberfly and beyond. How is it you discovered she was responsible for the queen's poisoning, Princess?" he asks, his voice tinged with curiosity.

"Larkin... I... I have a lumina," I say, instantly full of regret for letting my secret slip.

CHAPTER THIRTEEN

The morning sun filters in through the tall windows of the dining hall, casting warm golden light across the long table. I sit between my mother and father, trying to focus on the breakfast spread before me, but my thoughts are a flurry of nerves.

Today is the day we leave for Haravik.

Across the room, Larkin stands at attention in the corner, quiet, vigilant, every inch the royal guard. But every now and then, when he thinks I'm not looking, I feel his eyes on me. And when I glance up, I catch him just before he looks away. It's a dance we've mastered. Secret glances, small tells.

Whispers hidden in the pauses of a heartbeat.

My father sits straight-backed and proper next to my mother, slicing into his egg. His eyes flick from me to Larkin once, just once, but he doesn't say a word. I wonder what he's thinking. If he knows.

My mother, gentle but radiant even in her fragility, smiles softly as she lifts her cup. Her hand rests absently on her rounded belly, fingers tracing small circles.

"Kestral says any day now," she says. Her voice is calm but certain. "The babe is eager. I can feel it."

My father's hand moves to hers, protective and grounding.

"You should rest today, my love," he murmurs.

There's a strange ache in my chest. Guilt, maybe. I hate leaving her now, like this, on the cusp of something so important. But the journey is necessary. The alliance is necessary. I know that. Still, my heart stays tethered to this castle. I imagine the portrait of Brynn in the hall just feet away. My chest tightens.

A servant clears away the dishes, and I stand, smoothing the folds of my cloak. My mother rises slowly, and I step forward to embrace her. She holds me tightly. Her hand brushes my hair like she used to when I was small.

"Be careful, Winnie," she whispers. "And stay true to yourself."

I nod, swallowing hard.

I turn to my father. He clasps my shoulders firmly, meeting my eyes with pride.

"Be strong, my sweet girl."

I nod again.

He brings me in for a hug. "I'm proud of you, Winnie." His voice is barely above a whisper.

I freeze.

The words are a soft storm—gentle and powerful—that loosens a tension in my chest. He has never said that to me before, not once. Not after my studies, not when I learned to wield a blade, not even when I learned to perfect my magic. Now, just as I'm about to leave, he says it.

I nod, fighting back the sudden sting behind my eyes. "Thank you, Father," I whisper, my voice thin.

He lets go, and I turn away before he can see the emotion written across my face. Larkin is already at my side. His posture is straight, and his eyes are gentle when they land on me.

We walk down the long, echoing hallways of the castle. Our boots click softly on the polished stone. Sunlight streams in through the stained glass, painting the marble floor in patterns of red and blue. We walk in silence. His presence beside me is grounding. As we near the main corridor that leads to the entrance of the castle, I stop.

The portrait hangs high on the wall, framed in old and shadow. Brynn. Her eyes look out beyond the canvas, full of life, fire, defiance, everything she was. The ache blooms within me, a wound I thought had healed. I reach out and touch the edge of the frame. My fingers brush the gilded wood.

"I miss her," I say softly, not sure if I'm speaking to Larkin or myself.

Emotion swells in my throat: grief, guilt, longing. All of it. Larkin steps closer behind me, not saying a word. He doesn't have to. And for a moment, I just stand there, breathing through the ache in my heart, before we continue. As I'm still standing in front of Brynn's portrait, letting the sorrow settle in my chest, slow footsteps scrape from behind.

Igor. He bows stiffly, as he always does, deep, formal, precise.

"Princess," he says with his usual cool courtesy, "the carriage carrying our belongings is ready. I'll be departing ahead of you to ensure everything is in order before your arrival."

I nod.

"Thank you, Igor. That's appreciated."

He glances at Larkin. "If I may... a brief word. Alone."

That strikes me as odd. There's a clipped edge in Igor's tone, respectful but pointed. I glance at Larkin, who's already watching Igor with a sharpness in his eyes.

He nods once and steps away with Igor toward the far end of the corridor. I hesitate for a moment, watching them as they begin to speak in hushed tones.

I give them space. Whatever it is, it's probably some security matter, something beneath the surface of Nobel travel that I'm not to worry over. With silent steps, I make my way through the castle's western passage and out toward the cliffs.

The wind is stronger here, rushing up from the sea, laced with salt and sun. I look out to the horizon, wondering if I'll ever see my hero again, the dragon who's saved my life, maybe more than once. As I stand here recalling the dream, I begin to think it was more a memory than a fictional story during my slumber.

I kneel beside my cakile friends, their earthy scent lifting into the breeze. I lace their soil with a bit of my magic, just enough to keep them thriving until I'm able to visit. The cliffs have always been a place of comfort, of clarity. I let the winds carry away my doubts, my grief, my fear of the unknown.

My hand rests on a cluster of cakile, with its pale green leaves and soft lilac flowers trembling in the sea breeze.

But the moment I touch it, my vision turns white.

My sight blurs, and the world tilts. The cliffs are here, but not the present. A memory. *I'm sitting in the same place, sunlight painting my skin golden, hair a wild mess down my back. Laughter bubbles from my throat.*

There's a blanket spread over the grass, a basket of food half opened beside me. I can feel the warmth of the day, the fullness of my heart. No weight of court. Just sun, wind, and freedom. It's peace. A moment I forgot I had.

Then, it fades.

My eyes flicker with the memory lingering like the warmth of the sun on my skin.

I whisper to the cakile, "Thank you."

Then I rise and turn back toward the castle, with the wind at my back.

By the time I make it back to the castle, the sun has climbed higher, casting sharp golden light over the stone walls and tiled roofs. The halls are busier now. Servants carry linens, footmen adjust armor, and the bustle of a noble departure. But none of it slows me. My steps carry me straight to the stables.

Larkin is already there, tightening the last strap on his saddle. He looks up the moment he hears my approach. There's a calm steadiness in his eyes, but I know him well enough now to recognize the tension beneath it.

He gives me a soft nod. "All set. Your mare's ready when you are."

I glance around, then lower my voice. "Any word on Maya?"

His expression tightens, just for a second. "No. Nothing yet."

I frown, the disappointment settling deep in my stomach.

He steps closer. "But they'll find her," he says firmly. "The guards are still sweeping the outer towns and every merchant route out of the city. She won't go unnoticed forever. And when we do find her, we'll get to the bottom of it."

I nod slowly. "I just... trusted her. I don't understand why she'd do something like this. Unless—" I trail off.

Unless someone *made* her.

Larkin doesn't press. He just places a hand gently on my shoulder. "We'll find the truth. I swear it."

That calm warmth of his presence alleviates my nerves enough to breathe again.

I mount my horse, settling into the saddle as Larkin swings up onto his own. The stable doors are thrown open. Guards clad in silver glistening armor line in formation along the path. Igor is long ahead.

I take one last look at the castle, the towers, the emerald and silver banners fluttering in the wind, the place that has held every version of me so far. Then I turn my gaze forward. With a solemn nod, Larkin nudges his horse into motion, and I follow.

Together, we ride off to Haravik.

"Larkin, are we not bringing any other guards?" I ask, nudging my horse closer to his.

He doesn't answer right away.

His jaw shifts slightly, and his eyes stay on the road ahead.

"No, Princess, it's just us."

I frown. "Why? We're leaving the kingdom. Shouldn't we at least have a detail? Even a scout."

Larkin finally looks at me. His expression is unreadable, and his eyes are sharper than before. "Because we don't need them."

I study him, waiting for more.

He pauses. "I can handle whatever comes. I *will* handle it."

The way he says it, calm, certain, but with a weighty presence beneath the words, sends a small chill down my spine. Images of the night in Orospire flash through my mind, with the way he cut down four men in an instant.

"Between the search for Maya, the extra rangers in Orospire, and the new prince coming, the kingdom is shorthanded."

"Right," I say, straightening at the reminder of why I have to wed Prince Rome.

The silence stretches between us as the horses fall into a consistent beat, with hooves crunching against the gravel path that cuts through the forest. My mind keeps circling the same question over and over again.

I glance at Larkin again. His posture is upright, and his eyes constantly scan the trees ahead like they might breathe danger at any moment.

"Do you think she's working with Nyxlandia?" I ask, my voice low.

His gaze doesn't shift.

He rides on for a few seconds, and just when I start to wonder if he heard me, he answers. "No, Princess," he says simply, firmly. "I don't think it's them."

I narrow my eyes.

"Then who?" I ask.

He finally looks at me, his face unreadable. "She may be working with someone. But not Nyxlandia. If it *was,* we would know," he says confidently.

He's right. Nyxlandia doesn't bother with whispers. They deal in devastation.

"But someone *is* behind this," I press. "Someone who Maya trusts or fears."

I fall silent, my heart twisting.

Larkin's voice softens.

"Whatever it is, Princess... we will get to the bottom of it. I promise."

And somehow, I believe him, even if it means walking straight into the fire.

We continue down the winding path. The castle is long behind us now. The forest around us is full of shifting leaves, blushing into shades of amber, rust, and gold. The air has that crisp edge to it, the kind that bites softly at your cheeks and smells faintly of woodsmoke and the turning season.

I tug my cloak a little tighter around my shoulders and exhale, watching the puff of my breath disappear into the breeze. Larkin rides next to me, quiet as always. His eyes are alert, with his hand resting casually near the hilt of his sword. But then, without a word, he reaches into his saddlebag and pulls something out, wrapped in cloth, small, warm.

He leans toward me with a crooked smile.

"Hungry?" he asks, holding it out.

I take it, unwrapping the cloth eagerly, and I can't stop the grin that spreads across my face.

A cinnamon roll, still warm, and glazed just the way I like it. The scent alone makes my mouth water.

"Hard to forget the way your entire mood shifts when one of these is near," he says, chuckling.

I laugh under my breath, touched in a way I can't quite put into words. It's such a small thing, but it's *so* Larkin. Thoughtful. Never showy. Always watching. Always *knowing*.

The sun begins its slow descent beyond the treetops, setting the forest aglow in hues of gold and rose. The light filters through the thinning canopy in soft streaks, and the shadows grow longer with each passing minute. The air has turned colder now, brisk and whispering with the promise of night.

Larkin glances up at the sky. "We're losing daylight," he says. "There's a town not far off. Should be an inn there. We could stay there for the night, rest properly."

I think for a moment, then shake my head gently.

"Can we make camp instead?"

He raises a brow. "Camp? You'd rather sleep under the stars than in a warm bed with supper and firewood someone else has already chopped?"

I frown, images of the four men from the inn in Orospire flash through my mind.

Larkin's brows come together, and he gives me a nod. "Of course, Princess." His voice dipped with affection.

We veer off the road and follow a narrow path through the trees until we come across a small clearing beside a creek. The water trickles over smooth stones, soft and rhythmic, peaceful. The setting sun glints off the surface in dancing gold.

"This'll do," Larkin says, already hopping down from Doc.

While he starts setting up camp, unpacking the bedrolls, gathering dry branches, and checking the perimeter, I lead the horse down to the creek. They lower their heads eagerly to drink, steam rising faintly from their nostrils in the evening chill. The farther we travel north, the cooler the air grows.

I crouch beside the water, brushing my fingers over the surface. The cold rush of it stings a little, grounding and sharp. The woods around us are hushed, and the breeze carries only the rustle of leaves and the distant call of birds settling in for the night.

I glance back toward Larkin. He's smoothing out my blanket with more care than necessary, always making sure I'm comfortable before he even considers himself. Warmth stirs in my chest.

I stay by the creek a moment longer, letting the horses drink their fill while the cold water rushes over the stones beside me. But I can't keep my eyes from drifting back to camp.

To him.

Larkin stands near the edge of the clearing, splitting wood with natural skill. The last rays of sunlight dance across his figure, casting shadows over the sharp lines of his jaw, the strong curve of his shoulders. His dark hair is tied back into a tight knot, though a few stubborn strands have broken free, falling across his brow in a way that somehow makes him look more rugged.

He grips the axe with both hands, his forearms flexing with each powerful swing. The blade bites cleanly through the logs, again and again. There's nothing hurried or showy in the way he strikes. It's simple and strong. I watch his brow furrow as he lines up another piece. The muscles in his arms coil and release.

Gods, he's handsome.

Not just in the way he looks, though there's that, undeniably, but in the way he *moves*, the way he *is*. Grounded. Unshakable. Nothing could touch him unless he let it.

And yet... he lets me.

That thought lingers in my chest like a spark, warm and bright. I turn back to the horses, with my cheeks flushed. I run my fingers along the mare's neck, pretending to be focused, but all I can feel is the echo of *him*. His presence behind me. His strength... and the part of me that's beginning to crave it.

I steal one more glance over my shoulder. Larkin kneels at the fire pit now, with one knee bent and his forearm resting across it casually. One moment, there was only the rustling of leaves and the hum of the creek… and now, a full flame, dancing high and eager. The fire glows bright and warm, but it's the way it moves that catches me. It *leans* toward him.

Like it recognizes a familiar force in him and rises in answer.

The flames don't sputter or hesitate. They curl and coil as if they belong to him, as if he didn't light the fire but owns it. He's staring into the blaze, unaware of me watching. His face is calm, grounded. The fire is a loyal beast, coiling at his feet and breathing soft warmth into his presence. A shiver runs down my spine. Not from the cold.

The fire crackles low and persistent beside us now, casting amber light over the clearing as night settles in fully. The stars peek through the canopy overhead, cold, and the sounds of the forest hush into a lullaby. We sit side by side in our bedrolls, legs stretched out toward the fire. Larkin rummages through his pack and pulls out a wrapped bundle.

With a small grin, he lays it out between us, a loaf of bread, a wedge of sharp-smelling cheese, and when he unwraps the last bit of cloth, chocolates fall out onto his lap.

I laugh, eyebrows raised. "What *don't* you have in that bag? Is there a full kitchen in there?"

He shrugs, a smirk tugging at the corner of his mouth.   "Wouldn't be very good company if I let the Princess starve, would I?"

He hands me some bread and cheese, and we eat in easy silence. The fire crackles, the breeze rustles gently in the trees, and the world feels... far away.

After we finish, we lie back on our bedrolls. The night air grows colder, and I pull my blanket tighter around me, but the chill seeps in. I try to ignore it at first, but my toes are practically frozen.

I glance at Larkin beside me. He lies with his hands behind his head, eyes half closed, the firelight painting soft shadows over his face. He looks so peaceful. But he turns slightly, sensing me shiver.

"You cold?" he asks, already reaching for his blanket.

I hesitate for a beat, then scoot closer, tugging my bedroll along with me until my side brushes his.

"Just a little," I whisper.

He shifts without a word, adjusting the blanket over both of us and letting me settle into the space beneath his arm.

His body is *so* warm, a living furnace, and I melt against him almost immediately.

His arm curls around my shoulders, holding me gently but protectively. I sigh, my breath slowing. We lie there in the firelight. His heartbeat is even beneath my cheek, and the cold night is forgotten. The forest wraps around us, silent and watchful. I close my eyes, feeling safe, wrapped in warmth. We drift to sleep that way, tangled together, breathing in rhythm.

CHAPTER FOURTEEN

By the time we're back on the road, the sun has climbed just above the trees, casting soft golden light across the path. The cold air nips at my cheeks, but the sun cuts through it just enough to be pleasant. The leaves crunch under the horses' hooves, and our breath forms mist in front of us as we ride.

After a while, Larkin glances over at me.

"There's a town just ahead, a small one. We should stop," he suggests. "Thought you might want a warm meal, and perhaps a coffee too."

I nod, my tummy grumbling.

As we ride on beneath the canopy of amber leaves, the silence between us settles into a soft and thoughtful calm. The sun warms my back, and the cold air stings just enough to keep me alert, awake. I shift slightly in my saddle, glancing ahead at the road as it winds toward the distant hills, toward Haravik, my future.

I wonder what my new home will be like. Will the castle be cold, all stone and steel, or filled with music and sunlight like my last home? Will the people there be kind? I imagine long halls with unfamiliar tapestries, gardens I'll have to learn from the roots up, and rooms that don't yet carry any of *me* in them.

Then my thoughts drift off to *him*.

The prince.

Will I love him? Will he be kind?

The questions gnaw at the edge of my mind. I imagine a wedding, a cold smile, a duty-bound kiss. And then I imagine another face, one just beside me now. A crooked smile. A grounding hand. Amber eyes.

I glance at Larkin, who rides silently beside me, scanning the trees with his usual awareness. How will I even *feel* love for the prince... when I already feel something for the man riding next to me? My heart twists, but I say nothing. And we keep riding.

We turn off the main path, hooves clopping over cobblestone as we enter the little town tucked between the trees. It's quiet, sleepy, but it has its charm that immediately draws me in. The homes and shops are built from warm wood and dark stone, with red and orange ivy creeping up the sides of buildings. Nature reclaims the edges. The remnants of the autumn equinox celebration still hang in the windows and along the fences, bundles of dried corn, orange and gold ribbons, carved gourds stacked in corners.

A smile tugs at the corner of my mouth. It feels like the kind of place where time moves slower. Where people know each other by name. We find a place to tie up the horses just outside a cozy-looking building with smoke curling from the chimney and frosted windows fogged with warmth from within. A wooden sign swings gently above the door—*Basil and Ivy's Eatery*.

The moment I step inside, I'm wrapped in a blanket of scent, cinnamon, roasted meat, and spiced pumpkin. My mouth waters instantly. It's warm and golden-lit, with only a few patrons scattered across the wooden tables.

A beautiful woman with long red hair and freckles greets us with a nod from behind the counter. Her apron is dusted in flour, and her name tag reads *Basil*. Larkin gently touches my arm, motioning to a small table near the hearth.

"Go on. Sit. I'll get the food."

I nod, letting the warmth settle into my bones as I peel off my riding gloves and slide into the chair.

The fire crackles nearby, and I glance around, taking in the crooked shelves lined with dried herbs and the vase of fresh autumn wildflowers at the center of our table. Through the flicker of firelight and the haze of scent, I watch Larkin step up to the counter. His height towers over the woman, but his voice is low and calm as he speaks to her.

He's ordering for *me*.

He always remembers the things I'm fond of. And somehow, even in a strange town, in a room full of strangers, I feel more at home than I have in weeks.

Larkin pulls the chair out from across the room from me and sits down. He leans forward with his forearms resting on the table and offers me a smile. We fall into easy conversation about the road ahead.

Then, a soft voice interrupts us. "Here ya go, darlings."

A small woman with short black hair approaches the table. She carries two steaming plates, one in each hand. She sets them down gently in front of us.

The smell is a warm hug, wrapping around me.

The venison is cooked perfectly tender with golden potatoes and roasted vegetables with flecks of herbs. A warm, fluffy roll is perched on the edge of each plate. And between us, a slice of pecan pie on a small ceramic dish, still glistening with warmth.

Her name tag reads *Ivy*.

"Let me know if you need anything else." She says, before turning on her heel and retreating to the kitchen.

The fire cackles beside us, the wind whispers on the other side of the windows. The venison warms my body as it settles in my tummy.

This moment, this table, this man sitting across from me—it's a treasure I want to bottle and keep.

I speak without thinking. "What if we just stayed here in this town, forever?"

Larkin looks up and meets my gaze. "Say the word, Princess." His voice is even.

I chuckle. "If only we could."

We step back into the crisp afternoon air. The door to the eatery closes behind us with a soft clink. The smell of cinnamon and roasted meats still clings faintly to our clothes, and my belly is full in that comforting, content sort of way. Larkin reaches into his pocket and pulls his hand out, presenting two apples, offering them to Tally and Doc.

Larkin unties the horses, brushing a bit of leaf from my saddle before helping me up. His touch is gentle and familiar now. We exchange a glance, one of those silent looks that need no words.

The town slowly shrinks behind us as the trees fold in around us.

The cadence of the horses' steps drums a soothing pulse. The sunlight is a river of molten gold spilling through the trees. With our bellies full, we ride on, ready to put some distance behind us.

"You never told me about your lumina, Princess."

My heart skips for a moment, unsure what to say. "I don't quite understand it myself, Larkin."

He nods, getting the hint that I don't want to talk about it.

My body grows sorer with every mile that passes by. Hues of rose and lavender peek through the tree line as the sun makes its descent.

Larkin slows his horse and looks my way. "We should make camp," he suggests. "We've made good distance today."

I nod, welcoming the idea of rest. My muscles ache from the long ride. The weight of thoughts I've tried to ignore is starting to press against me again.

We veer off the main road and down a narrow, overgrown path that eventually opens into a clearing nestled between tall trees. A narrow stream runs by, catching the last glimmers of light. Larkin dismounts first and immediately gets to work, gathering wood and preparing the fire pit like it's second nature.

I slide down from my saddle, stretch, then turn to the horses. I remove their saddles and packs slowly, speaking soft thanks to them for the long day's journey. The air is growing colder by the minute. I lead them to a patch of soft grass near the stream where they begin to graze, tails flicking contentedly.

Behind me, the sound of wood splitting slices through the air as Larkin swings his axe. I glance back to see him in motion, focused, capable, the very image of safety. There's never a moment that I am not in awe of this man.

We lay our bedrolls out side by side beneath a sky dotted with stars, with the fire cracking softly beside us. I curl beneath my blanket, facing Larkin and watching the golden light dance across the planes of his face. For a long moment, neither of us says anything.

Then I whisper, "How are you going to be able to handle it? Me being married to someone else?"

His jaw tightens, but he doesn't look away. "I don't know," he says quietly. "I try not to think about it. Doesn't do me any good."

My chest aches at the hollowness in his voice.

"But I *do* know," he adds, shifting closer, "that no matter what happens... I'll be here, protecting you, at your side, even if it breaks me."

A hitch rises in my chest.

Before I can think, I close the space between us and kiss him, soft at first, like a question. But he answers without hesitation, pulling me closer. His mouth is warm and sure. The kiss deepens, charged and unspoken. His hand curls behind my neck, and the other slides over my waist, my back.

I move over him slowly, with my knees on either side of his hips. His hands are gentle but hungry, exploring the curve of my body through the layers between us.

The rest of the world disappears as my hands roam his solid form. My palms tremble with his hard muscles beneath them. His hands settle firmly at my hips, holding me closer as our kiss deepens, growing slower, more intense.

He guides me with a subtle motion, rocking me gently against him. The heat between us mirrors the fire beside us, thick and undeniable.

I can feel the tension in him, the restraint. And yet, there's no hiding the way his body responds to me. The steel in his pants is hard and aching beneath me, pressing through layers of fabric and sending a wave of warmth spiraling low through my belly down into my core.

My breath hitches against his mouth, and he pulls me tighter. I trace his jaw with trembling fingers, pressing my forehead to his for a brief moment, needing to breathe him in.

"Princess," he murmurs. His voice is gravel softened by rain, rough and quiet.

He rocks me again, slow, purposeful, building a rhythm that sends heat coiling deep in between my thighs.

I gasp softly against his mouth with my forehead still pressed to his. Every layer of clothing stands between us is unwanted and suffocating.

"Do you want me to stop?" he whispers. Though his voice is strained, his body trembles with control.

I shake my head, barely able to speak. "No."

His hands move up my stomach beneath my tunic, to my breasts, and his fingertips trail fire across my skin. Each kiss deepens, more urgent, yet controlled. There's a desperation in how he touches me. He must know this moment might never come again. I feel the unspoken things between us press closer than our bodies. The ache of craving what's forbidden.

"Do you want to keep going?" he asks, voice low and rough.

I meet his gaze, breath shaky but certain. I nod. "Please."

A shift passes through him, like a man who's been given a piece of his soul back. Our gazes meet, and his eyes are full of hunger. He trails my body as he removes my tunic, taking in every inch of me. His gaze drops to my chest and lingers there. His expression fills with a desperate want.

Larkin's fingers slip beneath the edge of my pants, sliding down into my underclothes. His fingers trail the most sensitive part of me, plunging deep into my core. My breath trembles, and I gasp at the feel of his touch.

He kisses me, slow, deep, and I instinctively begin to move with him, rocking gently into the thrusts of his fingers.

Just as I start to feel deep waves of pleasure crashing into me, the night cracks.

A sharp *snap* from the bushes nearby.

Then another.

He freezes.

The warmth between us vanishes in an instant as instinct takes over. His eyes narrow, focused, and before I can even process what's happening, he rolls me gently but swiftly off him and rises to his feet in one fluid motion, dragging me up with him.

"Behind me," he commands, voice firm but hushed.

I barely have time to grab my cloak and wrap it around myself before he steps forward. His body is a living shield between me and whatever is lurking just beyond the shadows. The fire crackles behind us, casting flickering shapes across the trees as the underbrush rustles again.

Larkin draws his sword with one hand, the black blade gleaming in the firelight, and raises his other arm slightly, centering me behind him.

We wait.

CHAPTER FIFTEEN

The the leaves part, and out of the darkness lumbers a massive bear. Its coat is dark brown, and its breath steams in the cold air.

It pauses, sniffing, with its small eyes fixed on us.

The drum of my heart thunders in my chest, yet my body stays still.

Larkin doesn't flinch.

His stance is low, sword held at the ready. His shoulders are tight and waiting for a signal to strike. I know he's calculating everything, its distance, its posture, whether it's here for food or a fight.

The bear grunts, showing its teeth. It takes a few steps toward us and pauses again.

Larkin doesn't falter; he whispers back at me, "If it charges, you mount a horse and run."

I nod, even though he can't see it.

As the bear steps closer, the flames rise.

The heat is a swelling wave, pressing against my skin. The firelight stretches long shadows across Larkin's wide back.

It climbs higher, hotter, until it becomes almost unbearable.

Larkin steps forward, slowly, his sword ready at his side, but his presence feels... different.

More than human, commanding.

The bear halts.

It lifts its head, sniffing the air again, but this time, its posture shifts. It looks *afraid*.

Its eyes lock with Larkin's, and an unspoken exchange unfolds between them.

And then, as if it recognizes the primal and powerful strength in him, the bear snorts and lowers its head. It takes slow steps back, turns, and disappears into the tree line, vanishing into the night from where it came.

Larkin exhales, lowering his sword, but his jaw is tight.

The fire settles, and the heat fades.

He finally turns to me, checking me over with that same protective intensity. "Are you okay?"

I barely breathe. "What just happened?"

An inscrutable shadow lingers in his eyes— no fear, never fear.

"You're safe."

The morning comes cloaked in a fine mist. Dew clings to the grass like tiny diamonds. I wake to the gentle clatter of Larkin packing up camp. His silhouette moves in the soft gray light. He hands me a small bundle wrapped in cloth, with dried fruits and nuts inside. I nibble on a piece of fig as I stretch out the sleep in my limbs.

"We should make it to the castle by nightfall," Larkin says, tightening a strap on one of the saddle bags. His voice is calm, but his eyes scan the horizon, like they always do. "Good chance of rain today."

We mount our horses and begin the slow ride back to the road.

I glance at him.

"Do you think I'll like Haravik?"

He doesn't answer right away. "I think it's… different," he finally says. "You will miss the warm seaside. It's colder. Harsher. But you'll adjust, Princess."

"What about the king? What's he like?"

Larkin's jaw tightens. "I've never met him. Only stories from the other guards."

"What kind of stories?"

He glances over at me, and there's a shadow in his expression. "That he is brutal. Ruthless. A man who rules with fear."

The weight of his words sinks into me like stones in a river. I try not to show it, but the chill that runs through me is sudden and sharp.

The road narrows as we ride deeper into the hills. Silence is a soft thread stretched between us. The sky has turned a gentle gray, and a cool drizzle begins to fall, making the air smell of wet earth and moss. I pull the hood of my cloak over my head. The fabric clings to my shoulders. Around us, the plants whisper in contentment.

I glance over at Larkin, with the reins loose in his hands and rain dotting his tanned skin.

"I don't know how to control my lumina," I admit.

He turns his head slightly toward me. "But you've used it?" he asks.

"Yes... but not on purpose. Sometimes, it just takes me, and I don't know how to stop it."

"Princess, it's your magic. It is a part of you. Not something outside of you. Command it."

"Well, that's the thing, Larkin. It *is* something outside of me. I *am* just the receptor," I say, my brow pulling together. "I thought you didn't have magic, Larkin."

He meets my gaze, calm and unreadable. "I never said I didn't have magic, Princess."

I look forward again, heart picking up speed. The rain falls a little steadier now, and a hush falls over the forest around us. He doesn't say more. Silence settles between us. The only sound is the gentle clops of hooves on the damp earth and the soft patter of rain through the forest canopy. Leaves glisten, with droplets clinging to their edges before falling with soft plinks onto mossy ground.

My thoughts drift, as they often do when the road stretches long and quiet. I imagine a warm hearth with a grand stone fireplace crackling with a dancing fire.

I picture curling up beside it, wrapped in a thick wool blanket with a steaming cup of coffee and a good novel. I could really go for a cinnamon roll too, soft and fresh, the icing melted into the warm dough. I can practically taste the cinnamon and sugar dissolving on my tongue.

I glance over at Larkin again. He's still calm, still quiet, broad shoulders hunched slightly against the rain. I wonder if he's cold, too, or if he's too stubborn to admit it.

He looks over at me. "You okay, Princess?" His voice is genuine.

"Yeah, I just hope Haravik has good coffee," I murmur under my breath with a tired smile.

The rain, once a gentle mist, suddenly turns violent, sheets of water hammer down from the sky, soaking through my cloak in seconds. Thunder cracks overhead, loud and sudden, shaking the very air around us. The horses whinny and toss their heads, hooves skittering on the muddy road as lightning splits the sky.

"Princess!" Larkin yells over his shoulder, pointing ahead, but the wind steals most of his words.

I follow the line of his arm and spot it, faint trails of chimney smoke curling into the gray sky. A town. I nod, even though I'm not sure he sees me, and urge my horse after him as he veers off the main path. We take the side road, muddy and narrow. Branches whip against our shoulders as we ride hard through the downpour.

We ride into the town half-blinded by the storm. Rain pelts down so fiercely it feels like needles on my skin. The world blurs around us, shapes and rooftops only barely visible through the curtain of water. I can barely see, barely breathe through the chill and the chaos. Larkin spots a covered stable up ahead.

He steers us toward it, and we rush inside. The sound of the rain suddenly muffles under the wooden shelter. The stable is dry and dim, with the smell of hay and wet gorse thick in the air.

Larkin dismounts first, moving fast.

He speaks to the stable hand, a gangly blond boy. His face is dusted with freckles, and he looks no older than sixteen. Larkin slips him a few coins, saying words I can't quite catch over the sound of the storm.

The boy nods quickly and points just across the road. I follow Larkin's gaze to a small, cobblestoned building. Golden light spills from its windows.

We dash through the downpour. My cloak is soaked, and my boots splash through the puddles. We slip through the door into the little eatery. Warmth rises in a solid wall of glorious, dry heat, wrapping around my frozen limbs.

The scent of roasted meat, herbs, and something sweet greets me next. My eyes sweep the space. The floors gleam, and the tables are polished. Every corner is clean and warm.

The fireplace, massive and roaring, dominates the far wall. Mounted above it is the largest elk head I have ever seen. Its antlers are so wide they nearly graze the mantle. I quickly move to the table nearest the fire, already feeling my fingers begin to thaw as I slip off my wet cloak.

Larkin, as always, handles the ordering without needing to ask what I want. He speaks to the innkeeper at the counter.

I settle into my seat and stretch my hands toward the flames, exhaling a long, relieved breath. As I settle into the warmth, my gaze drifts around the cozy eatery, soaking in every detail.

Movement catches my eye.

A broom sweeps across the marble floor with no hands to guide it, gliding with purpose. The bristles brush rhythmically back and forth. A towel hovers just above one of the empty tables, wiping away crumbs and drops of water with delicate, circular motions.

Curious, my eyes follow the movement, revealing an older woman behind the counter. She has long, snow white hair pulled into a thick braid down her back. She's not looking at the broom or the towel. With a single flick of her finger, the towel zips to the next table, cleaning with the same easy motion. With a subtle turn of her wrist, the broom shifts direction, sweeping closer to the door. She's commanding it all effortlessly and silently with her magic.

Larkin returns and sets a warm mug in front of me. The smell of chocolate and cinnamon hums against my senses.

"What's this?" I ask, looking down at the unfamiliar liquid.

Larkin leans back in his chair, that familiar tugging at his lips. "It's chocolate and cream," he says. "Try it."

Intrigued, I lift the mug to my lips and take a small sip.

The taste bursts across my tongue, velvety, sweet, and spiced with a hint of cinnamon. It's a tide of warmth. Luxurious comfort floods me entirely.

My eyes widen, and I let out the softest gasp of delight.

"Oh… gods," I whisper, staring into the mug like it just changed my life.

Larkin chuckles, the sound low and pleased. "I knew you'd love it."

I take another, longer sip, cradling the mug with both hands. "This is the best delight I've ever tasted."

He smiles at me, eyes soft, like watching me enjoy something so simple is the greatest reward.

I finish the delicious contents of the mug.

"More, please," I say, nudging the mug toward Larkin.

He laughs as he gets up with the mug. "Be right back, Your Highness."

Moments later, Larkin returns, and he's not alone.

Two plates float behind him, gliding through the air, like they have done it a thousand times before. My mouth drops slightly as they land gently on the table, one in front of each of us. He sets the fresh mug down in front of me, and I wrap my fingers around it instantly, already enchanted.

Another smaller plate floats toward us. It stops and lowers itself delicately between us. On it is a thick slice of cake dusted with powdered sugar, still warm from the oven.

I glance toward the older woman with white hair, standing behind the counter. She lifts her hand slightly, a single wave guiding the plate to its rest. I smile, with gratitude and wonder. She catches my gaze and smiles back kindly.

I look down at my plate, steaming mashed potatoes piled high with roasted poultry, blistered tomatoes, and sweet-glazed carrots. My stomach practically sings. I take a bite and nearly melt right there in my chair.

The crackle of the fire and low murmurs of nearby diners are a blanket around me. As I'm cutting another bite, I catch a voice behind us, rough and confident.

"Not lettin' up 'til morning, mark my words."

Larkin turns in his seat to glance at the man behind him. "You a storm watcher?"

The older man nods slowly, his heavy wool cloak still steaming from the rain. "Yes, sir. Storm rolled in fast off the coast. Heavy with salt and pressure. She won't let go 'til sunrise."

I glance toward the window, watching the rain blur the world beyond.

"So, we're stuck here for the night, then?"

Larkin meets my eyes and nods.

"Looks like it." He offers a soft smile. "There are worse places to be stranded."

Larkin stands and says he'll ask the keeper where the closest inn is. I watch him stride confidently to the counter. He ducks under the hanging chandeliers as he passes by. He speaks with the woman behind the counter. She smiles kindly, nodding at his questions.

He thanks her and returns to the table.

"The nicest inn in town is just two buildings down," he says, placing a generous pile of coin on the table.

I nod and gather my things, wrapping my cloak tighter around me. As we head toward the door, Larkin places his hand on the small of my back, gently guiding me.

I wonder... how much does my father pay him? Larkin is always so generous, almost careless with his coin. Either he's paid far more than I thought, or he gives without ever counting the cost.

We walk along the covered sidewalk, with the rain still falling steadily just beyond the awning. Every few steps, a gust of wind curls through, tugging at my cloak and making my hair whip across my face. Larkin's strong hand is firm at the small of my back, supporting me as I walk.

We reach a tall stone building. The door is glass, trimmed with polished brass that gleams even under the gray sky. Larkin opens it for me.

Warmth wraps around me instantly as I step inside, with the scent of cedar and aged parchment drifting through the air. The floors are a dark black marble, peppered with white and gold streaks. Plush rugs and velvet chairs fill the lobby, and a chandelier of crystal and brass hangs above, reflecting every flicker of light.

We approach the counter together, the soft clack of our boots on the polished marble floor the only sound besides the distant crackle of the fireplace behind us. Larkin leans forward slightly and asks the innkeeper for the nicest room they have. I pull out my coin before he can stop me.

"I'll get it," I say quickly.

He looks at me, a little amused, a little exasperated.

The tender, a small woman with a round face, porcelain-like skin, and a neat bun, nods approvingly and counts out the payment. She hands us a brass key with an etched number on the head and gives Larkin directions to our room. I grab a few of the parchment pamphlets from the countertop.

We head up a wide staircase to the second floor, with the plush carpet muffling our steps. We find the door with the matching number, and

The room is warm and softly lit, with tall windows draped in velvet. The bed is massive, four-postered, with a thick down comforter and piles of inviting pillows. A sitting area rests near the fireplace, with a table and two cushioned chairs. To the right, through an arched doorway, is the bathroom.

It's spacious, with polished marble floors, a long counter lined with golden fixtures, and a deep, luxurious tub that looks like the one back home in my chambers.

Larkin looks around the room and sets our bags down.

"Go ahead and bathe, Princess. I'll get the fire going and hang our things to dry."

I nod, thankful, and slip into the bathroom.

The tub is already calling to me. I draw the bath. The warm water fills quickly, with steam curling into the air. I glance at myself in the mirror. My hair is a tangled mess, and there are faint purple shadows beneath my eyes. I barely recognize the reflection. I look… worn. The last few days have carved themselves into my face.

When I'm done with my bath, I towel myself off and slip into the soft robe hanging by the door. It's thick and warm, cinching nicely around my waist. With my thighs chafed from riding, I waddle out of the bathroom to find Larkin already seated in one of the chairs by the fire. The flames crackle happily in the hearth. The room smells faintly of cedar and clean linens.

I settle into the chair beside him and start brushing my hair. Long wet strands fall down past my hips. I glance up and find him watching me with that look again, soft, amused, a little bit in awe.

"What?" I ask, meeting his gaze.

He shakes his head slightly, that familiar cooked smile pulling at his lips. "Nothing, Princess."

He rises from his chair with a quiet stretch and murmurs, "I'll take my turn."

He disappears into the bathroom, and I stay, brushing through the last tangles in my hair. The warmth is starting to lull me. My eyes feel heavy.

I finally stand and make my way to the massive bed, pulling back the thick quilt. The mattress is soft, with crisp and cool sheets. I sink into it with a sigh. The weight of the day finally catches up with me. By the time Larkin returns, I'm half asleep, curled on my side facing the fire.

He moves quietly, not wanting to wake me.

But I feel the mattress shift as he climbs in beside me. His warmth finds me instantly beneath the covers. Without a word, he wraps an arm around my waist and pulls me gently toward him.

I sigh again, softer this time, feeling safe and warm in his arms.

We fall asleep close, quiet, and still as the storm continues to murmur against the windows.

CHAPTER SIXTEEN

The closer we ride, the more the land opens into wide, empty fields, the forest thinning until it's just us and the wind. The clouds hang low and gray, the air bites sharper than yesterday.

The castle is a shadow carved from the storm, looming in the distance. Tall, jagged towers, dark stone, cold and imposing even from miles away, it looms closer with every step.

I tug my cloak tighter around me, trying to calm my nerves swirling in my chest. After a long moment, I glance over at Larkin. His jaw is set, and his eyes are fixed on the path ahead.

"I hope your room is close to mine," I say, my voice barely louder than the wind.

He turns to look at me, the corner of his mouth lifting. "I'll make sure of it, Princess."

His words warm a quiet space deep within me, though the cold still clings to the air around us. After a pause, I ask the question that has been sitting on my tongue since the castle came into view.

"What do you think of the prince?"

Larkin doesn't answer right away. He exhales slowly through his nose, his brow furrowing. "I think he's shrewd," he says finally. "And cocky."

He's quiet for a moment. Then. "His craft is... inconvenient. And his lumina, it's dangerous."

Dangerous.

"I thought his lumina was kept a secret," I say.

"It's not widely known. If my... sources... are correct, that is, it's very dangerous."

I glance sideways at him, studying his profile, his strong jaw, the set of his mouth. "Are you... afraid of him? *The* Larkin Steelborn, afraid?" I tease.

Larkin laughs under his breath, but it fades as quickly as it came. He turns his head to look at me, and his gaze carries a heavier shadow now. "I'm not afraid of anyone," he says, voice firm and confident.

But then he pauses. "What I do fear... is that he might change *you.*"

That catches me off guard.

"Change me?" I repeat, unsure what he means. "Change me how, Larkin?"

He looks ahead again, jaw tightening. "It's what his lumina allows him to do, Princess. I'm afraid he will dim that light that burns so bright in you."

The weight of his words settles deep inside my chest. I look at him, really look, and see the fierce protectiveness hiding just behind his amber eyes. He's not afraid of swords or power.

He's afraid of losing *me*.

We fall back into comfortable silence, the kind that says enough on its own. I let Larkin's words echo in my mind, tracing each one, like a thread I can't let go. The wind brushes across my face, colder now. It carries with it the scent of stone, snow, and something foreign.

The castle looms closer, its towers like a knife slicing into the gray sky.

I glance at Larkin. His expression is unreadable, with his eyes ahead and his jaw set. He's still close enough to reach for, but I know the space between us is about to change.

Everything is.

My heart aches for him. I try to imagine myself in his place, watching the person you love marry someone else, sworn to protect them, stay by their side, and never once get to call them yours.

I imagine it the other way around, *him* marrying someone else. Standing beside another woman, smiling at her the way he smiles at me, holding her the way he's held me. My hands tighten around the reins before I even realize it.

The thought burns. It makes me angry. I draw a slow breath, trying to calm the storm that's stirring inside me.

The silence between us stretches, the kind that feels too full of things unsaid.

My voice is softer than intended when I ask, "Have you ever been in love before?"

He doesn't answer right away. He keeps his eyes on the road ahead. The reins are loose in his hands. For a moment, I think he didn't hear me, or maybe he's choosing not to answer.

"Princess, had you asked me that a few moons ago, the answer would be no."

I swallow hard. My fingers fidget with the edge of my cloak as my heart nearly beats out of my chest.

We ride in silence, with only the soft thudding of hooves against the damp earth. Eventually, the trees begin to thin, and the path widens into a clearing on a gentle rise. As we crest it, West Cravenmore becomes visible. My diaphragm clenches, and my nerves twist a little tighter with each passing mile. The air is colder now, sharper.

The city sprawls beneath us, carved into the surrounding mountains like it's always been there. The buildings are tall and close together, made of deep, dark stone that almost looks black against the cloudy sky. Everything gleams faintly with dampness. The rooftops are sharp, folded metal rising against the sky. Even from here, the narrow streets look alive. Lanterns glow a warm amber, with voices rising and falling in laughter and chatter. Despite the grayness, there's joy in the air.

I watch a little boy tug his mother's hand near a bakery, and a couple pass beneath a string of glimmering lights, arm in arm. There are wreaths of green and red berries through the streets, thin and lovely. It's cold, much colder than I am used to, but the city feels... warm somehow. Lived in. Loved.

A snowflake drifts lazily down from the sky and lands on my shoulder. I glance at it, delicate and fleeting, before it disappears into my cloak.

"It's beautiful," I whisper.

Beside me, Larkin is silent. When I look over at him, he's watching me, not the city.

"It is," he finally says, but the way he says it... I don't think he means the city at all.

Inside the city walls, the streets are crowded but calm. People bustle about their day with purpose. I catch snippets of conversation, someone joking about the snow, someone bartering for fabric, the rhythmic clang of a blacksmith's hammer. The smell of spices and roasted meat drifts from food stalls, and I feel the sudden pang of hunger despite the knot in my stomach.

We slow our pace to a walk. The horses weave through the narrow-cobbled roads. The buildings lean over the streets just slightly, tall and elegant in their age. There's something hauntingly beautiful about Cravenmore. Its shadows feel rich with stories.

"This way," Larkin says, nodding to a side street that climbs toward the higher part of the city.

I follow him.

The castle soon rises into view, perched on a ridge that overlooks everything. It's massive, made of the same dark stone as the city, with towers that reach into the low-hanging clouds. It looks as if it was carved from the mountain itself.

We stop just outside the outer gates. Guards wear deep blue cloaks lined with fur and polished armor beneath. They recognize Larkin at once and open the gates after a brief exchange. I'm too nervous to hear what was said.

The path winds up again, and when we reach the castle doors, several servants come out to greet us. My stomach drops with anxiety.

I glance at Larkin, and he dismounts Doc and helps me down. His hands linger at my waist for just a second longer than they need to. I grip his forearm and alleviate my aching muscles.

The castle doors open with a groan of old wood and iron, and we step inside together. The grand hall is glowing with firelight and golden chandeliers. The air smells of pine and old stone.

My heart beats wildly in my chest. Somewhere in this castle, the man I'm meant to marry is waiting. And beside me, the man my heart truly belongs to walks in silence.

A young woman with honey-blonde hair twisted into an elegant braid steps forward as we enter the front hall. Her dress is a deep sapphire blue, and her eyes are almost the same color. Her face is dotted with freckles.

She curtsies low, her expression warm but precise.

"Princess Winifred," she says with a gentle voice, "I'm Layla, your new lady's maid. I'll be assisting you during your stay in Haravik."

I glance at Larkin quickly before turning my full attention to her.

"It's nice to meet you, Layla."

She straightens and gestures toward a grand staircase curling up the far wall. "If you'll come with me, I'll escort you to your rooms. Your belongings have already been delivered and unpacked. I've prepared a bath and selected a gown for your greeting with the prince."

Larkin steps closer and lowers his voice near my ear. "I'll be nearby."

I nod once, unable to speak past the emotion lodged in my throat.

I follow Layla up the stairs. My boots quietly shuffle against the dark marble floor. I feel his presence behind me even after he stops at the base of the stairs.

The halls we walk through are quiet, lined with tall windows that let in the pale, cold light of the overcast skies. Stone walls are dressed in deep tapestries in shades of blue, cream, and gold. Every detail feels old and regal.

And completely foreign.

We reach a set of heavy double doors, and Layla pushes one open with surprising strength.

The room beyond is enormous.

A fire crackles in the large fireplace, and warm light reflects off carved wooden furniture. A thick fur rug is laid over the cold stone floor, and the far wall is draped in midnight blue and cream silks. A changing screen sits to one side of the room, and beyond it, peeks the edge of a large, steaming tub.

As I step past the screen, the scent of rose oil grows stronger. The walls are smooth, dark stone polished to a soft sheen. The flickering sconce light dances gently across their surface.

"Would you like some assistance undressing, Your Highness?"

"No, thank you," I answer.

At the center of the room is a large sunken tub. Steam curls lazily from the surface of the water. The tub is surrounded by a small ledge that holds neatly folded towels, glass jars of bath salts, and a crystal decanter of scented oil.

Above it hangs a brass chandelier with soft glowing orbs, casting a golden warmth that softens the room's cool stone. A single narrow window is fogged from the warmth; through it, a view of the gray sky stretches.

I undress and slip into the steaming bath. The heat of the water embraces me all at once. I sink lower with a sigh as the warmth soaks deep into my aching muscles. Every knot of tension and the soreness from days on horseback begin to melt away.

Layla moves lithely. She kneels behind me and starts to gently unbraid my hair. Her fingers are quick but careful. The scent of roses intensifies as she lathers a soft soap into my scalp, massaging in small, calming circles.

I close my eyes for a moment and let myself lean into the comfort of it, feeling more human with every breath.

After she rinses my hair, I take the washcloth and finish cleaning the rest of my body, scrubbing away the last traces of the road. When I'm done, she offers a thick, soft towel, warm from sitting by the fire, and I wrap it around myself as I step out.

The mirror over the sink is slightly fogged, but I wipe it clear and look at my reflection. My pale gray eyes stare back, haunted, tired. My long auburn hair hangs damp and darker than usual, curling at the ends.

I return to the bedroom, where I sit, allowing Layla to brush the tangles from my hair.

Paintings of wild florals in rich, moody colors, violet, deep greens, and stormy blues hang above the fireplace. The canopied bed is dressed in thick, layered linens, cream and deep blue silks with a velvet throw draped carelessly across the foot. The bedposts are dark wood, sturdy and ornately carved, and the mattress itself looks decadently soft.

I quickly slip into the gown laid out for me.

It's a deep navy blue, long-sleeved and fitted through the waist, with a subtle shimmer that catches the candlelight with every movement. The fabric feels smooth against my skin, and the neckline is modest but elegant.

I drape the thick white cloak over my shoulders. The fur-lined hood rests softly at the base of my neck and fastens at the collar.

Layla returns to my side, holding a small case of cosmetics.

"Just a touch," she says with a warm smile.

She smooths something soft over my cheeks, dabs a bit of color across my lids, and gently darkens my lashes. I try not to fidget under her close attention.

"You have a lovely round face," she murmurs as she tilts my chin upward. "Delicate but strong. And these lips…" She laughs lightly, applying a touch of gloss. "Full and perfectly shaped. You are far more beautiful than the portraits I've seen of you. They didn't do you justice, Your Highness."

I feel my cheeks flush beneath the powder. "Thank you," I whisper, unsure what else to say.

Her words ease a tight tension in my chest, a small comfort as I prepare to see the man I am meant to marry.

Layla's fingers move deftly through my damp hair, weaving it into a tight, elegant braid. She twists it into a neat knot at the nape of my neck, securing it with ease. I watch her in the mirror as she lifts my delicate rose gold crown from its velvet-lined box. She places it carefully atop my head.

"Perfect," she says softly, stepping back to admire her work.

Layla meets my eyes in the reflection. "Are you ready to go, Princess?"

I take a breath and nod, even though I'm not sure I'll ever feel ready. "Yes."

She opens the large doors, and together, we step into the corridor.

The castle halls are quiet. Grand torches flicker against stone walls softened by tapestries and polished wood trim. Our footsteps echo faintly as we walk.

The corridor bends and opens into a vast hall. Warm light spills from the golden sconces and a towering chandelier overhead. Ahead, at the end of the room, is a set of carved double doors, and beyond them is the dining hall. And the prince.

As the heavy doors to the dining hall open, I take in the large space. The black marble floors gleam like still water beneath the soft glow of the chandeliers, reflecting flickers of candlelight. A long dining table of dark, polished wood stretches down the center of the room, smooth, grand, and intimidating in its elegance.

Only three men sit at the table: Prince Rome at the head, with Igor seated to his left with an empty space between them, and an older man with sandy brown hair and a long beard, whom I do not recognize, to his right.

All three stand as I approach. My steps echo across the glossy marble, but the sound of my own heartbeat is somehow louder. Layla gives a respectful nod and pulls out the chair next to Rome. She silently retreats behind me.

Prince Rome's eyes never leave mine. There is a slow, satisfied smile curling his lips.

"It's very nice to see you again, Winifred," he says, his voice smooth and commanding. "You're even more beautiful than I remember."

"Thank you," I say. "And... please, just Winnie."

I lower into the seat prepared for me next to him, with the rich navy of my gown glimmering under the light.

I feel his gaze linger as I settle.

The doors open again behind me, and I glance back to see Larkin entering the room. He takes a post near the doors. His expression is unreadable, but still, his presence grounds me.

Prince Rome leans forward slightly, folding his hands.

"How was the ride, Winnie?" he asks, politely.

Just as I begin to form my reply, the dining hall doors swing open once more, revealing a stream of servants moving in perfect coordination. Each of them carries a vessel: silver trays covered with domed lids, decanters of deep red wine, and golden cider.

They glide around the table, placing dishes down in front of each of us. The scent of roasted meats and warm spices fills the air. A platter of honey-glazed duck rests before me, surrounded by roasted root vegetables and buttery rolls still steaming from the oven. A glass of bubbly cider is poured beside my plate, and a smaller dish of some sort of creamy soup is placed just beyond it.

The warm aroma is comforting, and my stomach clenches in anticipation. Prince Rome smiles, gesturing to the meal.

"Please eat, Little Flower. You must be famished after such a long journey."

I nod politely, casting a quick glance toward Larkin. He's watching, always watching, unmoving at his post. I wonder if he's had the chance to eat.

Prince Rome lifts his goblet in a quiet toast. "Allow me to formally introduce my most trusted adviser," he says with a smooth tone. "Olaf, this is Princess Winnie."

The older man across from me nods with a warm but sharp expression. He has bright green eyes and a long white streak through his sandy brown beard.

"An honor, Your Highness," he says, bowing his head slightly.

The table fills with a hum of quiet conversation, with Olaf discussing trade routes, Igor making a comment about the mountain snowpack this year, and Rome occasionally asking me questions about my homeland. It's smooth, diplomatic, almost relaxing.

I feel Rome's hand under the table.

Through the high slit in my dress, his fingers find the bare skin of my thigh.

They stir slowly, tracing small, gentle circles against me. My breath stumbles ever so slightly, and I glance up at him. He's still smiling, still engaged in casual talk with Olaf and Igor.

Across the room, Larkin's posture is still rigid at the door. His jaw is set tighter than usual, and the muscle along the side of it ticks. His eyes, though they shift across the room as a proper guards should, keep finding their way back to me.

Or maybe Rome.

He's seen the prince's hand on me.

The heat of Rome's fingers trails up just a bit higher, and I shift in my seat, pressing my knees together.

Dinner concludes with the soft clink of cutlery and the murmur of polite farewells. Servants quietly clear the table, and Rome rises. He offers me his hand with a gentleman's refinement that doesn't match the possessiveness I felt under the table.

I hesitate only a moment before taking it.

"I'll walk you to your room," he says smoothly, with his ice-blue eyes scanning mine. "It's been a long day. You must be exhausted."

I nod. "Yes, sleep sounds perfect."

As we walk the dim corridor, the soft hush of our footsteps is the only sound between us. He glances sideways at me.

"Is there anything you need? Anything I can do to help you feel more... at home?" His voice is gentle.

I offer a small, tired smile. "Thank you, but I'll be fine. I just need some good sleep."

He nods. "You have a very loyal guard," he says, voice casual, though there is an undertone to his words. "He stays close... always watching. Protective, isn't he?"

I glance up at him, surprised, unsure how to respond.

"Yes," I say finally. "Larkin takes his duty seriously."

Larkin's steps echo on the marble floors a few feet behind us.

Rome hums thoughtfully, his gaze shifting forward again. "Loyalty like that is rare, especially when it's... personal."

I don't reply. I'm not sure I can even if I wanted to.

"I heard he made quite the fuss about the room he was given," he says quietly. "He was displeased it was too far from yours."

I gape, surprised.

"He wouldn't stop until his room was moved. He really doesn't like being far from you, does he?"

Rome chuckles lightly.

"He takes his duty seriously," I say quietly, unsure what else to say.

"Mm," Rome muses.

"That's one word for it."

We stop at my door, with the quiet tension taking over.

Rome turns toward me, his expression softening. "If there's anything else you need to feel more at home, I want you to tell me."

I nod.

His eyes linger on me before he leans in and kisses my cheek. "Goodnight, Winnie."

CHAPTER SEVENTEEN

I wake to the soft sound of a knock at my door, followed by a quiet creak as a servant steps inside, carrying a silver tray.

She places it gently on the small table by the window and gives me a polite bow before slipping back out. The smell of pastries and fruit fills the air, delicate and inviting. I wrap myself in the plush robe that was placed across the tuffet at the end of the bed.

Outside the tall arched window, snow falls softly, blanketing the dark stone in shimmering white. My heart flutters at the sight. It looks like something out of a storybook.

I sit by the window, cradling the warm mug in my hands, watching the flakes drift lazily down. I bring the cup up to my lips, take a sip, and frown. Tea. Floral, citrusy, fine, just not what I crave first thing in the morning. What I really want is a strong, hot coffee.

Just as that exact thought crosses my mind, there is a soft knock, and then the door opens. Larkin steps inside, holding a familiar-looking mug in his hands. *My mug.* He crosses the room and holds it out with a small, knowing smile.

The first sip is everything I needed, rich, sweet, and creamy, just the way I prefer it.

"Good morning," a strong voice says from the doorway.

Larkin and I both turn to see Rome stepping into the room, wearing a long black coat lined with fur.

Larkin nods to me and retreats to the hallway.

"How did you sleep?" Rome asks.

"Much better than expected. This bed may be the most comfortable thing I've ever laid on."

"I'm glad," he says, stepping further into the room.

"Do you enjoy the snow?" He gestures to the window.

"I love it. It's...peaceful."

He seems pleased.

"Then maybe you'd want to get a better look. If you're feeling up to it, I'd love to take you into town today. Let you see the heart of Cravenmore," he says with a soft smile.

He is rather handsome.

He stands tall in the center of my room. His presence is striking, undeniably princely, and every bit as polished. His raven-black hair is immaculately groomed, not a strand out of place. It shimmers slightly under the morning light, thick and full.

His face is clean-shaven, skin smooth and pale, with a healthy glow. When he smiles, his white teeth contrast starkly against the deep hue of his well-shaped lips, perfect and straight, the kind of smile one doesn't easily forget.

His jawline is strong and angular, sculpted as if it had been carved with a chisel. And when that charming smile breaks across his features, a single dimple appears on his left cheek, just enough to soften the lines of his face.

"Winnie?" Rome's voice pulls me from my thoughts.

"Oh, yes. I would like that... very much."

"Perfect," he says, already turning toward the door. "I'll have a carriage prepared. Dress warmly. I'll meet you in the hall shortly."

As the door closes behind him, I curl my hands tighter around the mug, letting its heat soak in.

I quickly finish the last bite of breakfast and take the final, comforting sip of coffee from my special mug. The warmth lingers in my chest as I rise from the table and move to dress for the day.

I slip into a warm, forest-green wool dress with long sleeves and silver embroidery tracing the edges. It hugs my figure comfortably, perfect for a chilly outing.

Over it, I fasten a thick cream-colored cloak with a fur-lined hood, and I tug on my tall leather boots.

I quickly braid my hair into a loose knot before placing my crown gently over the braid.

With a final glance in the mirror, I step out of my room.

Larkin stands just outside my door, as if he'd been waiting all morning. His eyes scan me for a second.

Rome is already waiting in the hallway. When he sees me, his expression brightens.

He turns toward Larkin. "You can stay here today, Guard. Enjoy the comforts of the castle."

Larkin's eyes flick to mine, uncertain.

"I'll be okay," I assure him softly, placing my gloved hand briefly on his arm. "Enjoy your day. Rest."

He doesn't say anything, but his jaw clenches before he nods. I can feel his eyes on me even as I follow Rome down the hall.

"You look lovely," he says, as we sit in the carriage. His bright eyes settle on me with a subtle smile that reveals a hint of a dimple.

"Thank you," I reply, offering a small smile in return, though my fingers play nervously with the edge of my glove. The carriage wheels crunch softly over snow-covered stone roads.

Outside, the city of Cravenmore unfolds, a place as dark and moody as it was breathtaking. The buildings are tall and narrow, constructed from charcoal-colored stone. Their steep rooftops are dusted with snow. Gothic ironwork lines windows that are decorated with small, enchanted lanterns giving off a soft golden glow.

Though the sky is overcast, the streets are alive with movement. Candles and garlands line shop windows, and wreaths made of dried berries and dark green pine hang from doors.

Vendors in long coats sell roasted nuts, spiced cider, and little paper bags of sugar-dusted pastries. The city feels timeless, proud, and touched with celebration.

We stop outside a grand building with tall glass windows and intricate stone archways. It's carved from the same dark stone as the rest of the city, though its entrance is marked by massive carved doors flanked by statues of angels.

Rome offers me his hand as we step down, and we enter the beautiful building together. The warmth of the space embraces us as we leave the snow behind.

Their building's gallery is quiet, with the muffled sounds of footsteps echoing softly against the marble floors.

I look around, my breath catching slightly at the beauty of it all.

Massive oil paintings in gilded frames line the walls, each one a masterpiece. Some depict sprawling landscapes, others elegant figures frozen in time.

Between them are tall pedestals encased in glass, holding delicate sculptures of stone, bronze, and crystal. The lighting is soft and warm, creating shadows that dance gently across the floor.

Rome walks beside me, with his hands clasped behind his back. His presence is confident but not imposing. I slow as we reach a large canvas tucked into its own alcove. It's breathtaking.

Bright gray eyes stare out from the painting, striking and luminous, almost alive. The woman's face is half concealed, shrouded in winding ivy and blooming flowers of every shade, soft roses, violet bellflowers, and little white blossoms. Only her eyes, her finely arched brows, the bridge of her nose, and wisps of long, wavy hair are visible. The rest of her fades beneath the foliage, nature having claimed her gently, delicately, turning her into a creature of the beyond.

I stare at it for a long moment, pulled into the mystery of her gaze, something so familiar to it.

Rome stops beside me.

"Do you like it?" he asks softly.

"It's... stunning," I say, my voice hushed. "Nothing I have ever seen compares to this."

He smiles, with a flicker of pride in his eyes. "It's mine."

I look at him. "You bought it?"

"No," he says with a small shake of his head, stepping closer to the canvas. "I painted it."

I look down at the corner of the painting, and there it is, R.A.R., his signature.

"You're an artist?" I ask, eyes flickering in surprise.

He nods.

My gaze drifts back to the canvas.

The eyes are a complete match to the ones I see in the reflection of the gilded frame.

"It's... magnificent, Rome."

We admire each painting, but my mind still goes back to the familiar set of eyes on the wall behind me.

Rome steps away, leaning toward a gallerist standing in the corner of the room and whispering into his ear.

The man nods. Rome returns to my side, his hand at the small of my back.

I turn to him slowly.

"Where did you learn to paint like that?" I ask, my voice soft.

Rome's expression shifts, with a flicker of tenderness in his eyes.

"My mother. She was a magnificent artist. She taught me everything she knew... before she died."

I glance at him. The vulnerability in his tone catches me off guard.

"When she passed, I kept painting. It's the only thing that still makes me feel close to her."

I can see it now, the grief, the memory, the love tucked into every brushstroke.

"She would be proud."

Rome gives me a small smile, quiet and grateful. "Thank you."

We step out of the gallery and into the soft hush of snow falling on the cobbled streets. Rome and I wander from shop to shop. Each storefront is more charming than the last.

In a cozy little jeweler's shop, he speaks to the jeweler manning the counter. They exchange coin and a small velvet box. With a sly smile, he turns to me and fastens a delicate rose gold necklace around my neck. A tiny rose charm shimmers just above my collarbone.

"For you," he says, his voice unusually soft.

I touch it gently, momentarily speechless.

"It's beautiful... Thank you."

He only smiles in reply and leads me back out onto the snow-dusted street.

He turns to me.

"Ready to go home?"

Home.

I nod.

My heart hammers as he leans closer, and I can feel the heat of him even before our lips meet. His lips brush against mine, soft, gentle, and somehow... pleasant.

He steps back, and I'm not sure if I want more or if I want to run into Larkin's arms. Maybe I want both of those things.

He holds out his hand, and I take it, letting him lift me into the carriage. Then he disappears.

He quickly returns with two steaming cups and a brown paper bag.

"Chocolate?" he asks, handing me a piping hot cup.

With a playful grin, he hands me the bag of honey-roasted nuts. Sipping from our cups and sharing the warm, sweet nuts, we ride quietly back to the castle. The snow falls, soft and unbroken, blanketing the city in peace. I force my shoulders to relax, my breaths to come smoother. My mind refuses to obey, refuses to ease the tug of war inside me. My heart is torn in two, and I want something I shouldn't. Both of them. And that thought terrifies me.

CHAPTER EIGHTEEN

Moonlight pools through my chamber window, casting silver across the bed sheets and my bare arms. The air is thick with quiet heat and longing, the kind that lives just beneath the skin.

Larkin is behind me, his body flush to mine. His breath is warm on my neck. His hand settles low on my waist, anchoring me, grounding me.

Rome is on one side of me, his hand brushing a lazy path down my arm. There's a gentleness in him tonight. His touch is reverent, almost unsure.

I should feel torn, but I don't. There's no jealousy here. No bitterness. Only the feeling of being wholly seen, wholly adored, by two men who have carved themselves into different chambers of my heart.

Their hands move in tandem. Rome's fingers trace my collarbone. Larkin's hand grazes the inside of my thigh.

I melt into the moment, into them.

Rome leans down. His lips brush my cheek, featherlight.

Larkin kisses the back of my neck. My body arches, caught between their warmth, their power, their devotion. I'm cradled between them, with their strength surrounding me.

I tilt my head back against Larkin's shoulder, and he presses a kiss behind my ear. His hand cups my breast in a gentle massaging motion. A soft moan slips from me.

Rome watches, eyes smoldering like winter flames, electric and hungry. His hand trails down my side, and he leans in. His lips crash into mine.

When he pulls back, Larkin turns me slightly and kisses me. I feel consumed by them both.

Larkin shifts behind me, trailing kisses along the curve of my spine, slow and sure.

They are in no rush.

Rome's lips trail a soft, heated path down the center of my body, igniting my skin with every lingering kiss. I arch under his touch. My breath catches as his mouth presses gently to my hipbone.

Larkin, solid and warm, shifts beside me. He guides me gently to lie flat. His large hands cradle me with care, as though I am a rare and precious relic.

He leans in, brushing his lips over the soft swell of my breast. His tongue flicks over the sensitive peak. My fingers bury in his long hair, unable to suppress the soft moan that escapes my lips when his warm mouth takes in the whole of my stiff peak.

One of his hands trails to the other breast, thumb rubbing in slow strokes that make my back arch from the bed.

Rome glances up from where he kneels. His eyes are dark with focus and desire. His fingers hook into the delicate lace between my hips, and he draws it down slowly. His lips follow the path.

The press of his mouth against the inside of my thigh sends sparks through every inch of me.

He pauses, with his lips brushing the sensitive skin at my center with such aching tenderness that I gasp. His hands grip my thighs, pulling them farther apart.

He plunges two of his fingers deep into my core, coaxing waves of pleasure from deep within me. His mouth remains pressed to my center, and his tongue moves in sync with the rhythm of his hand.

I can't stop the way my hips rise to meet him, seeking more, aching for the edge building fast and bright behind my eyes.

Larkin's mouth stays fastened to my breast. His tongue circles the sensitive peak as his hand roams over the other, teasing it gently with his thumb.

My fingers grip the sheets beneath me. I arch against them, overwhelmed, caught in the slow rhythm they've created together. Their hands and mouths work in tandem, in a perfect, maddening sync that sends tremors through me.

My back bows off the bed as Larkin groans against my skin, and Rome's fingers curl just right inside me. Pleasure coils deep, tighter, hotter.

Between the two of them, it builds like a rising tidal wave. I feel myself teetering on the very edge that will surely undo me.

And just as I'm about to fall—

I wake with a sharp gasp.

The room is hushed, dark with twilight seeping through the curtains.

My body is burning, slick with sweat. My breath comes in frantic waves.

My pulse thunders in my ears, the lingering echo of their hands, their mouths, still haunting my skin.

I close my eyes again, trying to breathe, to ground myself in silence.

A dream. Only in a dream could I ever truly have what *I* want. I don't even have the option of choice. There's not even a choice to be made yet the weight of it presses down as if there were. I still have to beg my heart to settle on one, to pray that the one it chooses won't ignite a war between nations.

Every beat feels like a negotiation I can't win.

Surprisingly... I enjoyed myself yesterday. The city has a charm to it, and Rome, well, he is not what I expected. He made me laugh. He's been kind.

I smile faintly to myself as I sit up, brushing my hair from my face. I dress for the day in a warm cream-colored wool dress and thick fur-lined boots. I drape a dark green fur-lined cloak over my shoulders and fasten it at the collar.

I step out of my room and into the corridor.

Larkin stands here, as always, like a silent sentry. His posture is rigid with his arms folded across his chest.

"Good morning," I say softly.

"Morning, Princess." His voice is quiet, careful.

We walk in silence. I want to say something. Anything. But the words hang in my throat. The weight between us shifts. He doesn't look at me. His jaw is tight. His silence says more than he ever would.

"The city was beautiful," I murmur, trying to fill the space between us.

He nods once. "Glad you enjoyed yourself."

I glance at him, and hurt flashes beneath the mask. I feel the ache in my chest. My heart breaks for him.

We reach the kitchens where the air is warm and filled with the smell of bread and breakfast meats.

Rome walks in, brushing snow from his coat and flashing me a bright, easy smile.

"Good morning, Winnie. Did you sleep well?"

I return the smile. "I did. Thank you."

We sit at a small table in the tearoom near the window, while Larkin stands in the corner, sipping coffee, silent, watching.

A servant brings out a silver tray filled with breakfast foods, and Rome takes it with a flourish. He sets a plate in front of me with three perfectly arranged slices of ham, buttered bread, and a cup of steaming tea.

"There you go," he says with a smile, clearly proud of the gesture. "A royal breakfast for a beautiful princess."

Before I can respond, Larkin's voice cuts through behind me.

Calm. Quiet. Firm.

"She doesn't like ham. She finds swine to be... revolting."

I look up in surprise.

Larkin steps forward from his spot in the corner of the tearoom. His eyes are fixed not on me, but on Rome.

"And she prefers coffee," he adds, glancing at the tea. "Sweet and creamy. Three sugars and a weighty splash of cream."

Rome blinks, slightly thrown. "I see. Thank you, *Guard*."

There's an awkward silence.

The space between them hums with tension—electric and sharp.

Larkin doesn't say it with malice, but the meaning behind his words isn't hard to read. He steps back without another word, retreating to his corner with a quiet sip of his own coffee.

After a while, Rome leans forward. "Would you like to see the snow in the courtyard?"

I nod, welcoming the chance to breathe some fresh air.

Outside, the courtyard is a scene from a fairy tale. Snow covers every surface, and the sky is pale and still.

As we walk, we chat about unimportant things, like how the snow was expected to fall all night, how his afternoon will be filled with meetings.

He leans into me slightly, with his expression brightening. "Tomorrow, you'll start planning the wedding."

The words freeze me for half a second, but I mask it with a nod.

"You'll meet with the castle's coordinator in the afternoon," he continues. "Her name is Valeria. She's very good at what she does. I think you'll like her."

"That's good," I say, my voice softer than I intend.

I force a smile. He looks pleased, content in the way things are progressing. And I... I'm not sure what I feel. I like him, I really do. Maybe it is guilt. Maybe it is Larkin's voice, still echoing somewhere in the back of my mind.

In the center of the courtyard, a massive stone fountain bubbles peacefully. The water is unfrozen despite the cold.

Rome gestures toward it.

"It's enchanted. Flame magic, so it stays warm all year. My mother loved this fountain, so I made sure it would never freeze."

I smile, warmed by the sentiment.

A snowball hits my arm.

I gasp, turning in time to see him, grinning with the wonder of a child. "Oh, it's on," I say, scooping snow into my hands.

We toss snowballs back and forth, laughing like fools. My cheeks sting with cold, my ribs with laughter.

For a moment, I forget everything. But when I turn to look across the courtyard, Larkin stands near the archway, watching. His face is still, but the pain in his eyes is impossible to ignore.

Rome brushes snow from his gloves and shakes flecks of snow from his midnight-black hair.

"I have work to get to. I'll see you at dinner?"

I hesitate. "Wait... Do you have a library?"

He brightens. "Of course. Come, I'll show you."

We walk back through the castle's winding halls. Larkin trails behind, a silent shadow.

Outside the doors to the library, Rome turns to me, his bright ice-colored eyes catching mine.

"See you at dinner, Little Flower," he says. He reaches for my hand and kisses it gently.

I feel the heat rise in my cheeks from the towering presence behind me. Larkin stands just feet away. Rome looks past me, smirking at him before turning and walking away.

I step into the library. It's magnificent. The ceiling is arched high overhead, and carved beams support sparkling chandeliers that bathe the space in soft, golden light. Floor-to-ceiling shelves line every wall, stuffed with books both dusty and new.

The scent of parchment, ink, and leather fills the air. Ornate rugs stretch across the stone floor, and a fireplace at the far end crackles with a low, comforting tone.

Floating several feet above the ground, a librarian moves quietly through the air, with his arms folded behind his back. Around him, his long robes drift, like silk submerged in water, moving with a calm, hypnotic rhythm. He gently nudges books back into their places. His eyes scan the spines as he hovers up and down, while he occasionally mutters to himself.

We each select a book. I find a dusty old story about two lovers. Larkin picks something I couldn't quite read the title of. We sit side by side, with the silence stretching on. Outside, snow continues to fall. Inside, we turn page after page with the cackle of the fireplace and the soft shuffle of parchment filling the background.

Then the atmosphere thickens.

The double doors at the end of the library creak open.

King Veric enters the room. The librarian floats down swiftly and bows midair before landing lightly on his feet.

"Your Majesty," he says, dipping his head.

Veric's expression is unreadable.

"Did you find what I asked for?" he asks the librarian.

His hard eyes scan the room before settling briefly on me. Ice blue, the twin of Rome's, yet colder, sharper. Lines etch his face like chiseled stone weathered by time and war. His dark hair, streaked with white, is perfectly combed. Not a strand is out of place. Every inch of him seems carved and controlled, down to the crisp fold of his coat.

The librarian nods and hurries to a locked cabinet tucked behind a thick column. With a whispered spell, the lock clicks open. He draws out a small chest, old and iron-bound. He unlocks it with a brass key and opens it with care.

Inside, he retrieves a scroll, frayed and yellowed with age, and he hands it to the king. Veric accepts it, glancing only briefly at the contents before rolling it closed again. Their conversation drops to a whisper. I strain to listen, but it is no use.

The librarian keeps his head bowed, and Veric's words are hushed and fast. Their secrecy is obvious. Larkin has straightened slightly, alert but still silent. His eyes narrow, tracking every movement with quiet caution.

As the king turns to leave, he looks at me again. His gaze lingers, cold and assessing. There is nothing warm in his look, no nod of welcome.

Without a word, he sweeps out of the library, his cloak a dark shadow trailing after him. The doors shut behind him with a soft thud. I realize I have been holding my breath.

I glance at Larkin. His eyes are still fixed on the librarian, narrow and sharp. His posture hasn't relaxed. His shoulders carry tension, like a tight thread straining beneath the surface.

Eventually, he turns to me. His expression is unreadable, but a shadow flickers behind his eyes.

"I should get you back to your room," he says, pushing his chair back with a quiet scrape. "So, you can prepare for dinner... with your *lover*."

There is a sharp edge in his voice.

I look at him. "And what are you going to do?"

"I need to see Igor," he replies.

I stand slowly, closing the book. He says nothing more as we walk from the library. The silence between us is full of everything we aren't saying.

Larkin walks just behind me. His hand is firm on my elbow, guiding me through the grand doors of the dining hall.

Rome is there, sitting at the head of the long table. The rest of the seats are empty, and a spot next to him is already waiting.

My heart flutters at the sight of him—candlelight highlighting smooth skin and the sharp lines of his handsome face. His gaze slides down me, slow and attentive, taking in the pale blue silk gown clinging to my body.

He stands as I approach. Larkin takes his post at the doors, leaving us in a bubble of quiet intensity. Rome pulls out my chair, and I sink into it.

"You look stunning."

I give him a smile and pour myself a glass of wine.

Rome tilts his head slightly, with a faint smile tugging at his lips. "And the library? Did you enjoy it?"

I nod, feeling the silk of my dress shift as I adjust in the chair.

"It was beautiful," I say softly. "I really enjoyed it."

He watches me for a long moment and leans back slightly, resting an elbow on the table.

"And what kind of novel did you pick up?" he asks, curiosity soft in his voice.

"Romance," I admit, feeling a faint heat creep into my cheeks.

A slow smile spreads across his face, and there's a hint of teasing in his eyes. "Romance, huh?" He murmurs. "Well... perhaps I could give you a love like the ones in your stories."

I gape at him, unsure whether to laugh or roll my eyes, but the words settle strangely in my chest.

A soft shuffle at the door makes me freeze. Larkin, no doubt, shifts uncomfortably at Rome's words. I don't dare glance up. I keep my eyes fixed on the table, on the rim of my glass, anywhere but him.

"It's fiction for a reason," I tease, letting out a soft sigh.

His fingers brush mine, and he gently takes my hand in his.

"I know it's not easy," he says quietly, with his gaze fixed on me. "I don't expect you to fall for me like they do in the fairy tales. But... I will do everything I can to make your time here easier, to make you comfortable, in every way I can."

His words settle over me like a warm, quiet weight. I squeeze his hand back and give him a small smile.

"I appreciate that."

Dinner finishes, and we rise from the table. Rome falls into step beside me as we move down the hall. The quiet click of our shoes echoes softly against the stone floors. He pauses outside my room and turns to me with his soft gaze.

"Do you... want some company before bed?" he asks, his tone casual. "You can read while I go over my notes from today's meetings."

I hesitate for just a moment. The corners of my mouth tug in a nervous smile.

"Um... yeah, sure," I say finally, letting him lead me inside.

I slip into the bathroom and change into something more comfortable, grateful for the chance to breathe. When I return, I climb onto the bed, pulling the blankets around me as I settle in with my book.

Rome has taken the chair next to the bed, scanning the pieces of parchment in his hands. The sight feels strangely domestic—me reading, him working.

I can feel his eyes on me long before I look up. Every so often, I catch the curve of a smile tugging at his lips as he pretends to focus on his parchment.

Finally, I lower my book with a sigh. "What?"

Rome laughs softly as he runs a hand through his raven-black hair and shakes his head.

"Nothing," he says, his voice warm. "You just look so... beautiful when you read, doing something you enjoy. It's a sight."

Heat prickles at the back of my neck, and I glance back at the page, pretending to be more interested in the words than the way my chest stirs at his.

I raise a brow at him, closing my book just enough to peek over the top.

"Beautiful when I read," I tease, lips curving. "That's a new one."

His laugh is low and warm, and instead of answering right away, he sets his parchment aside on the table. My pulse jumps as he rises from the chair and crosses the small distance to the bed.

The mattress dips slightly under his weight as he lowers himself onto it. For a long moment, we just sit there. The silence stretches between us like a held breath.

Then his hand settles on my thigh, warm and gentle. A flutter runs through me as he leans in, closing the space, and his lips press against mine.

The kiss is deep, insistent, and his other hand slides behind my neck, guiding me closer. My book slips forgotten to the side, and though my body responds, a tangle of guilt stirs beneath the surface.

Rome's hand glides up my thigh to my hip, pulling me closer as his body presses into mine. Heat spills from my core at his touch, quick and undeniable, leaving me breathless. As my lips move with his, guilt claws at the edges of my chest.

My thoughts betray me, drifting to Larkin. I break away, breathing heavy. My words tumble out in a stutter, "I-I..."

Rome rises quickly, his eyes searching mine. Worry spreads across his face.

"I'm sorry," he says, breathless. "Was it... too much?"

My chest is tight. My pulse is unsteady. I can still feel the heat of his hands on me, but beneath it all is the ache of Larkin's shadow, a weight I don't know how to set down.

"Don't be sorry," I manage, still catching my breath.

He doesn't answer right away. He only reaches for the parchment on the side table. His movements are calm.

When he steps closer again, his eyes soften into a calm, winter blue, searching, and he lifts a hand to gently caress my cheek. "I'll see you in the morning, Little Flower."

I find a smile for him, small but sincere. "Goodnight, Rome."

He lingers for only a moment before slipping from the room. The quiet click of the door fades into silence. I blow out the light and sink back into the bed. But my thoughts spin relentlessly, tangled with the memory of his kiss... and the image of Larkin's face, flashing unbidden across my mind.

My heart aches, pulled in two directions— one tethered to duty and honor, the other wild and forbidden.

The weight of everything I've kept inside finally crumbles, and I let the tears come, silent and relentless. I sob until the edges of my mind blur, and sleep gathers me in its dark, merciful embrace.

CHAPTER NINETEEN

The evening settles over the castle like a curtain drawing shut. Rome and I have spent the day together, wandering the halls and gardens, talking and laughing, and now we sit quietly after dinner.

He shifts, and the easy air between us tightens ever so slightly. He turns toward me. His gaze is serious, and my stomach twists in anticipation.

"There's something we need to talk about," he says quietly. "And I have something to show you."

Curiosity prickles at the back of my neck. I nod, trying to ready myself, unsure what he means or what I'm ready to hear.

I follow him through the castle, past the grand halls and tall doors, until we reach a narrow staircase tucked behind a heavy wooden door.

He unlocks it with an iron key from around his neck. The door creaks open, revealing a cool, dim corridor leading underground. The air grows damp as we descend. Stone walls close in around us. My heart is a drum—every beat a sharp warning. Sweat beads across my palms, slipping against the cool railing as we descend deeper into the dark.

Rome turns to me, placing his hand gently around my wrist.

"There's nothing to be afraid of, Winnie," he says. His voice is so soft it's almost inaudible.

He turns around, and we continue our descent.

Finally, we stop in front of another large door. He unlocks this one and pushes it open slowly. Inside is a long, shadowed chamber filled with large crates and troughs of soil.

Dozens of dark green buds rest in the soil, closed tight like secrets. Small orbs of bright fire rest just above the buds, casting a warm glow of light over them.

I step in cautiously. "Rome... what is this?"

He walks past me, stopping in front of one of the crates and gently brushes a bud with his fingers. "These are magus fur lilies...They were extinct. My father found a seed, left by one of our ancestors." His voice is quiet but tight with emotion. "When they flower, their petals can be used to cure a very particular illness."

I look at him, waiting.

"My little brother," he says finally. "He's five. He is sick, Winnie. The same sickness that killed my mother. And the only thing that can save him... are these flowers."

My lungs tighten. "But they haven't bloomed."

He nods. "We have tried everything. Light, tonics, heat, song. Nothing works. The keepers say they need something more... something like magic." He finally looks at me.

"Like my magic," I whisper.

"Yes, Winnie, like *your* magic. You're our only hope at saving Fader."

Flashes of Brynn's face cross my mind, soft and sudden, like ripples in still water. I take a deep breath. Despite every instinct in my body screaming at me—*stop, look closer, investigate, anything*—I let the grief of a sibling make the decision for me. I let my heart win.

"Of course, I'll help," I whisper.

I immediately start to work. The moment I begin channeling my magic into the little buds, I feel it, a burn. It bites into my chest like fire and spreads through my limbs, slow but sharp. *Odd.* The plants resist me. They *fight* me. My lungs skip a beat as I press both hands into the soil around their roots, forcing my energy into them, but it's like pushing against stone.

I grit my teeth and keep going, even as it drains me more than anything I have ever done before. My vision blurs slightly. My shoulders tremble. Every second stretches into an hour in disguise. I gasp and pull back just for a moment, breath heaving and body shaking. Dizziness takes over me, and a migraine creeps up my neck.

Rome is at my side instantly.

"Winnie?" His hands catch my shoulders, anchoring me. "Are you okay?" he asks, his voice trembling with panic.

"I'm fine," I whisper, though the words tremble. "Just need... a breather."

I shake off the dizziness and return to the flowers, placing my hands over the soil once more. The buds tremble, just slightly. I close my eyes, digging deeper into whatever I have left and letting it pour out.

It takes everything, more than I thought I had. My hands sweat, my back arches from the strain, and tears threaten the edges of my eyes from the sheer force of holding on. Just as I am about to give up, something changes.

A soft rustle. A stirring.

The buds slowly lift, stretching toward the stone ceiling, limbs awaking in green. One by one, they peel open. Large, full blossoms unfurl before my eyes. The petals are as black as midnight, brushed with tiny white flecks and swirling tendrils of dark blue and violet. They are a scattering of shimmering stars, haunting and beautiful. The scent is overwhelming, sweet, sharp, almost poisonous.

The moment they bloom, my legs give out beneath me. I collapse onto the stone floor, drenched in sweat, with my chest rising and falling in ragged gasps. My hands twitch with residual magic. The world spins softly around me.

Rome is beside me again, alarm in his voice. "Winnie!"

"I'm okay," I say between gasps. "Just... weak."

He tries to help me up, but I can't move. Lead fills my limbs. Without hesitation, he lifts me into his arms, one hand beneath my knees, the other around my shoulders. He locks the door behind us and carries me through the stone corridors of the castle.

"You did it, Winnie!" he says.

I fade in and out, focusing on the scent of pine and snow, *Rome's* scent.

That's when the familiar scrape of heavy boots sounds, fast and loud, echoing through the hall.

"What did you do to her?" Larkin's voice is sharp and furious, cutting through the air.

Rome turns as Larkin storms toward us. Larkin's eyes are locked on me with panic written all over his face.

"She's okay," Rome says tightly. "She used her craft. She just overdid it."

Larkin brushes past him and reaches for me. His hand cups my cheek, searching my face.

"Princess..."

"I'm fine," I whisper again, my voice a breath, just for him. "Just... tired."

Together, they get me back to my room.

The moment we arrive, someone is already calling for a healer. I catch one more glimpse of Larkin kneeling beside my bed, his brow furrowed in worry, and then my eyes drift closed.

I blink awake, and the room is blurry. The air is warm from the fire that must have been tended through the night. My body aches, my temples throb, and my neck is stiff. I let out a groan as I sit up. A figure catches my eye.

Larkin.

He's slumped in a chair near my bed, fast asleep with his arms crossed tightly. His legs are sprawled out like he lost the fight to stay awake. The moment I stir, he jolts awake, eyes flying open as he straightens.

"Princess," he says, already moving to the edge of the bed. "Are you okay?"

"I'm... fine," I whisper, rubbing the side of my head. "Just a headache."

His brows knit together as he moves to sit on the bed, with his hands reaching for mine.

"You scared the shit out of me," he murmurs, his voice rough with sleep. "What were you *doing* with him?"

I shake my head slightly. The memory is still foggy, but before I can answer, he suddenly stills. I follow his eyes and gasp. My hands are bruised a deep violet from my fingertips to my wrists.

"I— What?" I turn my palms upward, flexing my fingers. Soreness peaks with the motion. "Never before has my body reacted to my craft like this. Never."

Larkin gently presses his thumb to my wrist, watching me closely. His expression is heavy with worry. "You gave too much, Princess. Whatever those flowers were, they *took* from you."

I swallow, throat dry. "I had to," I say softly. "It was for his brother."

"I have to get you out of here," Larkin says suddenly, his voice trembling

I look at him. "What?"

He stands, moving toward the window and pulling back the curtain. He peers out at the mountain's cliff edge covered in snow, the morning cold and gray.

"We have to go, Princess. This castle... it doesn't feel right. There's an unease here. I don't trust them. I don't trust *him*."

I sit up straighter, heart beating faster. "Larkin..."

He turns back to me, his eyes intense, jaw set. "Rome is not what he seems. I feel it in my bones. I have been trying to ignore it, but last night, watching you like that. Something is *wrong* here. And I won't let you be caught in the middle of it."

I shake my head. "Larkin, I *can't* leave... I can't," I snap, sharper than I meant to. I press my fingers to my temples, trying to focus. "I have to marry him."

His expression falters. "No," he says, stepping closer. "He's using you, Princess."

I rise to my feet despite the ache in my body. "It's my duty to my kingdom. Besides, did you ever think that, maybe, I *like* him," I say through my teeth.

"You *want* to marry a man who forces you to drain your magic? Who touches you at the table like he *owns* you."

I flinch, a raw tremor shaking in my core. "Larkin..."

He shakes his head, angry now, eyes dark. "You *can't* marry him."

"And what, Larkin?" I shoot back. "Marry a *guard?*"

The moment the words leave my mouth, I regret them.

The hurt in his face is immediate. Sharp. A wound I've delivered. He steps back a fraction. His voice is quiet, but it shakes with untamed raw emotion. "Yes. Marry your *guard*."

My breath falters.

"Be with me," he says, stepping closer again.

I can't move. My hands tremble at my sides. "I have to marry a royal," I whisper, as if saying it out loud might make the cage shrink.

He stares at me for a long moment, breathing hard. "You want a royal?" he says, his voice cracking. "I'll be whatever you want." His eyes shift, darkening, red creeping into the rich amber like embers catching flame.

His whole body pulses in restraint.

"You want a king?" he growls. "I'll become a dammed *king* for you."

I instinctively take a step back, startled by the fire behind his eyes, the raw force in his voice. He sees me flinch, and his whole body softens.

He exhales and runs a hand through his long hair, stepping toward the door. Before he leaves, he looks over his shoulder. "I'll be whatever you need me to be," he says, eyes meeting mine. "As long as I get to call you mine."

Then he's gone. And I'm left standing here, heart pounding. My hands tremble, still aching.

Larkin's words linger in the air, like smoke curling around my ribs—sweet and dizzying.

A dull ache still lingers in my temples, and the absence weighs heavily in my chest. Rome hasn't come by. Not even a message. Not a single word since I collapsed trying to bloom those lilies. Are the healers working on the tonic?

There's a sharp knock at the door. The door creaks open, and a servant steps in.

"Your Highness," she says quickly, dipping her head. "A letter just arrived for you."

My eyes dart to the envelope in her hand. I recognize the seal instantly, my mother's crest. My fingers tremble slightly as I take it, murmuring a thank you. I turn away from the door, I break the wax and unfold the parchment.

My dearest Winnie, I write with the fullest heart. Your little brothers are here. Two of them. Twins. The midwife only sensed one, but our healer believes one of the boys must be a shield. His magic hid him from view, even in the womb. It shocked us all, but oh, what joy they have brought already. I have named them Jasper and Leif. I cannot wait to see you on your wedding day. You will be the most radiant bride. I am so proud of you, and I love you more than I can put into words.
Love always, Mother.

I read it again and again, holding the letter close to my chest. A thick lump forms in my throat as tears well in my eyes. New brothers. A shield. I fold the letter carefully and tuck it into a book on my bedside table. I wrap a cloak around my shoulders and head out the door.

The halls of the castle are quiet. The distant hum of servants and guards is the only sound. I follow the directions a guard gave me, winding through endless corridors until I reach a tall black door marked with Rome's family crest. I knock. Nothing. My hand trembles as I grip the handle and push it open.

His chambers are... magnificent. Vaulted ceilings with gold-trimmed beams, navy velvet curtains that drape like waterfalls, and ornate furniture carved from deep, rich wood. Everything smells faintly of him.

But he's not here. I take a few steps inside. The bed is made, not a wrinkle in the sheets. I scan the room. My eyes land on a tiny succulent perched on the bedside table. It's wilted, drooping, neglected.

I reach for the little plant, picking up the small ceramic planter. My fingers graze a soft leaf, and suddenly, the world shatters.

My vision goes white. I can't move. I can't speak. I'm no longer in control. I'm *here* in this room.

Dim candlelight flickers against the walls. The bed is no longer empty.

Rome is lying there, relaxed, shirtless. There's someone straddling him, under the blankets, laughing. Her voice is light, teasing. Familiar. Too familiar. She emerges from the covers, tangled brown hair falling around her face. Her full lips are parted in a smile.

My heart stops.

Maya.

My breath pauses in my throat. I can't scream. I can't move. I can only watch. Maya. The same woman who betrayed my family—no more than a shadow unraveling into the night.

She was *here* in his bed.

Rome reaches up, brushing her light brown hair from her face.

The vision rips away from me, and I stumble backward with a gasp, nearly dropping the planter. My hands are shaking.

No. No, this can't be real. The way they touched... the way he looked at her.

I rush from the room, skirts sweeping behind me as I race down the corridor.

I spot a servant and grab her arm, my voice sharp with urgency.

"Where is Prince Rome?"

She blinks, mouth open. "He's with the king, in the study."

"Where?"

She quickly gives me directions, and I don't wait for another word. My heart pounds in my ears as I follow her directions. My blood boils with betrayal and dread. I don't know what I'll do when I see him. I just know I need answers. *Now.*

I finally reach the study, only to find it empty.

I step into the quiet space. The door clicks shut behind me, and I am left standing in stillness, surrounded by towering bookshelves, old maps, and the faint scent of dust and ink. The room hums with secrets. I wander deeper, sweeping over parchment-strewn tables, quills in inkwells, and a globe perched crookedly beside an open ledger.

One sheet on the desk catches my attention. A list of names, rulers, and nobles. My eyes scan the column of names.

Then I see one that makes my heart shoot to my throat.

Alasdair Salem, weather wielder, storm watcher.

I scan further then...

Winifred Salem, plant influencer.

My name. My craft.

My gaze shifts again, and I freeze again.

Igor Wynfir, mind reader, earbane. There is a harsh red line through Igor's name. My heart drops. *Mind reader? Igor?* A cold sweat breaks across my skin.

And then, just below...

Larkin Steelborn, unknown.

My breath quickens. Why is he being watched like this?

I stumble back from the desk, heart pounding. The room spins with more questions than I can grasp.

My eyes catch on the tall, slender fern in the corner of the room. Its leaves tremble faintly as if it's waiting for me. I walk to it slowly, and my fingers tremble as I reach out to it.

"Please show me what I need to see." My hand brushes the leaf.

The world goes white. Suddenly, I'm standing in this same room, only Rome and King Veric are here.

Their voices are quiet and sharp.

"Did you get her to bloom the magus fur?" Veric asks.

"I did," Rome replies.

"Very good," his father says with a satisfied nod. "And Igor?"

"Taken care of," Rome replies.

"Good, now the guard next."

"They're in love," Rome mutters darkly.

"Even better reason to be rid of him," he growls.

A flicker of sadness flashes across Rome's strong features.

"Don't tell me you've grown to care for the girl," the king says. "Don't let her leave her room. Tell her that her adviser is missing, and it's too dangerous. Tell her the whole castle is on lockdown. I'll take care of the guard."

The words shatter through me like jagged stones breaking bones.

"And son," Veric says, "don't let your feelings for the girl get in the way."

I'm yanked back into my body, chest heaving. I stumble away from the fern, sickened.

They're going to kill Larkin.

I turn and bolt from the study. I *have* to get to him. I have to warn him. My arms pump as I sprint through the castle, trying to remember the way to my room. I'm feet away from Larkin's door, mine directly across from his.

"Winnie!" Rome's voice cracks through the air like a whip.

Before I can react, Rome grabs my wrist. His grip is firm, strong enough to make me panic.

"Larkin!" I scream.

Rome places a hand over my mouth, shushing me. He backs me into the wall beside my door, his expression tense.

"We'll talk," he says quickly. "I will explain everything. I swear it. I am so sorry."

"Rome, no—"

He opens the door behind me and pushes me inside. Before I can react, he slams it shut, and the lock clicks with menacing finality.

I yank on the handle—locked.

"Rome!" I slam my palm against the wood. "Rome, let me out."

Nothing.

My chest tightens. My breath catches as panic creeps in. I whirl around, trapped/ My mind races with every word, name, and betrayal. Larkin. I have to get to him. Before it's too late. I glance around the room. My eyes fall on a canvas that wasn't there before. The painting of the familiar eyes from the gallery. Rome's painting hangs there on the wall.

I see a piece of folded parchment tucked into the corner of the frame. I grab it. It's addressed to me. I shove it in my pocket as I rush to the large window in my room, heart hammering. I scan the ledge, the height, anything I could climb or leap to.

Then I freeze.

Sitting on the edge of the snowy cliffs below, alone on a jagged stone, is Larkin. His shoulders are slumped. His head is low, unmoving. I can feel the weight in him even from here. He's hurting. Tears prick my eyes, but then, a flicker in the corner of my vision shifts.

King Veric.

A viper in human skin, he stalks Larkin with a patience born of venom. My blood turns to ice.

His arm lifts, and from his palm, a cord of shadows lashes forward, writhing smoke, pulsing with malice.

It's aimed straight at Larkin's back.

"No!" I scream. My voice is raw with terror as I pound against the window. I grab the angel statue placed in the center of the table next to me and shatter the window, glass flying around me like a lethal mist.

"LARKIN!"

He turns at the sound of my voice, meeting my eyes, but it's too late.

The shadow slams into him with crushing force.

His body jerks violently, then he topples.

Off the cliff.

Gone.

"No!" I scream, shattering.

The sound that tears from my chest doesn't sound human. It's a hollow, breaking force that splits the silence like shattering glass. I collapse to my knees, clutching the windowsill as my world tilts on its axis. The pain in my chest is blinding. It cracks through my ribs and coils into my spine.

He's gone. He's *gone*. I scream until my throat gives out, until my soul aches, and there's nothing left but a trembling silence.

The door bursts open behind me.

Rome.

He rushes in, breathless. His eyes are wide as he sees me crumpled by the broken window. "Winnie."

But all I feel is rage.

Devastation and fury swirl together in my gut, and I rise to my feet, shaking with it. My hands ball into fists. My heart screams his name.

Just as I take a step toward Rome, ready to unleash everything inside me—

Boom.

An unseen force rocks the wall beside us.

With so much power, stone erupts inward, and the room fills with sunlight and debris.

I cover my face, stumbling back. When the dust clears, I see a shadow.

A massive form, scales as dark and rich as pine needles, wings stretching wide against the gray sky.

A dragon.

Towering, wild, eyes glowing fierce, hovering outside the gaping hole in my chamber wall.

I don't think.

I *move.*

"Winnie!" Rome yells, but his voice is nothing but static behind the pounding in my head.

I sprint across the ruined room, leap over fallen stone, and hurl myself through the breach.

The wind catches me midair.

I crash hard onto the dragon's back. My body slides before my hands clutch around one of the thick, jagged spikes at the base of its neck.

With a mighty beat of its wings, the dragon lifts, soaring high into the sky. My hair whips in the wind, stinging my cheeks as we fly over the snow-dusted forest far below.

The castle grows smaller behind me.

All I can see is Larkin.

Falling.

My last words to him were that he's not good enough for me.

And I sob into the dragon's scales.

CHAPTER TWENTY

We fly for miles, over the forest, past the snow, over frozen rivers, until the world below shifts from white to browns and reds. The dragon doesn't falter, just beats his wings.

Finally, he descends, gliding lower until we're just above the tree line.

A wide clearing opens below us, a secret meant only for us. Grass, soft and untouched, with a few wildflowers dancing in the breeze.

The dragon lands with a gentle thud, lowering his massive body until I can climb down. I slide off his side. My legs tremble the second my boots touch the ground.

I collapse to my knees, unable to hold myself up anymore. My hands cover my face as the sobs take over. The grief pours out in waves. Loud and ragged. I'm drowning in it. I'm choking on the pain. I can barely hear anything but the sound of my own heart bleeding out.

The sudden weight of a large, warm hand lands on my shoulder. I flinch and whip around, my breath snags in a panic.

And I see *him*.

Standing right in front of me.

Larkin.

My eyes blur. The earth tilts again, and I swear I'm hallucinating. "Larkin?"

His voice is calm and soft. "Yes, Princess, I'm here."

I stare, frozen.

"No... no, I *saw* you. I saw you fall. Off the cliff. I saw it."

He offers the faintest smile, one corner of his mouth tilting up. "The wings," he says with a shrug, "come in handy."

I gape at him. I can't think.

"What... what are you?"

He kneels beside me until his face is level with mine. His eyes are as warm and bright as ever.

"I'm yours, Princess."

I stare at him, my heart still raw and rattling, but steadier now with him here.

With Larkin.

"What... what do we do now?" I ask quietly, my voice cracked from crying and wind and fear.

He doesn't hesitate. "I could show you my home."

I stare at him. "I never want to set foot in Haravik again."

His lips curl into a smile. "Good," he says, "because we won't be going there."

I narrow my eyes at him, confused. "Larkin... you said you were from Mossvale."

"Did I?" He says casually, "I meant Syrias."

My stomach drops. "You're from Nyxlandia?" I whisper.

His face grows more serious. The joking fades into a heavier, but genuine tone.

"We have a lot to talk about, Princess. And I have a lot to show you."

I stare at him. "You lied to me."

He looks at me with shame in his eyes. "I had my reasons."

I glance at him again, the pieces finally clicking into place. The way he would always find me, the way he had fought like no man should.

"It was you... all this time," I whisper. "It was you who saved me. More than once."

His expression softens, his gaze fierce and tender.

His hand finds my waist.

I step toward him and wrap my arms around him, tight, like if I let go, the world would fall apart again. My lips find his. I kiss him, deep. There's nothing gentle about it. It's full of desperation and relief. He kisses me back just as fiercely, holding me close. His arms are locked around me, grounding in a way nothing else ever has.

When we finally part, we're both breathless.

He looks at me and grins. "I guess you got your birthday present a little late, huh?" He chuckles.

I freeze for half a second, then I burst into laughter, remembering. "I said... ride a dragon."

Realizing his birthday was coming up soon, I remembered his gift.

Doc. Tally.

"The horses," I say in a panic.

"I'll send for them when we are able to send post," he assures.

"Your birthday, Larkin. When is it again?" I ask.

"My birthday... is today, Princess."

Sadness and guilt wash over me. "Oh." I sigh, not sure what to say.

"Are you ready?"

I nod.

Completely unsure what to expect, I watch as Larkin takes several steps back. Head down, shoulders wide.

In a blur, his body morphs into a fury of scales and wings in an instant. One moment, a man stood before me, and the next, a magnificent beast. So large, my height caps at the beast's elbows. He bows low enough for me to climb up onto his back. In a few beats of his wings, we are in the sky.

We fly for hours. The wind is cold and sharp against my skin. I sit nestled between the powerful green scales of his back. My arms grip the thick ridge of his spine for balance. It's so hard to believe Larkin *is* this powerful beast beneath me. I trusted him without even knowing it was him, throwing myself out of a window into the air. It was him. It had *always* been him.

He lands in a quiet clearing surrounded by pines. The transformation is smooth, seamless. One moment, he is this giant beast, wings tucked and eyes burning gold. The next, he steps out of the glow of magic as a towering man pulling a shirt over his head with a quick grin.

"Just a few more hours," he says, tossing me a waterskin. "Drink some water, please."

I nod. "You never told me you could do *that*," I say quietly.

"My kind was hunted to extinction, Princess." He looks down, his expression shadowed.

"Your family?"

He nods.

My heart squeezes in my chest. I stare at him, overwhelmed, with my heart hurting. He had protected me, leaving himself vulnerable.

Once we are back in the air, I hold tighter, out of admiration, an understanding that makes my chest ache. The bond between us is more than I understand, but I know it's real. I trust him. More than anyone.

The sun begins to dip lower, casting fire across the sky. Then I see, far in the distance, where the mountains peel away into wide valleys and lakes edged in golden sunlight.

There it is.

A city of dark spires and glowing towers. Black stone bridges over shimmering rivers. We made it. To Syrias. We are now in the Kingdom of Nyxlandia.

CHAPTER TWENTY~ONE

We start our descent, with the air turning cooler as darkness wraps around us. Below, the training yard comes into view, shadowed now, but faintly lit by flickering torches and the moonlight. The sun has set, leaving the tall slate-gray stone castle and its stained glass windows bathed in a soft, mysterious light.

I slide off Larkin's broad, scaled back, balancing myself on the ground. He shifts smoothly back into his human form. His strong frame is outlined by the torchlight.

Together, we walk toward the castle's back entrance. We pass two giant dragon sculptures on each side of the walkway.

Inside, the kitchens buzz quietly with activity. Servants with wide, surprised eyes bow deeply as we pass. Larkin's voice is calm but commanding as he tells one of them to show me to a room and bring fresh clothes and food. Then, without warning, he pulls me close and presses a warm kiss to my lips.

"I'll come see you soon," he whispers.

And just like that, he slips away into the shadows of the castle, leaving me with a promise.

A woman with red curly hair, bright hazel eyes, and a warm smile greets me with a curtsy.

"I'm Magnolia," the lady says gently. "I'll be taking you to your room."

I follow her. Our footsteps echo through endless corridors. This castle is huge, far bigger than I imagined.

We finally reach a large door, richly adorned with gold trim that glints even in the dim light. Magnolia pushes it open, revealing a huge, luxurious room that takes my breath away. The soaring ceilings are decorated with intricate gold moldings, and rich burgundy velvet curtains frame windows that overlook the castle grounds.

Plush rugs in deep burgundy tones cover the reflective marble floor, and elegant furniture fills the space. A large four-poster bed draped with silk sits in the middle of the room. A large oil painting of a fleet of dragons hangs above a massive marble fireplace, completing the room's luxurious and comforting atmosphere.

Magnolia leads me into a spacious bathroom, asks what scent I would prefer for the bath, and starts listing off different names of smells.

I think for a moment before saying,
"Honey jasmine sounds lovely."

She pours salts and oils into the steaming water, filling the room with a soothing aroma.

I sink into the bath, letting the warmth wash away my exhaustion.

After a long soak, I slip into a soft robe hanging on the door.

Back in the room, I find food laid out on a small table. A spread of bread, cheeses, poultry, and fruit lay before me. As I eat, I can't help but think Larkin must hold a very high rank to grant me a room this fine. A room fit for a queen.

There's a soft knock at the door. I glance up from my seat just as Magnolia steps inside. Her arms are stacked high with folded fabrics, gowns, nightwear, soft tunics, and neatly pressed trousers. She opens the tall dresser and begins placing the clothes inside, carefully organizing each item like she's done it a hundred times.

She finishes and turns back to me, holding a small bundle wrapped in twine.

"I also brought parchment and ink, in case you needed to write anyone. If you write a letter, just place the envelope in the basket outside your door. I'll see to it that your post is sent."

I nod, grateful.

Glancing at the parchment Magnolia had set down, my eyes drift to the weight I'd nearly forgotten about, the folded parchment still tucked inside the pocket of my soiled trousers. My heart falls to my gut.

Rome's letter.

Magnolia moves toward the small pile of dirty clothes, reaching for them, but I spring up from my seat.

"Wait!" I call out, too sharp and sudden.

She stares slightly, pausing in place.

"I just… I need something from those," I say, moving quickly to the trousers. I dig into the pocket and pull out the folded parchment, already smudged and slightly crumpled from being carried through the journey I've just endured.

I settle onto the edge of the bed. The luxurious bedding dips beneath me. My fingers tremble slightly as I unfold the letter.

The moment my eyes meet the first lines, the room around me seems to still.

Winnie, if you are reading this, then I've failed you.

He writes of his shame. Of the madness coursing through his father's veins.

My father is not merely ambitious; he is consumed by greed. He wishes to rule all of Aerothias. He's creating something… a potion that allows one to steal another's craft and lumina. He made me lie to you. He made me abuse your kindness. He's using the magus fur lilies you coaxed to bloom.

My chest tightens as I continue to read.

He used the potion first on my mother, with the un-bloomed buds. She was powerful, brilliant. Her lumina was vast and beautiful. She could turn the realm upside down if she wanted.

It killed her. He killed her. He tried again on my little brother. His name was Fader. He inherited her strength. It... He killed him, too.

My hands begin to shake.

I have no lumina of my own, Winnie. Everything you felt for me was real. I did not manipulate you. I know you felt as I did. I sensed it with my craft. My father is ashamed of me and hides that truth with lies and whispers, says I can compel others, but it's not true. He is the one with the craft of compulsion. He uses it to force loyalty, to silence dissent. To control me.

I feel sick. Rome, so polished, so collected, was nothing more than another one of his father's pawns.

And I was, too. My heart aches for him. He must be living in absolute isolation.

He forced Maya to poison your mother. It was never her idea. It was punishment... for me. Because I loved her. When she returned, he had her killed.

My lashes flutter. The letters blur before my eyes.

He plans to kill your family. To take your throne. And with it, your father's lumina. He will stop at nothing. He wants to wear every crown, wield every power. Become a god among kings.

I know I betrayed you, I hurt you. But I never stopped caring. Maya...she was a sight. She said you'd leave when the truth was uncovered. She said you'd go on the back of a beast. I'm sorry. I'm asking you for help. I don't deserve it, but I can't do this alone. I want him dead.

p.s. Little Flower, I don't think your guard is who he says he is. My informants have no history of him ever working in Haravik...or anywhere for that matter. Please be cautious. I hope to hear from you soon. - Rome

I fold the letter slowly, numbly.

I press it to my lips, in grief. For what might have been.

Rome had been trapped in a kingdom of shadows. And he has nobody.

There's a knock at the door. I quickly wipe my eyes, trying to regain some composure, but the weight of the letter still lingers heavily in my hands.

The door creaks open, and Larkin steps inside, ducking his head as he steps through the doorway, moving quiet as a shadow. His eyes find mine immediately, and he closes the distance in just a few strides.

He sits beside me on the edge of the bed, his presence grounding, his warmth calming.

"You look pale, Princess," he says, his voice heavy with worry. "Are you all right?"

I don't answer.

Instead, I hold out the folded parchment with a trembling hand.

He takes it from me, eyes narrowing slightly as he begins to read. I watch his expression carefully. He doesn't flinch, doesn't speak until he finishes.

My voice comes out barely above a whisper.

"Have you never worked in Haravik? Was your father ever really a fisherman?" I hesitate, the question sitting heavy in my chest. "What were the truths, Larkin? And what were lies?"

He sighs, long and low. "You deserve every truth, and I'll give them to you... in the morning, Princess."

He places the letter on the bedside table and turns to me, brushing a stray curl from my cheek. "You need rest. We both do."

"We need to get Rome," I say, the fire rising in my chest.

He tilts his head slightly, studying me. "You still trust him? After everything?"

"I don't know," I admit. "But if what he wrote is real, if his father's trying to take every crown and steal everyone's lumina, then we don't have time to doubt."

Larkin is quiet for a moment, then nods.

I exhale, some small measure of peace settling into my bones. He leans in and kisses the top of my head, and I lean into his shoulder.

"Where do you sleep?" I whisper, tilting my head to meet his gaze.

"For now... in here," he says, giving me a soft smile.

We lay down together, with the heaviness of the day still pressing against my ribs. Larkin slips in behind me. His strong arm wraps around my waist, pulling me close. His warmth seeps into my back, melting the chill that's clung to me since I shattered that window.

The room is quiet, just the sound of the wind brushing the tall castle windows and the slow, steady rhythm of his breathing. I close my eyes, trying to drift, but my thoughts won't still. Rome's words echo in my mind.

I don't think your guard is who he says he is.

Is there anything else he isn't telling me?

I shift slightly. My fingers curl around the edge of the blanket. Larkin's grip on me tightens instinctively, grounding me, as if he senses the storm inside.

CHAPTER TWENTY~TWO

The next morning, the spot Larkin occupied before I drifted to sleep is empty. I pull myself up out of bed. I walk to the dresser Magnolia had stocked.

I slip into a mahogany-colored gown and throw a fur-lined shawl over my shoulders. As I'm sliding into my boots, I glance at the bundled parchment Magnolia left for me.

I grab some paper and sit at the desk. I quickly pen a letter addressed to my father.

I tell him where I am and what happened. I tell him of Igor and of King Veric's plans. I leave out the details of Larkin's beast form. I fold the parchment and place it in the basket.

I wander the halls. My boots are almost silent against the marble floor, following faint echoes until I reach a large stained glass double door that opens into the courtyard.

I step outside quietly. The early morning air is cool against my skin

Larkin is sparring. His sweat clings to his brow, hair damp from exertion.

He's training with someone tall, lean, and striking in a boyish way. He has short, sandy blond curls and a mischievous grin that never leaves his face. He looks a little younger than Larkin but carries himself like someone raised alongside power.

I find a bench tucked beneath a flowering vine. I sit, unnoticed, and I watch.

They move easily, with laughter breaking between strikes. The way they move, fluid and fast, speaks of years of practice. Each strike is met with ease, each parry followed by a grin or a quip.

The man laughs as Larkin nearly knocks the sword from his grip, and Larkin laughs right back, eyes shining.

I've never seen him so unburdened with laughter and light spilling from him.

There's familiarity between them, a silent understanding. A bond built through time and trust. It makes my heart ache inside me. For the months I've known him, he has always carried weight on his shoulders. He's protective, serious, always guarded.

But here... he's light.

"Malachai, you're getting slow," the other man calls, breathless from laughter.

Malachai.

I sit up straighter. The name rings through my head like a bell. It's familiar, but I can't remember where I had heard it before.

I stand. Larkin... or Malachai catches sight of me then. The joy on his face softens into a more cautious expression. He lets his sword fall to his side as the other man follows his gaze and gives me a wave before offering Larkin a small nod and heading back to the castle.

I step closer, my voice quiet but commanding.

"Who's Malachai?"

He sighs as he walks toward me, sweat glistening on his brow.

"Let's get some breakfast," he says gently. "I'll explain everything, Princess."

I follow him silently. The weight of that name is still heavy in my chest. But just before we reach the castle doors, a guard comes rushing toward us, panic in his eyes.

"Sir, there's been an attack. In Dragomir," the man says between ragged breaths.

Larkin's face changes in an instant. The joy, the lightness, it vanishes, replaced by a hard edge I recognize from Haravik.

He turns to me with urgency in his eyes. "I have to go. Make yourself at home. We will talk later."

"No." I step toward him, shaking my head. "You owe me answers."

"You'll have them," he promises, placing a hand briefly on my arm. "But right now, I have to go."

I don't fight him.

He's gone within seconds, disappearing in the sky over the castle gates. And I am left alone again, beneath castle spires that gleam like golden lies, wondering who Malachai truly was... and why that name haunted a fragment buried deep in my memory.

CHAPTER TWENTY~THREE
LARKIN

The wind roars past my wings as I soar above the clouds, with the castle fading into mist behind me. The air is cold and sharp, but it does nothing to settle my thoughts. Each beat of my wings is fueled by unease.

Rome's letter keeps repeating in my mind. His warnings. His plea for help. I want to believe it was manipulation. A final attempt to pull Winnie's heartstrings. But the more I think about it, the more his words claw at a truth that could be too real.

A potion to steal another's magic. A king driven mad by greed. It's not just poetic fear-mongering. And now there's been an attack.

In my own kingdom. Nyxlandia and Haravik are no strangers to tension, or even war.

I fly fast, pushing my wings harder, faster, until the trees below become a blur.

Nearly an hour has passed, and I finally see the perimeter of the guard outpost. Its flickering fire torches are arranged in a rough circle. The military camp surrounding it is tense. Armored guards run between tents and stone buildings, with every eye alert.

I land just beyond the outer wall, shifting back into my human form as I approach. Soldiers stare but quickly lower their eyes.

The camp's general meets me at the edge of the central tent. His face is grim.

"General Rafe," I say, nodding.

"Sir," he greets, dipping his head. "It's bad. You will want to see it for yourself."

He leads me across the camp, past the perimeter where soldiers stand in silence.

The duke's estate is barely a half mile from the guard outpost, but it might as well have been a graveyard.

The once grand house is scorched in places, with broken windows, blood-stained stone steps, and the distant scent of burned flesh still hanging in the air.

Inside, they've covered the bodies, but the general pulls back one of the cloths. I flinch. The duke's skin is darkened, purplish black, like it had rotted from the inside out. His veins are blackened vines, twisting and branching up his neck and jaw. His eyes are still open.

It's like something had consumed him from within.

"He died this way?" I ask quietly.

Rafe holds up an arrow. It looks like someone dipped the entire head in black tar. "We've never seen anything of its kind. So unnatural."

"How many others?"

"Fourteen. Guards, servants, anyone who stood in their way. Duke Jennings is the only one who looks... like this," he says, gesturing to the blackened body.

"And the Duchess?"

"Fine, left her sleeping in the bed."

"They only wanted him," I say, voice quiet.

Rafe nods grimly.

"It was precise. Fast. Brutal. As if they came with one goal."

"And they succeeded," I say. My mind spins back to Rome's warning. "What was Jennings's lumina, Rafe?"

I move through the rest of the estate, investigating everything.

Rafe follows.

"He was a cloak, sir. They got him in his sleep."

They must have known it would be the only way to catch an invisible man.

I move back to the body, looking at the wound. A black tar substance lines the edges of the entrance and seeps through his nightshirt.

He's using magus fur lilies potions to drain magic. He's coming for all of Aeorthias.

"Bring that arrow back to the castle," I say, gesturing to the substance-stained arrow lying on the table next to Jennings. "I have someone who may be able to tell us what that is."

If King Veric truly had a way to steal luminas, then none of us would be safe.

I took to the skies again, with my wings cutting through the wind as I left the camp behind. The cold air bites at my scales, but my thoughts are louder than the rush of wind.

Rome.

I need to speak to him.

The letter keeps replaying in my mind, line by line, and I hate how much of it makes sense now. The attack on the duke, the blackened veins, the stealth. No ordinary assassin or rogue kingdom would move like that. This was calculated, dark, and it stinks of the king's madness.

I clench my jaw. My wings beat harder, pushing me faster. My mind runs to Winnie. She is somewhere in the castle, maybe pacing, probably wondering why I hadn't come back yet.

And all I can think about is how much she didn't know.

How much I still have to tell her.

What I *hadn't* told her.

I spot the towers of the castle breaking through the clouds, its gray stone glowing in the low rays of sunlight. Hues of orange and pink dance across the stone walls. I tuck my wings and

dive toward the courtyard, landing with a thud
before shifting back into myself.

I find Rook in his study, tossing orbs of ice into the air and letting them float lazily above his head like winter stars. The frost shimmers under the warm lamplight, casting pale blue glows across the walls of the room.

He looks up as I enter, with one of the ice balls hovering between his fingers.

"Well," he says, running a hand through his blond waves. "You're back earlier than I thought."

I don't return the smile.

"Duke Jennings is dead. And fourteen others."

I throw Rome's letter on my cousin's desk.

His expression drops as he reads the words written on the parchment.

The air around us shifts, temperature falling ever so slightly as his lumina pulses and the orbs of frost still.

"So, it's true... The bastard is trying to steal luminas."

I nod, jaw tight.

"Then we prepare for war." He stands, the orbs vanishing into mist. "No hesitation. If he wants to play gods, then we don't sit on our hands and hope he fails."

I meet his eyes and nod.

He claps a hand on my shoulder, firm and familiar. "But you know you have to tell her, don't you?"

I let out a long sigh and run a hand through my hair. "Yeah. I know."

"She deserves to know everything, Kai."

He watches me for a moment, the way only someone who'd grown up alongside you could, reading more than just my expression.

I nod again, slowly this time. He's right. It *is* time.

I wander the castle halls, with my thoughts tangled and heavy. I'm not even sure where my feet are taking me, only that I need to find her. The smell of something freshly baked and sweet comes creeping from the kitchens.

I grab one of the sticky cinnamon delights and retreat into the halls.

After passing through another empty corridor, I push open the set of tall oak doors and step into the library.

The room is massive, lined with shelves that stretch toward a ceiling painted with constellations. Golden lamplight pools in the corners, warm and quiet.

And there she is.

Tucked into a corner of the room, legs curled beneath her, with a book resting in her lap. She hadn't noticed me yet. I stay where I am, just watching her. Her long auburn hair spills over her shoulders in waves of cashmere that catch the soft glow of the light.

I've always loved how long it was, wild and elegant, like her. Freckles dust her cheeks like stars scatter across her skin, subtle and soft. My gaze pauses on her lips, plump and pink, and parted ever so slightly in focus as she read.

She looks up.

And when her quartz gray eyes find mine, my heart jolts hard beneath my chest. Like it remembers a song my mind hadn't caught up with yet. The chord between us pulls so tight it almost brings me to my knees.

Gods, she's beautiful.

CHAPTER TWENTY~FOUR
WINNIE

I spot him in the hallway, holding a small plate in one of those ridiculously large hands of his. Relief washes over me at the sight of him, like I had been holding my breath the whole time he was gone.

He looks calm, stable, as always, and gods, so handsome it hurts. That broad chest and strong jaw, those wild amber eyes.

He meets my gaze and starts walking toward me. I sit cross-legged in the nest of floor pillows, with the book I had barely been reading still open in my lap.

When he reaches me, he eases down onto the pillows beside me. His thigh brushes mine. He hands me the plate.

A cinnamon roll. Still warm. I close the book, set it aside, and accept the pastry.

"Thanks," I whisper.

We sit in silence for a moment. The sugary warmth of the roll fills the space between us, but I can't ignore the quaking in my chest.

"How did it go?" I finally ask.

He looks straight ahead for a beat before turning to me. His voice is even, but there's a weight behind it. He tells me about his findings at the duke's estate, the death, the strange, darkened body, and the untouched duchess. I listen, but I'm floating outside myself, taking it in through a hazy veil.

Then, another silence.

He takes a breath.

"My name is Malachai Larkin Hawthorne," he says softly. "The beast form you've seen... they call it Steelborn."

The name echoes in my head, the familiarity of it stinging me, but I can't place it.

"And the man you saw me sparring with outside, his name is Rook Oren."

I freeze. My lips move before I can stop them.

"The crown prince," I whisper.

He nods.

Larkin... Malachai's voice lowers.

"King Veric killed my entire family, including Aurora, my little sister." His voice breaks on her name.

I cover my mouth with my eyes wide.

"I knew Igor had ties to the royal family of Odesa, and I got closer to him. He got me in, made me your guard. He knew why I was there. He lost his wife to Veric, too. She was my aunt."

My stomach twists.

"My whole plan was to get into Haravik, completely unnoticed, and kill Veric."

I can't move, can't breathe.

"But I fell in love with you, Princess, from the moment I saw you... the less I started to care about revenge. And now... the only thing that matters to me is keeping you safe." His voice is raw. Earnest.

But all I can feel is the sting.

I look down at the half-eaten roll in my hands.

"So... all of it? Getting close to me was that just part of your plan?"

"No," he says quickly. "Not like that. It started that way, but it changed. Everything changed."

My chest tightens. "You lied to me. About who you are. About everything."

"I had to," he says gently. "My kind were hunted to near extinction, remember? If anyone knew—"

"I'm not talking about you being Steelborn," I snap, standing up. My hands shake. "I'm talking about you letting me believe that you were just my guard, letting me fall for you while you carried around this secret mission."

He rises with me, slowly, like I might bolt.

"I never meant to hurt you," he says softly.

"But you did," I whisper. "I don't know what's real anymore. Or who to trust."

His voice cracks. "Princess, everything I've said to you, everything I've done for you, was real. I love you."

I take a step back, heart in my throat. The room spins a little. "You used me!" I shout, the words ripping through me before I can stop them.

Larkin flinches like I struck him. His face twists in hurt. Deep, raw hurt.

"Princess—" he says, reaching for my arm.

His touch is gentle, but I pull away.

"There's something else I want to tell you," he says quickly. His words are a bridge over the collapse between us.

But before he can say another word, a servant bursts into the library, breathless. She bows low.

"Your Highness. There's word for you, General Rafe awaits in your study."

Your Highness.

I freeze.

My chest stops moving. The air feels thick. Larkin's eyes flicker to mine. His lips part like he wants to say more, to explain.

But instead, he lifts my hand and presses a kiss to my fingers. "I'll be back."

I don't hear anything else. My mind is spinning so fast I can't focus on a single thought.

His name... it's more familiar now than before. It echoes in my bones like a half-remembered dream I can't grasp. Malachai Hawthorne. I stand motionless for a moment until my limbs move on their own. I turn toward the shelves and begin scanning the titles with shaking hands. I don't know what I'm looking for, only that I have to find it, some truth, answers.

Then I see a book titled *History of the Throne, Nyxlandia*. I yank it from the shelf and stumble to the nearest table. Flipping through the pages at a frantic pace. Names and dates blur past. Monarchs. Wars. Treaties. Then my gaze stops at *The Hawthornes*. A long lineage of kings, each bearing the surname Hawthorne.

Thorson Hawthorne - Deceased. Luna Hawthorne - Deceased. Aurora Hawthorne - Deceased. Malachai Hawthorne - Whereabouts Unknown. Shawniaus Oren (Regent Brother-in-law of Thorson) - Ruling in Absence of Heir.

My ears ring.

My hands tremble over the page.

Larkin... Malachai... He isn't just *close* to the royal family.

 He *is* the royal family.

My thoughts spin wildly as his words come crashing back to me.

"I'll be whatever you need me to be."

That's why his name sounded so familiar. I've heard it whispered in the halls growing up, during tense dinners and council meetings. Nyxlandia was always wrapped in secrecy. Its monarchy was shrouded in rumor. But I had heard of the missing prince.

And he has been beside me all this time. Protecting me. Kissing me. *Lying to me.* I sit in the library, book open, heart cracked open even wider. Malachai Larkin Hawthorne isn't just my guard.

He isn't just a dragon.

He's a *king*.

And I don't know what to do with that.

I can't sit here any longer. The words on the page blur as tears fill my eyes, from the weight of everything I don't know. Everything I still don't understand. I shove the book closed and rise to my feet, storming out of the library with no real destination, only a need to move.

To do something.

I reach my room. My hands shake as I tear out of the soft gown I'd worn to the library. I yank open the drawer of the tall dresser in my room and grab some trousers and a tunic. The fabric is rougher, my boots are worn, but right now, that feels right, familiar.

The courtyard is nearly empty when I arrive. The air is cool, and the stone beneath my boots is warm from the sun. I grab a training sword from the rack and stalk toward the row of dummies lined along the edges of the practice yard.

I don't hesitate. I strike. Once. Twice. I'm done being gentle. Done being a girl swept into the stories told by men.

Over and over again, I swing my sword. Every strike is a blow against a lie, a secret, a memory I can't trust. I let out a sharp cry and strike harder.

My arms burn, sweat slicks my skin, but I don't stop.

Each slam of the blade rings through the courtyard. I don't care who hears it. A breeze rushes past me, rustling the trees lining the walls.

The vines tremble. The flowers that cling to the far archway quiver, blooming faster than they should. The leaves... they're moving with me. A nearby vine pulses as though responding to my heartbeat, curling tighter around its post. The grass at my feet shimmers, rising just slightly, as if it's reaching.

He *used* me. And I'm pissed.

My breath comes in ragged bursts. The blade in my hand feels heavier with every swing, but I don't stop. Sweat clings to my brow, my chest a relentless beat echoing through my bones. The dummy in front of me begins to splinter at the edges from my relentless blows.

"Careful," comes a voice behind me, calm and amused. "You're going to break that thing's spirit."

I spin, sword lifted, only to see Prince Rook Oren standing a few feet away, arms crossed, with that crooked half smile tugging at the corner of his lips. His sandy curls are still tousled from earlier.

"I didn't hear you come up," I say, breathless.

"You were a little busy scaring the weeds into submission," he teases, nodding toward the trembling vines behind me.

I flush but say nothing.

He walks over to the weapons rack, selects a sword, and gives it a few test swings.

Then he faces me. "Care for a real opponent?"

I raise my brows but ready my blade. "Only if you're prepared to lose."

He lets out a low laugh and steps forward. "Show me what you got, Princess."

Our blades meet with a satisfying clang, and I grin in spite of myself.

We move across the courtyard like shadows cast by firelight, swift and purposeful. Rook is fast, but I'm not holding back anymore. Every strike I make, he counters with just enough resistance to challenge me but never overwhelming me. He's guiding me, pushing me harder, faster.

My heart rate increases, but my thoughts slow. I focus on my footing and my breath. The way the blade slices through the air.

Then, just as we pause to catch our breath, Rook tilts his head. "Kai was right. You are tough," he says, a smile tugging

He says it so simply. No teasing or condescension. My chest tightens. Larkin had been talking about me to Rook, praising me. I swallow hard, and I can't stop the smile that edges across my face.

I look away, letting out a breath. "Thanks," I say between breaths.

For a moment, I let myself forget everything else. The letter. The lies. The weight of my bloodline. Right now, I'm just a girl with a sword, and that's enough.

We circle back again, blades scraping, and laughter caught in our breath. There's a shift in Rook's eyes, softer now, less teasing.

He lowers his sword. "You know, Kai really cares for you."

My lashes flutter, caught off guard by the seriousness in his voice.

"He talks about you a lot," Rook adds, resting the practice sword on his shoulder. "Not just how strong you are. Not your magic. But little things. Like the way you smile when you're about to say something smart, or how you do a little dance when you have a sweet treat."

I stand still, with my heart quietly thudding in my chest.

Rook glances down at the sword in his hand, turning it slowly. "He has never been in love before. I don't even think he knows how to be."

That surprises me. "Really?"

He nods. "Yeah. There was no one around to teach him what love should be. Not real love, anyway."

I stay quiet. The weight of his words wraps around me.

"He's just guessing," he shrugs. "Doing his best with what he's got. And he might mess up sometimes, but I promise you, he's a good man. Loyal to a fault. If he's told you he cares for you, he means it. Even if he doesn't always know how to show it."

I swallow hard. My fingers tighten around the hilt of the sword.

A breeze sweeps through the courtyard. The leaves around us flutter. My chest feels tight. I meet his eyes, and he raises his sword again.

"All right. One more round before you wipe the floor with me?"

I smile, lifting my blade. "Of course."

The moon hangs low, casting a soft silver glow through the large windows, as I walk across the stone floor. My skin still tingles from the warmth of the bath. I pull on the only thing I can find in the armoire, a soft, ivory nightgown that clings in all the wrong places—or maybe the right ones. It is thin, almost sheer, the silk whispering against my skin like a second breath.

I finish brushing the damp ends of my hair when a knock sounds, followed by the quiet creak of the door opening.

I turn, and my gaze meets a pair of amber eyes. His tall frame fills the doorway, strong and still. A tray of food is balanced in his large hands. But his eyes stall when they meet me.

I watch his throat bob as he swallows, gaze dropping slowly over me. I pretend not to notice, though my cheeks flush with heat.

"I brought food," he says, his voice a little rough.

"Thank you."

I walk to the small round table near the window, acutely aware of the way his eyes follow me. He sets the tray down, but lingers close. Neither of us speaks as we take our seats.

We eat in silence for a moment, with only the sound of cutlery clinking against plates between us.

"There's something I need to tell you." His voice is low. He sets down his fork and looks at me.

I reach for his hand before he can finish. "I know," I sigh.

His eyes search mine. A pause, then a breath of relief passes through him.

"Malachi Hawthorne. The rightful heir of Nyxlandia."

He squeezes my hand gently. "I wanted to tell you myself. I just... needed to find the words." But then his expression shifts, hardens slightly. "There's more. Rafe brought word. Haravik troops were spotted near the border between Odesa and Haravik."

My stomach drops.

"What? Are they looking for me?"

"Possibly," he says grimly. "But I've already sent troops of my own. To help defend your kingdom."

I gape, the weight of it landing in my chest. "You sent your soldiers?"

He nods.

"Thank you, Larkin... Malachai."

A quiet moment passes again, only broken when I whisper, "I have to go home."

He nods again. "I know, Princess. And I'm coming with you."

A lump forms in my throat, touched beyond words. "You'd come with me? To my kingdom?"

He looks at me as if the question surprises him. "I'm not letting you go out into danger alone."

"But... what about your people? Your kingdom. Your coronation."

"They'll manage," he says. "We'll figure it all out, together."

The word *together* settles warm and heavy in my chest.

He leans back, and the corners of his mouth curve up slightly. "Besides," he adds with a wink, "how else are you getting there?"

A laugh slips from me before I can stop it.

Despite the weight of everything hanging over us, the potential war, the secrets, the pain, he still manages to make me feel safe, wanted—not alone. Whatever was coming, we would face it together.

"Where have you been this whole time?" I ask quietly. "After... after your family was murdered?"

He looks down for a moment, then meets my eyes. "Here," he says simply. "In this castle."

"Here? All this time?"

He nods. "After the attack, the staff who were loyal to my family hid me. They feared if word got out that I'd survived, I'd be next. So, they protected me, kept me in the shadows. I was too broken to take the throne," he says, his shoulders curving as he hangs his head.

"Shawniaus stepped in, took the throne, temporarily, until I'd be ready."

"I left shortly after, moved to a small town in Haravik, tried to live simply. I started as a footman, and yes, I really did work in the prison. But I couldn't get close to Veric without a proper background. No Nobel ties, no family history, it made people suspicious."

I see the frustration tighten in his jaw.

"I came back home. Decided if I wanted to ever get close to Veric, I'd need help. That's when I started working with Igor. He already had ties to Odesa's royal family and had the same hatred for Veric."

"So you became my guard," I whisper.

"That was the plan."

"And then?"

His voice drops, rough and sincere. "And then I met you."

I reach across the table and touch his hand. "And are you ready... to wear the crown?" I ask softly.

He nods.

CHAPTER TWENTY~FIVE

I awake slowly, tangled in warmth and quiet. For a moment, I forget everything, where I am, who I'm with. But then I feel the weight of his arm around me, the slow rise and fall of his chest at my back, and everything comes rushing back. Larkin. Malachai. King.

I turn slightly, just enough to see his face softened in sleep. His arm is draped over my waist like he is afraid to let go. I stay there for a little while, appreciating the way the morning light touches his jaw and the gentle crease between his brows that never fully fades, even in rest.

When he stirs and blinks his eyes open, he smiles sleepily. "Good morning," he says, his voice low and warm.

"Good morning," I whisper back.

He leans up on one elbow and brushes a strand of hair from my face.

"The castle's starting the preparations for my coronation," he says gently. "I told them you might want to be involved. If you do, the stewards can meet with you later this morning."

I look at him. "Your coronation."

His smile is small but real. "It's time."

I nod, unsure if I'm ready for what that actually means.

"I'll also be sending post," he adds. "To schedule a meeting with Rome. I want to speak to him, face-to-face. No more letters."

That eases the disquiet in my chest.

"Good."

He leans forward and kisses me, soft at first, then more thoroughly. The space between us disappears like it has been waiting to collapse. His hands roam over my body, drawing shivers as he traces the delicate fabric of my nightgown.

The tension between us ignites, slow and burning. My breath quivers when his hands roam the curve of my hip, slipping lower, coaxing a gasp from my lips.

"Kai..." I whisper. His name falls like a prayer to Odin.

His hands grip my thighs, firm and reverent, and I reach for him, surprised by the sheer length and hardness of him. My heartbeat thunders in my ears, with desire blooming fiercely in my core. His fingers make it under the soft lace covering my hot center.

There's a knock at the door.

"Kai?" Rook calls from behind the door. "Are you ready for the morning council?"

He exhales, resting his forehead against mine. "Of all the timing…" He presses a final kiss to my lips, lingering. "We'll finish this later," he murmurs, reluctantly rising from the bed. As he pulls on a loose tunic, he glances back at me with a hungry look in his eyes that makes my cheeks flush.

"I'll see you later, Princess," he says before exiting the room.

I slip out of bed, still warm from where his body had been. My legs feel a little weak, my lips still tingling from his kisses. I try to shake the heat from my cheeks as I move toward the wardrobe.

I choose a soft, flowing dress in pale lavender. The long sleeves drape around my wrists. I pull on my boots, still a bit dusty from the training courtyard, and smooth down the front of my dress before heading out the door.

The castle is already buzzing with activity. Servants and guards rush through the halls, carrying scrolls and armfuls of linens. Everyone feels the shift in the air. A king is returning to the throne.

The lost prince has found his way home.

I meet with the stewardess in a sunlit sitting room near the east wing. She curtsies low, and I smile, waving it off. We sit across from one another at a long table scattered with swatches of cloth, parchment, and silver-tipped quills.

Together, we go over the menu: wild pheasant, honey-glazed root vegetables, and blueberry tarts with sugared berries. I ask for something from every region of Nyxlandia.

For decorations, I describe the halls filled with glowing lanterns and soft, draped fabrics. The crest of House Hawthorne should be embroidered in gold on burgundy banners.

"This needs to be special, not just a coronation, a prince returning to his kingdom. Something that reminds them of who he is," I say softly.

The stewardess nods in agreement, jotting notes rapidly.

After the meeting, I thank her and slip away before anyone else can stop me. The greenhouse calls to me as it always does when I need space to think. When I push open the glass-paned doors, warm air greets me, sweet with the scent of roses and earth. The sunlight pours in, catching the petals in a golden shimmer. I roll up my sleeves and get to work.

I move through the rows, checking the blooms, pruning where needed, and whispering softly to the vines. They respond to my touch, leaves rustling gently and buds perking toward me like they understand. I run my fingers over the blossoms I plan to use in the ceremony: red roses, gold orchids, soft white lilies.

I place my hands in the soil and let the warmth of my craft pulse from my fingers, slow and nurturing. The energy flows into the roots, feeding every blossom, every leaf. The plants shimmer as if catching starlight. Petals unfurl wider, with their colors growing richer. Vines climb higher along the trellises, the roses glow with a dewy sheen, and the lilies pulse with a soft ethereal light.

These flowers will be a part of something bigger, something sacred. A broken boy reclaiming his power. They will be perfect for him, for the king, for the man who holds my heart.

The castle bells chime once from the far towers, signaling midday. And my stomach growls, reminding me I haven't eaten today.

I make my way back inside, slipping through the side entrance near the kitchens. The halls are still buzzing, but my mind is somewhere else, on Kai. I pause at a window and watch the sunlight dance around the courtyard below. I wonder if he's still in that meeting with Shawniaus and Rook. I wonder if he's thinking about me.

About us.

I grab a quick lunch and head down the corridor toward my room. Voices echo, guards murmuring about troop movements near Odesa. My heart clenches. As I turn down the quieter wing of the castle, sunlight spills across a gallery of old paintings.

I slow my steps, letting curiosity tug me forward. The portraits are grand, painted in rich detail, each face regal, familiar in a way I can't place until I spot *him*. My breath stills.

It's Kai, years younger, standing tall beside his family. He's smiling wide, eyes lit with a boyish joy I've never seen on his face before. His mother stands beside him, elegant and soft-eyed, draped in gold and burgundy.

There's his sister, Aurora, I assume— radiant with a mischievous grin that mirrors his. They look happy. Whole. Tears prick my eyes. The weight of what he's lost settles heavily on my chest. That light in his face... it's gone now, replaced by shadows and scars. Grief.

How is he still kind, still capable of love, after all his loss? I reach out and brush my fingers along the golden frame, as if I can touch that lost moment, preserved forever in oil and memory. I wish I could've known him then. I wish I could've saved some piece of that smile. I press forward, heart heavy and full, until I reach my room.

Back inside, I scrub the soil from my hands. The reflection in the mirror shows flushed cheeks and windswept hair. A gentle knock at the door draws my attention. I open it to find a woman with a warm, practiced smile. She's older, with deep tawny skin, soft brown eyes, and silver-streaked curls twisted into an elegant bun.

She wears a belt lined with measuring tapes, scissors, and bits of fabric swatches—a warrior armed with thread.

"Good afternoon, Princess," she says with a slight bow. "I'm Mira, the castle seamstress. I've come to take your measurements for the coronation gown."

"Oh," I breathe, surprised. "Of course, yes. Please, come in."

She steps inside, and her eyes scan the room briefly, assessing the lighting and space. Then she sets down a basket filled with spools of gold thread, silk ribbons, and shimmering fabric samples.

"His highness requested something special," she says with a faint smile as she unrolls her tape measure. "A garment worthy of a queen."

My cheeks flush at the word.

Queen.

Still, I nod and stand tall as she circles me like an artist before a canvas. Her fingers are gentle and quick, taking precise notes as she murmurs to herself.

"Strong shoulders... good waist... Hmm, you've got a beautiful frame. He was right."

My heart stumbles over itself. "He said that?" I ask softly, barely above a whisper.

She nods.

I manage a small smile, though it trembles. She finishes her notes, packs her kit, and promises a fitting in two days. And just like that, she is gone.

I finally settle into a cozy armchair near the balcony doors, the silver tray of food at my side. The sun is starting to dip low, casting amber light across the floor, soft and warm.

I pick up the book I left open earlier, a romance, light and full of yearning, and read as I nibble on a soft roll glazed in honey butter. For the first time all day, I relax.

The door opens, and I don't even have to look up to know it's him. Kai. His presence is magnetic. I close the book and gently smile as he enters the room, already loosening his belt.

"Rome should arrive in four days," he says, walking toward me. "The day after the coronation."

My stomach flips, nerves tangling with excitement. So much is changing, so fast.

"After the coronation, we will go to the Isles of Odesa," he adds.

I nod.

Without another word, he disappears into the bathing chamber, water splashing in the quiet. Steam begins to drift out, a curling fog slithering across the stone.

A moment later, the door creaks open slightly, and his voice calls out, low and inviting.

"Princess... you want to join me?"

My cheeks burn, but I don't hesitate.

"Yes," I say, trying to sound casual, but my voice cracks with excitement.

I rise from my chair, leaving the book behind, and I step into the warm, misty air of the bathing room. Kai is already in the tub. His dark hair is slicked back, and his strong arms rest on the edge. His chest glistens with water, and the dim light makes him look carved from a hammer and chisel.

His eyes roam slowly over every inch of me as I slide out of my dress. I try not to fidget, suddenly aware of the softer parts of me, the imperfections I usually hide beneath fabric. But his expression doesn't falter, not with displeasure, not even with hesitation.

My heart hammers as he lifts a hand from the water and gestures.

"Come here," he says, voice husked.

And I do.

I step into the tub, into the warmth of the water and the shelter of his arms, letting the world fall away. I ease myself into the warm water, and he pulls me gently into his lap, settling me against his chest like I belong there.

His arms wrap around my waist. His large hands are splayed possessively against my stomach. I melt into the sensation. The heat of the bath is nothing compared to the heat of his body beneath mine.

His lips brush against the curve of my shoulder. I tilt my head slightly, giving him more access, and he takes it, pressing soft kisses along my neck up to the corner of my jaw.

"You're so beautiful," he whispers. His voice is thick with sincerity.

I let out a breath I didn't realize I was holding. My insecurities still cling to the corners of my mind, but they dissolve with every touch of his mouth.

His hands slide over my hips, slowly tracing the shape of my thighs beneath the water. I can feel every movement, every subtle shift of muscle and skin.

One hand trails up. His fingers graze the inside of my thick thigh beneath the water. The touch is featherlight, almost teasing, but it ignites the longing deep inside me, a fire I have never known.

"Kai..." I whisper, the sound catching in my throat when he presses against me more firmly. His name leaves my lips again, this time as a moan.

He responds with a groan of his own, deep and low, his lips finding mine in a kiss that is slow but hungry. His tongue slides against mine, coaxing, exploring. One of his hands cups my breast while the other moves lower, rubbing firm circles that make my back arch against him. I reach behind me, fingers trailing down the ridges of his abdomen, dipping lower.

When I find him, hard and throbbing, I gasp, stunned by the thickness of him.

He exhales sharply. His breath is hot against my ear as I wrap my hands around his girth. He turns me to face him, water sloshing as he lifts me slightly to straddle him. His hands never stop moving, roaming my back, gripping my thighs, sliding over every inch of me.

My body aches for him, trembling with want. Every touch, every whispered word, seems to suspend time. I glide my hand up and down his thick column. He groans and hisses my name, and it has never sounded so sweet.

Slowly, softly, he starts to stand up in the tub, gathering me close around his waist as if drawing me into his heart. I cling to him. The water ripples around us as he carefully lifts me.

He carries me toward the edge of the tub and carefully steps over the lip, walking toward the plush bed waiting nearby. His strong arms wrap around me protectively as he lays me down on my back.

The cool air contrasts with the lingering heat between us, and I feel my pulse hammer in my ears, each beat echoing with both tenderness and deep, unspoken promise.

In that quiet moment, as his fingers trail lightly over my skin and his eyes lock with mine, all that exists is this connection, powerful, unyielding, and utterly transformative. Every doubt, every fear, fades into the background, replaced by the simple, raw truth of our closeness.

He stands at the edge of the bed, framed by the soft glow of the lantern light, between my thighs. His eyes trace every inch of me, dark and hungry with longing.

His hand drifts down his abdomen unhurried. He grabs himself from the base of his thick shaft. I watch, my breathing tight, as he moans, his gaze never leaving mine.

"After all this time crawling, begging, and clawing, the princess, finally, so graciously, lets me claim her. Now, spread those legs... good girl."

"Kai..." I whisper, barely able to speak.

He exhales a shaky breath, then steps forward, bending down to kiss me. His kiss is hungry now, desperate. He lowers himself slowly, carefully, as if I'm fragile and sacred all at once. My legs wrap around his waist, instinctive and trusting.

"I want you," I whisper, pulling him closer.

His forehead rests against mine for a fleeting heartbeat, and then he thrusts, gently. A sharp gasp escapes my lips as he slowly slides into my core. Time melts around us as his body presses into mine. The way he moves is patient and deep, a wave that builds with relentless rhythm. Each breath, each moan, is a thread stitching us back together. I cling to him. His name spills from my lips—a vow unbroken.

I reach for him, brushing trembling fingers over the lines of his jaw, the planes of his chest. His hand is gripping my hip, rocking me to meet him as he slams into me, repeatedly.

He lifts into a stance to better his momentum, with his eyes roaming my bouncing body. The pressure swells like a storm ready to break.

As he repetitively slides into me, his hands grip my hips like he's terrified I might vanish. His touch is possessive, desperate, grounding. It is overwhelming in the best way, as if he is claiming a sacred relic.

I cling to him, needing him closer, deeper. His rhythm grows more consuming, more insistent, and my body arches beneath him, aching.

As I near the edge, that familiar buzzing, the faint echo of the first time I saw him, roars to life within me.

This time, it isn't just a hum. It is electric, wild, and overwhelming, coursing through my veins with a fierce urgency.

The moment crests, and with a cry, I shatter, lightning racing under my skin. Every nerve is alight with that electric pull that only he has ever given me. It is as if the universe is aligning, sealing something sacred between us.

"I feel—" I gasp, but the words fail me.

He looks down at me, eyes meeting mine.

"I know," he whispers, with his voice full of awe.

When I come down, trembling and breathless, he's still here, forehead pressed to mine. His breath is ragged, and his arms are wrapped around me tightly.

"I was lost in the shadows, for what felt like an eternity. I had forgotten the warmth of light...

until you." His voice is husky, but there's a softness there that makes my chest ache. "I didn't think I'd ever deserve something like this. Like you."

I press my fingers to his jaw. I can't speak, not yet, so I kiss him instead. A slow, tender promise.

He finally pulls away and gently lays me down against the pillows, tugging the blankets over us. His arm wraps around my waist as he pulls me flush to his chest. His hand is splayed protectively over my stomach. We don't say anything else. Wrapped in his warmth, surrounded by the scent of him, I close my eyes.

CHAPTER TWENTY~SIX

"Good morning, Your Highness," Mira says with a curtsy. "I've brought the gown."

Behind her, two attendants follow, carrying boxes and small chests filled with accessories and cosmetics. She gently hangs the gown, still in the silk cover, over the changing screen. She turns to leave just as servants flood the room. I eat quickly, though my nerves flutter with every bite.

The servants sit me down at the vanity, and Magnolia begins with my hair. She brushes it carefully, letting my auburn strands spill over the back of the chair like melted sunset. She braids two sections from each temple, pulling them back and weaving them into a crown-like twist across the back of my head. The rest of my hair falls in soft waves down my back in a cascade of copper glass blazing in the light. Small, rose-shaped, gold pins are placed delicately throughout the braid.

My makeup is soft but defined. A warm glow dusts my cheeks, and my lips are painted a deep wine red. My eyes are lined with just enough coal to bring out the pale steel-gray of my irises, and a touch of gold shimmer rests at the inner corners, reflecting the light when I blink.

Then, with careful hands and murmurs, Magnolia and the others help me into the gown. It fits like a garment that was woven by dreams.

The gown is a deep, shimmering burgundy. The fabric is a mingling of fire and wine. Fine gold embroidery traces along the edges of the sleeves and neckline, twisting into delicate, curling vines. Tiny rosebuds, hand-stitched from deep crimson thread and dusted with flecks of gold, bloom along the hem and cascade up one side of the skirt.

The sleeves are fitted, ending in a slight point over the tops of my hands. The fabric clings to my waist, flares slightly at the hips, and pools behind me in a long train like a sweep.

As they fasten the last button at my back and place my delicate crown atop my head, Magnolia steps back and smiles with a glint of pride in her eyes.

I glance at myself in the mirror one last time. I barely recognize the girl staring back. She is strong, radiant, and I *feel* beautiful.

Magnolia holds up a gold and diamond necklace, preparing to fasten it around my neck. I look at the necklace, then down at the much less dazzling one resting on the vanity.

Gently, I reach for it.

"Oh... I'd prefer to wear this one instead."

I pick up Brynn's necklace, a dainty gold chain with a single diamond pendant that catches the light like a memory. I turn and hold it out to her, my fingers brushing the chain as if it might vanish.

Magnolia nods. Her smile is even warmer now.

"Of course, Your Highness."

She carefully fastens the necklace around my neck. Her touch is light and gentle. The pendant rests just above my heart. Meaningful and simple. Beautiful. Mine.

I whisper a quiet thank you to the staff. I might be dressed as a queen, but it's the small piece of home around my neck that makes me feel whole.

I meet my own gaze in the mirror one last time and touch the tiny diamond, thinking of Brynn. I wonder if she would be proud of me. What would she think of Larkin... Kai?

I stand at the edge of a future I never imagined, and I'm ready to step through it.

The heavy doors to the great hall groan open, and I step forward slowly. The air shifts as every head turns toward me. Candles flicker in the sconces, hundreds of them, casting golden light across the room's vaulted ceilings, and stone pillars are draped with deep burgundy banners.

The scent of fresh roses lingers faintly beneath the sweetness of candle wax and perfumed guests. My heels click softly against the stone floor. The shimmery burgundy fabric of my gown catches the light with each step. Gold embroidery curls into vines along the hem and sleeves, roses blooming at my wrist and collarbone.

I walk between nobles and royals, between lords and ladies dressed in their finest silks and satins, yet none of them matter. Because at the far end of the hall, atop the dais, stands Kai. For a heartbeat, I don't recognize him.

His face is clean-shaven, completely bare, for the first time since I've known him. The rugged shadow that once carved his jaw is gone, revealing striking, noble angles and full, expressive lips. His dark hair has been braided tightly and tied back in a thick knot at the nape of his neck, and even his brows are neatly groomed.

He's dressed in a black and gold formal jacket with the crest of Nyxlandia embroidered across the chest, bold, beautiful, unmistakably regal. He looks... breathtaking. He is every inch a king. And still, his golden amber eyes find me with the same softness, the same fire, as always.

The entire room fades around us. I forget the rows of musicians, the nobles whispering, the murmurs of royalty gathered from across the kingdoms. It's just him. He descends the steps slowly, towering over the crowd. Each movement is powerful and composed.

And when we finally meet in the center of the hall, he offers his hand. I place my hand in his. He leans in just enough for his lips to brush my ear.

"You wear the beauty of a goddess," he whispers, his voice low. "You're the most breathtaking thing in this room."

I smile, heart fluttering like wings beneath my ribs. "You are."

The orchestra begins to play softly as he leads me down the grand aisle to where the other royals are seated, right beside Prince Rook. As I settle in beside Rook, I glance once more at Kai as he ascends alone. My pulse quickens. The next time he descends those stairs, he'll do it as king.

The hall falls silent as Kai reaches the dais. Sunlight filters through stained glass, casting golden light over him. Shawniaus steps forward with the crown, blackened gold, sharp, set with rubies.

Kai kneels.

The crown lowers onto his head. The room erupts with applause, cheers echoing off stone walls. Bells ring in celebration. Rose petals rain from above—each one a blessing.

King Malachai Larkin Hawthorne rises. He looks out at the crowd, but his eyes find mine. He smiles that soft, real smile that's only ever meant for me. I rise with the crowd, clapping, with my chest full.

As he returns to his seat beside me, he leans in close and asks, "Did I do okay?"

"You were perfect," I whisper.

He squeezes my hand.

We're walking slowly through the halls, hand in hand, my heart still fluttering from everything that just happened. I glance over at him. His crown twinkles in the moonlight as I tuck a strand of hair behind my ear.

"I read in a book once that a long time ago, people used to bond with dragons," I say softly, remembering the worn pages and faded ink. "But it never mentioned that the dragons *were* people..."

Kai chuckles under his breath, warm and low. "We try to keep that a secret," he says. "At least from the other kingdoms. It keeps us safer that way." Then he gives me a crooked grin. "Come on. Want to go for a ride?"

"Right now?"

He nods. "The sky's perfect."

I look down at my dress, then grin.

"Give me two minutes."

I rush into my room and change quickly into a soft tunic and trousers, lacing my boots tight before hurrying back out to him. He's waiting for me in the hallway. He takes my hand, and we stride through the halls toward the courtyard.

As we step into the open air, he steps away from me, and with a flash of golden light and a low rumble, he shifts.

His beast form rises before me, magnificent and powerful. The moonlight casts a pale glow over his dark scales. I step forward, breath still in my throat, and he lowers himself so I can climb up. I settle onto his back, gripping the warm ridges of his spine.

Then we launch into the night sky.

The wind rushes around us, cool and wild, and the stars stretch endlessly above us. The moon lights our path, soft and glowing. I press myself close to him, with my heart soaring right along our flight.

"Humans did bond with dragons," he says, his voice smooth. *"The others just didn't know... we were humans too."*

His voice. In my head. My chest seizes. My heart pounds, and a thought forms before I can stop it. *I'm bonded to him?*

His voice answers immediately, rich with warmth. *"Yes, Princess."*

I'm stunned.

His voice echoes in my mind, even as the wind rushes past us. We're not speaking, but we're *talking*. I don't know how it's possible, but I feel him—his warmth, his presence. I'm bonded to him. It's overwhelming and beautiful and terrifying.

His wings tilt as we glide down toward a massive rock ledge jutting from the mountainside. The castle lies below us in the distance. Lights glow like stars scattered across the land. The city stretches out far beyond that, quiet and silver in the moonlight.

He lands softly, claws scraping stone, and lowers his body for me to slide off. As soon as my feet touch the stone, there's another flash of warm light, and he's Kai again, standing tall before me. Moonlight spills over his broad shoulders.

Without a word, he shrugs off his coat and places it around my shoulders. It smells of him— warm leather, smoke, and untamed air. I pull it tighter and glance out at the view.

"This place is beautiful," I whisper.

His gaze follows mine.

"I used to come here with Aurora," he says quietly.

We stand side by side, staring at the stars. The wind dances around us. I glance over at him. The moon casts silver on his cheekbones, the tension in his jaw, the distant look in his eyes.

I don't speak. I just let the silence hold us, hoping that in this quiet, he can still feel the way my heart beats for him.

The cool night air kisses my skin, and the stars stretch endlessly above us. Taking my hand in his, he turns to face me, brushing a soft kiss to my lips.

Then, to my surprise, he lowers himself to one knee.

My heart stops.

"I told you I'd become whatever you needed me to... if it meant I could call you mine."

From his pocket, he pulls a ring, rose gold, wrapped in delicate vines and tiny roses, a sparkling diamond set at its center. It's the most beautiful ring I've ever seen.

"Can I call you mine, for forever?" he asks, his voice thick with emotion. "Will you marry me?"

Tears rise in my eyes, and a breathless laugh escapes me.

I nod quickly, barely managing to say, "Yes. Yes, of course."

He slips the ring onto my finger, rises to his feet, and pulls me into him. Our lips meet in a deep, soul-stirring kiss, and in this moment, the whole world quiets around us.

Then, Kai turns to me, his voice is low and gentle. "Let's get you back to the castle."

I nod, reluctant to leave, but grateful for the warmth of his presence.

He shifts again. His body glows before expanding into that magnificent, dark-winged form. I climb onto his back, wrapping my arms around the spike at the base of his neck as he steps to the edge of the cliff. And then, we're flying.

The wind whips through my hair as we dive off the mountainside, soaring into the night sky. The castle grows closer, bathed in the soft golden light of torches and moonbeams. My heart pounds from the thrill of the ride, but more than that... from him.

We land in the courtyard.

I slide off his back, and he shifts again, taking my hand as we quietly walk inside.

Back in the soft golden glow of the bedroom, I sit on the edge of the bed, brushing out my hair.

"Turn around," he says.

I obey, glancing over my shoulder. "Why?"

"I have something for you," he says, his voice carries that deep, velvet seriousness he only uses when it really matters.

I do as I am told and turn my head back around, heart fluttering. The shuffling sounds of metal against leather fill the quiet.

Then silence.

Then...

"In my culture," he begins slowly, "it's tradition for a man to give his mate a hand-forged gift on the night of their engagement."

A grin breaks across my face before I can stop it.

"Turn around."

I do, and there he stands, beaming.

My gaze meets his, with a smile erupting from my lips.

In his hands is a long sword. Its silver blade gleams with mirrored polish, but it's the hilt that steals my breath. Rose gold, sculpted with delicate detail. Vines curl around the grip, and a small blossom is carved into the pommel.

"You made this?" I whisper, eyes wide.

He nods.

"Yes, I did, Princess. For you."

I step forward and take it gently from him, with my hands trembling. The balance is perfect. It molds to my grasp, belonging as though it always has. A tear forms in the corner of my eye. No one has ever fashioned something so entirely for me.

"It's perfect. Thank you," I say, setting the blade aside and throwing my arms around him.

His arms tighten around me instantly. His lips brush against the top of my head before finding mine. The kiss is slow, fiery, and full of commitment.

When we finally pull away, neither of us says a word. We just crawl into bed, still wrapped in each other's warmth, breath synchronizing. The sword rests on the table beside us—a symbol of strength and love, hand forged.

I press my cheek to his chest, feeling the soft beat of his heart.

After a moment, I lift my head slightly and ask, a little shyly,   "Are you... always in my thoughts?"

He chuckles, warm and soft, and brushes his thumb along my jaw. "No, Princess. Only Steelborn can access your thoughts."

I sigh in relief, and maybe a little disappointment, and bury my face against him again.

I inhale deeply, savoring the scent of him. It had become the scent of home. Not a place, not a castle, nor a crown, but *him*.

"Good," I murmur. "I think."

He kisses the top of my head. "Sleep, Princess."

"*Mate.*"

My eyes fling open. "You said 'mate,'" I say, my voice louder than intended.

"I did."

CHAPTER TWENTY~SEVEN

Rome is sitting in one of the leather chairs at Kai's desk. Two guards flank the far corners of the room, stiff and silent. Rome looks up at us, his gaze unfocused until it lands on my hand, on the ring. A flicker of something passes over his face, hurt, maybe regret, but he schools it quickly.

Kai gestures to the chair behind his desk. "Sit, Princess."

I obey, settling into the seat. Kai stands behind me, his hands resting lightly on the top of the chair. He takes the form of a shield, protective, possessive, like I'm not alone in whatever is about to unfold.

Rome leans back in his chair and exhales slowly.

"Well," he says, his voice quieter than I expected. "A king enters the room, and a future queen sits before me."

The weight of his gaze moves from Kai to me, lingering for just a beat too long. I can see the questions behind his eyes, but he doesn't voice them.

Kai reaches into the desk drawer and pulls out something long, thin, and wrapped in cloth. He places it gently on the surface between them.

"Tell me what this is," Kai says, his voice cool and composed.

Rome unwraps the object with slow fingers. The cloth falls away to reveal an arrow, its tip coated in a thick, black tar-like substance, dried blood clinging to its edge. A sickly sweet, venomous stench fills the room. My stomach churns.

Rome doesn't touch it. He doesn't need to. His jaw tightens. "It's laced with the magus fur potion."

I glance up at Kai. His fingers are still and firm against the chair. My pulse quickens.

"If it's ingested," Rome continues, his voice hollow, "the victim lives... but loses their power entirely. If it enters the bloodstream through a wound, it kills instantly. And strips the magic from their blackening body."

I swallow hard, inching my hand closer to Kai's.

Rome's eyes darken. "But that's not the worst of it. After a few days... the body vanishes. No explanation. Just gone."

A cold chill creeps over my skin.

Kai speaks quietly, "And who gains the stolen power?"

Rome meets his gaze, solemn. "Whoever uses their own blood to create the potion. So, when it's used, he inherits everything."

We all sit in silence for a moment. The stench of the arrow curls through the air like a promise of death.

"I tried to kill the flowers, but..." Rome's voice catches.

His eyes widen in pain. His neck strains visibly, muscles tightening as though something inside him is fighting back. Veins rise under his skin, dark and sharp. The air in the room stills.

I straighten in my chair, panic prickling up my spine.

"He's forbidden it," I whisper.

Rome doesn't nod. He doesn't need to. His eyes lock onto mine, haunted, apologetic, restrained, and I know that's all I need to understand.

"Do you know where the bodies are going?" Kai asks.

Rome tries to speak, but nothing comes out, just gasps.

He coughs hard, once, and then forces out. "I am...limited... on the information I can give."

I don't look at Kai. His energy shifts behind me. His anger mounts, but I can't tear my gaze from Rome. The man was trapped in the grasp of his own father. And my heart hurts for him, truly.

Kai's jaw tightens, and he calls for a servant. "Find General Rafe," he commands. "Tell him to inspect Duke Jennings's body."

The servant bows quickly and hurries off. The air is thick, tense.

Then another servant rushes in, breathless and panicked.

"Your Majesty, there's been another attack. In Deerhaven."

Everything stops.

Kai and I lock eyes—a silent panic shared between us. Without a word, he storms from the room. I'm already moving, my boots slapping stone as I run after him. Rome is right behind us. We reach the courtyard just as guards are gathering, weapons drawn, orders being shouted.

"Let me come with you," I say, reaching for his arm.

Kai turns to face me. His eyes are dark and heavy with conflict.

"It's too dangerous. It's about to storm. Send Rome home and stay where the guards can see you."

"Kai, I—"

Before I can finish, he pulls away, already shifting. His body expands, bones reshaping, wings unfurling with a powerful gust of wind. In seconds, the dragon stands before me—fierce and glowing beneath the rising sun.

"*I love you, Princess.*"

He launches into the air with one powerful thrust, and I lift my arm to shield my face from the wind.

"*We will lose the connection just as I pass the mountain range. Avoid being alone with him,*" he says into my thoughts.

"*I love you, Kai.*"

He's gone.

I stand there in the courtyard, breath caught in my throat, watching the sky where he disappeared, my heart pounding like a drumbeat of dread. I turn to face Rome, his eyes wide in disbelief.

"A king *and* a dragon," he whispers in awe.

Rome and I walk through the courtyard in silence. The hush between us is louder than words. We don't speak as we slip into the gardens, where the scent of roses curls through the air. The world hangs in stillness—a single breath caught between moments.

We find a bench tucked beneath the shade of a tree. Rome drops down onto it hard, elbows braced on his knees. He bows his head like the weight of it is too much. I hesitate, eyes scanning the area, then sit beside him. I *trust* him. I know I shouldn't, but I do.

"Are you okay?" I ask, my voice soft.

He doesn't respond at first.

When he finally looks up, something's wrong. His neck tightens, the veins bulging under his skin like he's fighting. Pain etches his face—shadows struggling to force their way out of him.

"I'm sorry, Little Flower..." he manages to grit out, voice strangled.

I recoil slightly, confused.

"Rome?"

Before I can move further, he slams his fist into my thigh. I gasp, a sharp prick, a burn that spreads beneath my skin like wildfire.

"Rome?" I slur, blinking fast as the world tilts sideways.

Everything around me spins.

I can't focus. I try to steady myself, to grab onto anything solid, but it's all slipping. My hands reach for nothing. My vision blurs, colors blending, sounds stretching into distant echoes. My breath falters. My heart is a drumbeat beneath water, each pulse heavy and distant.

The last thing I see is Rome's face, twisted with guilt. Then... blackness swallows me whole.

CHAPTER TWENTY-EIGHT
MALACHAI

The storm lashes at me—alive and merciless. Rain pelts against my scales, wind howling past my wings. I push through the dark sky. Each beat of my wings is harder than the last. Lightning cracks above me, close enough to feel its sting in the air, but I don't slow down.

I descend fast, the village coming into view through sheets of rain. The estate and its courtyard are dim, with torches barely flickering against the storm. I land hard. My claws scrape against the wet stone. Rafe is already waiting at the gate, soaked to the bone, his jaw tight.

"Your Majesty," he says with a quick bow. His voice is grim.

"I'll never understand how you fly so fast, Rafe. What happened?" I ask, already walking.

He falls into step beside me.

"Three dead. All gone."

I stop.

"What do you mean, gone?"

He glances at me, rain dripping from his brow.

"It was Captain Kellan, a brawny. Lord McKelvin, a flight, and Lady Willow, a sight. All powerful."

I clench my jaw. "The bodies?"

He shakes his head.

"Servants said they saw them, but by the time I got here..." He pauses. "They were gone. The servants described them as strange, blackened, eyes empty, skin a purpled coal. Just like Jennings."

My stomach turns.

"Vanished without a trace," Rafe adds. "Just like the others."

The rain lashes down, the sky relentless, scrubbing at the truth as if it could vanish. But I already know, we are too late, and the enemy is moving.

"Have you checked Jennings's body? Is it still... in the grave?" I ask.

"No, Your Majesty, it's not." Rafe looks away.

I grab him by the shoulder. "Close the borders. Effective immediately."

He nods. "Understood."

"No one in without proof of residency. I don't care who they are," I command.

He doesn't question it. I turn, already moving, rain pouring own my face. I shift mid-step, wings spreading wide, and launch into the sky with a roar that splits the air. The storm has not let up. It only worsens. Lightning forks across the clouds above me, thunder cracks—a chorus of drums pounding through the heavens.

I fly harder, faster, but there is this feeling in my chest. It grows every mile I leave behind. Something is not right. I beat my wings faster, pushing beyond what I know I should.

Just a little farther.

Just get in range. Then I can reach her. I can feel her. I crest the mountain ridge, wind shrieking past my ears. I stretch my senses, reaching out with my mind.

"Princess?" Silence. *"Princess, answer me."* Nothing. No warmth. No spark. No bond.

Panic crushes my chest. I dive, reckless and fast, slicing through the storm clouds. Trees blur below me as I descend, landing hard in the courtyard near the tree line, stone cracking beneath my claws.

I shift the second I hit the ground, boots slapping against wet stone as I run toward the castle.

"Where is she?" I shout, grabbing the nearest servant by the shoulder. "Where is the princess?"

They hesitate. I don't wait for an answer. I take off down the corridor, shouting for her. Room after room, nothing. Empty halls. No laughter. No scent. No trace.

She's gone.

So is Rome.

I grab the nearest servant by the collar, voice shaking with fury.

"Sound the alert bells. Now. Close the gates, lock down the entire castle."

Their eyes widen, but they nod and take off running.

"Stop everything. I want every guard, every servant, every soul in this place searching for her," I growl. "Don't breathe until she's found."

I spin on my heel and storm back into the courtyard. Rain still falls in sheets. My body shifts mid-stride, the shift nearly violent. Scales ripple down my arms, bones cracking and reforming as I surge back into my beast form.

With a roar that splits the sky, I throw my head back and unleash everything I'm feeling—rage, fear, desperation. The very ground quakes beneath me. I launch into the air again, wings slicing through the storm. I circle the castle, repeatedly, scanning the grounds, rooftops, gardens, anywhere she could be.

"Winnie."

My voice echoes through the bond like thunder. Nothing.

"Please answer me."

Still nothing. A hollow ache coils in my chest. I can't feel her. I can't reach her. It's like she's been pulled from the world without a trace.

The only way to break a bond is death unless she's too far away. She's not dead. No.

Wherever she is, I'll find her or burn the world down trying. I bank hard, heading for the tree-lined path to Haravik, my wings straining against the wind as I follow the only trail that makes sense. My mind races as fast as my body does. If they're on foot, I should catch up to them soon. She's smart, she'd leave some kind of sign, something.

But then a shadow of doubt creeps in, slow and poisonous.

What if she left with him... willingly?

No.

I grit my teeth and beat my wings harder. The rain stabs my scales. Each drop is a tiny dagger. She's strong, fierce, stubborn. She can hold her own, especially against someone like Rome. If she's with him... *What if she does not want to be found?*

"No." I snarl under my breath, the sound rolling low in my throat. I *will not* believe that. And I will tear apart every stone in Haravik if I must.

I *will* find her.

"*Winnie?*" I call for her through the bond.

Nothing. Silence. Nothing but the sounds of the storm and my roars echoing through the gray skies.

CHAPTER TWENTY~NINE
WINNIE

Cold stone presses against my cheek as I stir awake, the damp seeping into my skin. My head is heavy, thick with fog and choking inside my skull. My lashes flutter, once... twice. Everything is a blur. My throat is dry and aching.

"Rome?" I call out, my voice barely above a whisper.

No answer.

I push myself upright. The chain at my ankle clinks as I move. The sound sends a shiver through me. I squint into the dark, my heart beating faster as I take in the crumbling walls, the moldy stone, the single flickering torch barely lighting the room. Am I in... a cell?

"Rome!" I cry again, this time louder, with panic threading through my voice.

Nothing but silence and shadows. I try to remember what happened. Flashes come in broken pieces. Rome on the bench. His voice is tight with pain. The sting in my leg. The way the world spun and went black.

Gods.

A sob tears from my throat as I drag myself into the corner of the room, curling in on myself. I cover my mouth with my hands, but I can't stop. The realization crashes like a wave. He poisoned me. He took me. Rome betrayed me. *Again.*

The metal around my ankles bite into my skin with every shift of my legs. I don't know how long I sit here—minutes, hours—time stretching into an eternity.

Then... footsteps, heavier with each breath.

I scramble to my feet, chains dragging across the floor. Shapes emerge down the corridor, three of them. The flickering torchlight catches the outline of a crown, a long coat, and armored shoulders.

I freeze as they stop at my bars.

The king, Rome, and a guard. The same guard from before, who accompanied Rome to our meeting.

"Well done," the king says, turning to Rome with a cold smile. "You know what to do."

He turns and walks away, with his velvet, sapphire robes dragging behind him.

The guard steps forward, unlocking the cell door with a sharp *click*. I stagger back, instinct tightening in my chest, but he grabs me roughly by the arm.

"Careful with her," Rome snaps, his voice lethal. "I'm so sorry, Little Flower," Rome says. His eyes are haunted.

I can barely look at him. I follow, dazed and trembling, disbelief thick in my throat as they lead me out of the cell and down the stone corridor. My heart pounds like an iron hammer striking within my chest. Where are they taking me?

"Kai will kill you all," I say through my teeth.

"I can only hope he does, Little Flower," he replies, but the words strain against the raw hurt shadowing his expression.

The quiet ache in his words pulls at my heart. We stop at a familiar door. Rome pulls out a key and unlocks the heavy door.

My stomach twists. The scent hits me first, faint, fading lilies. My heart drops. They lead me inside and all but one of the flowers are dead. And it's barely hanging on. The petals are wilted, with brown leaves, and the soil is cracked and dry. It hangs there, spent, bowing beneath its own weight. It's like it doesn't *want* to survive—ready to surrender.

Rome turns to me. "Heal it."

I glare at him. "I'd rather die than help you." My voice cracks at the words.

His jaw tightens. "Winnie... they'll kill your family. There are spies in your castle right now... waiting. All they need is the word."

My breath catches. Maya's betrayal flashes behind my eyes.

I sob.

My hands tremble as I lift them up toward the wilted flower. I press my hands into the cold soil. I close my eyes and push my magic into the roots. It's like bleeding out slowly. Every drop of magic tears from my chest, leaving fire in its wake. I can barely breathe. My head swims. I pause, gasping, shoulders shaking.

Then I push again.

The petals quiver, uncurl, stretching with light ripples across the stem. The bloom opens, whole and bright. I stagger back so dizzy I nearly collapse.

They grab me, drag me out, and throw me back into my cell. I hit the stone floor hard. Everything aches. I try to keep my eyes open, but the exhaustion pulls me down, drowning me in slow, suffocating waves.

Somewhere between waking and sleep, there's voices, muffled, clipped. I can't make out the words, but I hear his voice.

The king.

"Force it down her throat if you have to," he snarls, and doors slam.

I drag myself to the bars, barely able to hold myself up. Down the hallway, Rome grabs the guard's arm, and then they vanish.

Gone like smoke curling into nothing.

The guard. He's a port. That's how we got here so fast. I choke on another sob, stunned and shaking. My forehead presses against the bars.

Kai...

"Are you looking for me?" I whisper.

I must have fallen asleep because the next thing I hear are footsteps. My eyes open. My heart lurches. Three figures stand outside my cell: Rome, the guard, and a servant. The servant carries a tray. My stomach twists before I even see what's on it.

Then the smell hits me. That awful, sweet, rotting, floral scent. The same one from before.

Poison.

My body tenses as the cell door creaks open. The servant doesn't meet my eyes. She rushes in, sets the tray of food down, and rushes out like she's afraid.

Rome stays. "I'm so sorry," he says, voice quivering.

The guard doesn't waste a second. He lunges for me, grabs me by the jaw so hard there's a faint crack. "Don't—" I try to scream, but my mouth is wrenched open.

Glass clinks. A vial.

I twist, claw, scratch, anything to stop him. Iron fingers dig into my cheeks. I gag, shaking my head, trying to clamp my mouth shut, trying anything, but then his knee slams into my stomach. The pain knocks the breath out of me. I crumple into him.

He catches me.

He dumps the contents into my mouth and forces my mouth closed. He reaches down and pulls out a dagger. The cold blade touches my throat.

"Swallow," he growls.

Tears streak down my face. I try not to. I try to hold it back, but my throat moves on instinct.

I swallow.

The taste lingers—rot crawling across my tongue. The smell fills my nostrils. They drop me to the floor like I'm nothing. Rome lingers for a breath too long, then turns and walks out. The door slams. I curl in on myself, sobbing, gagging. The scent of poison is still heavy in the air. I'm alone again.

A sound drifts in, static and faint, a whisper threading through the storm.

Then... a voice so faint I almost miss it.

"Winnie."

I sit up, heart pounding.

"Winnie..." Faint, reaching.

"Kai?" I whisper into the silence of my mind, desperate.

The connection crackles.

"Where are you?" His voice is clearer now, sharper, like a blade drawn in rage.

A sob escapes me, violent and raw. *"Kai,"* I cry. *"Kai, Kai, Kai."* I clutch my head. *"The dungeons... beneath the castle. I'm in a cell,"* I cry out.

"Are you hurt?" he demands, fury lacing every word.

"Not dead."

The ground trembles. Tiny pebbles on the stone floor begin to bounce. The castle quakes and the walls shudder as a roaring sound tears through the air. Dust falls from the ceiling as if the very bones of the place are afraid.

Familiar footsteps grow louder. Rome.

He bursts into the dungeon corridor like a storm. His eyes are wide with panic and rage. He throws open my cell's door and staggers in. The roar grows louder, closer. I can feel him now.

Kai.

The floor trembles beneath us. The torches flicker violently. Rome's fighting an invisible storm. I can see it in his body. His face is contorted. His veins bulge like his soul is being split in two. He clutches his head, shaking. Then he reaches into his pocket.

He pulls his hand out, presenting a dagger. His fingers tremble so violently, I think he might drop it.

He takes a step toward me.

"Rome..." My voice shakes.

"I'm sorry," he growls through clenched teeth, chest heaving. "I'm so sorry."

I glance down at the dagger, quickly noticing its tip impregnated with the thick black potion.

He lunges.

I flinch, but the blade doesn't come from me.

It turns.

And Rome drives it into his own gut.

Blood pours instantly, hot and fast. He drops to his knees. The chaos in his body stops. The tension breaks. Relief floods his face like sunlight. He collapses into me, his weight heavy and final.

"I failed you... Little Flower," he whispers. A single tear carves down his cheek.
My hands catch him. His blood soaks into my skin. He fumbles something into my palm.

Keys.

His voice is barely a breath now. "Go." His hand goes still.

The roar outside splits the stale air hanging around me and I run.

I grip the keys in one hand and pocket Rome's dagger with the other. My legs are shaking, but I run out of the cell, into the stench of death. The air is sodden and weighty, like breathing through rotting cloth.

I gag. A cell door flashes past. Blackened bodies. A pile of them burned or cursed, I can't tell. I cover my mouth with my hand and keep moving, heart hammering.

"I'm coming for you," Kai says in my mind, a sound sweet as music.

Then, as I pass the last cell, I see a petite figure.

A woman.

For a breath.

Then I'm at her door, shoving keys into the lock with trembling hands. One after the other. *Come on.* Last key. It doesn't work.

"No, no, no, no." My voice breaks, and I press my forehead to the bars. "I'll come back for you," I swear through the metal.

The girl just watches, eyes wide and wordless.

"I promise."

Then I run.

I reach the large door at the end of the hall, slam the biggest key right in, and burst through. The castle is chaos: screams, footsteps, and shadows moving fast.

A guard grabs my arm. I don't think. I just turn and drive the dagger into the gap between his helmet and breastplate, right into the hollow of his neck. His body stiffens, then drops. I don't wait. I run. And then, I see the magnificent beast.

Kai.

In the gardens, surrounded by smoke and blood and flame.

"*Come to me,*" he says. His voice is low, deadly, calling me home.

He shifts mid-stride. His human form rises, and a massive dark green-black sword materializes in his hand. His scales follow, covering his chest and arms—forged emerald armor gleaming in the light.

Strong. Unbreakable.

He is a force. He dances through the courtyard, swinging his sword, cutting down soldiers like they're paper dolls.

Nimble.

Lethal.

Unstoppable.

He lifts his arm and fire erupts from his palm in a blinding column, mowing down a wave of guards in front of him.

I slow, unable to do anything but watch in awe. My mouth falls open. The fire reflects in my eyes.

He's fire and fury. And he's mine.

Shouts ring out behind me. I turn to find more guards. Their blades flash. My lungs burn, pumping.

I glance over my shoulder to see the guards, fumbling, faltering.

Vines.

They shoot up from the ground, wrapping around the guards' legs, yanking them down. I sob, breathless and grateful.

The plants are helping me.

I look down, my hand is outstretched, fingers curling as more vines erupt. A wall of winding ivy spreads across the tall glass doors of the castle, barricading a retinue of guards inside.

I snap my head toward Kai. In a blink, he shifts into his beast form, towering, furious. Running to him, I pull at every fiber in my well of magic. "Please," I sob.

The willow tree in the courtyard shudders, its branches swaying like whips. Then a chorus of snaps—suddenly several guards are yanked off their feet. They slam their swords into the earth, but it does nothing to anchor them.

The tree drags them across the courtyard, tossing them through the air like puppets. They hit the ground with thuds; one guard flies toward the castle, arms flailing as his body shatters a tall window. Glass rains down around him as he tumbles inside.

I scramble up Kai's side, climbing onto his back as the sounds of pursuit grow louder. I glance over my shoulder.

Dozens of archers.

They lift their bows in one synchronized motion.

"Kai!" I scream.

But he's already moving.

He throws his wing up over me.

The arrows hit.

Thud after thud.

He roars, pain ripping through him, but he shields me completely. Then he unleashes. Fire pours from his mouth in a blinding ray that sweeps across the line of archers, turning them to ash.

His muscles tense beneath me. And we take off into the sky.

Smoke behind us.

Fire below.

Freedom ahead.

The arrows are still buried deep in Kai's wing, dark against the glint of his scales. Every beat of his wings must hurt like hell, but he doesn't slow. Not once.

"Kai, are you okay?"

His voice rumbles back, low and rough in my mind, *"I'm better now that you're safe."*

Tears prick my eyes again. *"You need a healer. You shouldn't have come alone. You shouldn't have risked your life—"*

He cuts me off gently. *"I vowed to protect you. And if I ever must die for you, just know, I'll do it smiling, because I got to love you first."*

Those words break me.

The sob tears from my chest before I can stop it. I bury my face into the warm scales between his shoulder blades, clutching him as tightly as I can, my body shaking with silent cries. We fly through storm clouds and smoke, blood on his wings and love in his heart, and I hold on, never letting go.

Kai's wings begin to falter, just slightly.

"I need to stop for a break," he says, breath ragged. Without waiting for my response, he angles down toward a clearing below. Trees part like they know he needs room.

He lands softly for his size, but the moment his claws touch the earth, his body trembles.

"Kai..." I breathe, taking in the damage.

"The arrows," he grits out. *"Take them out."*

My hands shake as I approach.

"Are you sure?"

He growls low in his throat.

"*Just do it.*"

I plant a hand on his scales and wrap the other around the shaft of the first arrow. I pause for a moment, then... yank.

He roars. The sound splits the air, shaking the ground beneath my feet. My heart breaks at the sound. I move to the second, heart pounding, tears stinging my eyes.

"*I'm sorry.*"

Another roar as it rips free.

The moment the last arrow leaves his wing, his form starts to shift, bones cracking and folding inward, scales peeling away.

He's human again, on his knees. His chest heaves, with blood slick on his side.

I rush to him. "Kai, are you—"

"I'm fine," he mutters. "Just... need a moment."

I kneel beside him, pressing my hands to his wound. It's still bleeding.

Too much.

Then a flicker in the sky catches my eye. I look up. Lightning cracks in the distance, followed by a deep rolling boom that shakes the ground beneath our feet. The wind howls—a wounded beast tearing at my hair and stinging my eyes.

I hook my arm tight around Kai's waist, nearly buckling beneath his weight. He's so much heavier than he looks, solid muscle.

My eyes scan the open field frantically, desperate to find any shelter.

My eyes land on a break in the rocks.

A shallow cave tucked beneath the ridge.

"There!" I shout over the howling wind. "It's not that far."

Kai grunts. His breath is ragged, and I feel him shift more weight off me, pushing forward on his own. The wind roars louder, almost screaming now, clouds churning in furious spirals overhead.

We limp across the field together, with his arm braced over my shoulders. My legs burn from the effort.

"Almost there," I tell him between breaths.

Just as the sky splits open and rain comes lashing down in violent sheets, we stumble into the cave. I ease him down to the stone floor. My arms tremble. I turn to Kai, crouching beside him. Water is streaming down his face. I catch rain in my cupped palms from the entrance of the cave, barely managing to hold it long enough to splash it over his wounds.

He winces, gritting his teeth and making the muscles in his jaw flex.

"Sorry," I murmur.

I rip the bottom hem of my tunic, wrapping the makeshift cloth around the worst of his injuries with shaking hands. I press it tight, trying to stop the bleeding. It's not perfect, not even close, but it'll have to hold, a least for now.

Outside, the storm rages. Trees groan and bend. The sky is alive with lightning, dancing violently across the horizon. Thunder crashes in vicious, cannon-like bursts that shake the very bones of the earth. Leaves whip across the entrance, torn free by the wind. The smell of ozone and wet earth clogs the air.

Lightning crashes again so close it makes my ears ring. For a moment, the entire cave glowed blue-white.

Kai's eyes flutter open.

"When the storm settles," he murmurs, voice barely audible above the chaos, "we'll go."

I nod. "How long would it take us to walk the rest of the way?" I ask.

"We're about halfway, so a full sun, at least."

I nod again, swallowing down the fear rising in my throat.

After hunkering in the cave for nearly an hour, the thunder fades into distant grumbles, the lightning grows sparse, and the torrential rain slows to a drizzle. The wind, once feral and violent, softens into a restless gust that rustles the battered trees outside.

Then, a sound cuts through the silence.

A voice.

Faint.

Muffled by the rain. But unmistakably human. Kai and I freeze, locking eyes. Neither of us breathes. Friend or foe, we can't tell. On the border, it could be either.

I slowly rise, heart pounding, and creep to the cave's mouth. I peer out, scanning the field as the mist begins to settle. My breath stills. In the distance, cutting a path through the soaked grass and scattered debris, is a tall figure.

CHAPTER THIRTY

I spin back toward Kai.

"It's Rafe," I whisper, barely able to believe it myself.

The breath shoots from his lungs. His shoulders sag with relief. He tries to rise but stumbles. I'm at his side in an instant, slipping under his arm and aiding him.

Together, we step out into the gray light of the clearing. Kai's steps get stronger at the sight of salvation. The storm has left everything drenched and broken, but Rafe is moving toward us with purpose. Kai lifts one trembling arm and waves. Rafe sees us and starts running.

Rafe skids to a stop in front of us, chest heaving, rain still dripping from his soaked clothes and dark curly hair. His eyes roam over Kai, taking in the blood, the torn tunic, and the way he leans into me for support.

Relief and worry clash across his face.

"I smelled your blood," Rafe says, voice raw. "Back at the edge of the mountains. I thought I'd lost you. The storm..." He shakes his head, frustrated. "It scattered everything. Washed the scent clean. I've been running in circles trying to pick it up again."

Then he turns his gaze to me, his golden eyes narrowing.

"But your father... your father has a very strong lumina."

My heart skips.

"My father?" I breathe.

Rafe nods.

"Yes. He's back at the castle. And he's not happy. He's been tearing through the forest looking for you, with no rest. He's been unable to control it."

Of course.

The tremors in the earth. The rage in the wind. The pressure in the air felt like it would snap the trees in two.

That was him. My father. It should have been obvious. A warm, overwhelming feeling blooms in my chest. He came for me.

Rafe turns to Kai, eyes scanning the blood still soaking his side, but his voice is firm and sure. "Let's get you back to the castle, Your Majesty."

Kai groans but offers a weak nod.

"We should fly before the storms start again," Rafe adds, casting a wary glance toward the sky, where ominous clouds still churn at the edges of the horizon, grumbling like they might return at any moment.

I tighten my arm around Kai's waist.

"He can't fly right now," I say firmly. "He's too wounded."

Rafe smirks. "Princess... he won't be flying." He takes a step away from us, his smile morphing into arcane mischief. "He'll be riding."

And with that, Rafe turns toward the clearing. His stride is confident and heavy.

Then, in one fluid leap, his form blurs mid-motion as it expands and twists, bones stretching, wings opening. His skin is replaced by rows of thick, glossy scales.

A dark burgundy dragon lands with a thunderous weight. His body is sleek and coiled with power. His wings stretch wide as the wind whips through the clearing. The air hugs with his magic. He's not nearly as big as Steelborn, but still an impressive size.

Kai huffs a laugh beside me. "Show off," he mutters.

Rafe lowers one massive, talon-tipped arm, the scales along his limb shifting with the smoothness of armor. I guide Kai forward first, helping him place one foot, then the other, into the crevice between two ridged scales. He groans softly, but he doesn't protest.

With effort, I hoist him up, guiding him as he settles into place along Rafe's broad back. I climb up after, sitting just in front of him. My legs straddle the wide base of his spine. Kai's arms wrap tightly around my waist, strong even in his weakened state. I feel his breath on my neck, ragged and constant. His grip grounds me.

I grip the large spike rising from the center of Rafe's back, bracing myself. With a powerful thrust of wings, Rafe darts into the air.

The ground disappears beneath us in a rush of wind and speed. The treetops blur into streaks of green, and the sky opens wide around us. The air up here is sharp and crisp, carrying the distant scent of rain.

The clouds swirl close, gray and vast, and we pierce them—a blade through the sky. I close my eyes for a breath, letting the wind whip through my hair, and lean back into Kai's chest. He traces slow circles on my arm.

He leans forward and presses a soft kiss to the back of my neck. Goosebumps rise across my skin. I let myself melt into him, safe, warm, loved.

But then, her face flashes in my mind.

The girl in the cell.

My ribs constrict. My pulse jumps.

I sit up straighter, my chest tightening.

"I promised her," I whisper, more to myself than to Kai.

What if she's like me?

What if that's why she was there? Why were there so many bodies near her? My thoughts

345

spiral. Panic grips me. Guilt wraps its claws around my ribs and squeezes. We'll return. I have to. I made a promise.

My mind is now tangled in memories, looping back to that cold, damp cell. Back to the guard's hand clamped around my jaw, the vial, the force, the sting of betrayal in Rome's eyes.

Rome.

Why did he bring that poison-dipped dagger if they already gave me the potion?

The vines... they rose to protect me.

Obeyed me.

My heart stutters.

Did the potion not work? The roots still knew *me*. Maybe the magic in me is stronger than the potion.

Rome.

He died for me.

He died *in place* of me. He decided to take his own life over taking mine. He fought it. And he thought he failed me.

My tears sting against my wind-blasted cheeks, but I can't stop them from falling.

Back at the castle, I help Kai down from Rafe. His weight is heavy against me. Rafe moves in quickly, slipping under Kai's other arm to help support him.

"I've got him," he says, stabilizing Kai with ease. "I'll get him to the infirmary."

I nod, watching them disappear through the corridor.

I walk through the large double doors of the front sitting area. My father is slumped in one of the large velvet chairs near the marble fireplace. I stand there at the doorway quietly for a moment.

His long, white hair is disheveled. His chest rises and falls in deep, steady breaths. His storm gray eyes are closed, finally resting.

I cross the room slowly, needing to be close.

As I kneel beside him, his eyes flutter open.

"Winnie?" His voice is rough, disoriented.

"I'm here, Dad," I whisper.

He sits up straight, eyes scanning me with urgency. "Are you hurt?"

Taking his hand in mine, I say, "I'm fine."

He exhales a breath. He stands and pulls me into his arms, holding me so tightly I can barely breathe.

"I looked for you everywhere," he murmurs into my hair.

"I know," I whisper.

We sit in silence for a few moments.

Then I pull back and smile at him.

"It's nearly twilight, Dad. You need rest. We will talk more in the morning."

His tired eyes linger on me, and then he nods. He gently runs a finger along my cheek, taking in the damage.

"Winnie..." he whispers.

"I'm okay, Dad. I promise." I hug him tight once more.

Then, I find a servant down the hall to escort him to a room.

I walk slowly through the castle halls. The lights are dim and flickering, casting long shadows against the stone walls. My whole body aches with each step. My ribs throb with every breath, and my jaw feels tight and bruised, a dull reminder of everything I've just survived.

I pass a tall mirror in one of the alcoves and pause.

For a moment, I don't recognize myself. My hair is wild, tangled from wind and rain. Faint scratches mark my cheek and neck. There's a dark bruise blooming along my jawline, and my eyes look tired and hollow.

I stare at myself, taking it all in.

What I've endured.

What I've become.

But I don't let myself linger. I turn away from the mirror and keep walking toward Kai. I keep walking down the quiet hall. Each step is slower than the last.

The castle is hushed, as though holding its breath in mourning. The torchlight flickers low on the stone walls, casting shadows that stretch long.

The occasional flicker follows behind me. I reach the infirmary doors, slowly pushing them open.

The room is quiet, with the scent of lavender, sage, and mint hanging in the air. A thick woven rug muffles my footsteps as I walk past rows of beds. Thin white curtains hang around some of the beds and a long wooden table in the center holds trays of tools I'd rather not look at too closely. Silver instruments gleam in the low light. Clean bandages are folded neatly beside jars of salves and powders.

Kai lies on a narrow bed in the farthest corner of the room. His massive frame looks almost too large for it. He's shirtless. His chest moves with slow, shallow breaths, his skin absent of his usual dark tan. \His eyes are closed. His thick lashes are dark against the pale bruising of his skin. He looks peaceful, though unease lingers. His brow is faintly furrowed. His jaw is slightly clenched.

Dried blood streaks across his ribs and down his side. The white sheets are rumpled beneath him, stained crimson near his waist where the wounds were the deepest. The muscles along his arms and torso are coiled, still battling ghosts that linger in his sleep.

The healer at Kai's side stands in perfect stillness, focused entirely on his wounds. Both her gentle hands hover just above his battered skin. Bright white light pours in wisps from her palms, soft and warm, threading itself into the open wounds along his side.

Each puncture slowly pulls together, sealing shut one by one, though deep bruising remains like shadows beneath the surface. He looks as if he's been through war.

And he has.

All for me.

The sting of guilt hits me as I step closer, quietly, afraid even the sound of my breath might disturb the fragile stillness between pain and healing. I take a shaky breath and ease down into the chair beside his bed. The cushions are soft, but doing nothing for the ache in my bones.

The healer moves with focus. Her hands are stable as radiant white light pulses gently from her palms. I watch her work, sealing the rest of the wounds that tore through Kai's side.

Her light reflects off the silver strands threaded in her dark hair hanging low beneath her waist. She looks almost astral, like a being completely out of this world.

One of Kai's hands rests on his stomach, bandaged, and the other hangs loosely off the side of the bed, fingers curled slightly. My eyes keep drifting back to his face, still and pale. His chest rises in heavy waves. Even like this, he still looks every inch a warrior.

My warrior.

I rest my elbows on my knees and lean forward, chin in my hands, unable to tear my eyes away.

The healer gives me a faint smile as she steps back, her work finally finished.

A servant quickly takes her place, and without a word, she begins gently cleaning the dried blood from Kai's side. I watch silently. My hand curls around his.

Once his skin is clean, she sets a tray down on the nearby table with crackers, fruit, cheese, raisin bread, and two tall glasses of water. The scent makes my stomach tighten with hunger, but I can't bring myself to move. I just don't have it in me.

The servant gives me a sympathetic glance and quietly leaves.

The room stills again.

Carefully, I lean forward and rest my head on the edge of the mattress, right beside his arm. His skin is warm, solid, grounding. I let my eyes close. My grip on this hand stays firm as I let my eyes fall closed.

The soft clink of a tray rouses me. My eyes open, my cheek still pressed to the mattress beside Kai's hand. A servant places a tray of breakfast with steaming coffee, honey-drenched biscuits, sliced fruit, and porridge. The smell stirs an emptiness in my stomach.

The servant gives me a warm glance and slips out.

Kai shifts beside me. "Princess?"

I lift my head groggily. His voice is stronger, smooth again, almost like nothing happened. His golden eyes find mine immediately, and when he sees my face, his expression falls. He sits up so abruptly, I can tell he's no longer in pain. His wounds are gone. His skin has color again. He looks whole.

"You stayed," he says softly, in disbelief.

"Of course, I did."

His hand reaches for my cheek. His thumb brushes just under the worst bruise on my jaw. "Gods," he mutters. "What did they do to you?"

"I'm okay," I reassure him.

"You are not. Look at you..." His jaw clenches. "You must be exhausted." He tosses the blankets off and starts to swing his legs over the bed.

"Kai, don't—"

"I'm fine," he insists, standing. "You need rest. You should not have slept in a chair."

Before I can argue, he's already coming around the bed, taking my hand with gentle insistence.

"I'm taking you to your room."

We finally make it to my room. The world is still gray with early morning light. Kai nudges the door open and helps me inside. I collapse onto the edge of the bed. My body is heavy, with screaming ribs. He doesn't say anything, just crosses to the bathing room, the water running in his wake.

When he returns, he pauses by the fireplace. With a casual lift of his hand, flames shoot from his palm, roaring to life in the hearth. The warmth spreads quickly through the space, casting golden light across the stone walls. That will never fail to amaze me.

"Bath's ready," he says gently.

I nod, sluggish, and let him help me to my feet. His hands move to the hem of my tunic, lifting it carefully over my head. He lets out a gasp when he sees the bruises sprawled in angry purples and sickly blues across my ribs and stomach.

I watch his jaw tighten. His eyes darken.

"Gods," he breathes. "Winnie..." His hands tremble as he lowers the rest of my clothes, slow and gentle. He moves as if I might shatter. "I'm going to kill whoever did this to you," he says through his teeth.

"I already did," I murmur, voice raw. "It was a guard. I stabbed him in the neck with a dagger on my way out."

He goes still, then his lips twitch, revealing a dark and proud smirk. "That's my girl." His voice is carved with pride.

I let out a quiet, tired laugh as he helps me step into the warm bath.

The water stings at first, but then soothes, wrapping around me like a balm. I sink into it with a soft sigh. Kai kneels behind me, gently gathering my tangled hair in his hands. He starts working through the knots with featherlight fingertips.

"You could call for a servant, you know," I say, eyes half lidded.

"I know," he says. "But I want to." His voice is tender.

He washes my hair, combing his fingers through the strands.

I close my eyes, relaxing in the safety of his hands, the warmth of the water, and the flicker of firelight dancing on the walls.

His fingers trail gently down the length of my hair, rinsing the soap out with handfuls of water. I lean back slightly, letting myself rest. There is a profound intimacy about this moment.

The room is warm and quiet. The fire crackles softly behind us.

Then his voice comes, low and rough. "You know I have to kill him now... Rome."

I stiffen, my heart falls to my gut. My voice is shaky. "Kai... Rome is dead." There's a beat of silence, weightier than thunder. "He... he killed himself." I stare down at the water. "So, he wouldn't have to kill me."

Kai's hands freeze.

The only sound is the gentle drip of water falling from my hair. I feel his breath stumble.

"I'm sorry," he finally says.

"I know," I breathe, fighting back the tears.

He stays quiet, gentle as his hands move over me with the cloth washing away the dirt and dried blood. There's so much care in his touch. His thumbs graze the bruises along my ribs, his jaw flexing again, but he doesn't speak.

When he's finished, he sets the cloth aside and helps me to my feet, wrapping an arm around my waist to aid me. He grabs a thick towel, dabbing it over my shoulders, then down my back tenderly.

From the back of the door, he takes down a long, plush robe and unfolds it. He drapes it over my shoulders like I'm made of porcelain, then meets my eyes as he closes it gently in the front.

"Thank you," I murmur. My voice is coated in exhaustion.

He leans forward, kissing my forehead.

I sit in a plush chair in front of the fire, nibbling on warm bread and fruit. Kai kneels behind me, fingers gently working through the tangles in my hair. The brush works through, tugging less with each pass. Once he's done, he sets the brush aside and comes around to face me.

"You should sleep," he says softly, crouching in front of me. "Even if it's for a few hours."

I shake my head a little, but he lifts a hand, brushing his thumb over my cheek.

"I'll call a council meeting soon. I bring your father in, tell him everything. But you... you need rest." His voice is firm but gentle.

"Okay."

He leans in and presses a soft kiss to my lips, tender, lingering, and filled with unspoken things. When he pulls back, his eyes linger on mine for a moment longer, full of warmth and care.

"I'll be back soon," he murmurs, brushing a strand of hair behind my ear.

After he leaves, I move to the bed and bury my face into my pillow, finally letting the sobs take over.

My body shakes with each ragged breath. I struggle to keep them coming. My fingers curl around the edge of my pillow as I force the screams away.

I tremble, gasping for air between sobs, until darkness swallows me whole and sleep finally claims me.

CHAPTER THIRTY-ONE

The sound grows louder the closer I get to the training fields. I push open a heavy door and step outside into the crisp afternoon air. The clang of swords and grunts of sparring soldiers ring through the clearing ahead.

I step fully into the sunlight, and my eyes are immediately drawn to the sparring ring. My breath pauses at the sight. Kai and my father, circling each other, with wooden practice swords in hand.

They move with ease, parrying and ducking with grins on their faces. Their laughter drifts across the field, light and genuine. It pulls a smile from me, despite everything.

Kai looks so alive again. His color is restored, and the strength in his movements has returned. My father's long, white hair is pulled back. His eyes are focused. They look... happy. So, at ease with each other. And seeing them like this fills a restless ache inside me.

To the side of the ring, I spot Rook near the edge of the field. His hand is outstretched, focused, releasing sharp shards of ice that fly like arrows toward the battered training dummy. Each one hits with a satisfying *crack*. The air around him shimmers with cold energy. His brow dips as he concentrates.

I watch them all from a distance. The breeze tugs gently at my braid, and the sun warms my face, a nice contrast to the biting chill of the air. I linger by the edge of the training grounds and move to sit on a nearby bench nestled against a tall rose bush. The blossoms are in full bloom behind me. I shift to get comfortable. The laughter and thud of training blades play like a melody behind my thoughts. But my mind drifts.

The potion.

I wrap my arms around myself, brows furrowed. I glance behind me at the rose bush. The petals also enjoy the sunlight.

I whisper under my breath. The response comes easily, a soft, silky voice brushing against my thoughts—petals drifting on the wind.

Kai glances in my direction, and when he spots me, his whole face lights up. That wide, bright smile of his never fails to make my chest flutter.

He looks so effortlessly handsome, with the sun dancing off the sharp lines of his face and the sweat on his brow.

He waves, and I lift a hand in return, unable to contain the small smile tugging at my lips. My father turns, notices me, and grins wide. Kai jogs toward me, dropping the wooden sword at his feet. He drops onto the bench beside me with a soft huff.

"You're awake," he says, brushing a loose piece of hair behind my ear.

"I am," I say softly. "You two looked like you were having fun."

He grins again. His thigh presses against mine. "He's relentless, your father, strong. Claims he's 'rusty,' but I swear he's just showing off."

Across the training yard, my father walks over to Rook, already deep in what looks like an animated conversation. Mostly filled with unsolicited advice on wielding magic, if I know him.

My father lifts his hand leisurely, with his palm glowing faintly. A massive bolt of lightning crashes from the sky, striking the training dummy in a flash of blinding white and roaring sound.

The wood splinters and smolders, leaving the dummy smoking and half-charred. He turns toward me with a sheepish wince, and he grins in a boyish, mischievous way that makes him seem far younger than he is.

"Yeah, definitely showing off." I shake my head and laugh, leaning into Kai.

Rook, unfazed, lifts his hand in response. A swirl of frost gathers at his fingertips, and a flurry of snow drops onto the dummy, covering the flames and dousing the smoke in a soft hiss.

Kai chuckles, leaning back on the bench, one arm draped behind me. "I like your dad."

My father walks toward us in long strides, brushing his palms on his trousers as he nears. Kai stands up as he approaches, giving my hand a soft squeeze before walking off toward Rook. My father settles into the empty space beside me on the bench, glancing after Kai.

"So... he's a king," he says, exhaling with a hint of a grin. "Who knew, huh?"

I smile, watching Kai from a distance. "Yes. He is." There's a beat of quiet between us before I say softly but surely, "I'm going to marry him."

My father turns to me then, eyes searching mine. A long pause is followed by a slow, thoughtful nod.

"That would be very good for you," he says, voice even. "And for our people. Two powerful kingdoms, united." His hand covers mine for a moment, warm and grounding. "I would love to see that, Winnie. You deserve to be happy, and you would make a lovely queen."

He squeezes my hand gently and looks at me with those weathered gray eyes of his, tired and soft. "I'm so proud of you, my sweet girl. For fighting. For surviving. For staying true to yourself, even when all odds were against you."

Emotion rises in my chest, unexpected and full. I blink fast, nodding, unable to speak for a moment.

He gives me a small smile, brushing a strand of hair behind my ear like I'm five again. "You've grown into someone truly remarkable, Winnie."

The warmth of his words fills my chest, wrapping around the ache that's always quietly lingered there. My eyes stutter again, trying to keep the emotion from spilling over.

But when he says, "Brynn would be proud of you, too."

My composure cracks.

One tear falls, then another. I turn my face just slightly, trying to wipe them away before he can notice. Whether he does or not, he doesn't say anything about it, just gives my hand another gentle squeeze. "Your two brothers... they look just like her."

The image of my sister floods my mind—her laugh, her warmth, her strength. I nod, pressing my lips together, and rest my head lightly on his shoulder. We sit there quietly for a while. Just the two of us, with the sound of sparring echoing in the background.

The scent of roasted meats and spiced vegetables greets me as I step into the dining hall. The golden light from the chandeliers overhead glints off the polished wood of the long table. My heels echo softly across the marble floor as I make my way toward the familiar faces already seated.

Kai sits at the head of the table, with the seat next to him waiting for me. His hair is in a tight braid down the center of his head with two smaller twin braids on each side. The braids meet in a knot tied at the nape of his neck. He is once again clean-shaven. My father is seated directly to his left. His long, white hair is tied back loosely.

Shawniaus and Rook sit across from each other. Shawniaus is next to my father. Kai looks up the second I walk in. He smiles, slow and warm, as if I'm the only one in the room. He rises, and the others follow suit. He pulls the chair beside him out just slightly. I take the seat, and everyone sits in unison.

Kai leans in a little. "We were just talking about Shawniaus," he says. "He's officially taken the role of the Crown's official adviser."

Shawniaus offers a rare smile and nods as he lifts his glass in thanks.

The conversation around the table shifts as everyone digs into their food.

A servant appears beside me, stacking my plate high with roasted chicken, glazed sweet potatoes, soft rolls, and sliced carrots. She fills my cup with Brumble Berry Ale, its deep fuchsia hue catching the firelight in my glass. I nod my thanks, offering a soft smile, and she bows before slipping away.

"We've had fifty new recruits arrive since yesterday," Kai says, cutting into his meat. "Thirty more expected by fortnight's end, all young men eager to start training."

Rook raises a brow. "That many?"

Kai shrugs. "Word spreads fast when the Crown starts offering decent coin and fair treatment." He chuckles, winking at Shawniaus.

My father gives a small approving grunt, sipping from his goblet.

"They'll need breaking in." Kai turns to Rook. "As lord commander, they're yours tomorrow sun up."

Rook smirks. "Good. I have been itching to knock some sense into fresh blood."

Shawniaus chuckles under his breath. "Try not to break them all on their first day, Rook."

"I make no promises," Rook says, grinning.

I sip my ale. The tart, sweet taste of the berries tingles on my tongue. We settle into the easy rhythm of the conversation.

My father sets down his goblet, turning to Kai with a nod of genuine gratitude. "Thank you for the extra rangers on our northern border."

Kai wipes his mouth with his napkin. His expression is calm but resolute.

"It's no problem. Our kingdoms are one now," he says, placing a large hand on my knee.

My father turns to me, his expression darkening just slightly beneath the candlelight.

"We found one of my own servants to be a spy," he says, voice low. "Working for Haravik."

I sit up straighter. My fingers tighten around the stem of my goblet.

"He broke under interrogation," my father continues. "Told us everything. Told us all in the kingdom had orders to bring you back to Cravenmore, willingly or not."

A chill runs down my spine.

"I left at that very moment," he says, his voice thick. "I searched everywhere. I wasn't going to stop until I found you."

My heart twists.

He looks to Kai then, eyes sharp but grateful. "I'm glad you got to her first. Because if you hadn't," his jaw clenches, "I would have turned that city to dust."

Kai leans back in his chair, arms crossed, with a smirk. "Well, we still might need you to turn that city to dust."

My father huffs a short laugh, but his eyes stay serious. "We do need to start planning for war. Nobody sends spies into my kingdom and stays untouched," he says, placing his goblet down with a *clink*.

Kai nods. The room grows quiet. Even the crackle of the fire in the hearth feels louder.

My father leans forward. "I've already begun sending blizzards north. One after another. The innocents will be forced to move south, away from the worst of it. Let their livestock starve. Let their supply routes vanish beneath ice. Let their ships freeze before they ever reach Nyxlandia." His voice is low but coated with steel.

I glance at Kai, watching his expression shift, impressed, calculating. My father is a man who commands the skies and the seasons, and he's ready to use them like blades.

Kai finally nods.

I clear my throat softly. "They have a large population of flames. Their heat can cut through the cold."

My father turns to me, the corners of his mouth lifting slightly, but his eyes stay hard. "No number of flames," he says, "can make a ripple in the force of me."

The room falls silent.

Rook lets out a low whistle. "Remind me to never get on your bad side."

Kai leans forward slightly, resting his forearms on the edge of the table. His eyes flick between my father and me.

"Good," he says, a sharp edge to his tone. "Let them keep their most powerful on defrost duty. That should keep the flames away from the border and out of our way." Kai's eyes glint with a dark fire as he leans back in his chair. "By the time you're done, they'll be on their knees begging me to burn that wretched castle to the ground."

Everyone at the table laughs.

The conversation shifts naturally, with the mood lightening as my father brings up the new trade routes being opened between our kingdoms. The scent of chocolate pulls my focus as the servants return, placing down a decadent chocolate cake.

Kai's hand finds my leg beneath the table, warm and gentle. He traces soft circles just above my knee. His thumb moves in slow, rhythmic patterns.

My father's eyes meet mine. "So," he says, his tone casual, "what's the date for the wedding ceremony?"

Kai turns to me, smiling. "Whenever she's ready."

CHAPTER THIRTY~TWO

The next morning, the sun barely peeks over the horizon. I stand at the castle doors, bundled in a long cloak over my training clothes, saying goodbye to my father. He pulls me into a warm, familiar hug. His long white hair brushes my cheek. He pulls back, eyes shining.

With a nod to his guards, he mounts his horse and rides off down the stone path, disappearing through the castle gates.

I turn to Kai, who's leaning casually against one of the pillars with his arms crossed. The morning light casts gold across his sharp features.

"You ready to train?" I ask, toying with the pommel of my new sword.

"Not today, Princess," he says, pushing off the column and walking toward me. "We're having fun."

I gape. "Fun?"

"We're exploring the city," he says, brushing a strand of hair behind my ear. "And... I have a surprise for you." His eyes twinkle.

I raise a brow, with my lips tugging into a curious smile. "What kind of surprise?"

He only winks and offers his hand. "Come on, Princess. You'll see."

We walk side by side through the quiet castle corridors. The early morning light filters in through the tall stained glass windows, casting colorful patterns on the stone floors. My sword shifts gently at my hip with each step, and my crown sits balanced on my head, catching the sun as we turn toward the courtyard.

As we step outside, a light snowfall drifts from the pale sky. The flakes catch in my hair, clinging to my dark fur cloak. The air is crisp and cool, filled with the hush that only fresh snow brings.

He leads me down the stone path to the stables. The scent of hay and leather greets us as we step inside, warm and earthy. A few stable hands glance up and quickly bow before returning to their duties.

I glance around, eyes searching. "What are we doing here?" I ask.

Kai only grins wider and leads me past the stalls. He leads me to the second-to-last stall, and my heart nearly stops.

"Tally?" I breathe, barely able to speak.

There she stands, her eyes bright and gentle as she steps forward, ears twitching. In the next stall over, Doc tosses his head. His black mane catches flakes of snow drifting in from the open stable doors.

Joy crashes into me like a wave. I throw the stall door open, wrapping my arms around Tally's strong neck. She lets out a soft, familiar huff, nuzzling into me.

"You're here," I whisper into her coat, blinking back the sting in my eyes. "I'll never leave you behind again, I swear it."

Kai leans against the frame, arms crossed, watching with a proud smile. "My men retrieved them. They arrived late last night."

I turn toward him, speechless for a moment, then smile so wide it hurts. "Kai... thank you."

He calls the stable hand over and instructs him to ready our two horses.

We stand together in a quiet embrace, with the snow dusting our cloaks and hair. I rest my head against his warm chest, still holding onto the joy of seeing Tally again. His arms stay around me, tender and grounding.

The stable hand finishes readying the horses, adjusting the saddles, and looping the reins carefully over their necks. With a respectful nod, he steps back, giving us space.

Kai pulls away gently and offers me a hand as I swing up into the saddle. Tally shifts beneath me like she remembers my weight. I smile down at her and give her a grateful pat.

Kai mounts Doc with ease, casting a glance at me as he clicks his tongue and nudges the horse forward. I fall in beside him. The snow crunches softly beneath hooves. The castle fades behind us as we make our way down the winding path toward the city. The quiet snowfall paints the world in calm.

We ride slowly into the city, and the sounds of winter festivities grow louder with each step. Snowflakes drift lazily from the sky, landing in my lashes, and the scent of spiced cider and pine floats through the crisp air.

People are outside their homes, bundling in cloaks and gloves, busy hanging garlands of holly and pine across doors and windows. Ribbons in deep red and gold twist between lanterns, and children chase each other with arms full of glittering snowflakes they've cut from parchment.

The city itself is breathtaking. Built from rich, dark red stone, its buildings rise tall and proud. Their roofs are now frosted with white. Tall dragon-shaped shrubs line the street.

The cobbled streets shimmer faintly under the light snowfall. Kai leans over slightly. His voice is low and full of warmth. "Looks like the whole kingdom's getting ready for Yule."

As we ride side by side through the festive streets, I glance up at the snowflakes swirling gently from the sky, then over to Kai.

"Does it snow a lot here in Syrias?" I ask, brushing a flake from my cheek.

He shakes his head slightly, smiling. "Not for long, only between the twelfth moon and the third. It's usually light. Nothing like the storms up north."

I nod, watching a pair of older women laughing as they try to wrangle a string of golden bells around a lamppost.

We bring our horses to a slow in front of a small stone eatery tucked between two shops. Its windows glow warm and golden. The scent of baked bread and sweet cinnamon drifts out with the breeze. A little bell above the door jingles as people come and go, with laughter and chatter spilling into the street.

Kai looks over at me, with one brow raised. His grin is easy and boyish. "You hungry, Princess?" he asks, tilting his head toward the door. "Feel like some breakfast?"

My stomach chooses that moment to growl softly in response. I nod, smiling. "Starving."

He hops down from his horse with ease, then offers me his hand. "Come on then."

We step inside. The eatery's warmth hugs us like a blanket draped in comfort.

The scent of burning oak, roasted meats, and something sweet fills the air. It's cozy, with mismatched chairs and worn wooden tables. Herbs hang from the ceiling beams, and a fire crackles in a small stone hearth.

Kai heads to the counter, exchanging a few cheerful words with the older woman behind it. He orders for us without even asking. He nods to her with a charming smile, then turns to me and gestures toward the back.

"We'll sit out back."

I follow him through the narrow walkway between tables, brushing past the scent of lavender and warm bread. He opens the back door, letting in a cool breath of snowy air, and guides me out of the door.

The moment we step through the back door, it's like entering another world. The air, though frosted just moments ago, is suddenly warm and honeyed with the scent of smoke and pine. Magic hums through the space, gentle and inviting. The chill lifts from my shoulders.

The courtyard is circular, surrounded by low stone walls decorated with beads and garland.

Smooth stone benches and rounded tables form a wide ring around a massive fire pit at the center, where golden flames dance and crackle. The warmth it gives off is almost unreal, gentle and deep, like sunlight resting against your skin.

Dozens of people are here, bundled in embroidered cloaks and laughing as they twirl to music drifting through the air with lively strings and soft drums, a sound that makes it impossible not to smile.

Children dart between legs with flushed cheeks, while elders sway slowly near the fire with mugs in hand. Lanterns hang from arching wooden posts, their golden glow flickering like stars caught in glass.

We find an empty stone table near the fire. The warmth wraps around us like a molten current flowing over our skin. I sink onto the bench. My hands hover near the flames, soaking in the cozy glow.

Kai sits across from me.

"This is amazing," I murmur. My eyes roam over the joyful chaos, the dancers, the flickering lanterns, and the way the fire makes everything golden.

Kai smiles, the flames casting a soft shimmer over his features. "This is where my sister and I used to come when we needed to get away from the castle." His voice is low and warm with memory. "We would dance around this fire for hours. Laugh until we couldn't breathe."

His words tug at a raw chord within me, and before I can brace against it, a wave of sadness crashes over my chest. My throat tightens as I picture it, him and his sister, young and free and full of laughter. And now... she's gone. My lashes flutter quickly, trying to keep my emotions from surfacing too loudly.

"Thank you for sharing it with me," I say softly, voice barely carrying over the music.

A cheerful table maid weaves through the dancing crowd and sets two wooden trays down in front of us with a warm smile. The smell makes my stomach tighten with hunger.

In front of me sits a steaming bowl of hot oats, thick with butter and cream. The surface is dotted with dark, glistening berries that burst with color. Next to it, a generous hunk of toasted bread soaked in melted cheese with crisp edges and topped with a pile of eggs.

In front of me, she places a mug of hot cider. Steam curls from its surface, spiced and sweet. The scent of cinnamon coils around me like a warm, familiar veil.

"This looks incredible," I say, already cradling the cider in my hands. The mug is warm, and I let it heat my fingers for a moment before taking a sip. It tastes like hearth fire and winter memories.

We sit by the fire, plates nearly clean. I sip what's left of my cider, letting it linger in my mouth as I watch the courtyard come alive around us.

A woman across the fire is moving her hands slowly, elegantly, and between her palms, tiny sparkling stars begin to form, like snowballs made of stardust. One by one, she hands them to the waiting children, their delighted giggles lighting up the air more than her magic itself.

Kai follows my gaze. "A light weaver," he says.

My eyes meet his, curiosity stirring.

"I've seen you... pull a sword from thin air. That armor, too. And the flames." I tilt my head. "How do you do all of that?"

He leans back, his amber eyes glowing slightly in the firelight.

"It's because I'm not only man or dragon. I'm everything in between, too."

I frown slightly. "What do you mean?"

"I can summon any part of the dragon when I need to," he explains, lifting his hand. "Bones become blades. Scales become armor. I can call the strength, the speed... the fire."

A flicker of flame blooms on his fingertip, swirling and twisting with a life of its own—wild and untamed. It dances there, playful, obedient.

"I don't carry weapons. It's a part of me."

I stare, completely in awe. His gaze falls on mine, serious now.

"That's why bonding with me isn't like bonding with a dragon. Or a man. It's both... Winnie, we're mated... for life... My magic is threaded to you."

He turns his palm over. The flame vanishes, and a tiny dark green sword appears through the curl of smoke.

His voice lowers, rich with a timeless depth that feels older than either of us. "When I say I'll protect you until death..." He pauses, eyes fixed on mine. "I don't mean it the way most people do."

My breath stills.

"I mean it *literally*," his eyes soften. "I have no choice. The pull to guard you, to keep you safe. It's in my blood, in my bones. It's instinct. It's not even something I can fight." He leans forward slightly, voice almost a whisper. "Not protecting you... it would be like defying gravity. Like trying to stop the moon from rising. It would be against the very laws of what I am."

His eyes search mine. "It's nature."

I stare at him, completely stunned. My lips part, but the only thing that escapes is a soft, breathless, "Oh."

His words shatter the stillness within me, unleashing a flood of longing. Warmth builds low in my stomach, curling tight. I shift slightly, thighs pressing together as the heat spreads. My pulse quickens. I try to ease my breathing.

Kai leans in, with his breath brushing my ear. His voice lowers—rough velvet woven with fire. "I can sense when you feel like this, too."

A shiver rakes down my spine. A flush kisses my cheeks. I don't dare look at him right away. My face suddenly feels hot.

"When did you know we were mated?" I manage to say.

"The minute I first saw you," he replies quickly.

My mind drifts for a moment back to the very first time I met him.

That day feels like forever ago now, and yet it lives in me like it just happened. I remember the *feeling*. The electricity that shot through my chest. I didn't understand it then. I do now. It was *him*. It was *us*. It was the beginning of the powerful bond we share.

I glance at him, still reeling from everything he's told me, and I ask softly, "So... what kind of magic *is* it that you have if it's not a craft or a lumina?"

He looks into the fire for a moment, quiet. Then he turns to me, voice low but certain. "We're a race, Princess, created by the gods. As time passed, we were hunted to near extinction. We're trying to rebuild what was lost."

I raise a brow. "As in... having children?"

His lips twitch into a grin, and he glances at me. "Yes, Princess."

I look at him carefully. "And do you... Is that something *you* want?"

His smile softens. "I think so, Princess," he says, taking my hand in his.

"The dragon's blood... was that... yours?" I ask.

He nods.

Warmth swells in my chest, aching and beautiful. "You saved her," I whisper.

"*We* saved her."

Suddenly, our little world explodes into chaos. A deafening boom cracks through the sky, followed by another, and another.

The ground shakes beneath our feet. Screams erupt around us as people scatter. Panic floods the warm courtyard like a wave. Arrows rain through the air, fast and merciless.

Kai is on his feet in an instant.

His hand grabs my wrist. His eyes burn with purpose. His fingers find the charm bracelet around my wrist, his gift. He grips the small horse charm and yanks it.

A burst of dark green flashes.

In seconds, sleek dark green armor shimmers into place over my body, piece by piece, molding to me like a second skin. It's the same dragon-forged armor I've seen him wear, made from his scales. Only now, it shields me.

I barely have time to breathe before he turns and takes off into battle armor-less. Men wearing all black storm the courtyard. Their faces are masked. Their weapons are drawn.

With no hesitation, I bolt into the chaos, scooping up a screaming child. I herd every child I can find into the stone eatery behind us, with my heart pounding. I throw open the doors and shove them through, shielding them as arrows thud against the walls.

I draw the sword at my hip and step back outside. Just as Kai taught me: feet light, knees bent, core strong.

I duck under an oncoming blade, twist, and slam my shoulder into the attacker's chest, sending him stumbling.

My blade meets his with a sharp clang. The vibration hums up my arm. I pivot, sidestep, and drive the edge of my sword into his side.

The armor glides with me—an eternal twin of steel, strong and seamless. Every breath I take sharpens my focus. My heart beat drums in my ears, but I stay grounded.

Another man rushes toward me, and I lift my blade just in time, blocking his strike with a satisfying spark of steel. I duck low and sweep his legs from under him, knocking him flat.

Out of the corner of my eye, I see a flash of light, bright and dancing. I turn just long enough to see the light weaver, the woman who had just been making stars for children. She's no longer smiling, but fierce and radiant, hurling brilliant sparks of gold and silver from her palms.

The magic crackles in the air as she blasts a man backward, then binds another in a ring of searing light.

A pair of attackers moves toward her flank.

"Behind you!" I shout and sprint in her direction.

She sees me coming and whips her hand around in a wide arc, sending a wall of glittering white fire between us and the attackers.

The enemy tries to push through. I meet the first one with steel. I sidestep, pivoting on my heel, and drive my sword upward, catching him under his ribs. He gasps, dropping his weapon, and I shove him back with my boot.

Another grabs my arm, trying to yank me backward. I twist hard, slamming my elbow into his nose. He stumbles, clutching his face, and I bring my sword down across his shoulder before he can recover.

The light weaver moves behind me, blazing and merciless. She tosses another ribbon of pure magic forward, snaring an attacker by the neck and flinging him into the wall with a flash.

We stand back to back. Around us, the chaos still reigns. I spot an attacker nearby raising a crossbow toward Kai. *No.* I lunge without thinking, knocking the man's arm up just as he fires.

The bolt goes wild, burying itself in a tree. He snarls and swings at me, but I duck. He raises his hand, finger curling, and the world narrows.

My lungs seize. There's no air. I gasp, but nothing comes. A crushing weight bears down on my chest.

I claw at my throat, stumbling backward, panic consuming me.

He grins, twisted and vile, watching me suffocate with a calm cruelty. Black dots bloom at the edges of my vision. My knees threaten to give. My sword slips from my grasp.

"Wrong target." Kai's voice is a blade slashing through the roar of panic. It's low, lethal, and thunderous with restrained rage.

The man turns. His concentration slips. Air rushes back into my lungs all at once. I gasp, collapsing to my knees, coughing violently.

In a blur of motion, he grabs the man by the throat, lifting him with terrifying ease and slamming him into the stone wall.

The man thrashes, but it's useless. Kai leans in close, eyes glowing like molten gold, lips curling into a cold and dangerous smirk.

"Your little tricks won't work on me."

He opens his mouth, wide and unnatural, and from deep within, fire erupts. A brilliant, roaring blaze of flame engulfs the man's face.

I shield my eyes as the fire crackles. When I look again, there is nothing left but a pile of ash.

Kai exhales slowly, with smoke trailing from between his teeth. His breath is still heavy as we move through the wreckage.

The air is thick with smoke and panic. He scans the area, looking for lingering attackers.

There's a pained wheeze from our left. One attacker is still alive, crawling, blood trailing beneath him. Without hesitation, Kai lifts his hand, and the man's body ignites. No scream, just silence and ash.

We step over debris and broken benches as we make our way back to the center of the courtyard. The fire spits embers around us, glowing specks dancing like fireflies.

Kai kneels beside one of the fallen rangers. His fingers move to the man's neck. A black cord. A pendant. He rips it free and stuffs it in his pocket.

Kai's expression softens as he looks at me with the glow of the fire dancing in his golden eyes. His hand finds my wrist gently, fingers brushing over the bracelet he gave me.

Without a word, he hooks his finger around the rose charm and gives it a soft tug.

A warm shimmer pulses across my skin. One by one, the pieces of dark green armor begin to pull away from my body, disassembling as if carried by invisible threads. The metal disappears into thin air, dissolving like dust in the wind.

His hand lingers on my wrist briefly. His thumb brushes over my pulse.

He reaches up and straightens my crown.

"You didn't even lose your crown," he says, smiling softly.

"Because of your armor," I replied, giving a grateful smile.

We step back into the warmth of the eatery. The heavy door closes behind us.

The moment we cross the threshold, cheers erupt. Dozens of voices rise at once, some relieved, some grateful, all full of awe.

Kai gives a small nod, offering them a quiet smile in return, but I can see the tension in his shoulders, the way he scans every face, still alert, still watching.

While he strides toward a small table to grab us some waters, I slip away from his side, weaving through the crowd toward the young woman who fought beside us, the one with the sparks at her fingertips.

She stands near the far wall, catching her breath. Her palms still faintly glow. Her long, pale blonde hair is tangled, sticking to her temple with sweat. Her skin is sun-kissed, and her ice-blue eyes are striking against the warm glow of the fire behind her.

"You were incredible," I say, stepping closer.

She looks at me, a wide grin spreading across her face. "So were you. I didn't know I was fighting alongside a princess, Your Highness." She curtsies and laughs lightly. "I'm Piper."

"Winnie," I say, offering her my hand.

She shakes it, her grip firm. "Thanks for helping with the children," she says. "I saw you pulling them into the building like an armored angel."

I smile. "You were kind of hard to miss. Commanding light sparks like a goddess."

She grins. "It was very nice to meet you, Winnie."

I nod, already liking her. "You, as well."

"See ya around," she says over her shoulder as she walks out the door.

Kai returns with two cups in hand.

He hands me one of the waters, and I take it gratefully. The coolness is already soothing the ache in my throat. I tilt my head back and nearly drink the whole thing in one go, not realizing how badly I needed it.

"You all right?" he asks.

I wipe my mouth with the back of my hand and nod. "I'm good, just ready for a bath," I say, setting the glass down.

"Then a bath it is." His voice is low and warm as he places his hand gently on the small of my back, steering us toward the door. "Let's get you home."

CHAPTER THIRTY~THREE
MALACHAI

I sit in the quiet of my study, with my fingers turning over the circular pendant I took from the fallen ranger. The metal is old, tarnished, but the design etched into it is unmistakable and familiar in a way that makes my stomach turn. I trace the lines absently with my thumb.

The door creaks open behind me. I don't look up. I already know it's Rook. He steps in. The heavy sound of his boots echoes across the stone. He drops into the chair across from me, eyeing the pendant still in my hand.

I set the pendant down on the desk between us. The light from the window catches on the engraved design: a silver tree, branches sprawling wide. Twisting around its roots is a coiled serpent forged in gold with eyes made of obsidian. Above the tree, a crescent moon hovers.

Rook leans forward, and for a second, his face pales. "Is this…" he starts.

"The crest of Draugrune," I finish for him, and my jaw tightens.

"Draugrune burned to ash fifty years ago," Rook mutters. "That Kingdom was wiped off the map."

I nod. The weight of the pendant between us feels heavier than iron.

Rook's eyes flicker from the pendant to the globe resting on my desk. His brows furrow. "What does this mean?" he asks, voice low.

I exhale slowly, and my shoulders tense. "I don't know," I admit, running a hand through my hair. "I should have kept one alive."

"How many dead?"

"Nine." I lean back in my chair, with the weight of the pendant still lingering in my palm. "I'll start an investigation. Quietly."

Rook nods once.

"I'll send Rafe," I say. "Have him scout the ruins of Draugrune. See if anything is stirring there. Or anyone."

Rook leans back, arms crossed. "You really think some survived?"

I look down at the pendant again. The metal feels colder now. "I think someone wants us to believe they did. Or maybe they've rebuilt."

Rook shifts in his chair, glancing down at the pendant once more. "I was planning to visit my mother in Valkygard," he says after a moment. "Just for a few days, after the new recruits are settled into training."

I look up at him, see the hesitation in his eyes.

"You want me to postpone my leave?"

I shake my head. "No. Go see your mother, Rook."

He studies me for a beat longer. "You sure?"

I nod. "I've got this. And she'll be glad to see you. I will send Rafe to Draugrune and keep things quiet here."

A flicker of relief crosses his face. "All right. But if anything changes, you let me know."

I nod, watching Rook rise to his feet. "And tell my aunt to send some of her stew back with you."

He laughs under his breath. "You know she will."

"And Rook, don't tell anyone about this."

He nods and turns to leave the room. He gently closes the door behind him. The faint clinking echoes in the quiet study.

My thoughts drift—to *her*.

Winnie.

The way she moved through the chaos, how she threw herself between danger and the innocent without hesitation. How she gathered those children and shielded them. How she fought for them.

She didn't falter or run. She stayed.

With me.

Like a true queen.

A soft smile pulls at the corner of my mouth. She's more than just brave. She's fierce. I press my palms together, rest my forehead on my thumbs, and exhale slowly.

CHAPTER THIRTY-FOUR
WINNIE

It's been nearly a full moon since the attack, and the weight of it all has slowly eased. Things have been calm, peaceful even. The castle has returned to a kind of quiet order. Stillness lives between the stone walls again.

I sit curled beside Kai in the library with the fire flickering low in the hearth. A blanket is draped across my lap, and I absently trace the edge of it with my fingers.

Outside, snow falls in slow, lazy drifts past tall windows, dusting the world in quiet. The scent of old parchment, strong coffee, and Kai's warmth surrounds me.

"We should probably have the wedding soon," I say softly, breaking the silence. "It would make a statement. Show the kingdoms we are united. It might put people at ease, give them something to celebrate."

Kai turns his head to look at me, his expression unreadable at first. Then he frowns slightly, gently setting the book in his lap aside. "I don't want you to marry me just to make a statement, Princess. Not for peace, politics, or pressure."

I gape, caught off guard. "Kai..."

He leans forward, his voice low. "I want you to marry me because *you* want to. Not because it's good for the kingdoms or because it's expected. Because you want me."

My chest tightens. I reach out and take his hand. "I *do* want you. I want to marry you. I've dreamed of a life with you since that first dance when you pulled me close and made the whole world fall away. I've already given you my heart."

His expression softens. His stormy eyes warm like fire on snow, and he squeezes my hand, bringing it to his lips, pressing a kiss to my fingers.

"Then let's not wait," he whispers. "Say the word, and I'll have it arranged." Kai leans back into the cushions beside me, brushing his thumb over the back of my hand.

"We still need to move rooms," he says, glancing toward the doorway leading down the hall. "Into the royal chambers."

I glance at him. "Is Shawniaus still staying there?"

"He is," Kai says, his expression thoughtful. "But it's time he moves out. I'll speak with him soon."

There's a pause. I watch the firelight flicker across his face, see the weight of everything he carries.

"I haven't stepped foot in that room since my parents lived in it," he says quietly. "Not since they died."

My heart aches at the weight in his voice. I reach over and take his hand, giving it a gentle squeeze.

His eyes are warm but shadowed. "It's time. It is where the king and queen are meant to be. And I want it to be ours."

The sound of heavy footsteps echoes from the hall. A moment later, Rafe steps through the tall arched doorway. His cloak is dusted with snow. He bows low. Kai rises at once, and I take his offered hand as he helps me up. Together, we walk to the long table nestled between high bookshelves and settle into the worn chairs.

Rafe wastes no time. "I scoured the lands," he begins, voice gruff with travel. "From the gulfs to the mountains. There's nothing left of Draugrune. Not a flicker of life on the continent. Just ash and ruin."

A hush falls over us.

"But..." His eyes darken. "I did find something. Ships. Haravik vessels. Dozens of them, heading straight for Draugrune's shores."

I tense. "Did you see what they were carrying?"

Rafe shakes his head. "No. I couldn't get close enough to see. I'll return in a fortnight," he says. "If a storm is building... I will find it."

Kai nods. "Thank you, Rafe."

He dips his head low. "Your Majesties," he says, his voice firm but tired.

With a sweep of his cloak, Rafe turns and strides toward the tall library doors. The quiet thud as they close behind him leaves the room wrapped in silence once more.

Kai turns to me, a sly smile pulling at the corner of his mouth. "Why don't we return to our chamber?" he says. "Have dinner delivered... start planning our wedding... maybe read one of those smutty books you hide behind all the dragon books."

I bite my lip, my heart fluttering. "That sounds like something I would be interested in," I say, trying not to grin too wide.

His smile blooms eagerly. He offers me his arm, and I take it, letting him lead me out of the library. Our footsteps are light and quick.

The rest of the walk drifts by in a haze of warmth and quiet conversation. Before long, I find myself alone in the bathing chamber, soaking in fragrant water. The flicker of candlelight dances along the tiled walls.

I wrap myself in a soft robe with the steam from my bath still clinging to my skin as I step back into the room.

The warm glow from the fireplace flickers across the walls, casting golden shadows that dance with the flames.

Kai is standing by the hearth, shirtless, with his back to me as he adjusts the logs. The firelight plays along the hard lines of his muscles, each one carved and perfectly sculpted.

His presence is so large, so commanding, it somehow makes the spacious chamber feel small.

Dinner waits on a large tray set at the foot of the bed. The scent of roasted meats and herbs curls through the air.

He turns toward me, and when his eyes meet mine, heat blooms low in my belly.

"Looks like dinner's ready," he says, his gaze trailing my full form.

Heat creeps up my neck at his words. Gods, he is so damned handsome. I can barely breathe.

We climb into the bed, settling on the plush mattress, with a pillow propped behind us.

I sit cross-legged, while Kai leans back against the headboard, one arm stretched behind me. The tray of food sits between us, and we eat slowly, savoring the quiet.

I glance at his side of the bed and grin. "You've already got a stack of books ready?"

He smirks, brushing a crumb from his lip. "What can I say? I love a good story."

I chuckle and lean into him.

Between bites, we start discussing the wedding. Just small details, like if it should be outside or in the great hall, what kind of flowers, and who will officiate.

We finish eating, and Kai sets the tray carefully on the footrest at the end of the bed.

He brushes his hands off on a cloth and reaches for the top book in his little smutty stack.

"This one's supposed to be especially scandalous," he says, flipping it open with a mischievous glint in his eye.

I giggle, settling beside him as he begins to read out loud. His voice is deep and smooth, adding far too much emphasis on the steamy words. I find myself biting my lip, not at the words, but at him. The way his hand grips the book, large, veined, and strong.

My gaze trails up his forearm, thick with muscle, to his bicep, flexed slightly from holding the book upright.

I follow the line of his chest, broad and perfectly sculpted, down to his abdomen. Gods. My chest quivers as my eyes linger on the sharp ridges of his lower stomach and those deep lines that disappear under the edge of his trousers.

My skin flushes with heat. A knot forms low in my belly. I shift slightly, trying to focus on the words he's saying, but I can't.

He pauses mid-sentence, tilting the book down slightly as he glances at me. "You're not listening," he says, amused. A smirk tugs at the corner of his lips.

I blink, forcing my eyes back up to his face. "I was," I lie terribly with my cheeks burning.

"Oh really?" he asks, closing the book slowly and setting it aside. "Then what did I just read?"

I open my mouth, but nothing comes out.

He raises a brow, and I groan, tossing myself back.

"You're distracting."

The bed shifts as he leans over me. His eyes are molten gold in the firelight, warm and intense. "Distracting?" he murmurs, lips hovering just above me. "What part of me is distracting, Princess?"

I trail my fingers over his chest without answering.

He catches my wrist, placing a soft kiss on my palm. "You're flushed," he whispers, voice dropping. "Warm all of a sudden?"

I tilt my head back. My heartbeat is wild. "Maybe."

His mouth brushes against my jaw, trailing down my neck. "Tell me what you want, *Queen*."

"You," I say, breathless. "Every inch of you."

He growls low in my ear. The sound is primal and full of promise, and my skin breaks into goosebumps.

I hold my breath as he lifts his hand. Flames flicker to life at his fingertips. They dance there for only a moment before he closes his fist, and they vanish into sparks.

Then, slowly, he trails his warm fingers down the center of my stomach.

The heat of him brands my skin, stealing the air from my lungs. My body arches instinctively toward him as his touch melts through every nerve, leaving fire in its wake.

His lips touch the shell of my ear as he whispers, "I want you to take every inch of me." His voice is molten.

And gods, I want to feel every ounce of him. Every brush of his fingertips feels like he's painting me in flames.

My pulse hammers, my breath turns ragged, and I swear I'd let him burn me alive if it meant being consumed by him.

His hand trails lower, slipping beneath the delicate lace that barely veils my most sensitive parts. The contrast of the cool fabric and the searing heat of his skin makes me gasp.

His touch is burning and all-consuming. My composure fractures under the weight of it. A soft moan escapes before I can stop it. He watches me with fire in his eyes, pleased and focused.

His lips find mine as he plunges two of his fiery hot fingers deep into my core. I clutch his shoulders with a gasp as he fills the tight space of me.

His fingers move with gentle mastery, drawing soft moans from my lips.

"Kai," I whisper against his mouth, my voice trembling.

My hips rock in time with his hand, finding that perfect rhythm, with our breaths syncing and our hearts pounding in unison.

Every thrust of his molten fingers sends sparks shooting up my spine. Heat curls low in my belly. His gaze is locked on mine.

I grip his strong arm, feeling the strength beneath my palm and anchoring myself as the pressure builds, overwhelming and consuming.

"Kai..." I pant.

We move together as I arch into his hand, wanting more, needing more.

And when the world finally splinters around me, he holds me through it, grounding me as my hot, wet center pulses around his grip.

As my body trembles, he kisses my collarbone, then lower, trailing heat across my skin. When he looks up at me again, there's nothing but thirst in his eyes.

MALACHAI

Her warmth wraps around me. Her breath trembles, and her body shakes as I position myself between her sweet, milky thighs. I grip them gently, holding her open for me. She's already undone, flushed, and soft beneath me.

I lower my trousers with my eyes locked on hers. She nods once. Her full, perfect lips are parted, and her ragged breaths finally slow.

I guide my throbbing, hot steel into her slowly. The world narrows to this moment, to the way she gasps, to her wide eyes and her trembling body beneath me.

I reach down. My fingers brush over the knot of her robe. She watches me with those soft, expectant eyes. I loosen the tie, and the fabric falls open like petals parting, exposing the soft curves of her form.

My breath stutters in my chest as I take her in, every line, dip, and curve. The fire crackles beside us, casting a golden light and highlighting the peaks of her breast as they rock in rhythm with my thrust. She watches me with eyes heavy with trust and hunger.

I reach down, cupping her soft, full breast with a tenderness that nearly undoes me. She gasps. Her back arches into my palm, and the sound rips straight through me. My thumb grazes across her hardened pink peak, and I watch every shift in her expression like it's a language to be learned.

I grip her hips and shift her body with ease. I turn her over, and her back arches as I guide her to her knees.

"That's it, good girl," I pant, running my hands along the generous curve of her waist. I anchor them on her wide hips, with my fingers splayed wide and my thumbs pressed into the dimples of her lower back.

I pause as I take in the sight of her beautiful, plump backside, letting her feel my molten heat before I dive into her drenched core.

She exhales a trembling breath. Her fingers grip the covers beneath her as I fill her.

My name falls from her lips like a prayer, and I answer it with a low growl. I hold her there, moving my hips at an even pace.

Her body meets mine repeatedly, thrust after thrust. I squeeze my eyes shut. My jaw is clenched so tight it aches.

The sight of her, the way her hips meet mine, it's almost too much. If I watch the way her backside rises and falls for a second longer, it will pull me under.

I can feel the edge creeping in, tightening every muscle in my body, but I can't give.

Not yet.

"Slow," I growl, voice hoarse, strained. "You're going to undo me."

She moans. Her body trembles beneath me. Her center is soaked and tightening around me like fire laced in silk.

Then she cries out, unrestrained, raw. The sound unravels me. With a deep, guttural groan, I slam into her tightness once more and pull out. I fist my engorged steel until I release. The waves of pleasure finally claim me, taking me under.

I grab my discarded shirt and gently wipe away the hot load I've shot onto Winnie's soft porcelain skin.

My head drops to her shoulder. One hand is locked around her hip, and the other is on the mattress, shaking beneath the weight of me. I hold her to me as we shatter together.

Every inch of me burns with her name, her scent, her warmth. There's nothing but the pounding of our hearts and the sound of our breath tangled in the air between us.

CHAPTER THIRTY~FIVE
WINNIE

I sit at the writing desk in our chambers. The soft light of morning casts a golden glow across the parchment a I dip my quill. The ink flows easily, and my hand moves quickly as I write:

Dearest Khristea,

I hope this letter finds you well. I am writing from Syrias with a hopeful request. I had to leave my wedding gown behind during my departure from Haravik, and though it pains me, I must ask for another. There's no one who can weave fabric to your caliber.

I've enclosed enough coin to last you for twelve moons—more than enough for the materials and your time. Expect a courier to retrieve the gown in a fortnight.

With all my love,

Princess Winifred.

I fold the parchment gently, then seal it with wax before fastening it to the box of coin. A servant enters at just the right moment, and I hand it to her with instructions to see it delivered by post.

After she leaves, I move to the sitting room just off the main hall, where the castle stewardess waits.

The warm scent of cinnamon and spiced honey lingers in the air as tea steeps between us, steam curling in the space.

"I'd like to keep the menu seasonal." I cradle my teacup between both hands. "Roasted roots, fresh breads. I'm thinking duck," I continue. "No swine, please."

She nods, scribbling notes. We talk more about wines, desserts, the decorations, and the layout of the outdoor gardens.

As the stewardess continues to speak, something about the length of table linens, I find my thoughts wandering. I nod as I stare down into my teacup, the amber surface rippling gently with each shift of my breath, and I realize with full force just how far we have come.

I was supposed to be married off for politics. A pawn on a map.

I used to believe that was all I could expect. All I deserved. But now, I'm marrying for love. The kind that crashes into you—a tidal wave that makes you forget how to breathe. The kind I used to read about in novels. A fire in the cold.

And somehow, with a war brewing just at our border and everything falling apart, he's what held me together.

The stewardess is looking at me expectantly. "The guest list, Your Highness. Shall we get started on it?"

"My apologies, of course," I say with a soft smile.

After the long stretch of planning, guest list, florals, and the endless talk of tapestries and table arrangements, I finally retreat to my room. The moment the door closes behind me, I let out a slow, tired breath and begin unlacing the bodice of my gown.

I cross the room to change into something more comfortable when my eyes catch on a small velvet pouch nestled beside a stack of folded linens.

My chest tightens. The bracelet. Rome's gift.

I sit on the edge of the bed, my fingers hesitant as I pull it out. The metal is cool in my palm, heavier than I remember. I run my thumb over the delicate silver work, the diamonds that once seemed so innocent.

Now they rest as secrets.

Memories flicker: his soft voice calling me *Little Flower*, the anguish in his eyes before he fell on his own blade, the keys pressed into my hand.

I can still feel the warmth of his final breath on my neck.

A sigh escapes me as I roll the bracelet between my fingers.

And then, I pause. There's something on the back. The surface is rough against the pad of my thumb. I squint, turning it in the light until I see it: a thin line of etchings hidden in the silver's curve. Not decorative. Runes.

I trace each symbol slowly. My heart thuds harder with each one.

What were you hiding, Rome?

I slip into a clean tunic and trousers and rush down the corridor with the bracelet clutched tight in my hand. My boots echo against the stone floors. My breath is shallow as I round each corner, scanning for any sign of him.

I finally find Kai in the royal chambers. He sits on the edge of the bed, his head bowed, fingers loosely threaded between his knees. My heart aches at the sight of him.

"Kai," I whisper.

He lifts his head slowly, and the moment our eyes meet, I cross the room and sink down beside him. I wrap my arms around his shoulders and press my forehead to his.

"Are you okay?"

He gives me a faint smile and nods.

"I found something," I say, pulling back just enough to show him the bracelet. "Rome gifted this to me on my birthday."

His brow furrows as he takes it from my hands.

"There are runes. Carved into the back."

He instantly turns it over in his hand, and his eyes narrow as he studies the markings. "I haven't seen script like this since I was a boy," he admits.

"You can read it?" I ask, voice eager.

He shakes his head. "No. But I know someone who can. Rook's craft... he's a linguist." Kai's gaze flicks up, intense and unwavering. "I'll have him look at it when he returns."

I glance at the bracelet again, my heart fluttering. "You think it's important?"

He meets my eyes. "If he left this for you... there's a message buried in it. And I will make sure we uncover it."

CHAPTER THIRTY~SIX

I can barely breathe as I unwrap the large parcel resting on the chaise in my room. The castle staff must have brought it in while I was visiting with Piper and the children in town. My fingers tremble as I untie the silk ribbon and peel back the delicate layers of tissue.

The gown. It steals the air from the room, leaving me breathless. It's more than I ever imagined. More than I ever dreamed. I press a hand to my mouth, stunned. My eyes are wide as I carefully lift the gown from its wrappings.

The fabric feels like moonlight, weightless and impossibly soft. A pure, radiant white, but when it catches the light, it shimmers with threads of silver and opal. The stars themselves were sewn into its silk.

Tiny crystals are hand-stitched into the bodice, twinkling like constellations across the heart of the gown. The sleeves are sheer and delicately embroidered with vines and celestial patterns, trailing down to wrists trimmed in soft lace.

I hold it up, stepping back, barely able to comprehend that it's mine. It's even more breathtaking than the first one. Tears prick at the corners of my eyes as I whisper to no one, "Khristea, you magnificent woman."

The gown looks as if she reached into the night sky and plucked each star, weaving them into the silk by hand. The fabric shimmers with starlight caught in motion, soft, ethereal, impossibly beautiful. It's more than a gown. It's a dream stitched into moonlight.

I place the gown gently back into its velvet-lined box, still breathless from its beauty. After tucking it away in my wardrobe, I head down the corridor toward the dining hall. The smell of roasted herbs and spiced cider drifts through the hall, warming the air.

When I step into the dining hall, I find Kai and Rook already seated. They both look up as I enter.

"Evening, Princess," Rook says, with a small bow.

I take my seat next to Kai, already piling my plate high.

"Are you ready for your wedding? It's coming fast," Rook asks.

I smile. "I am. And my gown arrived today."

Kai's eyes soften as he smiles at me. "I can't wait to see you in it."

Rook clears his throat and pulls a folded parchment from beneath his arm.
"Speaking of mysteries," he says, handing it to me. "I had some luck with the runes on your bracelet."

I take the parchment and unfold it. A list of items, some familiar, written in neat ink: *black salt, thistle, clove, moon water, victim's saliva, willow bark, thornapple husk: ground into a paste.*

I stare down at the parchment in my hands. The inked words still make little sense to me. "That's all it says... What is this?" I ask, lifting my eyes to them both.

They share a glance, then Kai shakes his head. "We're not sure," he says carefully.

Rook leans forward, tapping the edge of the parchment. "It's written as a recipe for a tonic, but the bracelet doesn't say what it's for."

I furrow my brow, my gaze returning to the list. "Maybe it's the potion? But it doesn't list the magus fur."

"Maybe he left that part out, too much of a risk if it fell into the wrong hands," Kai replies.

I let the paper fall into my lap and glance down at the bracelet sitting on the dining table. I run my thumb along the silver, pausing over the faint runes.

Rook stands from his chair, stretching slightly before tossing his napkin onto the empty plate. "You joining us for training in the morning, Princess?" he asks, his eyes bright with mischief.

I nod, with a small grin tugging at the corner of my mouth. "Wouldn't miss it."

Kai leans back in his chair, arms crossed loosely. "Where's your father, by the way? I haven't seen him since the briefing."

Rook shrugs. "Not sure. He said he would be absent for a few suns. Didn't say why." He scratches the back of his neck.

Kai nods slowly. "Goodnight, Rook," he says.

"Goodnight," I echo.

Rook offers me a wink, then strides out of the dining hall. His boots echo down the corridor behind him.

Kai leans in slightly, his voice low and gentle. "You ready for bed, Princess?"

I nod, feeling the weight of the long day finally settling into my bones. "Yeah," I murmur.

We rise from the table together. His hand brushes the small of my back as we leave the dining hall. The corridor is quiet, lit by soft golden sconces that flicker against the stone walls.

My steps slow as we reach our room. The familiar carved door opens easily beneath Kai's hand.

Inside, the fire crackles softly, casting warm shadows across the chamber. I slip out of my boots and begin unfastening the buttons on my tunic, trading it for the soft cotton nightdress folded at the end of the bed.

Kai changes too, shrugging off his shirt. He glances over his shoulder at me. His eyes are warm with a soft and silent affection.

We settle into the bed. The sheets are cool against our skin. The firelight flickers warmly on the stone walls. I nestle against Kai. His arms wrap securely around me. His chest is firm and warm beneath my cheek.

"Have you ever been to Odessa?" I ask softly, tracing idle shapes against his chest. "Before you became my guard, I mean."

He hums thoughtfully. "A few times. When I was young, I'd fly too far from the boundary lines. I would always get scolded, but I couldn't help it. Something about that shoreline always pulled at me."

I smile at the thought of a younger Kai, defiant and wild, chasing the sky.

"I had a dream... when I was little, I was playing too close to the cliff's edge, and I slipped. I toppled right over, falling, the wind rushing right past me. But... a dragon caught me. Dark, powerful, and gentle. It saved me."

He goes quiet. I glance up at him. His jaw tightens ever so slightly. Kai's fingers still for a moment against my side. Then slowly, he hums, a muffled sound deep in his throat.

"Strange dream," he murmurs, eyes fixed on the fire. "Sometimes, dreams are more than just dreams."

I turn my head to look at him. "What do you mean?"

He glances down at me. His lips curl ever so slightly into a smile. "Maybe someone was watching over you."

There's a warmth in his tone that makes my heart flutter.

I press myself closer to him, tucking my face into the crook of his neck.

"Whoever it was," I whisper. "I'm glad they were there."

His hand traces slow circles along my back.

"So am I, Princess."

CHAPTER THIRTY~SEVEN

The courtyard is alive with the rhythmic clash of blades and the crunch of boots against frost-dusted stone. A thin veil of mist still clings to the garden edges, the morning air sharp and biting.

I spar with Kai, both of us panting, sweat already clinging to our bows despite the cold. He doesn't go easy on me. Our blades sing as they meet, again and again. Each strike echoes across the stone.

Rook watches from the sidelines, arms crossed. His expression is sharp with focus. "Watch your footing!" he yells.

I duck, barely dodging a sweeping strike from Kai, then lunge forward and catch his side with a grazing blow. He grunts but grins, the fire in his eyes only igniting more.

We keep going until finally, I stumble back, chest heaving.

"Good," Rook says, stepping forward, clapping his hands once. "Now I want to see you stop holding back."

I look at him, lowering my sword. "What?"

He looks between us, then settles his gaze on me. "Your magic. I want to see you use it. *Offensively.*"

I frown, wiping sweat from my brow. "Rook, my magic doesn't work like that. It's not something I just... wield *offensively.*"

"Oh, yes, it is," he says, his tone suddenly serious. His brows narrow. "You've barely scratched the surface of what you can do. You think the vines that saved you that night in Cravenmore just acted on their own?"

I glance at Kai, who apparently told Rook the details of my plant friends graciously saving me that night. His expression is unreadable, watchful. Quiet.

Rook steps closer. "Then get mad, Princess. Feel something. Let the earth feel it too."

A silence settles between us, broken only by the whistle of wind through the training grounds. I stare at the frost-covered grass, remembering the girl in the cell, the blade at my throat, the guard's hand clamped over my jaw, and Kai's blood painting the stone.

My jaw clenches.

The air shifts.

I turn my eyes to the vines curling along the garden wall, stretching up the old stone like delicate green veins. I focus on them, reaching deep, searching for that thread inside me—that tether I have always felt between myself and the earth.

They shift slightly with a faint rusting, as if stirred by a breeze that doesn't exist.

I close my eyes and push harder, silently willing them to move, to do *something*.

Nothing.

Just the same subtle shuffle. They're acknowledging me but not answering. I sweep my gaze across the courtyard, at trees beyond the walls, at the flowerbeds edging the path, at the dried vines curling at the base of the sparring posts. Every living thing quivers faintly, almost like they're waiting.

But nothing happens. No eruption of roots. No snap of growth or surge of power. Just soft, wordless movement.

I let out a breath and turn to Rook, sword still in hand. "Happy?"

He watches me closely, arms crossed, his jaw tight in thought. He doesn't answer at first. Just stares at the vines as they slowly still.

Then, he shrugs. "It's something."

Kai steps forward, cracking his neck as he rolls his shoulders. "Your turn," he says, gesturing to Rook, flashing me a quick wink over his shoulder.

Rook grins, already raising his arm. "I thought you'd never ask."

Before I can blink, a massive shard of ice forms in Rook's palm, and he launches it across the courtyard.

Kai reacts instantly, lifting his hand with smooth control. A bolt of fire shoots from his palm and collides with the ice midair. The two elements clash with a loud hiss and explode into a shower of steam, a puddle sizzling as it hits the stone at their feet.

The sparring escalates quickly, ice against flame, wind against heat. Rook throws jagged spears of frost with precise strike, and Kai counters each one with a wave of fire—a serpent that curls through the air.

Their movements are swift and deadly. The air around them hums with power, and the courtyard is a battlefield of elemental fury.

I stand at the edge, jaw slack, completely awestruck. I've seen them fight before, but never like this. Never flame versus frost. Before me, two forces of nature collide—unstoppable and violent. Beautiful and terrifying.

The moment Rook begins to gain on Kai, the air thrums with a storm forming in its wake. Frost burst after frost burst, shard after shard of gleaming ice comes flying, relentless and sharp.

Kai stumbles back, caught off guard by the sheer speed. One shard aims directly for his face.

My pulse leaps into my throat. Before I even realize I've moved, I step forward.

A sharp crack tears through the courtyard as a vine explodes between the stone pavers, thick and fast.

It slams into the shard midair, knocking it clean off its path. The ice shatters into a dozen sparkling pieces.

Silence falls like a weighted blanket covering the space.

Kai straightens slowly, turning his toward me with wide eyes. Rook lowers his arm, staring at me like I have just become someone entirely new.

I gape, breathless. My fingertips tingle. The vine trembles beside me before curling in on itself like it's shy.

"Okay," Rook finally says, clapping his hands.

I catch my breath, stunned.

My chest rises and falls rapidly as I stare down at my hands, fingers trembling. I glance back at the shattered ice on the stones, then at the vine retreating slowly into the cracks of the earth.

"What was that?" I murmur, mostly to myself.

Neither Kai nor Rook answers.

They are both still watching me, one in awe, the other with the look of someone who has just found the edge of a map no one knew existed.

Rook looks at me, arms still crossed, his golden waves catching the morning light, tousled just enough to look effortless.

"I told you," he says with that familiar smirk tugging at his lips.

CHAPTER THIRTY-EIGHT

I'm seated at the long table in the sitting room with parchment scattered before me. A couple suns were left until the wedding, barely enough time to breathe, let alone second-guess the floral arrangements.

I scan the final list one more time before turning to the stewardess.

"Make sure Piper Sunniva is invited. The light weaver. I want her here."

The stewardess nods, scribbling it down with haste.

I rise from my seat, stretching my back with a quiet sigh. "Also, have the servants ready the guest wing. My family should be arriving at any time now," I say. "Thank you so much for your help, Tayanna."

"Yes, Princess," she says with a bow before hurrying out the door. Her dark curls bounce with every step.

My heart pounds a little harder with every passing moment. The wedding is so close now, I can feel it like lightning in the air.

I make my way down the quiet halls, the stone cool beneath my boots. My fingers trail absently along the wall as I walk. My thoughts are already in the greenhouse. The wedding florals need a touch of my craft, just enough to make sure they are faultless for the ceremony.

As I turn a corner, I nearly bump into Rook.

He flashes that easy grin, with his golden waves tucked behind his ear. "You off to do something suspiciously flower-related?"

I raise a brow. "Very suspicious. Want to join?"

He shrugs, falling into step beside me. "I could use some sun."

We walk together in companionable silence. The hallway opens up to the garden path. I inhale deeply as we step outside. The cool air is marked by the faintest promise of spring.

We walk through the heart of the garden, passing the winter bloomers.

The heavy glass doors of the greenhouse creak softly as they close behind us. Warmth wraps around us instantly, thick, humid, and scented with blooming things. The filtered sunlight makes everything glow in soft greens and golds, catching on the leaves and petals around us.

I breathe it in, grounding myself.

Rook looks around in quiet awe.

"I've never actually been in here," he says, brushing his fingers across a low-hanging vine.

I smile and walk toward the far table where rows of white orchids are perched. Their pale blooms droop slightly, still waiting for the touch of magic. I kneel beside them, already feeling the quiet hum of life beneath the soil.

Rook crouches beside me, watching as I slide my hand into the dark earth.

"What's it like?" he asks, tilting his head. "Talking to them?"

I glance at him, brushing my fingers gently through the soil. "It's not really talking. Not like you and I do. They don't form thoughts in words. It's more like... a current of feeling. Impressions. Instinct. They give me what they know, what they feel, what they need. It's less like a conversation and more like a song you just understand without hearing the lyrics."

He watches me for a long moment, his brows slightly drawn as he processes it. "So, they feel things?"

"Yes," I say, my voice soft as I coax my magic forward. "They know the sun. The cold. Hunger. Death. They know each other. They don't think, not exactly, but they know."

The pulse of energy leaves my hand and sinks deep into the soil, into the roots. The orchids respond immediately. The stems strengthen, straightening under their own weight. Petals brighten, blooming with renewed life. The air smells sweeter now.

"You make the world around you grow," he says, smiling.

Rook trails behind me as I move from one flower bed to the next, watching silently as I press my palms into the soil, coaxing life to surge through stems and unfurl blossoms. He stands just behind me with his arms crossed. His golden waves catch the dappled light that filters in through the glass.

"It's really something," he says softly.

I straighten up, brushing soil from my hands.

He meets gaze, expression firm. "We need to explore your lumina more," he says. "See what else you can do."

I exhale slowly, unsure if it's nerves or reluctance that presses in my chest.

He stares at me expectantly.

"You mean now?"

He grins, that mischievous spark lighting his green eyes. "Yes, now. Come on, Princess. Let's go outside. No better time."

I sigh and glance longingly at the greenhouse warmth and peace behind me.

"Fine," I mutter with a tired smirk. "But if a thorn bush attacks you, I'm not helping."

He laughs as we make our way toward the doors. "Deal."

We step out of the greenhouse and into the garden. The late afternoon sun hides beneath gray clouds. A soft breeze rustles through the hedges and tree branches, and I feel the hum of the earth beneath my boots, quiet and wanting.

Rook gestures to a clearing beside the fountain, where the grass is thick and undisturbed.

"Don't think too hard. Just... tug at that cord tethered to your magic."

I step into the clearing, I plant my feet shoulder-width apart and exhale, grounding myself. I reach into the quiet corner of the well where my magic sleeps. I close my eyes and focus on my breathing, calling for the same desperation I felt protecting Kai. I picture the vines coiling, stretching, responding.

I open my eyes and frown, exhaling slowly.
Nothing.
Just a few flowers rustling like they're caught in a breeze that doesn't exist. My palms are warm, tingling faintly, but the magic refuses to do anything real.

Rook meets my gaze with an unreadable expression.
Then...
He forms a snowball in his hand.

"No," I say flatly. "Don't you dare."

His lips twitch with mischief. "Too late."

He flings it. It hits me square in the face.

I stumble back a step, gasping. Cold drips down my neck. "You son of a—"

He laughs, already forming another.

"I swear, Rook—"

The second one hits my shoulder. I hiss through my teeth, swiping snow from my collar.

"Rook, I *will* kick your ass."

"Do it then." He grins, throwing a third.

I shriek and duck, narrowly missing it. More come, relentless. I spin and try to dodge, but my boots slip in the half-frozen grass. I'm drenched, humiliated, and furious.

"Stop it!" I yell.

The ground trembles beneath my boots. With a low groan, thick vines surge upward, weaving together in an instant and forming a towering wall in front of me. The snowballs hit it with soft thuds and fall harmlessly to the ground.

Rook lowers his arm, his mouth slightly open. "Well," he mutters. "There it is."

Applause echoes from the edge of the garden.

I turn to see Kai with a gleaming smile stretched across his face.

"Told you," Rook calls to him.

I narrow my eyes at both of them.

Kai walks closer, admiring the wall of vines. His arms wrap around my waist, pulling me into a warm, grounding embrace. I melt into him, with the adrenaline still thrumming in my veins. He brushes a damp strand of hair from my face. His touch is gentle.

When I look up at him, all I see in his expression is pride. Pure, unfiltered pride. The kind that makes my chest tighten and my heart pound.

Then he kisses me.

Deep and unrelenting—the world's gone quiet around us. His mouth moves against mine with a kind of hunger that sends heat spiraling down my spine. I grab the front of his tunic, holding on, kissing him back just as fiercely.

A voice clears from a few steps away. "Well," Rook says loudly. He waves a hand vaguely and backs away with a smirk. "Please, do continue."

I pull away from Kai just enough to glare playfully over his shoulder. "You're a menace."

Rook laughs and walks off, whistling.

Kai presses his forehead to mine. "I'm so proud of you," he whispers.

A gentle patter begins overhead. I tilt my face up to the sky, and cool droplets kiss my cheeks. A soft drizzle, just enough to make the leaves glisten and the air smell of fresh earth.

Kai leans in close, his breath warm against my ear. "Let's get you out of these wet clothes," he says lowly.

A flutter stirs deep in my belly. I bite my lip, trying not to grin too obviously as I glance sideways at him.

"I love the sound of that," I murmur.

He squeezes my hand gently and tugs me a little faster toward the castle. The rain falls steadily now, soaking through the back of my tunic. The castle doors loom ahead, warm and golden light spilling from the windows. We quicken our pace, laughing quietly as the wind picks up and the storm swells behind us.

By the time we reach the doors, we're damp and breathless, with our fingers still tightly entwined.

CHAPTER THIRTY~NINE

We finally moved into the royal chambers. The mattress beneath me is clouds—soft and endless. I stretch with a small sigh. A book is propped in my hands as I read under the soft glow of the bedside candle.

Kai walks toward me from across the room, shirtless, freshly washed, and impossibly sculpted. My eyes trail down his body, broad shoulders, lean waist, the ripple of muscles that move like a storm under his skin.

My gaze lowers instinctively, pausing at the bulge beneath the thin fabric of his trousers. My cheeks warm.

He tilts his head, his eyes narrowing as he nods toward the book in my hands. "Winnie, where did you get that?"

I blink, snapping my gaze back to his face. "The library," I say slowly. "What do you mean? It's just a romance novel."

"This," he mutters, voice suddenly sharper, more alert. "Where did you get *this*?"

"The place keeper?" I ask, confused. "It was in the nightstand. I found it just now. I just... thought it was pretty."

He turns the metal between his fingers. It's tarnished gold, oval-shaped, and etched with a symbol I hadn't paid attention to before.

"This is the crest of Draugrune," he says, eyes darkening. "Exactly the same as the pendant we found on one of the attackers."

I stare at it now, my stomach knotting. "Oh..." I whisper.

A quiet knock raps gently on the chamber door, breaking the heavy silence lingering after Kai's words.

He moves to answer it, pulling the door open just enough to speak in low tones with the person on the other side. From where I sit, I catch a glimpse of a servant.

Kai nods once, then shuts the door softly behind him.

He turns to me. His expression shifts with the edge in his features softening into a quiet warmth.

"Your family has arrived," he says, his voice gentle.

I sit up straighter. Butterflies stir in my stomach, nerves, and excitement. I throw back the blankets. My heart skips. I slide off the bed, slipping my arms through my robe and tying it quickly around my waist. My bare feet hit the cold stone, but I barely feel it. I'm already moving.

I burst out of the door. The soft patter of my steps echoes through the hallway as I rush toward the guest wing. My pulse thuds in my ears, anticipation building with every step.

I round the corner, breathless, and my eyes scan the corridor ahead, searching for the familiar faces I've longed to see.

Soft, familiar voices float down the corridor. My father's deep tone cuts through first, followed by my mother's gentle hum. I follow the sound around another corner, heart racing.

I reach the door, lift my hand to knock, but before I make contact, it swings open. My father stands there, tall and tired-looking from travel, but his gray eyes light up when he sees me.

"Dad!" I throw myself into his arms, squeezing him tightly.

He holds me just as hard, his hands cradling the back of my head like he used to when I was little. "Your mother felt you coming."

"Of course, she did."

I pull away only to dive into my mother's waiting arms. She smells of jasmine and the sea, sweet and familiar. *Home.* She smells like home. I hold back tears that sting my eyes.

Two tiny bassinets are near the bed. My baby brothers, fast asleep. Their little fists are curled at their sides, and their chests rise and fall in unison. My heart melts.

"They have our hair," I whisper, glancing back at my mother.

She nods with a small, bittersweet smile. I reach out, brushing a knuckle gently across one of their tiny brows. They don't stir.

I wrap my arms around my mother again, sinking into the warmth and comfort I've missed so dearly. She holds me close with her chin resting on my head.

"Tomorrow," she whispers, her voice thick with emotion, "you marry."

I nod against her shoulder, swallowing the lump rising in my throat.

She pulls back just enough to look at me, cupping my face in both hands. "And I'm so proud of you."

Tears sting my eyes, but I blink them away, smiling through the swell of emotion in my chest.

"I love you," I say softly.

"Now go," she says, brushing a lock of hair behind my ear. "We'll get some rest and see you in the morning."

I kiss her cheek and give her one last squeeze before slipping out of the room, heart full.

I run barefoot through the halls. The stone is cool beneath my feet. My robe flutters behind me. My heart feels light, full, overflowing. I push open our chamber door and find Kai already in bed, the fire casting a warm glow over his bare chest and strong shoulders.

He lifts the blankets as I climb in beside him, and I immediately melt into his side. His arms wrap around me without hesitation, pulling me close. He presses a kiss to my forehead.

"Goodnight, my bride." His voice is a low, sleepy murmur against my skin.

I close my eyes, smiling into his chest, and let the peace of that word carry me into sleep.

CHAPTER FOURTY

I'm standing in front of the mirror in my silk dressing robe, hair half pinned, when the door creaks open. My mother steps in, glowing in her soft lavender gown, holding one of the twins in her arms. A servant carries the other behind her.

"I thought you might want to meet them before the ceremony," she says gently, her voice thick with emotion.

I eagerly nod.

She walks over and places the baby carefully into my arms. "This is Leif."

The moment I cradle him to my chest, everything else fades. He's so perfect. He looks up at me with wide eyes, a hint of curiosity behind his sleepy haze.

My throat tightens as overwhelming joy surges in my chest, and before I can stop it, a tear rolls down my cheek.

"He looks just like Brynn," I whisper, barely able to get the words out. "They're already so big." I sniffle.

My mother smiles, brushing a hand over my arm. She gently lifts Leif from my arms and settles the other baby into them.

"And this," she says with a proud smile, "is Jasper. He's a shield."

I look down at him, awestruck. His little fingers immediately wrap around mine, gripping tightly. He stares right at me with bright eyes, and then, a wide smile breaks across his little face.

I laugh softly, pushing back another wave of tears. The weight of him in my arms, the feel of his warmth, the light in his eyes, it all roots into my soul like magic.

My mother leans in, brushing a kiss against my cheek as she gently lifts Jasper from my arms. Her eyes shimmer with pride.

"I'll see you at the ceremony, dear," she whispers, smoothing a strand of hair from my face.

I nod, unable to speak. My heart swells so full I think it might burst.

She turns and slips out of the room, the door clicking softly shut behind her.

The room buzzes quietly as servants begin their work. A young servant with smooth, olive-toned skin and nimble fingers begins brushing out my hair with a wide-toothed comb dipped in scented oil. The comb glides through my strands. The aroma of jasmine and honey calms the storm in my chest.

She separates sections with ease, twisting and braiding intricate loops and weaves at the crown of my head. Small golden pins shaped like ivy leaves and tiny blossoms are slipped into the plaits, catching the light as if they were kissed by starlight.

Another servant arrives with a small crystal bowl and begins carefully securing delicate pearl strands through the updo. Their opalescent glow gives my hair the illusion of holding moonlight.

Meanwhile, another servant tends to my face. She presses a cool lavender cloth over my cheeks, wiping away any traces of sleep or tears. She applies a light base of silken cream, feathering it over my skin until it glows with warmth and softness.

Her fingers are light as air as she brushes a soft rose tint to the apples of my cheeks. She paints my lips with a soft berry stain, subtle but rich, enhancing their shape.

For my eyes, she chooses a shimmer like dusted gold and applies it with a sweep of her fingertip, adding a faint outline in deep brown at the edges. A final pass of a small wand darkens my lashes, fanning them wide.

I bat my lashes, stunned at the woman in the mirror who looks back at me. She looks like me, only more... divine.

Soft powder is dusted over my collarbones and shoulders, giving a hint of shimmer, and when I move, I catch the faintest glimmer, as if a constellation had chosen to settle on my skin.

"You look radiant, Princess," one of them says softly.

And I do. I feel it, too.

They help me out of my robe, hands careful, and I step into the gown with the kind of care one might give to holding a relic. The silk cascades down my body, fitted to perfection.

It hugs and flows in all the right places, weightless and regal all at once. They tighten the laces at my back and smooth the train. One of them places the final addition, my crown, gently atop my head, anchoring it among the braids and pearls.

I turn to look in the mirror. And for a moment, I forget the battles, the pain, the war, the scars.

All I see... is the beginning of everything.

I step out into the hall, and the heavy oak door glides shut behind me. My gown whispers against the floor with every step, the silk trailing

433

long behind me like moonlight spilled across the ground.

My father stands there waiting, dressed in his formal cloak of deep emerald trimmed with silver, and when his eyes meet mine, his breath stops. He blinks once, then again, as if trying to ready himself.

"You are…" he starts, voice thick. "You're the second most beautiful bride I've ever seen."

A wide grin breaks across my face, warmth blooming in my chest. "I'd be offended if I didn't have the most beautiful mother in the realm."

He nods, smiling, but I can see the glassiness in his eyes. He offers me his arm, and I loop mine through it.

"You ready?"

I take a breath, soothing the flutter in my chest, and I nod.

Together, we start down the long hallway, each step echoing softly for the stone walls, toward the beginning of my forever.

The hush of my gown sweeping over the stone floor rises above the thunder of my heartbeat. As we round the last corner, the tall stained glass doors leading to the gardens come into view. My throat narrows.

Two guards, dressed in ceremonial armor, step forward and pull open the towering doors. Sunlight spills in, warm and golden, illuminating the gardens beyond. The wisteria trees are in full bloom, white blossoms cascading like waterfalls from their branches, forming a canopy of soft petals that sway gently in the breeze.

Every flower bed is bursting with hues of white and red—roses, tulips, orchids— all in full bloom.

Rows of guests—nobles, friends, guards, familiar and unfamiliar faces stand, all turning to look at me. My pulse tightens. I swallow. I feel my palms start to sweat.

But then I see him, Malachi Larkin Hawthorn, standing at the end of the aisle beneath a delicate arch woven with vines and white blossoms. His hair is braided neatly. His formal black and gold tunic is tailored to his perfect form, and his crown catches the light.

His expression is nothing but awe. His eyes lock on mine like I'm the only thing that exists in this entire garden. As if I'm his whole world.

And suddenly, I'm no longer nervous.

I'm home.

CHAPTER FOURTY~ONE

We sit at the long table beneath strings of hanging lanterns and silver glowing orbs. The garden is transformed with soft golden light and pulsing warmth from hundreds of candles hovering midair like floating stars.

Plates clink, music plays somewhere off to the side, and laughter rolls gently through the reception. Kai sits to the left of me at the head of the table, my father is to my right, and the two of them are deep in conversation, laughing over some tale my father is telling. Kai's hand rests on my knee under the table. His thumb brushes absentmindedly back and forth.

Rafe, seated next to Kai, leans forward and taps him lightly on the shoulder.

"Who's that?" he asks, voice low as he nods toward someone across the garden.

I follow his gaze and spot a familiar face. Her long golden hair glints in the candlelight, and her ice-blue eyes twinkle with amusement as she laughs at something one of the guests at her table said.

"Oh!" I smile. "That's my friend Piper. Piper Sunniva. She's a light weaver. I will have to introduce you two."

Rafe's gaze doesn't waver. "Please do," he says, tucking a strand of his black wavy hair behind his ear.

I raise a brow and grin, a teasing edge to my voice. "*Please do*?" I echo.

Rafe glances sideways at me, his hazel eyes meeting mine. "Yes, please do." His lips twitch into a shadow of a smile.

Rook strolls over with that easy grin of his. His golden waves catch the lantern light as he reaches us.

"You two," he says warmly, pulling Kai into an embrace, then wrapping me in one right after. "That was the most beautiful ceremony I've ever seen. Truly."

"Thank you, Rook," I say, hugging him back tightly.

Rook steps back, nodding. "I'll be over here if you need me."

He walks back across the garden and takes his seat beside Shawniaus. He looks over, raising his crystal glass toward us in a silent toast. His smile is subtle. Kai raises his own glass slightly in return, eyes shining in the soft candlelight as he laces his fingers through mine beneath the table.

I excuse myself and rise from the table.

On the way to the bath chamber, I pause in the corridor, drawn to the towering portrait hanging between the arched sconces.

Kai's family.

My gaze falls to the small girl beside Kai. Aurora. There's a whisper of her that gnaws at the edge of my memory. Her long brown hair tumbles over her shoulders like silk, and those eyes. They're Kai's eyes. But that's not what makes my stomach twist.

My heart beats louder, like my body knows a secret my mind can't place.

I shake my head softly, trying to clear the sudden weight pressing behind my eyes. Of course, she feels familiar. She is Kai's sister. They share the same features. Dark hair, sharp cheekbones, amber eyes.

I exhale and straighten my spine.

I turn to continue to the bathing chamber.

A deafening crack of thunder rips through the air, and in my peripheral, I see a bright light flash through the tall doors.

I rush to the gardens. Another blinding bolt of lightning splits the sky open. Guests scream, chairs scrape against stone, and guards rush toward the outer gates.

I bolt toward Kai, skirts flying, weaving through people until I finally reach him.

Fires bloom where the lightning strikes, licking at the garden edges. My heart lurches.

I spin around to find my father.

My mother screams.

My father collapses onto the table, goblet slipping from his hand. Plates clatter. My mother rises from her chair, catching him as he slumps.

I race toward them, but Kai is already moving. We reach him at the same time.

He's breathing, but unconscious.

My hands shake as I reach for him. I scream for a healer.

Kai grabs the goblet, staring at the remnants of deep red within. Slowly, he brings it to his nose, sniffing it once, then again.

His entire expression shifts, his eyes snap to mine, wide and panicked.

"Magus Fur," I whisper, my chest tightens as panic seizes me. "Who would do this?"

My mother cradles both babies as she runs for shelter.

I turn to the nearest guards. "Get him to the infirmary, now."

They nod and immediately begin to move him.

Lightning strikes again, closer. Guests scream and scatter, sprinting for the castle.

"Kai—" I start, but he's turning.

"Rook," he shouts, scanning the courtyard. "Where is your father?"

Rook is pale, visibly shaken.

"He was just here..." he says, his voice tight. "I... I don't know where he went."

"Start putting out the fires," Kai commands.

Rook nods.

Kai's jaw tightens. We all look around. The storm tears through the celebration like a curse unleashed upon the revelry.

My pulse tears through me—a drumbeat of panic and urgency. My eyes flick to the shadows beyond the stone arch.

Kai breaks out into a sprint toward the forest; I have no idea what he's after.

But I don't hesitate. I chase after him. The trees loom ahead, wind ripping through the canopy, and behind me, footfalls scrape the earth. It's Piper and Rafe, not far behind.

My gown tangles around my legs, soaked and heavy. I curse under my breath, grip the fabric, and rip the damn thing clean off, down to my underclothes. Rafe catches up, not even winded.

In one fluid motion, he pulls his tunic over his head and hands it to me without a word. I slip it over my head, the soft, satin fabric hanging to my knees. I toss my heels to the side and keep running. My bare feet pound against the earth.

Branches whip past. The trees blur. Kai is ahead, nothing but shadow as he moves. I glance over to Piper, still close. Her golden hair is soaked and plastered to her face.

"Piper!" I shout between breaths. We slow to a stop. "There's a piece of parchment in my jewelry box on my dresser."

She looks at me, confused.

"Take it to the healers," I command. "Tell them to make a tonic with those ingredients and give it to my father. Now!"

Understanding flashes in her pale eyes. She nods once, then takes off without another word, vanishing into the trees behind us.

Gods, I hope I'm right about this.

I face forward again and force my aching legs to churn. Wherever Kai is going, whoever he's chasing, I'll be right behind him.

Through the gaps in the trees, I spot him. Kai stands perfectly still in a clearing, his back to me. The air is thick with smoke and static, and the ground trembles beneath my feet.

A bolt of lightning splits the sky, a jagged streak of white hot light slamming into the earth just beside him. Flames roar to life, licking up the dry brush in angry tongues.

Rafe is already there, off to Kai's side, blade drawn.

I push harder, legs burning, lungs aching as I close the distance until I see who Kai's facing.

My heart drops.

Shawniaus.

He stands calm, almost serene, with his hands at his sides. His eyes are locked on Kai's, unmoving, even as smoke coils around him. Firelight flickers across his features.

I stagger to a stop just behind Kai. The wind tugs at Rafe's bare shoulders and the hem of the tunic, drowning my frame.

Shawniaus.

Suddenly, I understand.

He didn't just run from the chaos.

He started it.

With stolen power.

My father's lumina.

"You have nowhere to hide, Shawniaus," Kai says, voice low and lethal.

Shawniaus steps forward. His silhouette is jagged in the firelight. His calm mask fractures, revealing a twisted snarl beneath.

"You were never meant to return!" he shouts, his voice breaking with fury. "If you would've just gotten yourself killed like you were supposed to—this throne, *my* throne, would've been restored long ago!"

Kai doesn't flinch. He stands tall, broad shoulders squared. "That's what this is about? Nyxlandia was never yours, Shawniaus." Kai says, voice razor sharp.

Shawniaus shakes his head. His snarl returns. His voice is low, bitter, and stained with venom. "I *had* a throne until your kingdom burned it to the ground! Nyxlandia painted our banners in blood and called it *justice.*"

Kai steps forward, fire curling at his fingertips, his jaw forged of stone. "That kingdom died a half-century ago. Along with the war it tried to start."

Shawniaus points a shaking hand at him, trembling with fury. "It died because of your family! My people slaughtered. My crown buried under rubble. I was just a boy, left with nothing but ruins and a name no one dared to speak. Being forgotten—it made crawling into your aunt's bed easier. She has no idea she wed a forgotten prince."

Lightning forks across the sky, seeming to mirror his rage.

"You were supposed to die with your family," he shouts.

Kai doesn't hesitate.

He lunges forward. Fire bursts from his palms like twin jets of wrath. Shawniaus whips his cloak back, summoning a wall of rain that swallows the flames.

Rafe is already moving, sword drawn. Shawniaus hurls a spear of stone toward him, but Kai intercepts it mid-air with a flaming wall. The impact sends embers spiraling into the night.

Shawniaus spins and throws both arms wide. From the ground, gray stone rises, tall, jagged spikes forcing Kai to leap back.

With a guttural roar, Kai slams his hands together. Fire explodes in a ring around him, and out of it, something forms.

Armor.

His dragonbone armor. It plates over his chest and shoulders in interlocking, scale-covered pieces, molten light pulsing in every seam. His eyes glow gold.

"You should've stayed buried in your ruins," Kai says, voice deep and inhuman now. "Because tonight, Draugrune dies for good."

Shawniaus lets out a scream, one part fury, one part agony, and calls down lightning from the sky. It crashes into the earth, inches from Kai.

In a blur, Rafe shifts. He roars as he lifts into the air. His burgundy wings slice through the wind. With a single powerful beat, he hovers above the clearing.

Then his jaws open wide, and a massive column of flame erupts from his mouth, barreling down toward Shawniaus.

But Shawniaus barely flinches.

He lifts one arm and calls the storm, and a thick wall of water crashes from the sky, cutting off the fire with a deafening hiss. Steam explodes outward, blinding the clearing for a heartbeat.

In that moment, Kai moves.

He charges through the mist, sword raised, flame trailing behind the blade like a comet's tail. He roars as he strikes. Shawniaus turns just in time to parry with a burst of lightning, but Kai's momentum breaks through.

His blade slices across Shawniaus's ribs, searing flesh.

The traitor heir snarls and lashes out.

Two bolts of lightning tear from his palms.

The first misses Kai by inches.

The second slams into Rafe.

The dragon jerks midair, with a flash of pain ripping through his body. His wings falter. He roars, spiraling out of control, and crashes hard into the clearing. The impact sends a shockwave through the ground.

"Rafe!" I scream from the edge of the clearing. My voice is lost in the chaos.

I see his dragon form dissolve, his massive limbs folding inward and scales fading to skin, until he lies there, unmoving, back in his human form. Smoke rises from the burn across his chest. He groans but doesn't get up.

Shawniaus lifts his hand in Rafe's direction, palm crackling with lightning.

"No!" I scream.

My arm lifts before I can think.

I feel it. The surge, the tether, the *will*.

Vines erupt from the earth beneath Rafe, wild and fast—a beast awakened. They spiral upward and coil around him, thick and green, a living shield that swells over his body just as Shawniaus hurls the bolt.

It strikes.

The vines sizzle, curling at the edges, smoke rising from the impact, but they hold.

A beat later, a chorus of footsteps.

A dozen rangers step from the tree line behind Shawniaus, dressed in black—echoes of the attackers at the town center—blades drawn and eyes dead. My heart lurches, instinct kicking in. Rafe's sword lies inches away, where he dropped it mid-shift.

I dive for it.

My fingers close around the hilt, and I spin to my feet. My pulse is hammering. Rafe's tunic clings to my frame. With smoke in my lungs and barefoot, I move. I charge sword ready and fall into step beside Kai.

His eyes flick to me. He doesn't try to stop me. He motions to my wrist and simply turns his body, syncing with mine—an instinctive dance honed in memory, seamless as shadow and flame.

Do I pull it? No. He needs it more.

Shawniaus raises both palms, and chunks of jagged gray stone swirl into the air like they were pulled from the mountain's spine. They hover only for a heartbeat before they launch straight toward us.

Kai turns, already bracing, already trying to shield me with his body, his flames beginning to surge.

But I move faster.

I throw my hand out and *command*.

The earth answers.

Vines burst from the dirt, thick and serpentine, weaving together in midair like braids of living rope. They tangle and twist and *thicken* until a wall of green rises before us.

The stones slam into it, the impact rippling through my bones. The vines groan and splinter at the edges, but they hold.

Kai looks at me with wide eyes—stunned, breathless. And feral spark flashes across his expression. A *proud* flame.

He grabs my wrist, fierce, urgent, and yanks the small horse charm dangling from my bracelet. The pendant glows. My lungs seize as the air around us warps, a low hum rising.

His armor disappears from his body in a shimmer of green and gold. It pours over me in molten threads, piece by piece, scaling across my limbs like liquid metal. It latches to my chest, shoulders, thighs, and forearms until I am completely wrapped in his protection.

"Now let's end this," he says.

The ground is chaos.

Blades, screams, fire, rain. A ranger swings hard at me, but my body moves on instinct. I duck, spin, and drive my blade low through his thigh and twist free just as another comes from the left.

Steel clashes, my feet slide in the mud, and I swing with all my weight, knocking the attacker's blade from his hands.

A bright white light explodes in the corner of my eye.

I turn.

Piper stands on the edge of the clearing. Her hands glow with starlight, and her cloak whips in the wind. She raises her arms, and a thousand tiny sparks swirl into the sky, illuminating the battlefield with floating embers.

She flicks her fingers, and a burst of radiant energy slams into two rangers mid-sprint, knocking them flat.

I don't stop to watch.

I lunge, slicing a ranger's arm. Another charges me, and I block, parry, twist, and slam the hilt into his face.

He drops.

I see Kai out of the corner of my eye, fire blazing from his hands, spinning in elegant, violent arcs as he dodges Shawniaus's strikes of lightning and shards of sharp stone.

They clash in the heart of the clearing. Every swing of Kai's flaming blade meets a crash of thunder or a lance of lightning. Sparks fly, fire sizzles on wet earth, and magic tears through the trees—a storm of chaos splitting the world open.

Shawniaus snarls, hurling bolt after bolt of lightning from his palms. The strikes are so blinding and fast they leave ghost images across my eyes.

But Kai is relentless. He ducks, parries, with fire wrapping around his blade in a serpentine twist, countering every attack.

A massive crack of thunder shakes the ground as lightning strikes the edge of Kai's sword and splinters through the air. He grits his teeth, sliding back in the mud, smoke curling from his shoulder.

But he doesn't fall.

He never falls.

Across the battlefield, Piper is no longer touching the ground.

She hovers several feet above, robes billowing around her in waves of silk. Her eyes blaze bright white, glowing so fiercely they almost sear to look at. Her hands are raised—delicate, unmoving. And from them extends threads of glowing, misty magic.

Two attackers dangle in midair before her, suspended by their throats, their limbs kicking uselessly.

The mist writhes around them like ghostly serpents.

They choke. Claw. Tremble.

And still Piper floats. Her expression is serene, lethal, divine.

One of them sputters blood. The other goes still.

The wind howls louder. Trees bend. Fire burns.

Just ahead, Shawniaus and Kai circle again in a timeless dance of gods unfolding before me.

A change ripples through the air.

The air suddenly stills. The wind dies.

The rain stops mid-drop, frozen for the span of a breath before falling softly to the earth. The storm... ends.

Everything is silent.

Shawniaus stands at the center of the clearing, soaked and wild-eyed, his hand lifts toward the pastel-painted sky.

But nothing comes.

His brows furrow. He tries again, his fingers twitching with effort, reaching for the storm like a man grasping for a lover who's left him.

Still nothing.

Not even a spark.

His eyes dart upward, then around the clearing, panic slicing across his face.

He's lost control.

"No..." he whispers.

Then, with a snarl, he jerks both arms down, summoning stone instead. Chunks of jagged gray rock rip from the ground, whirling around him in a storm of shrapnel.

The stones launch in every direction—razor sharp, spinning so fast they howl. One slices past my arm, another slams into the vine wall beside me with a loud *thunk*. I drop to the earth, shielding my head.

"Duck!" Kai shouts. He throws up a wall of fire, the stone hitting it and cracking into steaming shards.

Piper, still hovering, spins midair, white magic blooming from her palms like flower petals in reverse. The stones aimed in her direction hit a bright white barrier and explode into dust.

I scramble back to my feet, heart thundering, ears ringing.

Shawniaus is unraveling.

Rafe groans as he lifts himself off the ground, clutching his side. Blood trickles from his temple. Relief floods me so fast my knees almost buckle.

Kai doesn't wait. He raises his hand, flame crackling and whirling, preparing to strike Shawniaus down.

A massive wall of ice erupts from the earth.

It slams between them with a deafening *crack,* so thick and tall it blocks even the light. Fire slams into it, hissing steam billows.

A second wall rises behind it, a towering stone barrier.

And behind us stands Rook.

Kai doesn't hesitate. He charges. Fury is painted across every line of his face.

Rook throws up his hands, palms out. "Wait, Kai— Wait! I swear I didn't know!"

Kai grabs him by the collar, fire curling up his arms.

"I didn't know!" Rook shouts again, voice shaking. "I swear it, Kai."

Kai's fist trembles, still burning.

I step forward, heart racing, unsure if I should intervene.

Rook's voice cracks. "It's still my father." His golden hair damp, his usually bright eyes dulled. "Let him go. Exile him. Don't kill him. Please."

The clearing is silent again. The fire crackles low. Rafe stands beside Piper now, arms crossed, jaw set, and bleeding.

Kai stares into Rook's eyes, long and hard, before finally releasing his tunic.

Rook stumbles back, chest rising and falling.

I reach for my wrist, pulling the rose charm. Kai's armor lifts from my form in green smoke and golden light.

The sound of ice meeting earth followed by stone pounding dirt breaks the silence. We turn to see the walls crumbling and Shawniaus disappearing between the trees.

We walk back to the castle through the charred trees and soaked earth. Smoke curls from the places where lightning struck. The skies have quieted, but my heart hasn't.

Dad.

It worked.

Rome gave us a cure.

As the castle towers come into view, Rook slows his pace.

He looks over his shoulder, his voice tight. "The castle was attacked."

I freeze. "What?"

He nods grimly. "Me and the guards took them down." His jaw clenches. "We lost a few."

My stomach twists. We won a battle. But the war is just beginning.

Everyone pours into the castle.

Kai and I linger.

The wind is cool against my damp skin, and my heartbeat slows from the battle. I grip his hand tightly. The ache of what just happened is still raw in my chest.

We both glance back toward the forest, toward the smoke still curling from the battlefield.

I squint my eyes as I see an outline form in the sky.

I freeze.

My ribcage stiffens.

High above the treetops, just visible against the fading storm clouds, something shifts, and massive wings slice through the air like blades of light.

A dragon.

White. A pure white dragon.

Moonlight and snow. Its scales shimmer with an iridescent sheen, catching the last golden rays of sun as it flies away, getting smaller with every beat of its wings.

Beside me, Kai is still.

He's staring at the sky as if the very foundation of his world just tilted.

"Aurora."

In loving memory of tally.
The best horse a girl could ask for.

Acknowledgements

To my alpha reader, Jenna—thank you for being the very first set of eyes on these pages. Your thoughtful feedback and encouragement kept me steady when I doubted myself. Maya, your opinions (and your hilarious commentary) made the long writing days brighter. You reminded me that stories are meant to be fun, even in their messiest drafts. To my mom—thank you for always believing in me, no matter what. Christopher, Savannah, Niki, Vanessa, Kyle, Laurel, Katie, Kailee, Taylor, Brian, Grandma Kelli, Nana and Papa—thank you for showing me nothing but love and support. You've been my foundation, and this book wouldn't exist without your belief in me. Piper, Layla, and Rafe thank you for helping me with name choices—you left your mark on these pages in ways you'll one day smile about. And finally, to my two boys, Hudson and Jasper— you are my greatest motivation, my reason to keep pushing forward, and the joy behind every word. This book is for you, always.